# THE
# LOST BOY

## CAMILLA LÄCKBERG

Translated by Tiina Nunnally

PEGASUS CRIME

NEW YORK LONDON

*For Charlie*

౷

This novel is entirely a work of fiction. The names, characters, and incidents portrayed in it are the work of the author's imagination. Any resemblance to actual persons, living or dead, or events is entirely coincidental.

THE LOST BOY

Pegasus Crime is an Imprint of
Pegasus Books LLC
148 West 37th Street, 13th Floor
New York, NY 10018

Copyright © 2009 Camilla Läckberg

English translation © 2016 Tiina Nunnally

First Pegasus Books hardcover edition October 2016

First published in Swedish as *Fyvaktaren*

Published by agreement with Nordin Agency, Sweden

Interior design by Maria Fernandez

Camilla Läckberg asserts the moral right to be
identified as the author of this work.

Library of Congress Cataloging-in-Publication Data is available.

ISBN: 978-1-68177-204-2

10 9 8 7 6 5 4 3 2 1

Printed in the United States of America
Distributed by W. W. Norton & Company

# 1

I t was only when she placed her hands on the steering wheel that she saw they were bloody. Her palms felt sticky against the leather. But she ignored the blood as she shifted into reverse and a bit too hastily backed out of the driveway. She heard the gravel spray out from under the tires.

They had a long drive ahead of them. She cast a glance at the backseat. Sam was asleep, wrapped up in a blanket. He really ought to be strapped in with a seat belt, but she didn't have the heart to wake him. She would just have to drive as carefully as possible. Immediately she let up on the accelerator.

The summer night had already started to brighten. At this time of year the hours of darkness were practically over before they even began. And yet this night seemed endless. Everything had changed. Fredrik's brown eyes had stared rigidly up at the ceiling, and she realized that there was nothing she could do. She had to save herself and Sam. She couldn't think about the blood. She couldn't think about Fredrik.

There was only one place she could go.

Six hours later, they reached their destination. Fjällbacka was just starting to wake up. She parked the car near the Coast Guard building, taking a moment to work out how she could manage to carry everything. Sam was still sound asleep. She took out a package of tissues from the glove compartment and wiped her hands as best she could. It was hard to get all the blood off. Then she took the suitcases out of the trunk of the car and quickly dragged them over to Badholmen, the island with the diving platform, where the boat was docked. She was worried that Sam might wake up, but she had locked the car so he wouldn't be able to get out and tumble into the water. With an effort she stowed the luggage on board the boat and unlocked the chain, which was meant to keep the vessel from being stolen. Then she ran back to the car, relieved to see that Sam was sleeping as calmly as when she'd left him. Picking him up, she carried him, still wrapped in the blanket, over to the boat. She kept her eyes fixed on her feet as she stepped on board so she wouldn't slip. Carefully she placed Sam on the deck and then turned the key in the ignition. The motor coughed but started up on the first try. Though she hadn't driven a motorboat in a long time, she was certain she could manage. She backed out of the mooring berth and then headed out of the harbor.

The sun was shining but hadn't yet had time to warm the air. She felt the tension slowly seeping away, and the horror of the night lost some of its grip on her. As she looked at Sam she wondered if what had happened would scar him for life. A five-year-old was fragile. Who knew what might have been destroyed inside him? She would do everything in her power to make him whole again. She would take away the evil with a kiss, just as she did when he fell off his bike and scraped his knee.

The route across the water was a familiar one. She knew every island, every skerry. She steered toward Väderöbad, heading further and further out along the coast. The waves were getting bigger, and the hull of the boat slammed against the surface after each swell. She enjoyed the feeling of the salty spray on her face, allowing herself to close her eyes for a few seconds. When she opened them again, she could see Gråskär in the distance. Her heart leaped. That always happened when the island came into view and she saw the small cottage and the lighthouse rising up white and proud against the blue sky. She was still too far off to see the color of the cottage, but in her mind she pictured the light gray of the façade with the white trim. She also thought about the pink hollyhocks that grew along the wall most sheltered from the wind. This was her refuge, her paradise. Her island called Gråskär.

⟨∞⟩

Every single pew in Fjällbacka church was taken, and the chancel was overflowing with flowers. Wreaths, bouquets, and beautiful silk ribbons inscribed with words of farewell.

Patrik could hardly make himself look at the white coffin that stood in the midst of the sea of flowers. It was eerily quiet inside the large stone church. At the funerals for old people, a hum of voices was almost always audible. Comments were exchanged, such as "she was in so much pain that it was a blessing" and the like. And everyone looked forward to the coffee served afterward in the church. Today those sorts of conversations were absent. Everyone sat in silence with heavy hearts and an unexpressed feeling of injustice. This should not have happened.

Patrik cleared his throat and glanced up at the ceiling, trying to blink away his tears. He squeezed Erica's hand. His suit was scratchy and itchy, and he tugged at his shirt collar to get more air. He felt as though he was suffocating.

The bells in the tower began to chime, the sound echoing between the walls. Many of those present in the church gave a start and glanced toward the coffin. Pastor Lena came out from the sacristy and walked over to the altar. It was Lena who had married them in this very church. That seemed like another time, another reality. Back then the mood had been elated, joyful, and bright. Now the pastor looked somber. Patrik tried to interpret her expression. Was she too thinking that this was all wrong? Or was she secure in her conviction that there was some meaning behind what had happened?

The tears welled up again, and he wiped them away with the back of his hand. Erica discreetly slipped him a handkerchief. The last chords of the organ faded away, followed by a few seconds of silence before Lena began to speak. Her voice quavered slightly, but then grew steadier.

"Life can change in an instant. But God is with us. Today as always."

Patrik saw her lips moving, but he soon stopped listening. He didn't want to hear what she said. The tenuous religious faith that had followed him through life ever since he was a child had now departed for good. There was no meaning to be found in what had happened. Again he squeezed Erica's hand.

⁀◌◌⁀

"I can proudly report that we're right on schedule. In a little over two weeks the Badhotel will be splendidly reopened in Fjällbacka."

Erling W. Larson beamed as he looked from one board member to the next, as if expecting applause. He had to settle for a number of approving nods.

"This is a real triumph for the region," he clarified. "A complete renovation of something that we might well consider a priceless historic icon. At the same time we can now offer people a modern and competitive wellness center. Or spa, which is perhaps a better word for it." He sketched quotation marks in the air around the word "spa," which was foreign to many Swedes. "All that remains is to take care of the finishing touches, invite several companies to try out the services in advance, and of course make preparations for the grand opening celebration."

"That sounds great. I just have a few questions." Mats Sverin, who had assumed the position of town finance officer a couple of months back, waved his pen to attract Erling's attention.

Erling, who detested anything to do with administrative work and financial reports, pretended not to notice. Hastily declaring the meeting adjourned, he withdrew to his spacious office.

After the fiasco of the *Sodding Tanum* reality show, no one had expected Erling to recover, yet here he was promoting an even bigger project which was on the brink of success. Personally, he'd never had any doubts, not even when the negative criticism had been at its worst. He was a born winner.

Of course it had taken a toll on him, which was why he had gone to the Ljuset wellness center in the Dalecarlian region of Sweden to recuperate. That had been a fortuitous turn of events, because if he hadn't gone there, he never would have met Vivianne. Meeting her had heralded a turning point for him, both professionally and personally. She had won him over as no other woman had ever done before, and it was her vision that he was now turning into reality.

He couldn't resist the temptation to pick up the phone and call her. It was the fourth time he'd done so today, but the sound of her voice always made him tingle all over. He held his breath as he listened to the ringtone.

"Hi, darling," he said when she answered. "I just wanted to hear how you're doing."

"Erling," she said, using that special tone of voice that made him feel like a lovesick schoolboy, "I'm as fine as I was when you called an hour ago."

"Good," he said, grinning sheepishly. "I wanted to make sure everything was all right."

"I know that, and I love you for it. But we still have so much to do before the opening, and you don't want me to have to work evenings, do you?"

"Absolutely not, my darling."

He resolved not to call and disturb her any more. Their evenings were sacred.

"Okay. Get back to work, and I'll do the same." He made a few kissing noises into the phone before he replaced the receiver. Then he leaned back in his chair, clasped his hands behind his head, and allowed himself a few minutes to day-dream about the impending delights of the evening.

⌒∞⌒

It smelled stuffy inside the cottage. Nathalie opened all the doors and windows to let the brisk wind blow through the rooms. A vase was nearly knocked over by the draft, but she grabbed it at the last second.

Sam lay in the small room next to the kitchen. They had always called it the guest room, even though it had been her bedroom when she was a child. Her parents had slept upstairs. She looked in on him, tucking a shawl around his shoulders. Then she took down the big, rusty key that always hung on a nail just inside the front door and went out onto the rocks. The wind cut through her clothes as she stood there, her back to the house, gazing toward the horizon.

The only other building on the island was the lighthouse. The little boathouse down by the dock was so small that it didn't really count.

She walked over to the lighthouse. Gunnar must have oiled the lock, because the key turned with surprising ease. The door creaked as she pulled it open. Nathalie only had to take a few steps inside before starting up the narrow, steep stairs, holding onto the railing as she climbed.

The view was so beautiful that it left her breathless. It had always had that effect on her. In one direction all she saw was the sea and the distant horizon; in the other direction the archipelago spread out below her, with all the islands, rocks, and skerries. It had been years since the lighthouse was in use. Nowadays it stood as a monument to bygone times. The lamp had been extinguished, and the metal plates and bolts were slowly rusting away from exposure to salt water and wind. As a child she had loved playing up here. It was so small, like a playroom elevated high above the ground. The only furniture that would fit into the confined space was a bed where the lighthouse keepers could rest during their long shifts, and a chair where they could sit and peer out across the waters.

She lay down on the bed. A musty smell rose up from the bedspread, but the sounds all around her were the same as when she was a child: the shrieking of the gulls, the waves crashing against the rocks, and the groaning sound of the lighthouse itself. Everything had been so simple back then. Her parents had been concerned that she would be bored on the island, since she had no siblings. They needn't have worried. She loved being here. And she had not been alone. But that was something that she couldn't have explained to them.

∼◦∽

Mats Sverin sighed and shuffled the papers piled on the desk in front of him. Today was one of those days when he couldn't stop thinking about her. Couldn't stop wondering. On such days, he got very little done, but they happened less frequently now. He had begun to let go; at least he wanted to think so. He could still see her face so clearly in his mind, and in a sense he was grateful for that. At the same time, he wished the image would start to blur and fade.

He tried to refocus his attention on his work. On good days he quite enjoyed his job. It was a challenge to immerse himself in the town finances, with the constant need to find a balance between political considerations and what was reasonable in terms of the marketplace. During the months that he'd worked here so far, much of his time had naturally been spent on Project Badis. He was pleased that the old hotel building was finally being restored. Like the majority of Fjällbacka residents, both those who still lived in the area and those who had moved away, every time he passed the beautiful structure he had bemoaned the fact that it had been allowed to fall into disrepair. Now it had been returned to its former grandeur.

Mats hoped that Erling's bombastic promises about the tremendous success this enterprise would enjoy were more than hot air, but he was skeptical. The project had already run up huge expenses for the restoration itself, and the proposed business plan was based on calculations that were far too optimistic. He had tried on a number of occasions to present his view of the situation, without success. And though he had gone over the figures time and time again without finding anything amiss—aside from the massive expenses accrued—nevertheless he had an uneasy feeling that something wasn't quite right.

He glanced at his watch and saw that it was lunchtime. It had been ages since he'd had any real appetite, but he knew that he needed to eat. Today was Thursday, which meant pancakes and pea soup at the Källaren restaurant. He should be able to get a few bites down, at the very least.

⁓

Only the closest friends and family members were to be present at the actual burial. The others silently disappeared in the opposite direction, headed toward town. Erica held on tightly to Patrik's hand. They walked behind the coffin, and it felt as if every step sent a stab of pain into her heart. She had tried to persuade Anna not to put herself through this ordeal, but her sister had insisted on having a proper funeral. Her desire to see it done right had temporarily roused her from her apathetic state, so Erica had given up trying to convince Anna to change her mind. Instead, she had helped make all the necessary arrangements so that Anna and Dan could bury their son.

On one issue she had refused to relent, however. Anna wanted all the children to attend the funeral, but Erica decided that the youngest should stay at home. Only the two oldest, Dan's daughters Belinda and Malin, were present. Patrik's mother, Kristina, was babysitting for Lisen, Adrian, Emma, and Maja. And the twins, of course. Erica had been a little concerned that this might prove too much for her mother-in-law, but Kristina had calmly assured her that she would have no problem keeping the youngsters under control for the two hours that the funeral would last.

Erica's heart ached when she looked at Anna's almost bald head in front of her. The doctors had been forced to shave off nearly all her hair in order to bore through her skull to relieve the pressure that had built up and might cause permanent brain damage if not dealt with at once. A downy layer of hair had started to grow back, but it was a darker color than before.

Unlike Anna and the driver of the other car, who had died immediately after the accident, Erica had come through with miraculously minor injuries. She had suffered only a bad concussion and several broken ribs. The twins were a bit underweight when they were born by emergency cesarean, but they were strong and healthy, and after two months they were allowed to go home from the hospital.

Erica almost burst into tears when she shifted her gaze from her sister's downy head to the tiny white coffin. Anna had not only incurred serious head injuries, she had also broken her pelvis. An emergency cesarean had been performed on her, too, but the injuries to the child were so extensive that the doctors gave Anna and Dan little hope. Only a week old, the baby boy had breathed his last.

The funeral had been delayed because Anna was unable to leave the hospital. Only yesterday had she finally been allowed to go home. And today they were burying her son, who would have had a life filled with so much love. Erica saw Dan place his hand on Anna's shoulder as he carefully parked her wheelchair next to the graveside. Anna shook off his hand. That was how she had reacted ever since the accident. It was as if her pain was so great that she couldn't share it with anyone else. Dan, on the other hand, needed to share what he was feeling, but not with just anybody. Both Patrik and Erica had tried to talk to him, and all of his friends had done what they could. But he didn't want to share his grief with anyone except Anna. And she was unable to respond.

Erica found Anna's reaction perfectly understandable. She knew her sister so well, and was fully aware of everything that she'd already been through. Life had not been kind to Anna, and this threatened to be the event that would finally prove too much for her. For all that Erica understood, she couldn't help wishing it wasn't so. Anna needed Dan more than ever, and

Dan needed Anna. Now they stood there, side by side, like two strangers as the little coffin was slowly lowered into the ground.

Erica reached out and put her hand on her sister's shoulder. Anna didn't brush it away.

⁘

Filled with a restless energy, Nathalie began cleaning the house. It had helped to air out the place, but the stuffy smell still clung to the curtains and bed linens. She threw them all into a big laundry basket, which she lugged down to the dock. Equipped with some laundry detergent and the old scrubbing-board that had been in the house for as long as she could remember, she rolled up her sleeves and began the hard work of doing the wash by hand. Every once in a while she would glance up toward the cottage to make sure that Sam hadn't awakened and come running outside. He'd been asleep for an unusually long time. Maybe it was in response to the shock. In that case, it was probably best to let him sleep. One more hour, she decided, and then she'd wake him up and see to it that he got something to eat.

Suddenly Nathalie realized that there actually wasn't much food in the house. She hung the laundry on the clothesline outside and then went in to have a look at the pantry. All she found was a tin of Campbell's tomato soup and a tin of Bullens pilsner sausages. She didn't dare look at the expiration dates. Surely that sort of tinned food would last forever? Regardless, she and Sam would have to settle for that today.

There was no temptation to go into town. She felt safe here. She didn't want to talk to anyone. She wanted to be left in peace. Nathalie paused to consider the situation as she held the soup tin in her hand. There was only one solution. She would have to call Gunnar. He had looked after the house for her after her parents died, and she could undoubtedly ask him for help.

The landline no longer worked, but she was able to get good reception on her cell, so she tapped in his number.

"Sverin."

The name stirred up so many memories that Nathalie shuddered. It took a few seconds before she composed herself enough to speak.

"Hello? Is anyone there?"

"Yes. Hi. It's Nathalie."

"Nathalie!" exclaimed Signe Sverin.

Nathalie smiled. She had always loved Signe and Gunnar, and the feeling was mutual.

"Sweetie, is that really you? Are you calling from Stockholm?"

"No, I'm here on the island." To her surprise she felt the words catch in her throat. She'd slept only a few hours, and fatigue must be making her overly sensitive. She cleared her throat. "I got here yesterday."

"But, my dear, you should have warned us so we could go out there and do some cleaning. The place must look terrible, and—"

"Don't worry about the cleaning." Nathalie interrupted Signe's torrent. She'd forgotten how much she talked, and how fast. "You've kept everything so nice out here. And it did me good to clean up a bit and do the laundry."

Signe snorted. "Well, you could have at least asked for help. We've got nothing to occupy ourselves these days, Gunnar and I. Not even any grandchildren to look after. But Matte has moved home from Göteborg. He's got a job working for Tanum council."

"That's nice for you. Why did he decide to do that?" She pictured Matte. Blond, tanned, and always cheerful.

"I don't really know. It all happened rather fast. He was involved in an accident, and afterward I had the impression that

. . . No, it's nothing. Don't pay any attention to an old woman who talks too much. So what's on your mind, Nathalie? Is there something we can do for you? And do you have the little guy with you? It would be so nice to see him."

"Yes, of course, Sam is here. Only he's not feeling very well."

Nathalie fell silent. Nothing would make her happier than to introduce Signe to her son. But not until they were settled on the island; not until she saw what effect the recent events might have had on him.

"That's why I thought I'd ask for your help. We don't have much food out here, and I don't want to make Sam get up so we could go into—"

Before she could finish her sentence, Signe interrupted.

"But of course we'd love to help. Gunnar is taking the boat out this afternoon anyway, and I can do your grocery shopping for you. Just tell me what you need."

"I can pay Gunnar back in cash, if you wouldn't mind buying the food for me."

"Absolutely. That's no problem, dear. So, what should I add to my shopping list?"

Nathalie could picture Signe putting on her reading glasses, sliding them down to the very tip of her nose as she reached for pen and paper. Gratefully Nathalie rattled off everything she could imagine they might need. Including a bag of sweets for Sam. Otherwise things could get difficult when Saturday arrived. He always kept track of the weekdays, and on Sunday he was already counting down to the next bag of Saturday sweets.

When she finished the phone conversation, Nathalie considered waking Sam. But something told her that she should let him sleep another hour.

∞

Nobody was doing any work at the police station. Displaying a sensitivity that was unusual for him, Bertil Mellberg had asked Patrik whether he wanted his colleagues to attend the funeral. Patrik had merely shaken his head. He'd only been back on the job a few days, and everyone was tiptoeing around him. Even Mellberg.

Paula and Mellberg had been the first officers to arrive at the scene of the accident. When they caught sight of the two cars, crumpled beyond recognition, they didn't think that anyone could have survived the crash. They peered in one of the windows and immediately recognized Erica. Only half an hour earlier an ambulance had come to the station to take Patrik to the hospital, and now his wife was dead, or at least seriously injured. The medics were unable to specify what the extent of her injuries might be, and it seemed to take an unbearably long time for the fire brigade to cut open the car.

Martin and Gösta were busy with another case and only heard about the accident and Patrik's collapse several hours later. They drove to the hospital in Uddevalla and spent the whole evening pacing the corridors. Patrik was in intensive care, and both Erica and her sister Anna, who had been seated next to her in the car, underwent emergency surgery.

But now Patrik was back on the job. Thankfully he hadn't had a heart attack, as was first thought; instead, he'd suffered a vascular spasm. After nearly three months on sick leave, the doctors had given him permission to return to work, although with strict orders to avoid stress. As if that's going to be possible, thought Gösta. With newborn twins at home, and considering what happened to Erica's sister. The devil himself would be stressed in that situation.

"Do you think we should have gone anyway?" asked Martin, stirring his coffee. "Maybe Patrik said no but he really wanted us to attend the funeral."

"No, I think Patrik meant what he said." Gösta scratched Ernst, the station's dog, behind one ear. "I'm sure there are plenty of people at the church. We can do more good here."

"How can you say that? We haven't heard a peep from anyone all day."

"It's the calm before the storm. By July you'll be longing for a day without any drunks, burglaries, or other sorts of trouble."

"That's true," said Martin. He'd always been the newbie at the station, but he no longer felt like such a beginner. By now he'd had a few years of experience on the police force, and he'd participated in several investigations that had been very difficult, which was putting it mildly. He had also become a father, and he felt as if he'd grown several inches the minute that Pia gave birth to their daughter.

"Did you see the invitation we received?" Gösta reached for a Ballerina cookie and began his usual routine of meticulously separating the vanilla top from the chocolate bottom.

"What invitation?"

"Apparently we're going to have the honor of acting as guinea pigs at that new place they're building in Fjällbacka."

"You mean at the Badis Hotel?" Martin woke up a bit.

"That's right. Erling's new project. Let's just hope that it goes better than all that *Sodding Tanum* nonsense."

"I think it sounds great. Lots of guys laugh at the idea of having a facial, but I had one in Göteborg and it was bloody marvelous. My skin was as smooth as a baby's bottom for weeks afterward."

Gösta gave his colleague a disgusted look. A facial? Over his dead body. Nobody was going to smear a load of muck all over his face. "Well, we'll have to see what they're offering. I'm hoping for at least some fancy grub. Maybe a dessert buffet."

"I doubt it," laughed Martin. "Places like that are usually more concerned with getting people to stay in shape than stuffing themselves with food."

Gösta looked offended. His weight was exactly the same as when he finished secondary school. With a snort, he helped himself to another cookie.

∞

Chaos reigned when they arrived home. Maja and Lisen were jumping on the sofa, Emma and Adrian were fighting over a DVD, and the twins were crying at the top of their lungs. Patrik's mother looked as if she might jump off a cliff at any second.

"Thank God you're home," she exclaimed as she handed Patrik and Erica each a screaming baby. "I don't know what got into these kids. They've been crazy. And I tried to feed the babies, but every time I fed one of them, the other would start crying, and then the first one would get distracted and couldn't eat and would start crying too . . ." She fell silent, trying to catch her breath.

"Sit down, Mamma," said Patrik. He went to get a bottle for Anton, whom he was holding in his arms. The boy's face was beet-red, and he was crying as loudly as his tiny body would allow.

"Could you bring a bottle for Noel too?" asked Erica as she tried to comfort her shrieking son.

Anton and Noel were still so small. Not like Maja, who had been big and robust right from the start. Yet the boys were actually enormous in comparison to their size at birth. Like tiny birds, they had lain in separate incubators, their thin arms hooked up to various tubes. They were fighters, according to the nurses at the hospital. And they had quickly gained weight, for the most part exhibiting a good appetite. But Erica and Patrik couldn't help worrying about them.

"Thanks." Erica took the bottle that her husband handed to her and sat down in an armchair, holding Noel. He greedily began drinking the formula. Patrik sat down in the other armchair with Anton, who stopped crying as swiftly as his brother. Erica thought that there were definite advantages to the fact that she hadn't been able to breastfeed. This way she and Patrik were able to share responsibility for the babies. That hadn't been possible with Maja, and it had felt as if her daughter were glued to her breast 24/7.

"How did it go?" asked Kristina. She lifted Maja and Lisen down from the sofa and told them to go upstairs to play in Maja's room. Emma and Adrian had already disappeared upstairs, so the two girls didn't need any further persuasion.

"It was fine. I don't know what else to say," Erica told her. "But I'm worried about Anna."

"Me too." Patrik cautiously changed position so he was sitting more comfortably. "It's as if she's shut Dan out. She's keeping him at a distance."

"I know. I've tried talking to her. But after all she's been through . . ." Erica shook her head. It was so terribly unfair. For years Anna had lived a life that could only be described as hell, but lately it seemed as if she'd finally found some peace of mind. And she'd been so happy about the baby that she and Dan were expecting. What had happened was unbelievably cruel.

"Emma and Adrian seem to be handling it relatively well." Kristina cast a glance upstairs, where the children could be heard laughing merrily.

"Yes, I suppose so," said Erica. "Right now they're probably just so happy to have their mother back home. I'm not sure that they've fully taken in what happened yet."

"You're probably right," said Kristina, and then looked at her son. "And what about you? Shouldn't you stay home from work a while longer until you're properly rested? No one's going to thank you for working yourself to death over at the station. What happened to you was a wake-up call."

"At the moment things are actually calmer over there than here," said Erica, nodding at the twins. "But I told him the same thing."

"It feels good to be working again, but I'll stay home if you really want me to," said Patrik. He set the empty bottle on the coffee table and placed Anton against his shoulder to burp him.

"No, that's okay. We're doing just fine now."

Erica meant what she said. After Maja was born, she'd felt as if she were walking around in a thick fog, but this time everything was different. Maybe the circumstances surrounding the birth of the twins left no room for her to be depressed. It also helped that they had developed a set routine while in the hospital. They slept and ate at specific hours, and always together. Erica wasn't the least bit concerned about being able to take care of the babies. She was happy for every second that she had with them, since she had come so close to losing both of them.

She closed her eyes, leaned forward, and pressed her nose against the top of Noel's head. For a moment his downy skin made her think of Anna, and she closed her eyes even tighter. She hoped she'd be able to find a way to help her sister, because right now she felt so powerless. She took a deep breath, drawing in Noel's comforting scent.

"My sweet baby," she murmured. "My sweet little baby."

∞

"So how's it going with your job?" Signe tried to strike a light tone as she piled meatloaf, peas, mashed potatoes, and cream gravy onto a plate. A huge serving.

Ever since Matte had moved back to the area, he'd hardly touched his food, even though she'd made his favorite meals every time he had dinner with them. The question was whether he ate anything at all when he was alone in his apartment. He was as thin as a rail. Thank goodness he at least looked better now that all traces of the assault had disappeared. When they went to see him at Sahlgrenska Hospital, she hadn't been able to hold back a cry of dismay. He had been beaten to a pulp. His face was so swollen that she could hardly tell whether it was really Matte lying in that hospital bed.

"It's fine."

Signe jumped at the sound of his voice. The answer to her question came after such a delay that she'd forgotten she asked it. Matte plowed his fork through the mashed potatoes and then stabbed a bite of meatloaf. She realized she was holding her breath as she watched him raise the fork to his mouth.

"Stop staring at the boy while he's eating," muttered Gunnar. He was already helping himself to seconds.

"I'm sorry," she said, shaking her head. "It's just that I'm . . . I'm so glad to see you eating something."

"I'm not about to starve to death, Mamma. See? I'm eating." As if in defiance, he loaded his fork and quickly stuffed the food into his mouth before it toppled off.

"They're not working you too hard at the office, are they?"

Signe received yet another annoyed look from Gunnar. She knew that he thought she was being overprotective, that she ought to leave their son in peace for a while. But she couldn't help it. Matte was her only child, and ever since that December day when he was born, which was almost forty years ago, she'd regularly woken up in the middle of the night, her nightgown soaked with sweat and her head filled with nightmares about the terrible things that might have happened to him. Nothing in life was more important to her than seeing him happy. She had always felt that way. And she knew that Gunnar was every bit as devoted to their son as she was. But he was better equipped to shut out the ominous thoughts that love for a child always entails.

She, on the other hand, was constantly aware that she might lose everything in a matter of seconds. When Matte was a baby, she'd dreamed that he had a heart defect, and so she had persuaded the doctors to do a thorough examination, which showed that her son was perfectly healthy. During his first year she slept no more than an hour at a time, because she kept getting up to make sure he was still breathing. As he got bigger, up until he started school, she would cut his food into small pieces so they wouldn't get stuck in his throat and cause him to choke. And she had nightmares about cars driving right over his soft little body.

By the time he was a teenager, her dreams had become even worse, filled with alcoholic comas, drunken driving, and fistfights. Sometimes she tossed and turned so much in bed that she woke Gunnar. One feverish nightmare after another until she forced herself to sit up and wait for Matte to come home, her gaze fixed first on the window, then on the telephone. Her heart gave a leap every time she heard someone outside, approaching the house.

The nights were a bit calmer after he moved away from home. Which was rather odd, because it seemed as if her fears should have grown when she was no longer able to keep watch over him. But she knew that he wouldn't take any unnecessary risks. He was a cautious person—that much she'd managed to teach him. He was also considerate and would never think of hurting anyone. In her mind, this meant that no one, in turn, would ever try to harm him either.

She smiled at the memory of all the animals he had brought home over the years. Injured, abandoned, or generally in a bad way. Three cats, two hedgehogs that had been hit by a car, and a sparrow with an injured wing. Not to mention the snake that she happened to find when she was just about to put his newly laundered underwear in his drawer. After that episode, he had to swear to her that he'd leave all reptiles to their fate, no matter how injured or abandoned they might be. He had reluctantly agreed.

It had surprised Signe that he hadn't become a veterinarian or a doctor. But he seemed to enjoy his studies at the business school, and from what she understood, he definitely had a head for numbers. He also seemed to like his job at the council. Yet there was something about him that worried her. She couldn't put her finger on what it was, but the bad dreams had started up again. Every night she awoke, bathed in sweat, with fragments of images in her head. Something was amiss, but her tactful queries were merely met with silence. That was why she had decided to focus her efforts on getting him to eat. If only he would put on a few pounds, everything would probably be fine.

"Wouldn't you like some more?" she ventured as Matte put down his fork. Half of the huge portion of food was still left on his plate.

"That's enough, Signe," said Gunnar. "Leave the boy alone."

"It's okay," said Matte, giving them a wan smile.

Mamma's boy. He didn't want her to suffer a scolding for his sake, even though after forty years with her husband, she knew that Gunnar's bark was worse than his bite. In fact, it would be hard to find a kinder man. She knew that the problem was hers, that she worried too much.

"I'm sorry, Matte. Of course you don't have to eat any more."

She called him by the nickname that he'd had since he first learned to talk but couldn't say his name properly. He'd called himself Matte, and everybody else had done the same.

"Guess who's home for a visit," she went on, cheerfully, reaching for the plates so she could clear the table.

"I have no idea."

"Nathalie."

Matte flinched and looked at her.

"Nathalie? My Nathalie?"

Gunnar chuckled. "I knew that would wake you up. You've always had a bit of a crush on her."

"Hey, knock it off."

Signe suddenly pictured in her mind the teenage boy, a lock of hair falling into his eyes, as he told her with a stammer that he had a girlfriend.

"I took some groceries over to her today," said Gunnar. "She's over on Ghost Isle."

"Oh, don't call it that." Signe shuddered. "Its name is Gråskär."

"When did she arrive?" asked Matte.

"Yesterday, I think. And she had the boy with her."

"How long is she staying?"

"She said she doesn't know." Gunnar stuck a wad of snuff under his upper lip and contentedly leaned back in his chair.

"Was she . . . was she the same?"

Gunnar nodded. "Sure, of course she was just the same, our little Nathalie. Exactly the same. Although I thought she had a slightly sad look in her eyes, but maybe that's my imagination. Maybe they had a quarrel back home. What do I know?"

"Don't go speculating about such matters," Signe scolded him. "Did you see the boy?"

"No. Nathalie met me down at the dock, and I didn't stay long. Why don't you go out there and say hello?" Gunnar said, turning to Matte. "I'm sure she'd be happy to have a visitor out there on Ghost Isle. Sorry. I mean, Gråskär," he added, giving his wife an annoyed look.

"That's all a bunch of nonsense and old superstitions. I don't think we should be encouraging that sort of thing," said Signe, a deep furrow appearing between her brows.

"Nathalie believes it," said Matte quietly. "She always said that she knew they were there."

"What do you mean by 'they'?" Much as Signe would have preferred to change the subject, she was curious to hear what Matte would say.

"The dead. Nathalie said that sometimes she saw them and heard them, but they didn't mean any harm. They just ended up staying there."

"That's awful. Now I think it's time for dessert. I've made rhubarb pudding." Signe stood up abruptly. "Pappa's right about one thing, though, even if he does talk a lot of drivel. It would make her happy to have you visit."

Matte didn't reply. He looked as if he were far away in his thoughts.

# Fjällbacka 1870

*E*melie was terrified. She had never even seen the sea, let alone sailed on it in what seemed to be a very unstable boat. She had a tight grip on the railing. It felt as if she was being tossed forward and backward by the waves, with no chance of putting up any resistance or governing her own body. She sought Karl's eye, but he was standing there with a resolute expression, staring out at what awaited them far ahead.

The words were still ringing in her ears. They were probably nothing more than the superstitious ramblings of an old woman, but she couldn't help thinking about them. The woman had asked where they were headed when they loaded their belongings onto the small sailboat down at the Fjällbacka harbor.

"Gråskär," Emelie had answered happily. "My husband Karl is the new lighthouse keeper on the island."

The woman didn't seem impressed. Instead, she had snorted and with a strange little smile she said, "Gråskär? Oh, I see. In these parts nobody calls it Gråskär."

*"Is that right?"* Emelie had the feeling that she really shouldn't ask, but her curiosity got the better of her. *"So what do you call it then?"*

At first the old woman didn't reply. Then she lowered her voice and said, *"In these parts we call it Ghost Isle."*

*"Ghost Isle?"* Emelie's nervous laughter had carried over the water in the early morning haze. *"How strange. Why?"*

The old woman's eyes glittered when she spoke. *"Because it's said that those who die out there never leave the island."* Then she turned on her heel and left Emelie standing there among all the bags and suitcases, with an awful lump in her stomach instead of the joy and anticipation that had filled her only a few moments ago.

And now it felt as if she might meet death at any second. The sea was so vast, so untamed, and it seemed to be drawing her toward it. She couldn't swim. If any of the waves, which looked so big even though Karl said they were only small swells, should capsize the boat, she was convinced that she would be pulled down into the deep. She gripped the railing harder, fixing her eyes on the floor, or the deck as Karl claimed it was called.

*"Over there is Gråskär."*

Karl's voice demanded that she look, so she took a deep breath and raised her eyes to stare in the direction he was pointing. Her first thought was that the island was so beautiful. The cottage, though small, seemed to sparkle in the sunlight, and the gray rocks gleamed. She saw hollyhocks growing at one end of the house, and she was amazed that they could thrive in such a barren setting. To the west the island shoreline was very steep, as if the cliffs had been sheared in half. But in the other directions the rocks sloped gradually toward the water.

Suddenly the waves didn't seem so rough. She still longed to feel solid ground under her feet, but Gråskär had already enchanted her. And she pushed the old woman's words about Ghost Isle to the very back of her mind. Something that was so beautiful couldn't possibly conceal anything bad.

# 2

She had heard them in the night. The same whispering, the same voices that she recalled from when she was a child. Her watch told her that it was three A.M. when she awoke. At first she didn't know what had caused her to wake up. Then she heard them. They were talking downstairs. A chair scraped. What did the dead talk about with each other? About things that had happened before they died? Or about what was taking place now, many years later?

Nathalie had been aware of their presence on the island for as long as she could remember. Her mother had said that, even as a baby, Nathalie would suddenly start laughing and waving her arms, as if she saw things that no one else could see. As she grew older, she became more and more conscious of them. A voice, something flitting past, the feeling that somebody else was in the room. But they didn't mean her any harm. She knew that back then, and she knew that now. For a long time she lay awake, listening to them until the voices finally lulled her back to sleep.

When morning arrived, she remembered the sounds as nothing more than a faraway dream. She made breakfast for herself and Sam, but he refused to eat his favorite cereal.

"Please, sweetie. Just one spoonful. Just a teeny bit?" she coaxed him but was unable to get him to take a single bite. With a sigh she put down the spoon. "You have to eat, you know." She stroked his cheek.

He hadn't uttered a word since everything happened. But Nathalie pushed her concern to a far corner of her mind. She needed to allow him time and not try to pressure him; she simply had to be available to him as he processed the memories, putting them away and replacing them with others. And there was no better place to do that than here on Gråskär, far away from everything else, near the cliffs, the sun, and the salty sea.

"You know what, let's skip breakfast and go out for a swim instead." When she received no answer, she simply picked him up and carried him outside into the sun. Tenderly she took off his clothes and carried him down to the water, as if he were only a year old and not a big boy of five. The water wasn't very warm, but he offered no objections as she sank down, immersing both of them while pressing his head protectively to her chest. This was the best medicine. They would stay here until the storm subsided. Until everything was back to normal.

⌒∞⌒

"I didn't think you'd come in until Monday," said Annika, peering over the tops of her computer glasses to look at Patrik. He had stopped in the doorway to her office, which was also the station's reception area.

"Erica threw me out. She claimed she was sick and tired of seeing my ugly mug at home." He attempted a laugh, but thoughts of the previous day were still with him, so the laugh didn't reach his eyes.

"I know exactly what she means," said Annika, but her expression was as melancholy as Patrik's. The death of a child affected everyone. Since Annika and her husband, Lennart, had learned that they would soon be able to bring home their long-awaited adoptive child from China, she was even more sensitive when it came to children who were hurt or harmed in some way.

"Is there anything going on?" asked Patrik.

"No, I wouldn't say that. Just the usual. Old Mrs. Strömberg has called for the third time this week to say that her son-in-law is trying to kill her. And a few kids were picked up for shoplifting at Hedemyr's."

"Super busy, in other words."

"Right. The big topic of conversation at the moment is that we've received an invitation to come and sample all the wonders on offer at that new place—Badis."

"That sounds tempting. I reckon I should volunteer for that particular job."

"At any rate, it's good to see the transformation Badis has undergone," said Annika. "The building used to look as if it might fall apart at any moment."

"Yes, it's great. But I doubt it's going to be profitable. It must have cost a fortune to restore the place. And do you think people will really want to go to a spa there?"

"If not, Erling's going to be in hot water. I have a friend who works for the local council, and she told me that they've invested a large part of their budget in the project."

"I can well imagine. And there's a lot of buzz in Fjällbacka about the opening festivities that they're planning. That's not going to be cheap either."

"The whole police force is invited, in case you hadn't heard. So we're all going to have to put on our best clothes."

"Is everyone out?" asked Patrik, changing the subject. He wasn't particularly keen on getting dressed up for a fancy party.

"Yes, except Mellberg. He's probably in his office, as usual. Nothing has changed, even though he claims that he came back to work before his leave was over because the station was on the verge of falling apart without him. From what Paula told me, they were forced to find another childcare solution before Leo started on a career as a sumo wrestler. Apparently the last straw was when Rita came home early one day and found Bertil stuffing a load of hamburger into the blender for Leo. She went straight back to her job and asked her boss to let her work part-time for the next few months."

"You're joking."

"No, it's the gospel truth. So now we're going to have to deal with him on a full-time basis. At least Ernst is happy about it. Mellberg left him here at the station while he was home with Leo, and the poor dog looked like he was pining away. He just lay in his basket and whined."

"Well, I suppose it's good to know that nothing has changed," said Patrik. He headed for his office, taking a deep breath before he stepped inside. Maybe work would make him forget the sad events of the previous day.

⌒∞⌒

She was never going to get up again. She would just lie here in bed and stare out of the window at the sky, which was sometimes blue, sometimes gray. For a moment she even wished that she was back in the hospital. Things had been so much simpler there. So calm and peaceful. Everyone had been so caring and considerate, speaking in low voices and helping her to eat and wash. Here at home there were too many noises disturbing her. She could hear the children playing, and their shouts reverberated through the house. Every once in a while they would come in to peer at her, their eyes big. It felt as if they were demanding something from her, as if they wanted something that she couldn't give.

"Anna, are you asleep?"

Dan's voice. She would have liked to pretend that she was sleeping, but she knew he wouldn't be fooled.

"No."

"I've made you some food. Tomato soup with toast and goat's cheese. I thought you might want to come downstairs to eat with us. The kids are asking for you."

"No."

"No, you don't want to eat? Or no, you won't come downstairs?"

Anna could hear the frustration in his voice, but she didn't care. She didn't care about anything anymore. There was nothing but a huge empty space inside of her. No tears, no sorrow, no anger.

"No."

"You have to eat. You have to . . ." His voice broke, and he set the tray down on her bedside table with a bang, making some of the tomato soup slosh over the side of the bowl.

"No."

"I lost a child too, Anna. And the kids lost a brother. We need you. We . . ."

She heard him searching for words. But in her head, there was room for only one word. A single word that had lodged inside of the emptiness. She looked away.

"No."

After a moment she heard Dan leave the room. She turned to look out of the window again.

It worried her that he seemed so distant.

"My dear Sam." She cradled him in her arms, stroking his hair. He still hadn't made a sound. It occurred to her that maybe she should have taken him to a doctor, but she quickly dismissed the idea. She wasn't ready to let anyone else into their world yet. If he just had some peace and quiet, he would soon be himself again.

"Do you want to take a little afternoon nap, sweetie?"

He didn't answer, but she carried him to his bed and tucked him in. Then she made herself a pot of coffee, poured some into a cup along with some milk, and went outside to sit on the dock, savoring the warmth of the sun on her face. Fredrik had loved the sun; in fact, he had worshipped it. He was always complaining about how cold it was in Sweden and how seldom the sun shone.

Why was she suddenly thinking about him? She had pushed all such thoughts to the back of her mind. He no longer had any place in their lives. Fredrik, with his constant demands and his need to have control over everything and everyone. Mostly over her—and Sam.

Out here on Gråskär there was no trace of him. He'd never been to the island; it was all hers. He had never wanted to come here. "I'll be damned if I'm going to park myself on some fucking rock," he'd said the few times that she'd asked him. She was glad that he'd refused to come. The island hadn't been sullied by his presence. It was a pure place that belonged only to her and Sam.

She wrapped her hands tightly around the coffee cup. The years had passed so swiftly. Time had flown by so fast, and in the end she was stuck. There was no escape, no possibility of fleeing. She had no one other than Fredrik and Sam. Where was she supposed to have gone?

At least now they were finally free. She felt the salt breeze brush her face. They had done it. She and Sam. After he recovered, they could live their own life.

⁓

Nathalie was home. He had thought about her all evening after having dinner with his parents. Nathalie with the long blond hair and the freckles on her nose and arms. Nathalie who smelled of the sea and summer. After all these years he could still feel her warmth in his embrace. It was true what they said: you never forget your first love. And those three summers on Gråskär could only be described as magical. He had gone over to see her as often as he could, and together they had made the small island their own.

But occasionally she had scared him. Her clear laughter would suddenly come to an abrupt halt, and then she seemed to disappear into a darkness where he couldn't reach her. She was never able to put words to the feeling that came over her, and eventually he learned to leave her alone whenever it happened. During that last summer the darkness had come more and more often, and she had slowly slipped away from him. In August, when he waved goodbye to her as she boarded the train for Stockholm with her luggage, he knew that it was over.

Since then, they hadn't been in touch at all. The following year he had tried to phone her when her parents passed away, one dying very soon after the other, but he got through only to her voicemail. She never called him back. And the cottage on Gråskär stood empty. He knew that his mother and father went out there once in a while to look after the place, and that Nathalie occasionally sent money to pay them for their efforts. But she had never come back, and over time his memories of her had faded.

Now Nathalie had returned. Matte stared into space as he sat at his desk. His suspicions about the spa project funding were getting stronger, and there were things he needed to tend to. But thoughts of Nathalie kept intruding. When the afternoon sun began sinking over the Tanumshede council building, he gathered up all the documents lying in front of him. He had to see Nathalie. With resolute steps he left his office, pausing to exchange a few words with Erling before he headed out to his car. His hand was shaking as he put the key in the ignition and started up the engine.

&c∞◦

"You're home so early, darling!"

Vivianne came to greet Erling, giving him a light kiss on the cheek. He couldn't resist catching hold of her, wrapping his arms around her waist to pull her close.

"Now, now, take it easy. We need to save our energy for later." She placed her hands against his chest to hold him off.

"Are you sure about that? Lately I've been so tired in the evenings." Again he drew her close. To his great disappointment, she slipped away and turned to head for her home office.

"You'll just have to wait. I've got so much to do that I couldn't possibly relax right now. And you know how things go when I'm not relaxed."

"Okay. All right."

Crestfallen, Erling watched her walk away. Of course they could wait until later, but he'd fallen asleep on the sofa for over a week now. Every morning he awoke to find himself lying under a blanket that Vivianne had tenderly spread over him, with one of the sofa pillows under his head. He couldn't understand it. It must be because he was working too hard. He really ought to get better at delegating tasks to others.

"I've brought home a treat, at any rate," he called after her.

"That's nice of you. What is it?"

"Shrimp from Olsson Brothers, and an excellent bottle of Chablis."

"Sounds wonderful. I'll be done around eight o'clock, so it would be lovely if you had everything ready by then."

"Of course, sweetheart," murmured Erling.

He picked up the grocery bags and took them out to the kitchen. It still felt a bit strange to him. When he was married to Viveca, she had always taken care of the cooking. But since Vivianne had moved in, she had somehow shifted the responsibility to his shoulders. For the life of him, he couldn't comprehend how that had happened.

He sighed heavily as he put the groceries in the refrigerator. Then he thought about what was in store for him later in the evening, and his mood lifted. He would make sure that she was properly relaxed. It would certainly make up for the time he had to spend in the kitchen.

⁙

Erica was breathing hard as she walked through Fjällbacka. Being pregnant with twins and then undergoing a cesarean hadn't exactly helped either her weight or her physical condition. But that sort of thing now seemed terribly unimportant. Both of her sons were healthy. They had survived, and the gratitude she felt every morning when they started crying at six thirty was so overwhelming that it still brought tears to her eyes.

Anna had suffered a much worse fate, and for the first time Erica had no idea how to approach her sister. Their relationship had never been easy, but since the time they were kids, Erica had been the one to take care of Anna, blowing on her bruises and cuts, wiping away her tears. This time things were different. The pain wasn't some minor scrape but a deep hole in Anna's soul. Erica felt as if she were standing off to the side, watching as her sister's life force seeped out of her. How was she going to help her heal? Anna's son had died, and no matter how sad Erica felt, she couldn't conceal her joy that her own children had lived. After the accident, Anna couldn't bear to look at her. Erica had gone to the hospital to sit next to her sister's bed. But not once had Anna met her eye.

After Anna came home, Erica couldn't bring herself to visit her. She had merely phoned Dan a few times. He sounded both depressed and resigned. So now Erica couldn't put it off any longer. She had asked Kristina to come over to babysit for the twins and Maja. Anna was her sister. She was Erica's responsibility.

Her hand felt like lead as she knocked on the door. She heard the children making a commotion inside, and after a moment Emma opened the door.

"Aunt Erica!" she cried happily. "Where are the babies?"

"They're home with Maja and their grandmother." Erica patted Emma's cheek. She looked so much like Anna when she was a child.

"Mamma is sad," said Emma, glancing up at Erica. "All she does is sleep, and Pappa says that it's because she's so sad. She's sad because the baby in her stomach decided to go to heaven instead of coming to live here with us. And I can understand why, because Adrian is always so noisy and Lisen keeps teasing me. But I would have been really nice to the baby. Really nice."

"I know you would, sweetie. But just think how much fun the baby must be having bouncing around up there on all the clouds."

"Like on lots and lots of gigantic trampolines?" Emma's face lit up.

"That's right. Exactly like lots of trampolines."

"Oh, I wish I had lots of big trampolines," said Emma. "All we have is a tiny one out in the garden. There's only room for one of us, and Lisen always gets to go first, and I never get a turn to jump on it." She turned on her heel and headed for the living room, still muttering to herself.

Only then did Erica realize what Emma had said. She had called Dan "Pappa." Erica smiled. It actually didn't surprise her, because Dan loved Anna's children, and they had loved him right from the start. The child that Dan and Anna were expecting together would have bound the family even closer. Erica swallowed hard as she followed Emma into the living room. It looked as if a bomb had gone off in there.

"Sorry about the mess," said Dan with embarrassment. "I just can't seem to keep up. It feels like there aren't enough hours in the day."

"I know what you mean. You should see what our house looks like." Erica paused in the doorway, casting a glance upstairs. "Is it okay if I go up?"

"Sure, go ahead." Dan rubbed his hand over his face. He looked totally exhausted and sad.

"I'll go with you," said Emma. But Dan squatted down to talk to her quietly, persuading her to allow Erica to look in on Anna alone.

Dan and Anna's bedroom was just to the right at the top of the stairs. Erica raised her hand but then stopped herself from knocking. Cautiously she pushed open the door. Anna was lying with her face turned toward the window. The late afternoon sun shone on her head, making it gleam under the downy new hair. Erica felt a pang in her heart. She had always been more like a mother for Anna, but that had changed over the past few years, and their relationship had become that of two sisters. Yet with one blow they were back in their old roles. Anna young and vulnerable; Erica concerned and protective.

Anna's breathing was calm and regular. She gave a little whimper, and Erica realized that she was asleep. She tiptoed over to the bed and carefully sat down on the edge so as not to wake Anna. Gently she placed her hand on her sister's hip. Whether Anna liked it or not, she intended to stay by her side. They were sisters. And friends.

⌒∞⌒

"Pappa's home!" Patrik shouted loudly and then listened for the expected response. He heard two little feet pattering along the floor, and the next second he saw Maja come around the corner at top speed, heading straight toward him.

"Pappaaaa!" She kissed his face over and over, as if he had returned from a voyage around the world and not just from a day at work.

"Hi, sweetie. Pappa's little girl." He gave her a big hug, burrowing his nose against her neck and breathing in that special Maja-scent that always made his heart leap.

"I thought you were working only half-days." His mother wiped her hands on a dishcloth as she gave him the same look he remembered from when he was a teenager and came home later than he'd promised.

"It felt so good to be back on the job that I stayed a bit longer. But I'll take it easy. We don't have anything urgent at the moment."

"Well, you know best. But you need to listen to your body. What happened to you should be taken seriously."

"Okay, okay." Patrik hoped his mother would drop the subject. She didn't really need to worry. He couldn't shake off the terror that had come over him in the ambulance on the way to

Uddevalla Hospital. He thought he was going to die; he'd been totally convinced of it. Images of Maja and Erica and the two babies that he would never get to see kept whirling through his mind, around and around, merging with the pain in his chest.

Not until he woke up in intensive care did he realize that he had survived, that it had been his body's way of telling him to take things easier. But then he was told about the car accident, and a new pain had descended on him. When they took him in a wheelchair to see the twins, his first impulse had been to turn around in the door. They were so tiny and defenseless. Their thin chests rose and fell with such effort, and every once in a while a spasm would pass through their bodies. He couldn't believe that anything so small could survive; he didn't want to go any closer, didn't want to touch them. If he did, he wasn't sure that he'd be able to say goodbye.

"Where are your brothers?" Patrik asked Maja. He was still holding her, and she had her arms wrapped tightly around his neck.

"They're sleeping. But they made a mess in their diapers. A big mess. Grandma wiped it up. It smelled yucky." She wrinkled her nose.

"They've been little angels," said Kristina, her face lighting up. "They each drank nearly two bottles of formula, and then they fell asleep without any fuss at all. Well, after dirtying their diapers, as Maja said."

"I'll go upstairs and look in on them for a minute," said Patrik. Ever since the twins had come home from the hospital, he'd gotten used to having them always within sight. While he was at work, he'd felt a terrible longing to see them.

He went upstairs to the bedroom. They hadn't wanted to separate the two boys, so they slept in the same crib. Right now they were so close that their noses touched. Noel's arm was draped over Anton, as if protecting him. Patrik wondered what their roles would be. Noel seemed a little more demanding, a little louder than Anton, who could best be described as content. As long as he got enough food and was allowed to sleep when he was tired, they never heard anything but delighted prattle from him. Noel, on the other hand, would utter loud protests if he wasn't happy about something. He didn't like being dressed or having his diaper changed. Worst of all was being bathed. Judging by his screams, he seemed to think that water was life-threatening.

Patrik stood for a long time leaning over their crib. Noel and Anton were both sound asleep, their eyelids fluttering faintly. He wondered if they were dreaming the same thing.

⁓

Nathalie sat on the steps in the fading sunlight as she watched the boat approach. Sam had already fallen asleep. Slowly she stood up and walked down to the dock.

"Permission to come ashore!"

His voice sounded familiar, and yet different. She could tell that he'd been through plenty since they'd last met. At first she wanted to shout: "No, don't come ashore! You don't belong here anymore." Instead, she caught the line he tossed her and out of habit tied a double half-hitch to moor the boat. The next second he was standing on the dock. Nathalie had forgotten how tall he was. She was used to being about the same height as most men, but she'd always been able to press her head against his chest. That was one of the things that Fredrik had teased her about—the fact that she was at least an inch taller than he was. She had always been forced to wear flats whenever they went anywhere together.

Don't think about Fredrik right now. Don't think about . . .

She found herself in his arms. She didn't quite know how that happened, or who took the first step. All of a sudden his arms were around her, and his rough sweater was scratchy against her cheek. Drawn into his embrace she felt safe, and she breathed in his familiar scent, which she hadn't smelled for so many years. Matte's scent.

"Hi, Nathalie." He hugged her even harder, as if trying to keep her from falling, and he succeeded. She wanted to stay there forever, touching everything that had been hers so long ago but that had vanished in all the confusion of darkness and desperation. Finally he released her, holding her away as he studied her face, as if seeing it for the very first time.

"You look just the same," he said. But Nathalie could see in his eyes that it wasn't true. She wasn't the same; she was someone else. It was evident in her face, in the lines etched around her eyes and mouth, and she knew that he could tell. She loved him for pretending otherwise. He'd always been so good at that—at pretending bad things would go away if only you closed your eyes tight enough.

"Come on," she said, holding out her hand to him. He took it, and then they walked up to the house.

"The island looks the same as always." The wind snatched at his voice, carrying it out over the cliffs.

"Yes. Here, nothing has changed." She wanted to say more, but Matte stepped inside. He had to duck as he went in the door, and then the moment was gone. That was how things had always been with Matte. She could remember words that she'd carried inside her and wanted to say to him, but they had refused to come out, rendering her mute. And making him sad. She knew that. Sad that she shut him out whenever the darkness descended.

She couldn't let him in now either, but she could allow him to sit here in the house with her. At least for a while. She needed his warm presence. She had been frozen for so long.

"Would you like some tea?" She took out a saucepan without waiting for him to reply. She needed to keep busy in order not to reveal that she was shaking.

"Sure, that would be nice. Where have you put that little man of yours? How old is he now?"

She gave him an inquiring look.

"Mamma and Pappa have kept me up-to-date," he said with a smile.

"He's five. And he's already asleep."

"Ah." He sounded disappointed, and that warmed her heart. It was important to her. She had often wondered what things would have been like if she'd had Sam with Matte instead of with Fredrik. Only in that case, he wouldn't have been Sam but some other child. And that was impossible to imagine.

She was glad that Sam was asleep. She didn't want Matte to see him the way he was now. But as soon as he was feeling better, she would introduce Matte to her little boy, whose brown eyes were always so filled with mischief. If only the mischief would return, then all three of them could spend time together. She looked forward to that.

They sat in silence for a while, sipping the hot tea. It was odd to feel like strangers, to know that they had let the passing of time bring them to this state. Then they started talking. It wasn't easy, because they were not the same people they used to be. Slowly they fell into a familiar rhythm that had been theirs alone, and they were able to strip away all that the years had placed between them.

When she took his hand and led him upstairs, it felt as if everything was as it should be. Afterward, she fell asleep with his arms wrapped around her and his breath in her ear. Outside she could hear the sound of the waves crashing against the rocks.

⌇

Vivianne spread a blanket over Erling. The sleeping pill had knocked him out, as usual. He'd started to wonder why he fell asleep on the sofa every evening, and she knew that she had to be careful. But she could no longer stand lying next to him, feeling his body touching hers. She couldn't do it.

She went into the kitchen and tossed the shrimp shells into the garbage. Then she rinsed off the plates and put them in the dishwasher. There was a little wine left, so she poured it into a fresh glass and went back to the TV room.

It was so close now, and she was beginning to get nervous. Over the past few days it had seemed as if the fiction they had so carefully constructed might collapse. Only one small part had to shift for the whole thing to come tumbling down. She knew that. When she was younger, she'd found a certain perverse enjoyment in taking risks. She had loved the feeling of teetering on the edge of danger. Not anymore. It was as if the older she got, the stronger her yearning for security became, the desire to lean back and not have to think. And she was sure that Anders felt the same way. They were so alike and knew what the other one was thinking without saying a word out loud. It had always been that way.

Vivianne lifted the glass to her lips but paused for a moment when she smelled the wine. The scent brought back memories of events that she had sworn to forget. It was all so long ago. She had been a different person, someone she could never be again, not under any circumstances. She was Vivianne now.

She knew that she needed Anders to keep her from falling again, sliding down into that dark hole of memories that made her feel sullied and small.

Giving one last glance at Erling lying on the sofa, she grabbed her jacket and went out. He was sleeping soundly. He wouldn't miss her.

# Fjällbacka 1870

**W**hen Karl proposed to her, Emelie was in seventh heaven. She could never have imagined that such a thing would actually happen, even though she'd dreamed about it. During the five years that she'd worked as a maid on his parents' farm, she had often fallen asleep with the image of Karl's face in her thoughts. But he was far beyond her reach, and she knew it. Edith's sharp rebukes had also chased away the last of her dreams. The farmer's son was not about to marry the maid, not even if she was in the family way.

Karl had never touched her. He had hardly spoken to her the few times he'd had free from the lightship and had come home to visit. He had merely treated her politely, stepping out of her way if she needed to get past. At the most he had asked after her health but had never given any sign that he felt the same as she did. Edith had called her a fool, telling her to push those thoughts out of her mind and stop being such a dreamer.

*But dreams could come true, and prayers could be answered. One day he had appeared and asked to speak with her. She was frightened, thinking that she'd done something stupid and that he was going to tell her to pack up her belongings and leave the farm. Instead, he had stared at the floor. A lock of his dark hair fell over his eyes, and she had to restrain herself from reaching out to brush it back. Stammering, he had asked whether she might consider entering into marriage with him. She couldn't believe her ears. She found herself looking him up and down to see whether he was joking. But he went on speaking, telling her that he wanted her to be his wife, and they could be married the very next day. His parents and the pastor had already been informed, so if she accepted his proposal, the whole thing could be arranged at once.*

*She hesitated for a moment but then whispered "yes." Karl had bowed and thanked her as he backed out of the room. She sat there for a long time, feeling the warmth spread through her chest. She offered up her thanks to God, who had heard the prayers she had silently repeated every night. Then she rushed out to find Edith.*

*But Edith hadn't reacted as she had hoped, with surprise and perhaps a little envy. Instead, she had drawn her dark brows together in a frown as she shook her head and told Emelie that she needed to be careful. Edith had heard strange conversations, voices that rose and fell behind closed doors, ever since Karl had come home from the lightship. He had arrived unexpectedly. At least no one who worked on the farm had been given any forewarning that the youngest son was on his way home. And that was unusual, Edith had said. But Emelie wasn't listening. Interpreting her friend's words as a sign that she was jealous of the happiness that awaited her, she had resolutely turned her back on Edith and refused to speak to her again. She didn't want to hear anything about such stupid talk and gossip. She was going to marry Karl.*

*A week had passed since then, and they had spent one day and one night in their new house. Emelie found herself walking around humming. It was wonderful to have her own home. Of course it was small, but it was lovely in its simplicity, and she had busily swept and cleaned since the day they arrived. The whole place now sparkled and smelled of fragrant soap. She and Karl hadn't spent much time together yet, but there would be plenty of opportunities for that from now on. He had a lot to do, putting everything in order. Julian, who was the assistant lighthouse keeper, had now arrived as well, and on the first night he and Karl had taken turns in the lighthouse.*

*She wasn't sure what she thought about sharing the island with this man. Julian had hardly spoken to her since he came ashore on Gråskär. Mostly he just stared at her, giving her a look that she didn't really care for. But it was probably because he was shy. It couldn't be easy to be suddenly living in such close quarters with a stranger. As she understood it, he knew Karl from their time together on the lightship, but it was going to take a while for him to get to know her. And if there was one thing they had in abundance out here, it was time. Emelie continued puttering about the kitchen. She wasn't going to give Karl any reason to regret taking her as his wife.*

# 3

Nathalie reached out her hand for him, just as she had always done back then. It had felt as if only a day had passed since they last lay together in this bed. But they were grown-ups now. His body was more angular and hairy, with scars that hadn't existed before, both inside and out. She had lain for a long time with her head resting on his chest, running her finger along the shapes of those scars. She wanted to ask him about them, but in her heart she knew that things were still too fragile to risk inquiring about what had happened during the intervening years.

Now the other side of the bed was empty. Her mouth was dry, and she felt exhausted. Lonely. She ran her hand over the sheet and pillow, but Matte was gone. It felt as if she'd discovered that she'd lost part of her own body during the night. Then she felt a spark of hope. Maybe he was downstairs. She held her breath and listened but didn't hear a sound. Wrapping the blanket around her, Nathalie set her feet on the worn floor-boards. Cautiously she tiptoed over to the window that faced the dock and looked out. His boat was gone. He'd left without saying goodbye. She slid down along the wall and felt the onset of a headache. She needed to drink something.

Slowly she got dressed. It felt as though she hadn't slept a wink all night, even though she knew that she had. She had fallen asleep in his arms and slept more soundly than she had in a very long time. And yet her head was pounding.

It was quiet downstairs. She looked in on Sam and found him awake but lying in bed and not making a sound. Without a word, she picked him up and carried him to the kitchen table. She stroked his hair before putting water on the stove to make coffee. Then she got herself a drink. She was so thirsty. She downed two big glasses of water before the dry feeling in her throat was gone. Nathalie wiped her mouth with the back of her hand. The fatigue was greater, more noticeable, now that her thirst was quenched. However Sam needed food, and she did too. She boiled some eggs, made herself an open-face sandwich, and fixed oatmeal for Sam, the whole time moving as if on automatic.

Then she cast a surreptitious glance at the drawer out in the hall. She didn't have much left. It was important to ration herself. But the exhaustion she felt and the memory of the solitary boat at the dock prompted her to take the few steps into the hall and pull out the bottom drawer of the bureau. Eagerly she thrust her hands underneath the clothing, yet her fingers didn't find what they were looking for. She searched again, and then pulled all of the clothes out of the drawer. Nothing. Maybe this wasn't the right drawer. She pulled out the two other drawers and emptied the contents onto the floor. Nothing. Panic washed over her, and suddenly she understood why her hand had found only an empty bed when she woke up. Now she realized why Matte was gone, and why he hadn't said goodbye.

She collapsed onto the floor and curled up in a foetal position, hugging her knees. In the kitchen she could hear the water
boiling over.

❦

"Leave the boy alone." Gunnar didn't look up from reading
*Bohusläningen* when he repeated the same thing he'd been saying
all day.

"But maybe he'd like to come over for dinner today. Or
tomorrow, since it's Sunday. Don't you think so?" Signe insisted.

Gunnar sighed from behind his newspaper. "I'm sure he has
other things to do over the weekend. He's a grown man. If he
wants to come over, he'll probably call or drop by. You can't
keep hounding him like this. He was just here for a dinner."

"I think I'll give him a quick call anyway. To hear how
he's doing." Signe reached for the phone, but Gunnar leaned
forward to stop her.

"Let him be," he said sternly.

Signe drew back her hand. Her whole body was aching to
call Matte's cell, to hear his voice and make sure that everything
was fine. After the beating she had become more concerned
than ever. The incident had confirmed what she'd always
known—that the world was a dangerous place for Matte.

Logically she knew that she needed to take a step back. But
what good was that when everything inside of her screamed
that she had to protect him? He was grown up now. She realized that. Still she couldn't stop worrying.

Signe slipped out to the hall to use the phone there. When
she heard Matte's recorded message on his voicemail, she put
down the receiver. Why wasn't he answering his phone?

❦

"I don't know what to do."

Erica slumped in her chair. They had a rare moment of peace in the midst of the chaos. All three children were asleep, so she and Patrik could sit at the kitchen table together, eating hot sandwiches and talking without being constantly interrupted. But Erica was having a hard time enjoying the moment. She couldn't stop thinking about Anna.

"There's really not much you can do except make yourself available when she needs you. And she does have Dan, after all." Patrik reached across the table to put his hand on Erica's.

"What if she hates me?" she said faintly, on the verge of tears.

"Why would she hate you?"

"Because I have two babies and she has none."

"But that's not your fault. It's just . . . I don't know really what to call it. Fate, maybe." Patrik stroked her hand.

"Fate?" Erica gave him a dubious look. "Anna has suffered enough at the hands of fate. She was finally starting to be happy, and she and I were getting so close. But now . . . She's going to hate me. I know she is."

"How did it go yesterday when you went to see her?"

They'd both been so busy that they hadn't had a chance to talk until now. The candle that Patrik had lit began fluttering so that Erica's face was alternately illuminated and in shadow.

"She was asleep. I sat with her for a while. She looked so small."

"What about Dan?"

"He seemed in despair. He's carrying a heavy load. I can tell, even though he pretends that everything is okay. Emma and Adrian are asking a lot of questions. And he told me that he doesn't know what to say to them."

"She'll make it through this. She's demonstrated in the past that she's a very strong person." Patrik let go of Erica's hand and picked up his knife and fork.

"I'm not so sure about that. How much can any human being stand before falling apart? I'm afraid that Anna has reached her limit." Erica's voice broke.

"We'll just have to wait and see. And help her if she needs us." Patrik could hear how hollow his words sounded, hovering in the air. But he couldn't think of anything else to say. He didn't know any better than Erica did. How did people defend themselves against fate? How could anyone go on after losing a child?

At that moment two cries from above made them both jump. Together they went upstairs to get the twins. This was their fate. They felt both guilty and grateful.

# 4

That was Matte's office. He didn't come in yesterday, and he's not there today either. And he didn't call in sick." Gunnar seemed frozen in place as he held the phone in his hand.

"And he didn't pick up all weekend when I called his number," said Signe.

"I'll drive over to his place and have a look."

Gunnar was already on his way to the door, grabbing his jacket as he passed. So this is how Signe feels, he thought. Fear was darting around in his chest like a wild animal. This was how she must have felt all these years.

"I'm going with you," Signe said firmly, and Gunnar knew better than to argue. He nodded briefly and then waited impatiently as she put on her coat.

They drove in silence all the way to Matte's apartment. Gunnar took the back roads, not the route through town.

Instead he drove past the Seven Hills, the place where kids went sledding in the winter. Matte had done that too when he was a boy. Gunnar swallowed hard. There had to be a logical explanation. Maybe he was running a fever and hadn't thought of calling in sick. Or maybe . . . He couldn't think of anything else. Matte was always so conscientious about everything. He would have rung the office if he couldn't make it to work.

Signe's face was pale as she sat next to him in the passenger seat. She was staring straight ahead, gripping her handbag, which rested on her lap. Gunnar wondered why she was holding on to it so tightly, but he had the feeling that the handbag was her lifeline at the moment.

They parked in front of Matte's building. Entrance B. Gunnar wanted to run, but for Signe's sake he tried to act calmly and forced himself to walk at a normal pace.

"Do you have the keys?" asked Signe, who had gone striding ahead and already had the front door open.

"Here." Gunnar held out the spare keys that Matte had given them.

"I'm sure he's home, so we won't really need them. He'll come to the door himself and then . . ."

He listened to Signe's incoherent chatter as she ran up the stairs. Matte lived on the top floor, and they were both out of breath by the time they reached the door to his apartment. Gunnar had to restrain himself from immediately putting the key in the lock.

"Let's ring the bell first. If he's home, he'll be cross if we go barging in. Maybe he has company and that's why he hasn't gone to work."

Signe was already pressing the doorbell. They heard it ringing inside. She tried it again. And again. Then they listened for approaching footsteps, Matte's footsteps coming to the door. But there was only silence.

"I think you'd better use the key." Signe gave her husband an urgent look.

He nodded, stepped in front of her, and began fumbling with the key ring. He found the right key, turned it in the lock, and pushed down on the door handle. The door didn't budge. In confusion he realized that the door had been open, and he had just locked it. He glanced at Signe. They could see the panic in each other's eyes. Why would the door be left unlocked if Matte wasn't home? And if he was home, why hadn't he come to the door?

Gunnar turned the key again, and heard the click of the lock. With fingers that were now shaking uncontrollably, he pushed open the door.

The moment he looked inside the front hall, he realized that Signe had been right all along.

⁂

She was sick. More ill than she'd ever been in her life. The smell of vomit filled her nostrils. She couldn't really remember, but she thought she'd thrown up in a bucket next to the mattress. She saw everything through a fog. Nathalie cautiously tried to move. Her whole body ached. She squinted. Her eyes hurt as she tried to see what time it was. What day was it? And where was Sam?

The thought of Sam gave her enough strength to sit up. She was lying on a mattress next to his bed. He was asleep. She was finally able to focus her eyes enough to read her watch. It was just after one. Which meant that Sam was taking an afternoon nap. She stroked his head.

Somehow she must have managed to look after him in spite of the fever. Her maternal instincts had proved sufficiently strong. Relief flooded over her, making the pain easier to bear.

She looked around. A bottle of water lay on his bed, and scattered on the floor were pieces of fruit, a hunk of cheese, and a packet of cookies. It looked as if she'd made sure he had food and water.

A bucket stood next to the mattress, and the smell coming from it was disgusting. She must have realized how ill she was and brought the bucket into the room. Her stomach felt empty, so she'd apparently thrown up everything she'd eaten.

Slowly she got to her feet. She didn't want to wake Sam, so she stopped herself from groaning aloud. Finally she was able to stand though her legs were wobbly. It was important for her to have something to eat and drink. She wasn't hungry, but her stomach was growling in protest. She picked up the bucket, careful not to look inside as she carried it out of the room. Using her shoulder to push open the front door, she shivered in surprise as she came out into the cold air. The summer heat must have disappeared while she was sick.

Cautiously she sat down on the dock and, averting her eyes, dumped the contents of the bucket into the sea. She picked up a rope and tied it to the handle. Then she lowered the bucket over the side of the dock and rinsed it out in the water.

The wind tore at her hair as she walked back to the house, arms hugging her chest. Her whole body was screaming from the effort, and she could feel the sweat pouring out of her. Disgusted, she peeled off all her clothes and washed up before putting on a clean T-shirt and a jogging suit. With trembling hands she made a sandwich, poured herself a glass of juice, and sat down at the kitchen table. It took several bites before the food began tasting of anything, but after that she quickly ate two more sandwiches. Gradually she could feel life returning to her body.

Nathalie glanced at her watch again, looking at the little window that showed the date. After doing some calculations in her head, she decided it had to be Tuesday. She'd been sick for almost three days. Three lost days, filled with all sorts of dreams. What exactly had she dreamed? She tried to grab hold of the images swirling through her mind. There was one that kept repeating. Nathalie shook her head but the movement made her stomach heave. She took a bite of a fourth sandwich, and her stomach settled down. A woman. There was a woman in her dreams, and there was something about her face. Nathalie frowned. There was something so familiar about that woman. She knew that she'd seen her before, but she couldn't recall where.

She got up. No doubt she'd remember sooner or later. But a feeling from the dream refused to leave her. The woman had looked so sad. With the same feeling of sadness, Nathalie went into the bedroom to see to Sam.

◌◦◦

Patrik hadn't slept well. Erica's concern for Anna had infected him, and he had awakened several times during the night with gloomy thoughts about how swiftly life could change. His own recent experience had made him lose his foothold a bit. Maybe it was good that he no longer took life for granted, but at the same time a nagging feeling of uneasiness had settled inside of him. He found himself behaving in a much more overprotective manner than he'd ever done before. He didn't like seeing Erica drive off with the children in the car. To be quite honest, he would have preferred her not to drive at all. And he'd feel much more secure if she and the children never stepped outside the house again but remained indoors, far removed from any dangers.

Of course he understood that such thoughts were neither healthy nor rational. But he'd been so close to losing his own life as well as Erica and the twins. Their family had been seconds away from disappearing altogether.

He gripped the edge of his desk, forcing himself to breathe calmly. Sometimes he felt overwhelmed by panic; he thought he might have to learn to live with it. That much he could manage, because in spite of everything, he still had his family.

"How's it going?" asked Paula, suddenly appearing in the doorway.

Patrik took another deep breath. "Okay. I'm a little tired, that's all. Night feedings, you know," he said, attempting to smile.

Paula came in and sat down.

"Oh, right." She looked him straight in the eye with an expression that revealed she wasn't buying his evasive answers and false smiles. "I asked you how it's going."

"It's been up and down," Patrik admitted reluctantly. "I think it will take a while for me to get back to normal. Even though everything is fine now. Except for Erica's sister, of course."

"How is she?"

"Not good."

"It takes time."

"I suppose so. But she's shut everybody out. She won't even talk to Erica."

"Do you think that's so strange?" asked Paula quietly.

Patrik knew that his colleague had the ability to get straight to the heart of a matter. She often said what people needed to hear—not necessarily what they wanted to hear. And she was usually right.

"You and Erica have two children who survived the accident. Anna lost her baby. I don't think it's so strange that she would shut her sister out."

"That's exactly what scares Erica. But what should we do?"

"Nothing. Not at the moment. Anna has her own family; she has a husband who is the baby's father. They need to find their way back to each other before Erica is allowed in. No matter how harsh it sounds, Erica needs to stay away for now. That doesn't mean she's giving up on Anna. She's still here if her sister needs her."

"I can understand that, but I don't know how to explain it to Erica." Patrik took another deep breath. The pressure in his chest had relaxed a bit as he talked to Paula.

"I think that—" Paula began, but she was interrupted by someone knocking on the door.

"Excuse me," said Annika, her face flushed. "We just got a call from Fjällbacka. A man has been found shot to death in his apartment."

At first no one said a word. Then Paula and Patrik sprang into action, and a minute later they were headed for the garage. Behind them they heard Annika knocking on the office doors belonging to Gösta and Martin, who would have to take the other police vehicle. They'd follow later.

∞

"This is fantastic!" Erling looked around with pleasure at everything inside the new Badis spa before he turned to Vivianne. "It certainly wasn't cheap, but it's worth every krona as far as the town is concerned. I think it's going to be a big success. And considering the amount of money that you've personally invested, there's going to be a nice little profit for us once we've covered expenses. You're not paying the employees too much, are you?" He cast a suspicious glance at a white-clad young woman walking past.

Vivianne linked arms with him to lead him over to one of the tables.

"Don't worry. We're very cost-conscious here. Anders has always been extremely tightfisted. It's thanks to him that we made so much at the spa at Ljuset, and that's the reason we could invest in this project."

"Yes, it's lucky that you have Anders." Erling sat down at the table in the dining room to have coffee. "Did Matte get hold of you, by the way? He mentioned last week that there were a few things he wanted to check with you and Anders."

He reached for a bun, but after taking a bite he put it back down on the plate.

"What are these?"

"Spelt buns."

"Oh," said Erling, and settled for sipping his coffee.

"No, I haven't heard from Matte, so it probably wasn't important. I'm sure he'll drop by or give me a ring when he gets a chance."

"It's rather strange, actually. He never showed up at the office yesterday, even though he didn't call in sick. And I didn't see him there this morning before I drove out here."

"Probably nothing to worry about," said Vivianne, reaching for a bun.

"May I join you, or do you lovebirds want to be alone?" Anders had appeared without either Erling or Vivianne noticing. Both of them were startled, but then Vivianne smiled and pulled out a chair so her brother could sit down next to her.

As always, Erling was struck by how alike they looked. Both were blond with blue eyes and similar mouths with bow-shaped lips. But while Vivianne was energetic and extroverted, possessing what Erling would call a magnetic charisma, her brother was introverted and quiet. An accountant type was what he first thought upon meeting Anders during his stay at Ljuset. And he didn't think that was a bad thing. With so much money at stake, it was reassuring to have such a dull numbers-person looking after the finances.

"Have you heard from Mats? Erling says he had a few questions," said Vivianne, turning to Anders.

"Yes, he dropped by briefly on Friday afternoon. Why?"

Erling cleared his throat. "Well, he mentioned at the end of last week that he was concerned about several issues."

Anders nodded. "As I said, he dropped by, and we were able to clear up a number of questions."

"Oh, good. It's nice to know that everything is in order," said Erling, smiling happily.

# 5

An elderly man and woman stood outside the front entrance, holding on to each other. Patrik assumed that they were the parents of the deceased. They were the ones who had found the body. He and Paula got out of the car and went over to them.

"Patrik Hedström, Tanum police. Are you the ones who called us?" he asked, even though he already knew the answer.

"Yes, we did." The man's cheeks were wet with tears.

His wife kept her face pressed against her husband's chest.

"It's our son," she said without looking at them. "He's . . . up there . . ."

"I'll go up and take a look."

The man made a move as if to follow, but Patrik stopped him.

"I think it's best if you both wait here. The medics will be arriving any minute, and they'll take care of you. My colleague Paula will stay with you until they get here."

Patrik gestured to Paula, who gently led the couple aside. Then he entered the building and went up to the third floor, where he found a door standing wide open. He didn't need to go inside the apartment to know that the man lying on his stomach on the hall floor was dead. A big hole was visible in the back of the victim's head. Blood and brain matter had sprayed out over the floor and walls and then congealed. This was obviously the scene of the crime, and there was no use doing anything until Torbjörn Ruud and his team of technicians examined the apartment. Patrik decided that he might as well go back downstairs and have a talk with the victim's parents.

When he came outside, Patrik hurried over to the couple. They were standing next to Paula and talking to the ambulance medics, who had just arrived. A blanket had been draped over the woman's shoulders, and she was crying so hard that she shook. Patrik chose to start with the husband, who looked more composed even though he too was crying.

"Are we needed up there?" asked one of the medics, nodding toward the building.

Patrik shook his head.

"No, not for a while, at least. The techs are on their way."

For a moment no one spoke. The only sound was the heart-wrenching sobs of the elderly woman. Patrik went over to her husband.

"Could I have a few words with you?"

"We want to help as much as we can. We just don't understand who would . . ." The man's voice broke, but after casting a glance at his wife, he followed Patrik over to the police vehicle. The woman didn't seem aware of what was happening around her.

They sat in the backseat of the car.

"It says 'Mats Sverin' on the door of the apartment. Is that your son?"

"Yes. Although we've always called him Matte."

"And your name is . . .?" Patrik took notes as they talked.

"Gunnar Sverin. My wife's name is Signe. But why—"

Patrik placed his hand on the man's arm to calm him.

"We're going to do everything in our power to catch who-ever did this. Do you think you could answer a few questions?"
Gunnar nodded.

"When did you last see your son?"

"Thursday night. He came over to have dinner with us. He's been doing that a lot since he moved back to Fjällbacka."

"What time did he leave your place on Thursday?"

"He drove home shortly after nine, I think."

"Have you heard from him since then? Have you talked to him on the phone, or had any other sort of contact?"

"No, nothing. Signe is the worrying kind, and she tried to call Matte all weekend without reaching him, but I . . . I told her she was being an old worrywart and she should stop both-ering the boy." Tears welled up in his eyes again. Embarrassed, he wiped them away on the sleeve of his jacket.

"So no one answered the phone at your son's apartment? And he didn't answer his cell either?"

"No, we just got his voicemail."

"Was that unusual?"

"Yes, I think so. Signe calls him up a little too often, in my opinion, but Matte has the patience of an angel." Gunnar again wiped his eyes on his sleeve.

"Is that why you came over here today?"

"Yes and no. Signe was getting really upset. I was too, even though I pretended not to be worried. But then I got a call from the council saying that Matte hadn't turned up for work . . . And that's not like him, not at all. He has always been very conscientious about being on time and so on. He gets that from me."

"What sort of work did he do for the town?"

"He's been the finance officer for the past couple of months. That was after he moved back here. He was lucky to get the job. There aren't many positions available for economists."

"How did he happen to move to Fjällbacka? Where did he live before?"

"In Göteborg," said Gunnar, answering the second question first. "We don't really know why he decided to make the move. But he was involved in a terrible incident not long before he came here. He was assaulted by a gang in the city, and he spent several weeks in the hospital. That sort of thing can make a person reevaluate his life. At any rate, he moved back here, and that made us very happy. Especially Signe, of course. She was overjoyed."

"Did they find the gang who assaulted him?"

"No. The police never caught them. Matte had no idea who they were, and he wouldn't have been able to identify them afterward either. He was really badly beaten. When Signe and I went to Sahlgrenska Hospital to see him, we could hardly recognize our son."

Patrik drew an exclamation mark on the page next to his note on the assault. He needed to find out more about that ASAP. He'd have to contact his colleagues in Göteborg.

"And you and your wife don't know of anyone who might want to harm Matte? Any individual or individuals who might have had a score to settle with him?"

Gunnar shook his head emphatically.

"Matte never quarreled with anyone. Everybody liked him. And he liked everybody."

"So how was his new job going?"

"I think he enjoyed it. He did seem a bit worried when we saw him on Thursday, but that was just a vague impression I got. Maybe he was feeling overworked. In any case, he never mentioned having fallen out with anyone. His boss Erling can be rather difficult, from what I understand, but Matte said that he was basically harmless, and he knew how to deal with him."

"And when he was living in Göteborg? Can you give me any details of his life there? Friends, girlfriends, work colleagues . . . ?"

"No, I can't say that we really know anything. He didn't discuss personal matters much. Signe tried prodding him to tell her what was going on in his life, regarding girls, and that sort of thing, but he never went into details. A few years ago he'd occasionally tell us about some of his friends, but from the time he started at that last job he had in Göteborg he seemed to retreat from socializing, and all his time was devoted to his work. Matte could get very immersed in his job."

"So what happened when he came back to Fjällbacka? Didn't he contact any of his old friends?"

Again Gunnar shook his head.

"No, he didn't seem at all interested in doing that. Besides, not many of his old friends still live here. Most have moved away. But he seemed to want to keep to himself. And that worried Signe."

"He doesn't have a girlfriend?"

"I don't think so. But of course, we wouldn't always know about such things."

"Didn't he ever bring anyone home to meet you?" asked Patrik with surprise. He wondered how old Matte was. When Gunnar told him, he realized that Matte was the same age as Erica.

"No, he never brought anyone home, but that doesn't necessarily mean anything," the old man added, as if he'd read Patrik's thoughts.

"Okay. But if you happen to think of any other details that might help us, you can call me at this number." Patrik handed

Gunnar his card. "Anything at all. We're going to want to talk to your wife too. And we'll need to talk to you again. I hope you understand."

"Of course," said Gunnar, taking Patrik's card.

He peered out of the window to look at Signe, who seemed to have stopped crying. Presumably the medics had given her a sedative.

"I'm very sorry for your loss," said Patrik. Then silence settled between them. There really wasn't much more to say.

As they got out of the car, Torbjörn Ruud and his team of crime techs pulled into the parking lot. Now the meticulous process of collecting evidence would begin.

❦

With hindsight, it was hard to understand why Nathalie hadn't seen through Fredrik. But maybe that wouldn't have been so easy. Outwardly, he seemed very polished, and he had courted her so ardently that at first she had laughed at him. That had merely goaded him on, and he increased his efforts until she eventually gave in. He had pampered her, taken her on trips abroad where they had stayed in five-star hotels, offered her champagne, and sent her so many bouquets of flowers that they practically filled her whole apartment. She deserved luxury, he said. And she believed him. It was as if he spoke to something that had always been inside of her. An insecurity and a desire to hear that she was special, that she deserved more than other people. Where had all the money come from? Nathalie couldn't remember ever asking that question.

The wind had picked up, but she stayed where she was, sitting on the bench on the south side of the house. Though her coffee had grown cold, she continued sipping at it. Her hands, wrapped around the cup, were shaking. Her legs still felt unsteady, and her stomach was churning. She knew this would go on for a while. It was nothing new.

Slowly she'd been drawn into Fredrik's world, which was filled with parties, traveling, and beautiful people and things. A lovely home. She had almost immediately moved in with him, all too willing to leave behind her cramped one-room apartment in Farsta. How could she possibly go on living there after spending so many nights and days in Fredrik's enormous house in the wealthy Stockholm suburb of Djursholm, where everything was new and white and expensive?

By the time she fully understood what Fredrik did for a living and how he earned his money, it was too late. Her life was intertwined with his. They had the same friends, she wore his ring on her finger, and she no longer had a job because Fredrik had wanted her to stay home and make sure everything ran smoothly on the domestic front. But the sad truth was that she hadn't really been very upset when she found out. She had merely shrugged, firmly convinced that he belonged to the upper echelons of a sleazy industry, that he was so high up that he wasn't touched by the muck far below. There was also a certain excitement about the whole thing. She got a little adrenaline kick from knowing what was going on all around her.

Outwardly, none of this was evident, of course. On paper Fredrik was a wine importer, and that was partially true. His company made a small profit every year, and he loved visiting the vineyard that he'd bought in Tuscany. He planned to launch his own wine label someday. That was the façade he presented to the world, and no one ever questioned it. Sometimes Nathalie would sit at the table, dining with upper-crust guests and important business associates, and she'd muse upon how simple it was to fool them, how readily they swallowed everything Fredrik said. They accepted that the enormous sums of money whirling around them came from his import business.

But maybe that was merely what they chose to believe. The same way she had done.

Everything changed when Sam was born. It was Fredrik who insisted they should have a child. He wanted a son. She'd had her doubts. Nathalie was still ashamed to recall her fear that being pregnant would ruin her figure, and that having a child might keep her from having three-hour lunches with her women friends and devoting her days to shopping. Nonetheless, when Fredrik had insisted, she'd reluctantly agreed.

The instant that the midwife placed Sam in her arms, her whole life changed. Nothing else mattered anymore. Fredrik finally had his longed-for son, but he found himself pushed to the periphery as she devoted herself to the baby. He wasn't the sort of man who tolerated being knocked out of first place, and his jealousy of Sam manifested itself in a strange way. Forbidding his wife to breastfeed the baby, against her wishes he brought in a nanny to take care of Sam. Nathalie, adamant that she would not be dismissed in that way, had put Elena in charge of ironing and vacuuming, leaving her to spend more hours in the nursery with Sam. Nothing was allowed to come between them. Previously she had behaved like a pampered and spoiled woman, but now she displayed a new confidence in her new role as Sam's mother.

But the moment she held Sam in her arms, her life also began falling apart. There had been incidents of violence before when Fredrik was drunk or high on drugs. She'd ended up with bruises that had hurt for a few days, or a bloodied nose. Nothing worse than that.

After Sam was born, her life became hell. Now the strong wind, combined with the memories, brought tears to her eyes. Her hands shook so badly that some of the coffee spilled over the side and onto her trousers. She blinked to get rid of both the tears and the images. The blood. There had been so much blood.

One remembered image overlapped another, like two negatives merging into one. She felt confused. And scared.

Abruptly Nathalie stood up. She needed to be close to Sam. She needed her son.

c○○ɔ

"Yes, this is truly a sad day." Erling was standing at the head of the conference table, looking at his colleagues with a somber expression.

"How could something like that happen?" His secretary Gunilla Kjellin blew her nose on a handkerchief. Tears were pouring down her cheeks.

"The officer who called didn't tell me much, but I gather Mats was the victim of some sort of crime."

"You mean somebody murdered him?" asked Uno Brorsson, leaning back in his chair. As usual he had rolled up the sleeves of his checked flannel shirt.

"As I said, I don't really know any of the details yet, but I trust that the police will keep us informed."

"Is this going to affect the project?" Uno tugged on his moustache, as he always did whenever he was upset.

"It won't change a thing. I want to assure you all of that. Matte put so many hours into Project Badis, and he would have been the first to say that we must press on. Everything will proceed exactly according to plan, and I will personally be taking charge of the finances until we can find a replacement for Mats."

"How can you already be talking about a replacement?" said Gunilla, sobbing loudly.

"Now, now, Gunilla." Erling was at a loss faced with such an emotional outburst, which even under the circumstances seemed to him highly inappropriate. "We have a responsibility to the town, to the citizens, and to everyone who has put their heart and soul not only into this project but into all that we're doing to make sure the community thrives." He paused, both surprised and satisfied with the way he had managed to formulate his thoughts. Then he continued: "As tragic as it is that a young man's life should be prematurely ended, we cannot simply stop everything. The show must go on, as they say in Hollywood."

Silence had descended over the others in the conference room, and the last phrase had sounded so good to Erling that he couldn't help repeating it. He straightened his shoulders, thrust out his chest, and with a strong western Swedish accent, he said in English:

"The show must go on, people. The show must go on."

⁓

In utter bewilderment they sat at the table across from one another. They had been sitting that way since one of the kindly police officers had given them a ride home. Gunnar would have preferred to drive himself, but they had insisted. So his vehicle was still in the parking lot, and he'd have to walk over there to retrieve it. But of course then he might have a chance to go up and visit . . .

Gunnar gasped for breath. How could he have forgotten so quickly? How could he forget even for a second that Matte was dead? They had seen him lying there on his stomach on the striped rag-rug that Signe had woven for him. Lying on his stomach with a hole in the back of his head. How could he forget the sight of all that blood?

"Shall I put on some coffee?" Gunnar forced himself to break the silence. The only sound he heard was his own heart, and he'd give anything to stop listening to those steady beats, which made him realize that he was alive and taking one breath after another while his son was dead.

"I'll get you a cup." He stood up even though Signe hadn't answered. She was still under the effects of the sedative as she sat there, motionless, with a blank look on her face and her hands clasped on the oilcloth covering the table.

Gunnar moved mechanically, putting in the filter, pouring in the water, opening the coffee container, measuring out the grounds, and then pressing the button. A hissing and bubbling started up at once.

"Would you like something with your coffee? A piece of sponge cake, maybe?" His voice sounded oddly normal. He went over to the refrigerator and took out the sponge cake that Signe had baked the day before. Carefully he removed the plastic, set the cake on the cutting board, and cut two thick slices. He put them on plates and set one in front of Signe, the other at his own place at the table. She didn't react, but he didn't allow himself to worry about that now. He heard only the thudding inside his chest, drowned out briefly by the clattering of the plates and the sputtering of the coffee maker.

When the coffee was ready, he reached up to take down two cups. Their daily habits seemed to have become more entrenched with every passing year, and they each had a favorite cup. Signe always drank her coffee from a delicate white cup with roses adorning the edge, while he preferred a sturdy ceramic cup that they had bought on a bus trip to Gränna. Black coffee with one sugar cube for him; coffee with milk and two sugar cubes for Signe.

"Here you are," he said, setting her cup next to the plate with the piece of cake.

She didn't move. The coffee burned his throat when he took too big a sip, and he coughed until the stinging sensation subsided. He took a bite of the sponge cake, but it seemed to swell inside his mouth, forming a big lump of sugar and egg and flour. Then he felt bile rising up in his throat, and he knew that he had to get rid of that lump, which was getting bigger and bigger.

Gunnar dashed past Signe out to the bathroom down the hall, and dropped to his knees to lean over the toilet. He watched as coffee, cake crumbs, and bile poured into the water that was always green from the cleaning fluid that Signe insisted on fastening to the side of the porcelain toilet bowl.

When his stomach was virtually empty, he again heard the sound of his own heart. Thump, thump, thump. Once more he leaned forward and threw up. Out in the kitchen, Signe's coffee was growing cold in the white cup decorated with roses.

∞

It was evening by the time they finished their work at Mats Sverin's apartment. Though it was still light outside, the hustle and bustle of the day had begun to taper off, and the number of people passing by had diminished.

"His body just arrived at the forensics lab," reported Torbjörn Ruud.

The head of the crime tech team looked tired as he came over to Patrik, holding his cell in his hand. Patrik had worked with Torbjörn and his team on several homicide investigations, and he had tremendous respect for the gray-bearded man.

"How soon do you think they'll get to the postmortem?" asked Patrik, massaging the bridge of his nose. He was beginning to feel the effects of what was turning out to be a very long day.

"I don't know. You'll have to ask Pedersen about that."

"What's your preliminary assessment?" Patrik shivered in the cold wind blowing across the small patch of lawn in front of the building. He pulled his jacket tighter around him.

"It's not all that complicated, from what I can see. A gunshot wound in the back of the head. One shot, killing him instantly. The bullet is still inside the skull. The casing we found indicates a nine-millimeter pistol."

"Did you find any evidence in the apartment?"

"We've taken fingerprints from all the rooms, and also a few fiber samples. That will give us something to go on, once we have a suspect."

"Provided that the suspect actually left any prints or fibers," said Patrik. Technical evidence was all fine and good, but from experience he knew that a large helping of luck was needed to solve a murder case. People came and went, and it could just as well have been friends or family members who left traces behind in the apartment. If the killer was among them, the police would be faced with a whole different set of problems in terms of trying to link the perpetrator to the crime scene.

"Isn't it a bit too early to be taking such a pessimistic view?" said Torbjörn, giving Patrik a poke in the side.

"Sorry." Patrik laughed. "I must be getting tired."

"You're taking it easy, aren't you? I heard that you hit the wall hard, so to speak. It can take a while to recover from something like that."

"I don't really like that phrase 'hit the wall,'" muttered Patrik. "But you're right. It was definitely a warning signal."

"Well, I'm glad you're paying attention. You're not exactly old and decrepit yet, and we're hoping you'll be working with the police for many years to come."

"What do you make of the evidence you've collected so far?" asked Patrik, attempting to steer the conversation away from his health.

"As I said, we've collected a few things. Everything will be sent over to the lab now. It's going to take a while to get the results, but I'm owed a few favors, so with a bit of luck, I'll be able to speed things along."

"We'd be grateful to get the results as fast as possible." Patrik was freezing. It was much too cold for June, and the weather continued to be unpredictable. At the moment it felt like early spring, yet during the day it had been so warm that he and Erica had been able to sit in the garden without putting on a sweater or jacket.

"So what about you. Have you and your colleagues made any progress? Did anyone hear or see anything?" Torbjörn nodded toward the block of apartments.

"We've knocked on every single door, but so far with only limited results. One of the neighbors thinks that he heard a sound in the early hours on Saturday, only he was asleep in bed when it woke him, so he's not sure what it was. Other than that, nothing. Mats Sverin appears to have kept to himself, at least when he was at home. Because he grew up in Fjällbacka, and his parents still live here, most people knew who he was and were aware that he worked for the town, and so on, but no one seems to have really known him. His neighbors were passing acquaintances, nothing more."

"At least the gossip mill is alive and well in Fjällbacka," said Torbjörn. "With luck, that should give you a few leads."

"Perhaps. At this point it seems he lived a hermit's existence, but we'll try to drum up some new leads tomorrow."

"Go home and get some rest." Torbjörn gave Patrik a friendly slap on the back.

"Thanks, I will," Patrik lied. He had already phoned Erica to say that he would be home late. The investigative team needed to devise a strategy tonight. And after a couple of hours' sleep, he'd be back at the station early in the morning. He knew that he ought to have learned his lesson after what he'd just been through. But his job came first. He couldn't help it.

Erica stared at the wood burning in the fireplace. She had tried not to sound concerned when Patrik called. Although she kept telling herself he was looking much better of late, with some color in his face again, and even though she knew this was one of those times when he needed to stay late at work, it worried her that he seemed to have forgotten his promise to take it easy.

She wondered who the dead man was. Patrik hadn't wanted to say much on the phone. All he told her was that a man had been found dead in Fjällbacka. She was eager to hear more. As a writer, a keen sense of curiosity was essential. She always wanted to find out the inside story of people and events. In time, she was sure that she'd hear all about it. Even if Patrik declined to tell her, the news would soon spread. That was both the advantage and disadvantage of living in a small town like Fjällbacka.

The thought of all the support they'd received after the car accident still moved her to tears. Everyone had offered help, be they close friends or people they hardly knew. Some had babysat for Maja and kept an eye on the house; others had left food on the doorstep when she and Patrik had finally come home from the hospital. And at the hospital they had practically drowned in all the flowers, boxes of chocolates, and toys for the children. All gifts from people in town. That was the way it was. In Fjällbacka, everyone stuck together.

Tonight, however, Erica was feeling lonely. Her first impulse after talking to Patrik had been to call Anna. She felt a pang in her heart, as usual, when she realized that she couldn't do that, and slowly she set the cordless phone back down on the table.

The children were asleep upstairs. The fire was crackling in the fireplace, and outside dusk was gathering. During the past few months she had felt frightened many times, yet never lonely. On the contrary, for she'd been constantly surrounded by other people. But not tonight.

When she heard the babies crying upstairs, she quickly got to her feet. It was going to take a while to feed the twins and get them to fall asleep again, but at least that would keep her from worrying about Patrik.

⸻

"It's been a long day, but I thought we should spend some time comparing notes and coming up with a plan before we all go home to rest."

Patrik glanced at the others. Everyone looked tired but focused. They had long ago given up any thought of meeting in any room other than the station's kitchen. And Gösta had proven to be unusually considerate tonight by making sure that everybody had a cup of hot coffee.

"Martin, could you summarize what we've learned by knocking on doors today?"

"We went around to all the other apartments and actually managed to find most of the tenants at home. There are only a few that we still need to talk to. Obviously our first objective has been to find out whether anyone heard noises coming from Mats Sverin's apartment. Loud voices, shots, or any other sort of commotion. But on that point we pretty much came up empty-handed. The one person who might have heard something was the man in the next-door apartment. His name is Leandersson. He was awakened early on Saturday by a sound that could have been a gunshot, but his memory of the sound is very vague. All he can say for sure is that he remembers being awakened by something."

"And no one saw anybody arriving or leaving?" asked Mellberg.

Annika was furiously taking notes as the others talked.

"Nobody recalls seeing any visitors at Sverin's apartment during the whole time he lived there."

"How long is that?"

"His father said that he had only recently moved here from Göteborg. I'm planning to have another talk with the parents tomorrow, when they've calmed down a bit. I'll ask them for a more precise date then," said Patrik.

"So we didn't get any useful information from knocking on doors," Mellberg concluded, staring at Martin as if holding him responsible.

"No, not much, at any rate," said Martin, staring back at his boss. Although still the youngest person at the station, he had lost the timid respect he'd had for Mellberg when he first joined the force.

"Let's move on." Patrik once again took charge of the meeting. "I talked to the father, but the mother was in such a state of shock that I wasn't able to interview her. As I mentioned, I plan to drive over to see them tomorrow and conduct a longer interview. I hope to find out a lot more, but according to the father, Gunnar Sverin, he and his wife have no idea who might want to harm their son. Apparently Mats hadn't acquired many friends since moving back to Fjällbacka, even though he was originally from here. I'd like someone to talk to his work colleagues tomorrow. Paula and Gösta, could you take care of that?"

They glanced at each other and nodded.

"Martin, you'll keep chasing down the neighbors that we haven't yet talked to. Oh, and I forgot to say that Gunnar mentioned his son had been the victim of a serious assault in Göteborg shortly before he moved here. I'll check up on that myself."

Then Patrik turned to his boss. It had become routine to make sure that Mellberg's often damaging interference in an investigation was kept to a minimum.

"Bertil," he now said solemnly. "We need you here at the station in your capacity as chief of police. You're the best person to deal with the media, and there's no way of knowing when an important lead will turn up."

Mellberg immediately cheered up.

"Of course. Absolutely. I have an excellent relationship with the media and a lot of experience in dealing with them."

"Great," said Patrik, without a trace of sarcasm. "So we all have assignments to get started on tomorrow. Annika, we'll submit our reports to you, since we need someone to collate all the information."

"I'll be here," said Annika, closing her notebook.

"Good. Now let's all go home to our loved ones and grab a few hours' sleep."

As he spoke those words, Patrik felt an intense longing to be home with Erica and the children. It was late, and he felt exhausted. Ten minutes later he was on his way to Fjällbacka.

# Fjällbacka 1870

**K**arl still hadn't touched her in that way, and Emelie was feeling confused. She didn't know much about such matters, but she was aware that certain things went on between a man and a woman that hadn't yet taken place.

She wished that Edith were here and that they hadn't parted under strained circumstances when she left the farm. Then she would have been able to talk to Edith about all this, or at least she could have written to her and asked for advice. Because a wife couldn't very well venture to discuss this type of thing with her husband. It simply wasn't done. Nevertheless, she did think it was all a bit strange.

Her initial delight with Gråskär had also diminished. The autumn sunshine had been replaced by strong winds that brought the sea crashing against the cliffs. The flowers had withered so that now only bare, sorry-looking stalks filled the flowerbeds. And the sky seemed to be forever hidden behind a thick layer of gray. She spent most of her time indoors. Outdoors she shivered with the cold, no matter how warmly she tried to dress. Indoors, the house was so small that it felt as if the walls were slowly closing in on her.

Sometimes she caught Julian glaring at her, but whenever she met his eye, he would look away. He hadn't yet spoken a word to her, and she couldn't understand why he was so antagonistic. Maybe she reminded him of some woman who had treated him badly. But at least he seemed to like the food she cooked. Both he and Karl ate their meals with good appetites, and she had to give herself credit for her ability to put together delicious dishes from limited ingredients, which at the moment was mostly mackerel. Every day Karl and Julian went out in the boat and usually came back with a large number of the silvery fish. She fried up some of them for dinner and served them with potatoes. The rest she salted so that they'd last all winter, since she'd heard that there would be even colder days ahead.

If only Karl would give her a friendly word once in a while—that would make her life on the island seem so much easier. But he never looked her in the eye, never gave her an endearing pat as he passed. It was as if she didn't exist, as if he hardly realized that he had a wife at all. Nothing had turned out as she'd imagined, and occasionally she would hear Edith's words of warning echoing in her mind. That she needed to take heed.

Emelie always shook off such thoughts as soon as they came. Life was hard out here, but she had no intention of complaining. This was the lot that she had been dealt, and she had to make the best of it. That was what her mother had taught her before she died, and that was the advice she planned to follow. Nothing ever turned out the way people thought it would.

# 6

**M**artin hated knocking on doors. It reminded him too much of when he was a kid and had been forced to go around selling lottery tickets, socks, and other idiotic rubbish in order to make money for class trips. Still, it was a necessary part of the job, all this trudging in and out of blocks of apartments, going up and down stairs, and knocking on every single door. Thankfully, he'd dealt with most of them the day before. He glanced at the list he'd pulled out of his pocket to see who was left and decided to start with the most promising candidate: the third tenant who lived on the same floor as Mats Sverin.

The nameplate on the door said *Grip*. Martin checked his watch before he rang the bell. It was only eight o'clock; he was hoping to catch the tenant at home before he or she left for work. When no one opened the door, he sighed and then pressed the bell again. The shrill sound hurt his ears, but there was still no response. He was just turning to head downstairs when he heard the sound of a lock turning behind him.

"Yes?" The voice was surly.

Martin hurried back to the door of the apartment.

"I'm from the police. Martin Molin."

The safety chain was on, but he caught a glimpse of a bushy beard in the door opening. And a bright red nose.

"What do you want?"

Hearing that Martin was from the police didn't seem to have made Mr. Grip any more amenable.

"A man died in that apartment over there." Martin pointed toward Mats Sverin's door, which was now sealed with police tape.

"Yes, I heard about that." The beard bobbed up and down in the doorway. "What's it got to do with me?"

"Could I come in for a few minutes?" Martin asked in the pleasantest tone of voice he could muster.

"Why?"

"So I can ask you some questions."

"I don't know anything."

The man started to close the door, but Martin instinctively stuck his foot in the opening.

"Either we have a brief chat here and now, or both of us will have to waste the whole morning while I take you down to the station and interview you there." Martin knew full well that he had no authority to haul Grip off to the station, but he took a chance that the old boy wouldn't realize that.

"All right. Come in," said Grip, unfastening the safety chain and pulling open the door.

Martin stepped forward to enter, a decision he regretted the moment he smelled the stench.

"Come back here, you little rascal. You're not getting out."

Martin caught a glimpse of something furry, and then the man threw himself forward and grabbed the cat by its tail. The creature meowed in protest but then allowed the man to pick it up and carry it into the apartment.

With the door closed behind him, Martin tried to breathe through his mouth so as not to throw up. The place was stuffy and reeked of garbage, but the overpowering smell was cat pee. It didn't take long to see why. Martin stood in the doorway to the living room and stared. There were cats everywhere—lying down, sitting up, and moving about. He did a quick count and realized there were at least fifteen. In an apartment that couldn't be much more than four hundred square feet.

"Have a seat," grunted Grip. He chased a few cats off the sofa.

Martin cautiously sat down on the very edge of the cushion.

"Okay, what do you want to know? I haven't got all day. This lot keeps me plenty busy."

A fat, ginger cat hopped onto the old man's lap, curled up, and started purring. The cat's fur was matted, and it had sores on its back legs.

Martin cleared his throat. "Your neighbor, Mats Sverin, was found dead in his apartment yesterday. So we want to find out whether anyone who lives in the building saw or heard anything unusual over the past few days."

"It's not my job to hear or see anything. I mind my own business and I expect everybody else to do the same."

"So you didn't hear any noises from your neighbor's apartment? Or notice any strangers in the stairwell?" Martin persisted.

"As I said: I mind my own business." The old man petted the cat's matted fur.

Martin closed his notebook, deciding to give up. "What's your full name, by the way?"

"My name is Gottfrid Grip. And I suppose you'd like to know what everyone else is named too, right?"

"Everyone else?" said Martin, glancing around. Were there other people living in this apartment?

"This is Marilyn." Gottfrid pointed at the cat on his lap. "She doesn't like women. She always hisses at them."

Martin dutifully opened his notebook again and jotted down word for word what the old man was saying. If nothing else, his report was bound to give his colleagues a good laugh.

"The gray one over there is named Errol, the white one with the brown paws is Humphrey, and then there's Cary, Audrey, Bette, Ingrid, Lauren, and James." Grip continued rattling off the cats' names as he pointed to one after the other, and Martin wrote all of them down. He was going to have quite a story to tell when he got back to the station.

On his way out the door, Martin paused for a moment.

"So neither you nor your cats heard or saw anything?"

"I never said that the cats didn't see anything. I just said that I didn't. But Marilyn here, she saw a car very early on Saturday morning, when she was sitting in the kitchen window. She sat there hissing like crazy."

"Marilyn saw a car? What kind of car did she see?" asked Martin even though it sounded like a strange question.

Grip gave him a scornful look. "Do you seriously think cats know about different kinds of cars? Are you out of your mind?" He tapped his temple and shook his head, laughing. As Martin stepped out into the hall, Grip closed the door behind him and fastened the safety chain.

◦◦◦

"Is Erling in?" asked Gösta, knocking lightly on the door jamb of the first room in the corridor. He and Paula had arrived at the council offices in Tanumshede.

Gunilla gave a start. She was sitting with her back to the door.

"Oh, you really scared me," she said, fluttering her hands nervously.

"I'm sorry. I didn't mean to do that," said Gösta. "We're looking for Erling."

"Does it have to do with Mats?" Her lower lip began quivering. "It's just so awful." She reached for a packet of tissues and used one to wipe away the tears that had welled up in her eyes.

"Yes, it does," replied Gösta. "We want to talk to all of you, but we'd like to start with Erling, if he's here."

"He's in his office. I'll show you where it is."

She got up and, after blowing her nose quite loudly, escorted them to an office further along the corridor.

"Erling, you have visitors," she said, stepping aside.

"Well, hello. It's been a while, hasn't it?" said Erling heartily as he stood up and shook Gösta's hand.

Then he looked at Paula and seemed to be feverishly searching his memory.

"Petronella, right? This brain of mine is like a well-oiled machine. I never forget a thing."

"It's Paula, actually," she told him, reaching out to shake his hand.

For a moment Erling looked a bit embarrassed, then he merely shrugged.

"We're here to ask you a few questions about Mats Sverin," Gösta told him. He sat down in one of the visitor's chairs in front of Erling's desk, which prompted Paula and Erling to sit down as well.

"Yes, it's awful," Erling said with a strange grimace. "Everyone in the office is very upset, and naturally we're all wondering what happened. Is there anything you can tell us?"

"Not much at this time." Gösta shook his head. "I can only confirm what you were told yesterday when we called your office. Sverin was found dead in his apartment, and we're investigating his death."

"Was he murdered?"

"That's not something we can either confirm or deny."

Gösta could hear how formal his words sounded, but he knew that he'd catch hell from Hedström if he gave away too much information, which might damage the case.

"We need your help," he went on. "From what I understand, Sverin didn't come to work on Monday, or on Tuesday either. That was when you contacted his parents. Was it usual for him to miss work?"

"On the contrary. I don't think he'd taken a single sick day since he started here. As far as I recall, he was never absent for any reason. Not even for a dentist's appointment. He was punctual, dedicated, and very conscientious. That's why we got worried when he didn't turn up or contact us."

"How long had he worked here?" asked Paula.

"Two months. We were really lucky to find someone like Mats. The job had been advertised for five weeks, and we'd brought in a few candidates for interviews, but none of them had the qualifications we were looking for. When Mats applied, we were concerned that he was overqualified, but he assured us that the job was exactly what he wanted. He seemed especially keen to move back to Fjällbacka again. And who can blame him? It's the pearl of the coast." Erling threw out his hands.

"He didn't give any particular reason for wanting to move back?" asked Paula, leaning forward.

"No, except that he wanted to get out of the big-city rat race and have a better quality of life. And that's precisely what our town has to offer. Peace and quiet and a great quality of life." Erling carefully enunciated every syllable as if giving a PR presentation.

"So he didn't mention anything about his personal circumstances?" Gösta was beginning to get impatient.

"He didn't talk about his private life. I knew that he was originally from Fjällbacka and that his parents still live there, but other than that I can't remember him ever saying much about his life outside the office."

"Sverin was involved in a very unpleasant incident shortly before he moved here from Göteborg. He was assaulted and beaten so badly that he ended up in the hospital. Did he mention that?" asked Paula.

"No, never," said Erling in surprise. "He did have several scars on his face, but he said that he'd got his trouser leg caught in his bicycle wheel and taken a fall."

Gösta and Paula exchanged looks of astonishment.

"Who attacked him? Was it the same person who . . . ?" Erling almost whispered the questions.

"According to his parents, it was an act of unprovoked violence. We don't think it has any connection to Sverin's death, but we can't rule it out," said Gösta.

"So he never mentioned his years in Göteborg?" Paula insisted.

Erling shook his head. "I can only repeat what I already told you. Mats never talked about himself. It was as if his life started when he took the job here."

"Didn't you find that rather odd?"

"Not really. I don't think anyone gave it much thought. He wasn't antisocial by any means. He laughed and joked and joined in the chat about TV shows and the sorts of topics that come up during a coffee break. I don't think anyone really noticed that he never discussed anything personal. It's only now, after the fact, that it's occurred to me."

"Was he doing a good job?" asked Gösta.

"Mats was an excellent financial officer. As I said, he was conscientious, methodical, and painstaking with his work.

Those are all desirable qualities in someone who's in charge of financial matters, especially in such a politically sensitive office as ours."

"You have no complaints about him?" asked Paula.

"None. Mats was extremely talented in his field. And he has been an invaluable resource for Project Badis. He came on the scene late in the game, but he quickly got up to speed and really helped us to move forward."

Gösta glanced at Paula, who shook her head. They didn't have any other questions at the moment, but Gösta couldn't help thinking that Mats Sverin seemed as anonymous and faceless as he had before they began this interview with his boss. And he couldn't help wondering what they might find when they finally started scratching the surface.

⌐∞⌐

The Sverins' small house was located down by the water's edge in Mörhult. It was warmer today—a lovely early summer day, and Patrik left his jacket in the car. He had phoned ahead to say that he would be coming, and when Gunnar opened the door, he looked down the hall to the kitchen and saw that the table had been set for coffee. That was how things were done here on the coast. Coffee and biscuits were always served, no matter whether the occasion was joyous or sorrowful. Over the many years that he'd spent on the police force, Patrik had downed countless gallons of coffee as he visited local citizens.

"Come in. I'll just go and see if I can get Signe to . . ." Without finishing his sentence, Gunnar turned to go upstairs.

Patrik remained where he was, thinking that he would wait in the front hall. But Gunnar was gone a long time, and finally Patrik moved toward the kitchen. The whole house seemed cloaked in silence, so he took the liberty of stepping inside the living room. It was a pleasant room, nice and tidy with elegant old furniture and doilies everywhere, as was customary in the homes of elderly people. Scattered about were framed photographs of their son. As he looked at them, Patrik was able to follow Mats's life from infancy to adulthood. He had an agreeable appearance, a likeable face. He looked happy. Judging by the photos, he'd had a good childhood.

"Signe will be right down."

Patrik was so immersed in his own thoughts that Gunnar's voice almost made him drop the framed picture he was holding.

"You certainly have a lot of nice photos." Carefully he set the photograph back on the bureau and followed Gunnar out to the kitchen.

"I've always enjoyed taking pictures, so we've accumulated a lot of them over the years. And we're glad to have them now. As a reminder of him, I mean." Embarrassed, Gunnar began fussing with the plates and filling the coffee cups.

"Do you take sugar or milk? Or both?"

"Black is fine. Thanks." Patrik sat down on one of the white kitchen chairs.

Gunnar set a cup in front of him and then sat down on the other side of the table.

"We might as well start. I'm sure Signe will be here soon," he said, casting a worried glance at the stairs. Not a sound could be heard from overhead.

"How's she doing?"

"She hasn't said a word since yesterday. The doctor said he'd look in on her later. All she does is lie in bed, but I don't think she slept a wink all night."

"Looks like you've received a lot of flowers," said Patrik, nodding at the counter where big bouquets had been placed in all sorts of containers serving as vases.

"Everyone has been so nice. They've offered to come over, but I can't stand the thought of having a bunch of people sitting around the house." He dropped a sugar cube in his cup and began stirring. Then he reached for a biscuit and dipped it in his coffee before putting it in his mouth. He seemed to have a hard time swallowing the mouthful and had to wash it down with some coffee.

"There you are." Gunnar turned around to look at Signe as she entered the hall.

They hadn't heard her come down the stairs. Gunnar stood up and went over to his wife. Gently he put his arm around her and led her to the table, as if she were a very old woman. She seemed to have aged several years just since yesterday.

"The doctor will be here in a while. Have some coffee and a biscuit. You need to get something in your stomach. Should I make you a sandwich?"

She shook her head. It was the first time she'd reacted, acknowledging that she had heard what he said.

"I'm terribly sorry," said Patrik, and he couldn't resist placing his hand over hers. She didn't pull it away, but neither did she respond to the gesture. Her hand felt limp and dead. "I wish that I didn't have to disturb you at a time like this. At least, not so soon after what happened."

As usual, he was having a hard time finding the words. Since becoming a parent, he found it harder than ever to deal with people who had lost a child, even if that child was grown up. What was he supposed to say to someone whose heart had been ripped out? Because that was how he imagined it must feel.

"We realize that you have a job to do," said Gunnar. "And of course we want you to find the person who . . . did this. If there's any way that we can help, we want to do that."

He was sitting next to his wife, and now he protectively drew his chair closer to hers. She hadn't touched her coffee.

"Have some," he said, lifting the cup to her lips. Reluctantly she took a few sips.

"We talked about this yesterday, but could you tell me a little more about Mats? Any details you'd like to share with me, no matter how big or small."

"He was always so nice, even as a baby," said Signe. Her voice sounded dry and raspy, as if she hadn't spoken in a long time. "He slept the whole night through, right from the start, and he was never any trouble. But I worried about him; I always have. I kept thinking that something terrible was going to happen."

"And you were right. I should have listened to you," said Gunnar, fixing his eyes on the table.

"No, you were the one who was right," said Signe, looking at him. She seemed to have suddenly woken up from her stupor. "I wasted so much time and happiness by worrying, while you were always glad and grateful for what we had, and for Matte. It's impossible to prepare for something like this happening. I've spent my whole life worrying about everything between heaven and earth, but I was never able to prepare myself for this. I should have been happier." She fell silent. Then she said, "What do you want to know?" And she picked up her cup to drink her coffee without waiting to be coaxed.

"Did he go to Göteborg when he moved away from home?"

"Yes, after secondary school he enrolled in the Business College. He received excellent marks," said Gunnar, obviously proud of his son.

"But he often came home on the weekends," added Signe. Talking about her son seemed to be having a positive effect on her. She now had a little more color in her cheeks, and her eyes were clearer.

"Naturally, in recent years he didn't come as often. But in those early years he was home almost every weekend," said Gunnar, nodding.

"And things went well with his studies?" Patrik had decided to stick to subjects that would make Signe and Gunnar feel calm and relaxed.

"Yes, he got good marks in college too," said Gunnar. "I never understood how he came to be so good at book learning. He didn't get it from me, at any rate." He smiled and for a moment seemed to forget why they were on this subject. But then it all came back to him, and his smile faded.

"So what did he do after he finished his degree?"

"His first job was for that auditing company, wasn't it?" Frowning, Signe turned to Gunnar.

"Yes, I think so, but for the life of me I can't recall the name of the firm. Something American. He was there only for a few years. It didn't really suit him. He said the job involved working too much with numbers and not enough with people."

"And where did he work after that?" Patrik's coffee had grown cold, but he kept on taking small sips.

"He worked at several different places. I'm sure I can find you the names if you like, but for the last four years he was responsible for the finances of a nonprofit organization called the Refuge."

"What do they do?"

"It's a group that helps women who have fled from domestic violence situations, seeing to it that they can rebuild their lives. Matte loved that job. He hardly talked about anything else."

"Why did he quit?"

Gunnar and Signe glanced at each other, and Patrik realized that they had wondered the same thing.

"Well, we think it had something to do with the assault. He didn't feel safe living in Göteborg any longer," said Gunnar.

"And he wasn't safe here, either," said Signe.

No, thought Patrik, he certainly wasn't. No matter what had prompted Mats Sverin to leave Göteborg, the violence had caught up with him.

"How long was he in the hospital after the assault?"

"Three weeks, I think," replied Gunnar. "It was a shock when we saw him there."

"Show him the pictures," said Signe quietly.

Gunnar got up and went into the living room. He came back carrying a small box.

"I don't really know why we saved these photographs. They're not exactly the kind that you'd want to show anyone." His callused fingers reached into the box and gently removed the photos.

"May I see?" Patrik held out his hand, and Gunnar gave him the small stack. "Ouch!" He couldn't hold back his reaction when he saw the pictures of Mats Sverin lying in the hospital bed. What he saw bore no resemblance to the young man in all the photos in the living room. His face, his entire head was swollen. And his skin was various shades of red, with tinges of blue.

"I know," said Gunnar, looking away.

"They said he could have died. But he was lucky, in spite of it all." Signe blinked away her tears.

"From what I understand, they never caught the perpetrators. Is that right?"

"Yes," said Signe. "Do you think this might have something to do with what happened to Matte? The young thugs who attacked him were complete strangers. It was because he told one of them not to take a leak outside the door to his building. He'd never seen them before. Why would they . . . ?" Her voice now sounded shrill.

Gunnar stroked her arm to calm her down.

"They don't know anything yet. The police just want to find out as much as possible," he told her.

"That's right," said Patrik. "We don't have any answers yet. We need to build up as complete a picture of Mats and his life as we can." He turned to look at Signe. "Your husband said that as far as you're aware, Mats didn't have a girlfriend at the moment. Did he?"

"No, or if he did, he kept that information to himself. To be honest, I'd started to give up hope of ever having a grandchild," said Signe. But when she realized what she'd said, and that now there was no hope of such a thing, the tears began to fall again.

Gunnar squeezed her hand.

"I think there was someone in Göteborg," Signe went on, her voice thick with sobs. "He never said so, but I had a sense there was a woman. And sometimes I could smell perfume on his clothes when he came home to visit. The same perfume each time."

"But he never mentioned a name?" asked Patrik.

"No, never, even though Signe couldn't resist asking him a few times," said Gunnar, smiling.

"Well, I didn't see why it had to be such a big secret. Why couldn't he have brought her home one weekend so we could meet her? We can behave ourselves if we make an effort."

Gunnar shook his head. "As you can tell, this was a rather sensitive subject."

"Did you have the impression that this woman, whoever she might have been, continued to be part of Mats's life after he moved back to Fjällbacka?"

"Hmmm . . ." Gunnar looked at Signe.

"No, she wasn't," she said emphatically. "A mother knows such things. And I would almost swear that he no longer had a girlfriend."

"I don't think he could ever forget Nathalie," Gunnar interjected.

"What do you mean? That was ages ago. They were just children."

"That doesn't matter. There was something special about Nathalie. I've always thought so, and I think Matte . . . You saw how he reacted when we told him that she was back, didn't you?"

"Yes, but how old were they at the time? Seventeen? Eighteen?"

"I still think I'm right," Gunnar stubbornly insisted. "And he was going to go out there to see her."

"Excuse me." Patrick broke into the conversation. "But who is Nathalie?"

"Nathalie Wester. She and Matte grew up together. As a matter of fact, they were in the same class as your wife. Both Matte and Nathalie."

Gunnar seemed a bit embarrassed to admit that he knew Erica, but Patrik wasn't surprised. Almost everybody in Fjäll-backa knew everyone else, but they also took a special interest in Erica because her books were so popular.

"Does Nathalie still live here?"

"No, she moved away years ago. She went to Stockholm, and she and Matte haven't been in contact since then. But she owns an island near here. It's called Gråskär."

"And you think that Mats went out there to see her?"

"He might not have had time to do that," said Gunnar. "But you can phone Nathalie and ask her." He got up to get a note that was stuck on the refrigerator door. "Here's her cell number. I don't know how long she's planning to stay. She's out there with her little boy."

"Does she come here often?"

"No, in fact we were a bit surprised. She's hardly been here since she moved to Stockholm. Her last visit was years ago. But the island belongs to her. Her paternal grandfather bought it, and Nathalie is the only descendent left, since she doesn't have any siblings. We've looked after the house for her, but if nothing is done with the lighthouse very soon, it'll end up beyond saving."

"The lighthouse?"

"Yes, there's an old lighthouse from the nineteenth century out there on the island. And a cottage. In the past, that's where the lighthouse keeper used to live with his family."

"It sounds like a lonely life." Patrik downed the last of his cold coffee, unable to stop himself from grimacing.

"Lonely, or beautiful and peaceful. It all depends how you look at it," said Signe. "But I could never spend a single night out there alone."

"Weren't you always the one who said that was just a load of rubbish and old wives' tales?" said Gunnar.

"What do you mean?" Patrik's curiosity was instantly sparked.

"The island is usually called Ghost Isle. According to legend, it was given the name because those who die out there never leave the island," said Gunnar.

"So there are ghosts?"

"It's nothing but gossip," snorted Signe.

"Well, it doesn't matter. I'm going to give Nathalie a call. Thank you so much for the coffee and biscuits, and for taking the time to answer my questions." Patrik got up and pushed his chair under the table.

"It was nice to talk about him," said Signe softly.

"Would you mind if I borrowed these for a while?" Patrik pointed at the photographs from the hospital. "I promise to take good care of them."

"Go ahead and take them." Gunnar handed him the pictures. "We have a digital camera, so I have the pictures on my computer."

"Thank you," said Patrik, carefully sliding the photos into his briefcase.

Signe and Gunnar both went with him to the door. As he got in the car, he replayed in his mind all those images of Mats

Sverin as a boy, a teenager, and an adult. He decided to drive home for lunch. He felt an overwhelming urge to give the twins a kiss.

∞

"How's Grandpa's little sweetie-pie today?"

Mellberg had also gone home for lunch, and as soon as he set foot inside the door, he grabbed Leo from Rita and began lifting him high in the air, making the boy shriek with delight.

"Typical! When Grandpa comes home, Grandma might as well disappear." Rita frowned but then a smile took over, and she gave them each a kiss on the cheek.

A special bond had existed between Bertil and Leo ever since Bertil had been present at the baby's birth, and no one was more pleased about this than Rita. Nevertheless she was relieved when Bertil had been convinced to return to work full-time. It had seemed like a good idea to have him fill in for Paula at home, but no matter how much she adored this unlikely hero, she had no illusions when it came to his judgement, which at times was questionable, to say the least.

"What's for lunch?" Mellberg carefully set the boy in his high chair and tied a bib around his neck.

"Chicken and my homemade salsa that you like so much."

Mellberg hummed with pleasure. All his life he had never eaten anything more exotic than boiled lamb with dill sauce, potatoes, and carrots, but Rita had managed to change all that. Her salsa was so strong that it practically burned the enamel off his teeth, but he loved it.

"You got home late last night." She placed a dish on the table with some less spicy food that she'd made for Leo, and Bertil began feeding the boy.

"Yes, we're all going at full throttle again. Paula and the boys are out doing the footwork, but Hedström pointed out, quite rightly, that someone needed to be at the station to deal with the media. And no one is better suited than me to take on such a big responsibility." He shoveled a little too much food into Leo's mouth, who fortunately just let half of it slide right out again.

Rita suppressed a smile. Clearly Patrik had once more succeeded in outmaneuvering his boss. She liked Hedström. He knew how to handle Mellberg: with patience, diplomacy, and a certain degree of flattery that could get Bertil to do exactly what he wanted. She did the same in order to ensure that their life together ran smoothly.

"You poor thing. It sounds as if you're really busy." She put some chicken on his plate along with a generous serving of salsa.

Leo had finished eating, so Mellberg dug into his own food. A couple of servings later, he leaned back and patted his stomach.

"Delicious. And I know exactly what would be perfect to follow that. What do you think, Leo my boy?" He got up and went over to the freezer.

Rita knew that she ought to stop him, but she didn't have the heart. She let him take out three big Magnum ice cream bars, which he happily handed out. Leo almost disappeared behind the huge bar. If Bertil kept on like this, the boy would soon be as wide as he was tall. For today, however, she decided not to worry about it.

# Fjällbacka 1870

She moved a little closer to Karl. He was lying on the side of the bed next to the wall, wearing long underwear and a shirt. In a couple of hours he would have to get up to relieve Julian in the lighthouse. Cautiously she placed her hand on his leg, stroking his thigh with trembling fingers. She wasn't the one who was supposed to take the lead like this, but something was wrong. Why didn't he ever touch her? He hardly even spoke to her. Merely mumbled his thanks for the food before leaving the table. And he seemed to be always looking past her, as if she were made of glass and barely noticeable, in fact almost invisible.

For that matter, he barely spent any time at home. During most of his waking hours he was in the lighthouse or doing work on the boat. Or he was out at sea. She spent all day utterly alone in the cottage, and her housework was soon finished. After that, she had many hours to fill, and she began to think that she might go mad. If she had a baby, she would have someone to keep her company, and other tasks to occupy her time. Then she wouldn't mind that Karl worked from early morning until late at night, and it wouldn't matter that he never talked to her. If only they would have a child.

But after living on the farm, she knew that certain things had to happen between a man and a woman before she could end up in the family way. Things that hadn't yet occurred. That was why she put her hand on Karl's leg and ran it along the inside of his thigh. Her heart was pounding with nervousness and excitement as she gently slipped her hand inside the fly of his underwear.

Karl sat up with a jolt.

"What are you doing?" His expression was darker than she'd ever seen it before, and she yanked her hand away.

"I . . . I just thought that . . ." She couldn't find the right words. How was she supposed to explain the obvious? Even he must realize how strange it was that they'd been married for nearly three months, and yet he'd never come near her. She could feel the tears welling up in her eyes.

"I might as well sleep in the lighthouse. I'm not going to get any peace here." Karl pushed past her, threw on his clothes, and stomped down the stairs.

Emelie felt as if he'd slapped her face. Up until now he had simply ignored her; this was the first time he'd spoken to her with that tone of voice. Harsh, cold, and contemptuous. And he'd looked at her as if she were some disgusting creature that had crawled out from under a rock.

With tears running down her cheeks, Emelie crept over to the window and looked out. The wind was blowing hard across the island, and Karl had to fight the gusts as he headed for the lighthouse. He tore open the door and went inside. Then she saw him appear in the window of the tower, where the beam of light transformed him into a shadow.

She went back to bed and wept. The house creaked and groaned, almost as if it might rise up and fly over the islands, out into the gray sky. But that didn't frighten her. She'd rather fly away, to anywhere at all, than stay here.

*She felt something caress her cheek, at the very spot where Karl's words had left a sting, as if he'd slapped her. Emelie sat up with a start. No one was there. She pulled the covers up to her chin and stared into the dark corners of the room. She saw nothing. She lay down again. It was probably just her imagination. Same as all the other sounds that she'd heard since coming to the island. Not to mention the cupboard doors she sometimes found open, although she was certain that she'd closed them. And the sugar bowl that had somehow moved from the kitchen table to the counter. She must have made up all those things. It had to be her imagination, combined with the island's isolation, playing tricks on her.*

*She heard a chair scrape downstairs. Emelie sat up, holding her breath. The old woman's words rang in her ears, the words that she'd managed to push aside during the past months. She didn't want to go downstairs, didn't want to know what she might find there, and what had been here in the room, stroking her cheek.*

*Shaking, she pulled the covers over her head, hiding like a child from unknown terrors. There she lay, wide awake, until dawn came. But she heard no more sounds.*

# 7

**W**hat do you make of all this?" asked Paula. Having bought themselves lunch at the Konsum supermarket, she and Gösta had now sat down to eat in the station's kitchen.

"It's certainly a bit odd," said Gösta, taking another bite of his fish gratin. "Nobody seems to know anything about Sverin's personal life. And yet everyone has a high opinion of him, telling us that he was a very open and sociable person. It doesn't make sense to me."

"I feel the same way. How can anyone keep everything except his work so secret? Something was bound to come out over coffee or lunch, don't you think?"

"Well, you weren't exactly forthcoming about your own life in the beginning."

Paula blushed. "I see your point. And I suppose that's exactly what I'm getting at. I kept silent because there was something I didn't want people to know. I had no idea how all of you would react if you heard that I was living with a woman. So the question is: What was Mats Sverin trying to hide?"

"That's what we have to find out."

Paula felt something brush against her leg. Ernst had smelled the food and was now sitting at her feet, hoping for a handout.

"I'm sorry, fella. I'm the wrong person to beg from. All I've got here is salad."

Ernst didn't budge but sat gazing up at her with a pleading look. Paula realized that she'd have to show him what she was eating. She removed a piece of lettuce from the plastic bowl and held it out to him. His tail thumped eagerly against the floor, but after sniffing at the lettuce he looked up at her with disappointment and turned away in a marked manner. Then he went over to Gösta, who reached for a cookie and discreetly slipped it to the dog.

"You're not doing him any favors, you know," said Paula. "He'll get fat, and it might even make him ill if you and Bertil don't stop feeding him treats like that. If it weren't for Mamma taking him out for long walks, that dog would have died long ago."

"I know. But when he gives me that look, I can't . . ."

Paula stared at Gösta with a stern expression.

"We'll have to hope that Martin or Patrik have come up with a lead or two," said Gösta, quickly changing the subject. "Because right now we're not really any wiser than we were yesterday."

"You can say that again." Paula paused and then went on, "It's so awful thinking about that scene. To be shot in your own apartment. The one place where you're supposed to feel safe."

"My guess is that it must have been someone he knew. The door hadn't been forced, so he must have let the person in of his own accord."

"That makes it worse," said Paula. "To be shot at home by somebody you know."

"It doesn't necessarily have to be a friend or acquaintance. There's been a lot in the papers lately about people who ring the bell and ask to use the phone and then steal everything in the place." Gösta stuck his fork in the last bite of fish gratin.

"Yes, but they usually target elderly people. Not someone who's young and strong like Mats Sverin."

"True, but that doesn't mean we should rule it out."

"We'll have to wait and see what Martin and Patrik come up with." Paula put down her knife and fork and got to her feet. "Want some coffee?"

"Yes, please," said Gösta. He slipped another cookie to Ernst and was rewarded by a wet tongue licking his hand.

⌒∞⌒

"Oh, I needed this," Erling groaned loudly as he lay on the narrow massage table.

Vivianne's fingers expertly kneaded the muscles in his back, and he felt the tension gradually disappearing. It wasn't easy to handle all the responsibilities that went with his job.

"Is this the type of service that we're going to be offering?" he asked, his face resting in the hole of the table.

"This is a traditional massage, so it will definitely be one of the services. In addition we have Thai massage, and a treatment with hot stones. Clients can also choose between a partial and a total body rub." Vivianne continued working on his back as she spoke in a calm, almost hypnotic voice.

"Excellent. That's excellent."

"Later we'll offer other treatments besides the basic spa package. Salt and seaweed scrubs, light therapy, algae facials, and so on. We're going to have a full line of services. But you already know that because it was in the prospectus."

"Yes, but it's still music to my ears. What about the staff? Is everyone on board?" He could feel himself getting drowsy from the massage, the muted lighting, and Vivianne's soothing voice.

"The staff will soon be fully trained. I've taken charge of that part myself. We've brought in some fantastic people—young, enthusiastic, and ambitious."

"Excellent. That's excellent," Erling repeated and then uttered a deep, contented sigh. "It's going to be a massive success. I can feel it." He grimaced as Vivianne pressed a tender spot on his back.

"You have some real knots right here," she told him, as she continued to rub the spot.

"That really hurts," he said, suddenly wide awake.

"It takes pain to get rid of pain." Vivianne pressed even harder, and Erling couldn't hold back a whimper.

"Why are you so tense?" she asked.

"It must be because of what happened to Mats," said Erling, his voice sounding strained. His back hurt so much that he felt tears welling up in his eyes. "The police came to the office this morning asking questions. The whole business is absolutely ghastly."

Vivianne abruptly stopped rubbing. "What sort of questions?"

Grateful that the pain had stopped, at least temporarily, Erling drew in a long breath.

"Mostly stuff about Mats and what he was like at work. What we knew about him, and whether he was good at his job."

"What did you tell them?" Vivianne was again massaging his back. Thankfully she had moved on to a different spot.

"Well, there wasn't much to say. Mats was so reserved, we never really got to know him. But this afternoon I went through the accounts, and I have to say that he was certainly meticulous. That's going to make it easier for me to take control of the finances until we can find a replacement."

"I'm sure you'll do a great job." Vivianne was now massaging the back of his neck in a way that gave him goose pimples. "So he didn't leave behind any question marks?"

"No, from what I could see, everything was in perfect order." Erling felt himself dozing off again as Vivianne's fingers continued their work.

*⸺*

Dan was sitting at the kitchen table and staring out the window. The house was quiet. The children were in school or at the day care center. By now he'd usually have gone back to work, but it was his day off. He'd have preferred to be working. Lately his stomach started to hurt the minute he was on his way home, because the whole house reminded him of what they had lost. Not just their baby, but also the life that they'd shared together. In his heart, he had begun to think that it might be gone forever, and he didn't know what to do. It wasn't like him to feel as utterly helpless as he did right now, and he hated the feeling.

His heart ached for Emma and Adrian. They couldn't understand why their mother refused to get out of bed, why she wouldn't talk to them or kiss them or even look up when they brought the drawings they'd made to show her. They knew that Anna had been in a car accident and that their little brother had gone to heaven. But they couldn't comprehend why that would make their mother lie so still, endlessly staring out of the window. And nothing that Dan did or said could make up for the emptiness they felt. They liked him, but they loved their mother.

With each passing day, Emma was becoming more withdrawn while Adrian got more aggressive. Both were reacting in their own way. Dan had talked with the teachers at the day care center about the fact that Adrian had begun hitting and biting the other children. And Emma's teacher had phoned to discuss the changes in her; she'd gone from a lively, cheerful child to one who sat through classes without saying a word. What was Dan supposed to do? They needed Anna, not him.

At least he was able to comfort his own three daughters. They came to him with their questions and seeking hugs. They were sad and upset, but not in the same way as Emma and Adrian. Besides, his girls went to stay with their mother Pernilla every other week, and there they could escape the sorrow that hovered like a heavy blanket over his whole life.

Pernilla had been a great help. Their divorce had not been without its problems, but since the accident she had been amazing. It was largely due to her that Lisen, Belinda, and Malin were coping so well. Emma and Adrian had no one else. Naturally, Erica had tried to help, but she had her hands full taking care of the twins, and it wasn't easy for her to make time for her niece and nephew. He realized that, and was grateful for the effort she made.

In the end, he and Emma and Adrian were left alone with their paralyzing fear about what was going to happen to Anna. Sometimes he wondered if she would spend the rest of her life staring out of the window. The days would become weeks and then years as Anna simply lay there, slowly getting older. He knew that it was his own dark thoughts making him feel this way. The doctors had said that she would gradually come out of her depression, but that it had to run its course. The problem was that he didn't believe them. Several months had now passed since the accident, and it seemed as if Anna was drifting further and further away.

Outside, a few titmice were pecking at the balls of suet that the girls had insisted on hanging up for the birds, despite the time of year. He watched them, enviously thinking how carefree their lives must be. Concerned only with the basic needs: eating, sleeping, and reproducing. No emotions, no complicated relationships. No sorrow.

Then he thought about Matte. Erica had phoned to tell him what had happened. Dan knew his parents well. Many times he and Gunnar had gone out in the boat, sitting there telling stories, and Gunnar had always talked of his son with such pride. Dan also knew who Matte was because they'd gone to the same school, although Mats had been in Erica's class, not his. But they'd never really been friends. Gunnar and Signe must be suffering terribly. That thought cast his own grief in a new light. If it felt this bad to lose a son that he'd never had a chance to know, how much worse it must be for them to lose a son that they had followed through life and watched grow into a man.

The titmice suddenly took off. They didn't fly off together but instead scattered in all directions. The next second Dan saw what had caused such an abrupt departure. The neighbor's cat had sauntered into the yard and was now looking up at the tree. This time the cat was out of luck.

Dan stood up. He couldn't just sit here all day. He had to try talking to Anna again, urge her to rouse herself from the dead and rejoin the living. Slowly he headed upstairs.

∞

"How'd it go, Martin?" asked Patrik as he leaned back in his chair. They had once again convened in the kitchen to discuss the investigation.

Martin shook his head. "I haven't got much to report. I contacted most of the people that we missed yesterday, but none of them saw or heard a thing. Except maybe . . ."

"What?" said Patrik. Everyone's attention was fixed on Martin.

"I don't know if this is any use. The old guy isn't quite right in the head."

"Let's hear it."

"Okay. There's a man named Grip who lives on the same floor as Sverin. As I said, he seems a bit nuts." Martin tapped his temple. "And he's got a load of smelly cats living in his apartment . . ." He took a deep breath. "Grip said that one of his cats saw a car early Saturday morning. About the same time that the other neighbor, Leandersson, was awakened by a sound that might have been a gunshot."

Gösta snickered. "His cat saw a car?"

"Quiet, Gösta," said Patrik. "Okay, Martin, go on. What else did he say?"

"That's all. I didn't really take him seriously, since he seemed so out of it."

"From the mouths of children and fools we will hear the truth spoken," murmured Annika as she continued taking notes.

Martin shrugged dejectedly. "That's all I have to report."

"Good job," said Patrik, wanting to encourage him. "Door-to-door inquiries are never easy. People either exaggerate what they might have heard, or they've noticed nothing whatsoever."

"Yes, this job would definitely be a lot easier without witnesses," muttered Gösta.

"What about you two?" Patrik turned to Gösta and Paula, who were sitting next to each other at the kitchen table.

Paula shook her head. "We don't have much to report either. Mats Sverin doesn't seem to have had much of a life outside work, if we're to believe his coworkers. At any rate, they couldn't tell us much. He never mentioned any outside interests, or friends or girlfriends. Yet they describe him as pleasant and outgoing. It doesn't really add up."

"Did he talk to them about his years in Göteborg?"

"No, not a word." Gösta shook his head. "As Paula said, he apparently never discussed anything aside from his job and more general, ordinary subjects."

"Did they know about the assault?" asked Patrik as he got up and began pouring coffee for everyone.

"Not exactly," said Paula. "Mats told them that he'd had a bicycle accident and was in the hospital for a while. That's hardly the truth of the matter."

"And his work—were there any problems on that front?" Patrik set the coffee pot back on the counter.

"He seems to have been very good at his job. They sounded extremely pleased with his performance. Apparently they felt it was quite a coup to hire an experienced economist from Göteborg. Besides, he had ties to the area." Gösta raised his cup and took a sip, burning his tongue. "Damn, that's hot!"

"So there aren't any leads that we can follow up on?"

"No, not from what we've found out so far," said Paula, now looking as dejected as Martin.

"Well, I suppose that's it for the time being. No doubt we'll have occasion to talk to his work colleagues again. I had a talk with Mats's parents, with pretty much the same results. He evidently wasn't very open with them either. But I did find out that one of his old girlfriends is living on Gråskär out in the archipelago, and Gunnar thought that Mats had been planning to go and visit her. So I need to contact her." Patrik then placed the photographs from Sahlgrenska Hospital on the table. "And I got these from his parents."

The pictures were passed around the table.

"Jesus," said Mellberg. "He really took a beating."

"Yes. Judging by the photos, we're talking about a case of aggravated assault. Of course it may not have anything to do with the murder, but I still think we should take a closer look at what happened. We need to request his hospital records and see what it says in the police report. We should also interview the staff at the organization that Mats worked for at the time. It's interesting that the purpose of the group is to help women who are victims of domestic violence. Maybe we'll find some sort of motive there. It would be best to go to Göteborg and talk to everyone in person."

"Is that really necessary?" asked Mellberg. "There are no indications that he was shot because of what happened in Göteborg. It's more likely connected to something local."

"Considering how little we've been able to find out so far, and how secretive Sverin seems to have been about his life, I think it's certainly justified."

Mellberg frowned as he pondered this. It took him a while to make up his mind.

"Well, if you insist," he agreed eventually. "But I hope you get some results. Because it sounds as though you'll be gone most of the day tomorrow."

"We'll do our best," replied Patrik. "I was thinking of taking Paula with me."

"What should the rest of us do in the meantime?" asked Martin.

"You and Annika need to search the public records for references to Mats Sverin. Was he ever secretly married or divorced? Does he have any children? Does he own any property? Does he have a criminal record? Check for anything and everything."

"Okay, we can do that," said Annika, casting a glance at Martin.

"And Gösta . . ." Patrik paused. "Phone Torbjörn and find out when we can get into Sverin's apartment to take a look around. And try to put some pressure on him to speed things up with the technical report. With so little to go on, we need the results as soon as possible."

"Okay," said Gösta without much enthusiasm.

"Bertil, you'll still be here to hold down the fort, right?"

"Absolutely," said Mellberg, sitting up straight. "I'm ready for the onslaught."

"Good. Then we'll all start fresh tomorrow." Patrik stood up to signal that the meeting was over. He looked shattered.

⁓

Nathalie gave a start. Something had awakened her. She'd fallen asleep on the sofa and was dreaming about Matte. She could still sense the warmth of his body, the feeling of him inside of her. And she could hear his voice, which was so familiar, so reassuring. But apparently he hadn't felt the same about her, and she could understand why. Matte had loved the Nathalie that she once was. The person she had become had disappointed him.

She was no longer shaking, and her joints had stopped hurting. Yet the restless feeling wouldn't go away. It had made her arms and legs prickle, prompting her to wander around the house as Sam watched her, his eyes wide.

If only she'd managed to explain why everything had gone so wrong. She'd told Matte some of it as they sat at the kitchen table. Confided in him the details that she could bring herself to say out loud. But she couldn't bear to utter the words that would describe the worst humiliations. The things that she'd been forced to do and that had fundamentally changed her.

She knew that she was no longer the same person. And Matte had noticed. He had seen how ruined and rotten she was inside.

Nathalie sat up. She was having a hard time breathing. She drew her knees to her chin and wrapped her arms around her legs. It was so quiet, but suddenly she heard a thump against the floor. A ball. Sam's ball. She watched the ball as it slowly rolled toward her. Sam hadn't touched any of his toys since they'd come to the island. Had he climbed out of bed and started playing again? Her heart filled with hope until she realized that wasn't possible. The door to Sam's room was on her right, and the ball had come from the kitchen, on the left.

Slowly she got up and went into the kitchen. For a moment she was frightened by the shadows moving over the walls and ceiling, but her fear vanished as quickly as it had come. A great sense of calm settled over her. There was no one here who wanted to harm her. She was certain of that, even though she couldn't have explained why.

Hearing a giggle from a dark corner of the kitchen, she glanced in that direction and caught a glimpse of him. A boy. But before she could take a closer look, he moved. He raced toward the front door, and without thinking she followed. She tore open the door and felt the blast of wind in her face, yet she knew that the boy wanted her to follow him.

He was sprinting for the lighthouse. Every once in a while he would look back, as if to make sure that she was behind him. His blond hair was ruffled by the wind, the same gusts that were so strong they nearly took her breath away as she ran.

She had trouble pulling open the heavy door to the light-house, but that was where he had gone, so she had to get inside. She dashed up the steep stairs, hearing the boy moving around overhead, hearing him giggling.

But when she reached the top of the lighthouse, she found the round room empty. Whoever the boy was, he had disappeared.

꒰∞꒱

"How are things at the station?" Erica moved closer to Patrik as they sat on the sofa.

He'd come home in time for dinner, and now the children were asleep. With a yawn she stretched out her legs and rested them on the coffee table.

"Tired?" asked Patrik, without answering her question. He stroked her arm as he kept his eyes fixed on the TV.

"Exhausted."

"Why don't you go to bed, sweetheart?" With a distracted expression, he gave her a kiss on the cheek.

"I should, but I don't want to." She glanced at her husband. "I need some grown-up time with you and the news stories on *Rapport* to counterbalance all the dirty diapers, vomit-covered shirts, and baby prattle."

Patrik turned to face her. "Is everything okay?"

"Of course," she told him. "It's nothing like when Maja was born. But sometimes it can feel too much of a good thing."

"In the autumn I'll take over so you can start writing again."

"I know. Besides, we have the summer vacation before then, which is great. It's been a hectic day, that's all. And what happened to Matte is so awful. I didn't really know him very well, but we were in school together. Secondary school too." She paused and then said, "So how's the investigation coming along? You didn't answer my question."

"We haven't made much progress." Patrik sighed. "We talked to Mats's parents and several of his coworkers, but he seems to have been a real loner. Nobody can tell us anything about him. Either he was the world's most boring person, or else . . ."

"Or else what?" asked Erica.

"Or else there are things that we haven't yet discovered."

"Well, I certainly didn't think he was boring when we were in school together. He seemed so outgoing and upbeat. And he was very popular. One of those boys who was bound to succeed, no matter what he did."

"Didn't you go to school with his girlfriend too?" said Patrik.

"Nathalie? Yes, I did. But she . . ." Erica hunted for the right words. "It always felt like she thought she was better than the rest of us. She didn't really fit in. Don't get me wrong—she was popular too, and she and Matte were the perfect couple. But I always had the feeling that he . . . How should I put it? He followed her around like a puppy dog. Happily wagging his tail and grateful for the slightest attention. I don't think anyone was surprised when she decided to move to Stockholm and left Matte behind. He was devastated, from what I could tell, but even he probably saw it coming. Nathalie wasn't the sort of person you could hold on to. Do you know what I mean? Am I making any sense at all?"

"Yes, I get what you're saying."

"Why are you asking about Nathalie? She was his girlfriend in secondary school. And though I hate to admit it, that was ages ago."

"Nathalie's here."

Erica looked at him in amazement. "In Fjällbacka? She hasn't been back here in years."

"Well, according to Mats's parents, she and her son are out there on that island her family owns."

"Ghost Isle?"

Patrik nodded. "Apparently that's the nickname for it, but I think they told me it has another name too."

"Gråskär," said Erica. "Although most people around here call it Ghost Isle. It's said that the dead . . ."

". . . never leave the island," Patrik finished her sentence and smiled. "Yes, I've heard about that superstition."

"What makes you so sure that it's just superstition? I once spent the night over there with my classmates, and at least half of us came away convinced that there really were ghosts on the island. It had an incredibly spooky atmosphere, and after everything we saw and heard, none of us ever wanted to spend another night out there."

"I don't put much faith in the imaginings of teenagers."

Erica poked him with her elbow. "Don't be such a spoilsport. A few ghosts always liven things up."

"Well, that's one way to look at it. At any rate, I need to have a talk with Nathalie. Mats's parents thought that he was planning to go out and see her, but they weren't sure whether he ever did. Even though it was a long time ago that they were dating, he might have told her more about his life now . . ." He seemed to be thinking out loud.

"I'll go with you," said Erica. "Tell me when you want to go, and we can ask your mother to babysit. Nathalie doesn't know you," she added before Patrik could voice any objections. "At least she and I went to school together, even if we were never good friends. Maybe if I'm there, she'll be willing to talk."

"Okay," Patrik agreed reluctantly. "But tomorrow I have to drive to Göteborg, so it won't be until Friday."

"Perfect," said Erica with satisfaction, snuggling into Patrik's arms.

# Fjällbacka 1870

*H*ow does it taste?" Emelie asked at every meal, even though she knew that the response would always be the same. A grunt from Karl and a grunt from Julian. The fare was a bit monotonous on the island, but she had no control over that. Most of what she put on the table came from the two men's fishing expeditions, usually mackerel and plaice. And since she still hadn't been allowed to accompany them on their trips to Fjällbacka, which occurred a couple of times each month, the grocery purchases hadn't been entirely satisfactory.

"So, Karl, I was wondering . . ." Emelie put down her knife and fork without even tasting the food. "Couldn't I come with you to Fjäll-backa this time? I haven't seen anyone else in so long, and it would be a joy to spend a bit of time on the mainland."

"That's out of the question." Julian wore that stern expression that he always did whenever he looked at her.

"I was talking to Karl," she calmly replied, but she could feel her heart skip a beat. This was the first time she had ever dared talk back to him.

Julian snorted and glanced at Karl.

"Did you hear that? Do I really have to put up with that sort of talk from a woman?"

Karl looked tired as he stared at his plate.

"We can't take you with us," he said, and it was clear that he considered the topic closed. But the solitude had begun to wear on Emelie's nerves, and she couldn't stop herself.

"Why not? There's plenty of room in the boat, and I could take care of the grocery shopping so that we'd have something besides mackerel and potatoes day in and day out. Wouldn't that be nice?"

Julian's face had turned white with rage. He kept his eyes fixed on Karl, who abruptly got up from the table.

"You're not coming with us, and that's my final word." He put on his jacket and went out into the gusty weather. The door slammed behind him.

This was how it had been ever since the night when she had touched Karl in bed in an attempt to draw him into a more intimate relationship. His indifference had been replaced with an attitude that was more like Julian's open disdain. Karl radiated an animosity toward her that she could neither understand nor change. Had she really done something so terrible? Was she that repulsive and disgusting? Emelie tried to recall what it had felt like when he asked her to marry him. The proposal had come unexpectedly, but there did seem to be some warmth and longing in his voice. Or had she imagined that because of her own feelings and dreams? She looked down at the table.

"Now see what you've done." Julian tossed his knife and fork onto his plate with a clatter.

"Why do you treat me like this, when I've never done you any harm?" Emelie didn't know how she'd summoned up the courage, but it felt as if she simply had to speak the words that had been weighing on her so heavily.

Julian didn't reply. He merely stared at her with that dark expression of his. Then he stood up and followed Karl out of the house. A *few minutes later she saw the boat leave the dock as they headed for Fjällbacka. In truth, she knew full well why she wasn't allowed to go along. The presence of a wife wasn't wanted at Abela's tavern on Florö, which was where the two men obviously ended up on their trips into town. They'd be back before dusk; they always returned in time to work their shifts in the lighthouse.*

*A cupboard door slammed shut, and Emelie jumped. She didn't think it was intended to scare her, but it had. The front door was closed, so a gust of wind couldn't be the cause of it. She stood very still, listening and looking around. No one else was in the house. When she shut everything else from her mind, she could make out a distant, muted sound. The sound of someone breathing, light and regular, although it was impossible to say from which direction the sound was coming. It was almost as if the house itself were breathing. Emelie tried to work out what this unknown person might want from her. But suddenly the sound vanished and the house was quiet once again.*

*Emelie's thoughts returned to Karl and Julian, and with a heavy heart she set about washing the dishes. Though she was a good house-keeper, nothing she did seemed satisfactory. She felt terribly lonely. At the same time, she wasn't alone. It was becoming increasingly hard to ignore their presence on the island. Emelie heard things, sensed things, just as she had a moment ago. And she was no longer afraid. They didn't wish to harm her.*

*As she leaned over the dishes, with tears dripping into the dirty water, she felt a hand on her shoulder. A comforting hand. She didn't turn around. If she did, she knew she'd find no one there.*

# 8

Paula stretched out her arms in bed, and her hand happened to touch Johanna's hair. She left her hand lying there, even though it made her uneasy. Over the past few months they had felt awkward about touching each other. It no longer came naturally, and they'd had to make conscious decisions to express themselves physically. They had made love to each other, but it had felt so strange.

In fact, it had been going on longer than a few months. If Paula were to be completely honest, it had started when Leo was born. They had both longed for him, and fought to have him. They thought that having a child would make their relationship stronger. And in one sense it had, but in other ways it had not. Paula didn't think she had personally changed very much; Johanna on the other hand had immersed herself in the role of mother. And lately she'd started to act as if she were superior in some way. It seemed as if Paula didn't count any more, or at least that Johanna counted more, since she was the one who had given birth to Leo. She was Leo's biological mother, while the baby possessed none of Paula's genes. All she could give him was the love that she'd felt for him ever since he was inside Johanna's womb. A love that had grown a thousandfold after he was born and Paula held him in her arms. She felt that she was as much Leo's mother as Johanna was. The problem was that Johanna didn't share this feeling, even though she refused to admit it.

Paula could hear her mother bustling about in the kitchen as she talked to Leo. They were really very lucky. Rita was a morning person, and she was happy to get up early so that Paula and Johanna could sleep in. And now that the ongoing murder investigation was making it hard for Paula to work only part-time, Rita had willingly stepped in to help. To everyone's amazement, Bertil had also shown himself ready to lend a hand. But lately Johanna had begun criticizing the way Rita took care of their son. In her opinion, she was the only one who knew how to care for Leo properly.

With a sigh, Paula swung her legs over the side of the bed. Johanna stirred but didn't wake up. Paula leaned over and brushed a lock of hair out of Johanna's face. She had always thought that their relationship was so strong and stable. That was no longer the case. And that thought frightened her. If she lost Johanna, she would also lose Leo. Johanna would never stay here in Tanumshede, while Paula couldn't imagine moving away. She was thriving in this small town, with her job and her colleagues. The only thing that didn't make her happy was the way things had changed between Johanna and herself.

In spite of everything, she was looking forward to driving to Göteborg with Patrik today. The Mats Sverin case had roused her curiosity. She wanted to find out all there was to know about him. Her instincts told her that they needed to examine his past and all the things that he'd kept quiet about if they wanted to find out who had put a bullet in the back of his head.

"Good morning," said Rita when Paula came into the kitchen.

Leo was sitting in his high chair. He reached out his arms toward Paula, and she lifted him up, holding him close.

"Good morning." She sat down at the table with Leo on her lap.

"Breakfast?"

"Yes, please. I'm super hungry."

"I can fix that." Rita placed a fried egg on a plate and set it in front of Paula.

"You spoil us, Mamma." Impulsively Paula wrapped one arm around Rita's waist and leaned her head against her mother's warm body.

"I enjoy spoiling you, sweetheart. You know that." Rita hugged her back and then kissed the top of Leo's head.

Ernst came sauntering into the room and with a hopeful expression sat down on the floor next to Paula and Leo. Before anyone could react, Leo tossed the fried egg to Ernst, who happily swallowed it whole. Pleased at having fed his favorite dog, Leo clapped his hands with delight.

"You little rascal," said Rita with a sigh. "That dog is getting so fat that it wouldn't surprise me if he were to die an early death."

She turned back to the stove and cracked another egg into the skillet.

"So how are the two of you doing?" Rita asked in a low voice without looking at her daughter.

"What do you mean?" said Paula, although she knew full well what her mother was getting at.

"I mean you and Johanna. Is everything okay?"

"We're fine. We've both been really busy at work lately, that's all." Paula looked down at Leo so that her expression wouldn't give her away if Rita happened to turn around.

"I just wondered whether . . ." Rita didn't have time to finish her sentence.

"Is there any breakfast?" Mellberg strolled into the kitchen, clad only in his underwear. He leisurely scratched his belly and sat down at the table.

"I was just telling Mamma that she spoils us," said Paula, relieved at the change of subject.

"How true, how true," said Mellberg, greedily eyeing the egg frying in the pan.

Rita cast an inquiring glance at Paula, who nodded.

"I'd rather have some bread and cheese."

Rita slid the egg onto a plate. Ernst watched her every move and then sat down close to Mellberg's feet. If he was lucky, he might get another helping.

"I've got to go," said Paula after wolfing down a big piece of bread and cheese. "Patrik and I are off to Göteborg today."

Mellberg nodded.

"Good luck. Hand over the boy, and let me hold him for a while." He reached out for Leo, who willingly allowed himself to be transferred to Mellberg's lap.

Out of the corner of her eye as she left the kitchen Paula saw Leo, quick as a flash, toss the second egg to Ernst. This really was the dog's lucky day.

⁂

Having settled the twins on a soft blanket on the floor, Erica headed for the attic. She didn't want to leave them alone for more than a few minutes, so she practically ran up the steep steps. Once she reached the top, she had to stop for a moment to catch her breath.

After rummaging about for a bit, she located the box she was looking for. Cautiously she backed down the attic stairs balancing the heavy box in her arms. The babies didn't seem to have missed her, so she sat down on the sofa and placed the carton on the floor at her feet. Then she began pulling out items and putting them on the coffee table. She wondered when she'd last looked through the contents. School yearbooks, photo albums, postcards, and old letters quickly joined the pile on the table. They were covered with dust, and the original colors had faded. She suddenly felt ancient.

A few minutes later she found what she was looking for. A school yearbook and a photo album. She leaned back against the sofa cushions as she leafed through the pages. The pictures of students in the yearbook were all in black and white. Some of the faces had been crossed out, some were circled, depending on who had been the object of hatred, and who had been well liked. Remarks had also been scribbled here and there. "Cute," "sweet," and "idiotic" were some of the labels that had been handed out without much finesse. Her teenage years were not something to be proud of, and when Erica came to the page with the picture of her own class, she blushed. Good Lord, is that really how she had looked? She couldn't believe her hair style and the clothes she was wearing. Obviously there was a good reason why she hadn't looked at these photos in a long time.

She drew in a deep breath and took a closer look. Judging by her hairdo, the picture must have been taken during her Farrah Fawcett period. Her hair was long and blond, and she had used a curling iron to flick up the ends. Her glasses were so big that they hid half her face, and she sent a silent thank-you to whoever it was that had invented contact lenses.

Suddenly her stomach gave a lurch. There was so much anxiety attached to those years in secondary school. The feeling that she didn't fit in, didn't belong. The constant searching for something that would admit her to the circle of kids who were considered cool and hip. She had tried. She copied their hair styles and clothes, used the same slang as the girls in her class—the popular ones. Girls like Nathalie. But Erica had never succeeded. She hadn't belonged at the very bottom either; she wasn't one of the students who was constantly bullied, the type who knew that they were such outcasts that it wasn't worth their trying to fit in. No, she had belonged to the invisible masses. Only the teachers had paid any attention to her, giving her encouragement and approval. But that hadn't been much consolation. Who wanted to be a bookworm? Who wanted to be Erica if they could be Nathalie?

She looked at Nathalie in the class photo. She was sitting in front, with her legs casually crossed. Everyone else had carefully posed for the camera, but Nathalie looked as if she had simply dropped onto the chair and hadn't bothered to change position. Yet she was clearly the center of attention. She had long, blond hair that reached to her waist. Straight and shiny, no bangs. Sometimes she had worn her hair pulled back in a simple ponytail. Nathalie seemed to do everything without effort. She was the original, and everyone else was a mere copy.

In the photo Matte was standing behind Nathalie. The picture was taken before they started dating, although with hindsight it was obvious that they'd end up together. Because Matte wasn't looking at the camera like his classmates. Instead, the photographer had caught him as he cast a glance at Nathalie, looking down at her beautiful long hair. Erica remembered thinking that Matte was in love with Nathalie, but back then all the boys were in love with her. There was no reason Matte should have been an exception.

"How nice he was," murmured Erica as she studied the picture. She couldn't recall having that thought at the time, but that was probably because she'd been so infatuated with Johan. He was in the same grade but in the other class, and she'd harbored an unrequited love for him throughout secondary school. She could see now that Matte was very cute. His blond hair was slightly tousled and shaggy; his serious expression was quite appealing. He was a bit lanky, but that was how all boys were at that age. She had no clear memories of Matte from those years in school. She hadn't belonged to the same group. He was one of the popular kids, although he never boasted of the fact. Not like some of the other cool boys who were loud and arrogant and so full of themselves and their status in that little world where they were the kings. Matte just seemed to quietly drift along.

Erica put aside the yearbook and picked up the photo album. It was filled with pictures from school trips, various end-of-term celebrations, and a few parties that her parents had allowed her to attend. Nathalie was in a lot of the photos. Always in the very center of the action, as if the camera lens sought her out. My God, she was pretty, thought Erica, and then found herself hoping rather mean-spiritedly that Nathalie was now over-weight, with her hair cut in a plain, old-lady style. There was something about her that stirred both desire and jealousy. All the girls wanted to be like her; second best was to be included in her circle of friends. Erica had been neither. Nor was she in any of the photos. She was the one holding the camera, after all, but nobody had ever taken it from her and said that she ought to be in the picture. She was invisible, hiding behind the lens as she greedily took snapshots of all those scenes that she longed to be part of.

It annoyed Erica that she was still overwhelmed by bitter-ness. She couldn't understand why her memories of that period had the power to diminish her and make her feel like the girl she once was instead of the woman she had become. She was a successful author, happily married, with three amazing children, a beautiful home, and great friends. Yet old jealousies rose to the fore, and she felt again the longing to fit in, accompanied by the terrible pain of knowing that she never would, that she would never be good enough, no matter how hard she tried.

The twins began whimpering as they lay on the blanket. Relieved to be forced back to the present, Erica got up and went over to her sons, leaving the yearbook and photo album on the table. Patrik would no doubt want to have a look at them too.

⟶⟵

"Where should we begin?" Paula was struggling with motion sickness. She had started feeling ill by the time they reached Uddevalla, and it was only getting worse.

"Do you want to stop for a while?" Patrik cast a glance at her face, which had taken on a disturbing greenish hue.

"No, we're almost there anyway," she said, swallowing hard.

"I was thinking we should start at the Sahlgrenska Hospital," said Patrik, negotiating Göteborg's dense traffic with a determined expression on his face. "We've been given permission to look at Mats's medical records, and I've phoned the doctor who was in charge of his care, telling him that we're on our way."

"Good," said Paula, fighting off the nausea.

Ten minutes later they turned into the parking lot at the hospital, and she jumped out of the vehicle the minute it stopped. She leaned against the door, taking in deep breaths until the nausea eased. A vague sense of discomfort remained, however, and she knew it would stay with her until she got some food in her stomach.

"Are you ready? Or do you need a few more minutes?" asked Patrik. But she could see that he was so impatient to get going that he was shifting from one foot to the other.

"I'm okay now. Let's go. Do you know the way?" She motioned with her head toward the vast hospital complex.

"I think so," he said and started for the main entrance.

After taking a couple of wrong turns, they were finally able to knock on the door of Nils-Erik Lund's office. He was the doctor who had been responsible for Mats's care during the weeks he'd spent in the hospital.

"Come in," said a voice, and they stepped inside.

The doctor stood up and came around his desk to shake hands.

"You're from the police, I assume?"

"Yes. We spoke on the phone earlier. I'm Patrik Hedström, and this is my colleague Paula Morales."

They exchanged the usual pleasantries before they all sat down.

"I've pulled out the information that I think you need," said Dr. Lund, shoving a file across his desk.

"Thanks. Could you tell us what you remember of Mats Sverin?"

"I have thousands of patients every year, so it's impossible to remember them all. But after reviewing his records, I've managed to recall a few things." He tugged at his shaggy white beard. "The patient came to us with extensive injuries. He had been severely beaten, probably by more than one individual. You'll have to ask the police for more details."

"We'll do that," said Patrik. "But feel free to tell us your own thoughts. Any information you can provide may prove valuable."

"Very well," said Dr. Lund. "I won't bother you with the medical terminology—you can read that in the file later on—but the patient had received blows and kicks to the head, resulting in bleeding in the brain as well as a number of broken facial bones, swelling, damage to the underlying tissues, and extensive discoloration of the skin. He had also suffered injuries to his abdomen, with two broken ribs and a ruptured spleen. His injuries were extremely serious, and we found it necessary to operate at once. We also took X-rays to determine the severity of the bleeding in his brain."

"Did you judge his injuries to be life-threatening?" asked Paula.

"The patient was in critical condition, and he was unconscious when admitted to the hospital. Having established that the bleeding in his brain was minor and did not warrant surgery, we focused our attention on his abdominal injuries. There was a risk that the broken ribs might puncture his lungs, which is a major concern."

"You were able to stabilize his condition?"

"I would venture to say that we did a superb job. Quick and effective. Thanks to excellent teamwork."

"Did Mats Sverin tell you what had happened to him? Did he talk about the assault?" asked Patrik.

Dr. Lund tugged at his beard as he tried to recall. It's a wonder he has any beard left, thought Patrik, considering the way he keeps pulling on it.

"No, I can't remember that he did."

"Did he seem scared? Did you get the sense he felt threatened or was trying to hide something?"

"Not that I recall. But as I said, it was several months ago, and a lot of patients have come and gone in the meantime. You'll have to ask the officers who were in charge of the police investigation."

"Do you know whether he had any visitors while he was here?"

"It's possible that he did, but I'm afraid I have no idea."

"Then we'll thank you for your time," said Patrik, standing up. "Are these copies?" He pointed at the file lying on the desk.

"Yes, you can take them with you," said Dr. Lund, getting up as well.

On their way out, Patrik suddenly had an idea.

"Shall we stop by and see Pedersen? Find out if he has anything for us?"

"Okay," said Paula, nodding. She followed Patrik, who now seemed to know which corridors to take. She was still feeling slightly ill, and she wasn't sure that a visit to the morgue was going to help matters.

⌒∞⌒

What was the point of living anymore? Signe had hauled herself out of bed to make breakfast, and later on she fixed lunch. Neither of them had any appetite. She had vacuumed the entire ground floor, washed the bed linens, and made coffee, which they didn't drink. She had done everything she usually did, but she felt as if she were as dead as Mats. She was merely moving her body about the house, a body without purpose, without life.

She sank down onto the bench in the kitchen. The hose to the vacuum cleaner fell to the floor, but neither of them reacted. Gunnar was sitting at the kitchen table. He'd been sitting there all day. They seemed to have switched roles. Yesterday he had been the one moving around, while it had taken her an enormous effort merely to get her muscles to cooperate with her benumbed brain. Today he sat there while she tried to fill the hole in her heart with feverish activity.

She stared at the back of Gunnar's neck, noticing as she had so many times in the past that Matte had inherited the same whorl of hair at the edge of his shirt collar. Now it would never be passed on to the little blond boy that she had pictured so often in her daydreams. Or it could have been passed on to a girl, for that matter. It didn't matter whether it was a boy or a girl; either would have been welcome. If only she'd been given a grandchild to pamper, offering sweets before dinner and far too many gifts at Christmastime. A child with Matte's eyes and somebody else's mouth. Because that was something she had always looked forward to, wondering what sort of girl-friend he would bring home. What would she be like? Would he find someone like his mother, or somebody who was the exact opposite? She couldn't deny that she'd been curious, but she had vowed to be nice. She didn't want to be one of those dreadful mothers-in-law who meddled. And she would have been ready to babysit whenever needed.

But as the years passed, she had begun to give up hope. Occasionally it occurred to her that Matte might not be interested in women. That would have required some get-ting used to, and she would have regretted not having any grandchildren, but she could have accepted the situation. All she wanted was for him to be happy. But he had never brought anyone home, and now all hope was gone forever. There would be no towheaded child with a whorl of hair at the nape of his neck; no grandchild to whom she could slip a sweet before dinner. No heap of Christmas presents that cost too much and fell apart in a matter of weeks. Nothing except emptiness. The years stretched ahead of them like a desolate country road. She glanced at Gunnar as he sat motionless at the kitchen table. Why should they keep on living? Why should she keep on living?

✧

"You really wanted to go to Göteborg, didn't you?" Annika glanced up from her computer screen and gave Martin a long look. He was her protégé at the station, and they had established a special bond.

"Yes," he admitted. "But this is important work too."

"Do you want to know why Patrik took Paula with him?" asked Annika.

"It doesn't matter. Patrik can take whoever he wants," he replied rather sullenly. Before Paula joined the force, he had almost always been Patrik's first choice. To be honest, that was because at the time the station didn't have anyone else worth considering, but Martin couldn't deny that it hurt.

"Patrik thinks that Paula has seemed a bit depressed lately, so he wants to give her something else to think about."

"Is that so? I hadn't noticed," said Martin, feeling a pang of guilt. "What's going on with her?"

"No idea. Paula isn't exactly a talkative person. But I think Patrik is doing the right thing. She hasn't been herself lately."

"Well, just the thought of having to live in the same apartment with Mellberg would be enough to break me."

"You can say that again," said Annika with a laugh, and then turned serious. "But I don't think that's the problem. We'll just have to let her be until she feels like talking. At least you know now why Patrik wanted her to go with him."

"Thanks for telling me." Yet Martin felt ashamed that he had reacted so immaturely. The important thing was that the job got done, not who was assigned to do it.

"Shall we get started on this?" he asked, stretching his spine. "It'd be great if we could find out more about Sverin by the time they get back."

"Good idea," said Annika, and she began tapping on the keyboard.

cⱺⱺ

"Do you ever think of him?" Anders took a sip of his coffee. He and Vivianne were having lunch together at the Lilla Berith restaurant, which they did almost daily in order to get away from all the construction noise at Badis.

"Who?" asked Vivianne, even though she knew exactly who he meant. Anders noticed how her knuckles turned white as she gripped her coffee cup.

"Olof."

They had always called him by that name. He had insisted on it, and nothing else had seemed natural. He deserved no other name.

"Of course. Once in a while." She looked at the patch of lawn at the top of Galärbacken. The town had started coming to life. More people were out and about, and it felt as if Fjällbacka was slowly thawing out, stretching its limbs, and getting ready for the onslaught. It was a dramatic transformation from the torpor that gripped the small town the rest of the year.

"So what do you think?"

Vivianne turned to face Anders, giving him a sharp look.

"Why are you suddenly talking about him? He no longer exists. He's of no importance."

"I'm not sure," he replied. "It's something to do with Fjällbacka. I don't know why, but I feel safe here. Safe enough to think about him."

"Don't get too comfortable. We're not going to be here long," she snapped, immediately regretting her tone of voice. She was angry at Olof, not Anders. But she was cross that he'd started talking about him. What good would it do? She took a deep breath and decided to answer Anders's question. He had always supported her, gone with her everywhere. She depended on him, and the least she could do was to give him an answer.

"I think about how much I hate him." She felt her jaw tighten. "I think about how much he destroyed, how much he took from me and from us. Isn't that what you think about too?"

She suddenly felt scared. They had always shared a hatred for Olof. That had been the glue that held them together, the reason why they hadn't gone separate ways but had always stayed together, through good times and bad. Mostly bad.

"I don't know," said Anders, turning to look at the sea. "Maybe it's time to . . ."

"Time to what?"

"To forgive."

There they were. The words she didn't want to hear, the thought she refused to entertain. Forgive Olof? When he had robbed them of their childhood, turned them into adults who clung to each other like victims of a shipwreck? He was the driving force behind everything they had done, everything they still were doing.

"I've given it a lot of thought lately," Anders went on. "We can't keep going like this. We're running away, Vivianne. But we're running away from something we can never escape, because it's inside here." He pointed to his temple as he fixed her with a penetrating, resolute stare.

"What exactly are you trying to say? Are you starting to get cold feet?" She could feel tears welling up in her eyes. Was he planning to desert her? Betray her, the way Olof had?

"It feels like we're always searching for the pot of gold at the end of the rainbow, and if only we could find it, then Olof would disappear. But we're never going to find it. Because it doesn't exist."

Vivianne closed her eyes. She remembered all too clearly the filth, the smells, the people who came and went, and Olof wasn't there to protect them. Olof, who hated them. He'd told them that quite bluntly, that they should never have been born, that he'd ended up with them because of his sins. They were disgusting, ugly, and stupid. And they were the ones who had driven their mother to her death.

She abruptly opened her eyes. How could Anders talk about forgiveness? He had thrown himself in between so many times, protecting her body with his own and suffering the brunt of the blows.

"I don't want to discuss Olof." Her voice sounded strained because of everything she was holding back. Terror overwhelmed her. What did it matter that Anders talked of forgiveness when that was something that could never happen?

"I love you, sister." Anders gently stroked her cheek. But Vivianne didn't hear him. The dark memories were roaring too loudly in her ears.

⌘

"Well, look at that. I've got visitors." Tord Pedersen, the medical examiner, peered at them over the top of his glasses.

"Yes. We thought it would be good if the mountain came to Muhammad for a change," said Patrik with a smile as he stepped forward to shake hands. "This is my colleague Paula Morales. We were over at the Sahlgrenska Hospital to make a few inquiries about Mats Sverin. So we thought we might as well drop in to see you and find out how things are going."

"Your visit is a bit premature, I'm afraid." Pedersen shook his head.

"Does that mean you don't have anything for us?"

"I've only had time to make a preliminary examination."

"And what do you think?" asked Paula.

Pedersen laughed.

"I thought it couldn't get any worse than having Patrik breathing down my neck."

"I'm sorry," Paula apologized, but her expression told Pedersen that she was still waiting for an answer.

"Come with me. Let's go to my office." The medical examiner opened a door on their left.

They followed him inside and took seats in front of his desk while Pedersen sat down across from them. He folded his hands.

"Based on an external examination, I can tell you that the only obvious injury is the gunshot wound in the back of his head. However, he does have other healed wounds that look relatively recent and probably stem from an assault that occurred a few months ago."

Patrik nodded. "That's why we called in at the hospital to talk to the doctor. How long had he been dead?"

"Not more than a week, I would say. The postmortem will tell us more."

"Do you have any idea what type of gun was used?" Paula asked, leaning forward.

"The bullet is still lodged in his head, but we should have an answer to your question as soon as I remove it. Provided it's in reasonable condition, that is."

"But you must have seen countless gunshot wounds," said Paula. "Can't you take a guess?" She deliberately didn't mention the empty casing and what it signified. She wanted to hear Pedersen's own opinion.

"Yet another officer who refuses to give up," said Pedersen with a laugh, looking almost delighted. "If you promise to take this as the educated guess that it is, I'd say we're dealing with a nine-millimeter gun." Pedersen held up an admonitory finger. "But it is only a guess, and I could be wrong."

"We understand," said Patrik. "When will you do the postmortem so we can get a look at the bullet?"

"Let me see now . . ." He turned to his computer and clicked the mouse. "The postmortem is scheduled for next Monday. So you'll have my report by Wednesday."

"Couldn't you get to it any sooner?"

"Afraid not. We've been damned busy the past month. People are dropping like flies for some reason, and besides, two of our staff suddenly had to go on sick leave for an unspecified length of time. Burned out, apparently. This job can have that effect on certain people." It was clear that Pedersen didn't see himself in that category.

"Okay, I suppose it can't be helped. Please give me a ring as soon as you know more. And I assume that the bullet will be sent ASAP over to the forensics lab?"

"Of course," said Pedersen, looking slightly offended. "We may be a bit understaffed at the moment, but we still carry out our work in a professional manner."

"I didn't mean to imply otherwise." Patrik held up his hands. "I'm just impatient, as usual. Give me a call when your report is ready, and I promise not to hassle you any more."

"No problem." Pedersen got up to say goodbye.

It felt as if Wednesday was a long way away.

⁂

"So you're saying that we can go inside the apartment now?" Gösta sounded uncharacteristically eager. "And we'll have your report tomorrow? That's great. Hedström will be glad to hear it."

He smiled as he put down the phone. Torbjörn Ruud had just told him that they'd finished the technical inspection so the police were now free to take a look at Mats Sverin's apartment. Gösta suddenly had a brainstorm. It would be silly to sit here, twiddling his thumbs and waiting until Patrik and Paula came back. For all that twiddling his thumbs was one of Gösta's favorite pastimes, it got on his nerves that Patrik was the one who always made all the decisions. Especially since he himself and Bertil were the station's most experienced officers. He had to admit to a certain desire to get back at Patrik. Though it went against the grain to put too much effort into his job, it would be nice to show those young whippersnappers how the job ought to be done. Gösta made a quick decision and hurried over to Mellberg's office. In his eagerness, he forgot to knock, and as he pulled open the door, he caught Bertil waking up from what looked like a very pleasant nap.

"What the devil?" Mellberg glanced around in bewilderment while Ernst sat up in his basket, ears pricked.

"Excuse me. I thought . . ."

"Thought what?" bellowed Mellberg, straightening his comb-over, which had slipped down as he slept.

"Well, you see, I was just talking to Torbjörn Ruud on the phone . . ."

"And?" Mellberg was still looking angry, but Ernst had curled up in his basket again.

"He said that we could go into the apartment now."

"Whose apartment?"

"Mats Sverin's. They're done there. The tech team, I mean. And I thought . . ." Gösta was beginning to regret his decision. Maybe it wasn't such a stroke of genius after all. "I thought . . ."

"Get to the point, why don't you!"

"Well, Hedström is always so bloody keen on getting everything done immediately, and preferably yesterday. So I was thinking that you and I could get going and do our own inspection of the place. Instead of waiting for him to get back."

Mellberg's face lit up. He was starting to understand what Gösta had in mind, and he liked the idea.

"Absolutely! It would be a shame to postpone things until tomorrow. And who has more expertise than we do to get this case moving forward?" He smiled broadly.

"Exactly what I was thinking," said Gösta, smiling as well. "It's time to show the young folk what us old guys can do."

"Brilliant, my friend."

Mellberg got up and they headed for the garage. The two veterans were about to take to the field.

⁕

Nathalie was bathing him again. She poured the warm, salty water over his body, wet his hair, and tried to avoid getting water in his eyes. Sam didn't seem to be enjoying it, but he didn't appear to hate it either. He lay quietly in her arms and allowed her to wash him.

She knew that sooner or later he would wake from his torpor. His brain was trying to process what had happened—an experience that no one should ever have to go through, especially someone so young. A five-year-old child should not be separated from his father, but she'd had no choice. It had been essential to flee; it was the only way out. She and Sam had paid a high price though.

Sam had loved Fredrik. He hadn't seen the side of him that she had seen, or experienced what she had gone through. For Sam, Fredrik was a hero who could do no wrong. He had idolized his father, and that was the main reason why it had been so hard to make the decision. To the extent that she'd had any choice in the matter.

In spite of everything, it pained her that Sam had lost his father. No matter what Fredrik had done to her, he had always meant a great deal to Sam. Not as much as she did, but nevertheless he was important to the boy. And now Sam was never going to see him again.

Nathalie lifted her son out of the water and placed him on the towel that she had spread out on the dock. Her father had always said that the sun was good for both body and soul, and the warm rays truly did feel as if they were having a restorative effect. Overhead the seagulls circled, and she thought that Sam might enjoy watching them when he was feeling better.

"My sweet, sweet little boy." She stroked his hair. He was still so small, so defenseless. It felt as if it were only yesterday that he was an infant and could fit so easily in her arms. Maybe she ought to take him to a doctor after all, but her maternal instincts told her no. He was safe here. He didn't need hospitals and medicines; he needed peace and quiet and her loving care. That was what would make him well again.

She shivered. A chill wind had started sweeping over the dock, and she worried that Sam might catch cold. With an effort she stood up, holding him in her arms, and walked toward the house. She pushed the door open with her foot and carried him inside.

"Are you hungry?" she asked as she got him dressed.

He didn't say a word, but she sat down on a chair and began feeding him cornflakes. In good time he'd come back to her. The sea, the sun, and her love would heal his damaged soul.

⁕

Erica tried to take a walk every afternoon before collecting Maja from the day care center. The babies needed fresh air, and she needed to get some exercise. Maneuvering the twins' stroller gave her quite a workout, and on the return journey, with Maja standing on the running board, it was a real challenge to push the stroller all the way home.

Today, instead of taking the direct route up Galärbacken, she decided to take the long route past Badis and the Lorentz jam factory. At the wharf below Badis she paused and shaded her eyes with her hand so she could look up at the old building. The newly painted façade was a gleaming white in the sunshine. It made her happy to see the place restored. Aside from the church, the spa hotel was the dominant feature of the town's skyline and the first thing people noticed when they approached the town by boat. For years the building had fallen more and more into disrepair until finally it looked as if it might collapse altogether. Now it was once again the pride of Fjällbacka.

She sighed with pleasure and then chuckled at herself, embarrassed that she could be so moved by the boards and paint of an old building. But it was more than that. She had so many fond memories of Badis. For Erica, as for most people who lived in Fjällbacka, the building held a special place in her heart. Badis was part of their history, and it had now been restored to the present and the future. No wonder she'd come over all sentimental.

Erica began pushing the stroller again, steeling herself for the long, steep path up the hill past the sewage treatment plant and the mini-golf course. Suddenly a car pulled up and stopped next to her. She paused, peering at the driver to see who it was. A woman got out of the car, and Erica recognized her at once, even though she'd never actually met her. The local grapevine had been rife with gossip about this woman since she moved to the area a number of months ago. It had to be Vivianne Berkelin.

"Hi!" said the woman cheerfully, coming forward with her hand held out. "You must be Erica Falck."

"Yes, that's right," said Erica with a smile as they shook hands.

"I've been meaning to say hello to you. I've read all your books, and I like them a lot."

Erica felt herself blushing, which always happened whenever she received praise for her books. She still hadn't grown used to the fact that so many people had read something she'd written. And after being on maternity leave for several months, it was refreshing to meet someone who viewed her primarily as an author and not as the mother of Noel, Anton, and Maja.

"I really admire anyone who has the patience to sit down and write a whole book."

"All it requires is a tough backside," said Erica, laughing.

Vivianne radiated an infectious enthusiasm, and Erica was filled with an emotion that she at first couldn't quite identify. Then she realized what it was. She wanted Vivianne to like her.

"It's looking amazing." She turned toward Badis.

"Yes, we're incredibly proud of it." Vivianne looked in the same direction. "Would you like a tour?"

Erica glanced at her watch. She had planned to pick up Maja a bit early, but her daughter loved being at day care, so there would be no harm in picking her up at the normal time. Besides, she was dying to find out whether the interior of the building was as lovely as the façade.

"That would be great. But I'm not sure how I'll manage to get the stroller up there," she said, looking at the steep stairs.

"Don't worry, I'll give you a hand." Vivianne headed for the steps without waiting for a reply.

Five minutes later they had maneuvered the twin stroller up to the entrance, and Erica was able to push it inside. She paused in the doorway, her eyes wide as she glanced around. Gone were all the old, worn furnishings, yet the original character of the place remained. As she surveyed her surroundings, memories of the summer disco when she was a teenager came flooding back, yet everything now looked so new and fresh. She parked the stroller next to the wall and lifted Noel out. She was about to lift out Anton's bassinet when she heard Vivianne say quietly:

"May I hold him?"

Erica nodded, and Vivianne leaned over and gently picked up Anton in her arms. The twins were used to being held by so many different people that they were never bothered by strangers picking them up. The baby gazed up at her, giving her a smile.

"What a little charmer, you are," prattled Vivianne as she carefully removed his jacket and hat.

"Do you have children?" asked Erica.

"No, I've never been so lucky," replied Vivianne, looking away. "Would you like some tea?" she asked as she carried Anton toward the dining room.

"I'd prefer coffee, if you have it. I'm not much of a tea drinker."

"Normally we don't recommend poisoning the body with caffeine, but I'll make an exception and see if I can find some real coffee."

"Thank you." Erica followed Vivianne. Coffee was what kept her going. She drank so much of it that she probably had coffee rather than blood flowing through her veins. "Everybody has their vices, and I can think of worse things than caffeine."

"I'm not so sure about that," said Vivianne, but she chose to say no more on the subject. She probably sensed that her words would fall on deaf ears.

"I'll be right back. Why don't you sit down here? We'll take a tour afterward." Vivianne disappeared through a swinging door which Erica assumed led to the kitchen.

For a moment she wondered how Vivianne was going to manage to make coffee while holding the baby. By now Erica had learned to do nearly everything using only one hand, but it definitely took practice. She pushed away the thought. Vivianne would probably let her know if she needed help.

After serving the coffee, Vivianne sat down across from her. Erica noticed that the tables and chairs were also new. Although they were stylish and modern, they fit in perfectly with the traditional setting. Someone with good taste had chosen all the furnishings. The view from the windows that lined the outer wall was spectacular. The entire Fjällbacka archipelago was spread out before them.

"When does it open?" Erica picked up a rather strange-looking cookie, and instantly regretted her choice. Whatever it was made of, there wasn't enough sugar; it was much too wholesome to qualify as a cookie.

"In about a week. Provided we get everything done on time," said Vivianne with a sigh as she dunked her cookie in a mug of tea. Probably green tea, thought Erica, looking with pleasure at her own pitch-black beverage.

"You're coming to the party, aren't you?" said Vivianne.

"I'd really love to. I got the invitation, but we haven't actually decided yet. It's not easy to find a babysitter for three kids."

"Try to come. That would be so nice. By the way, on Saturday your husband and his colleagues are coming here for a firsthand look at the place. We're going to let them try out all the services we offer."

"Really?" said Erica with a laugh. "Patrik didn't tell me that. I don't think he's ever set foot in a spa before, so it should be an interesting experience for him."

"Let's hope so." Vivianne stroked Anton's head. "How's your sister doing? I hope you don't mind my asking, but I heard about the accident."

"That's okay." To her annoyance, Erica felt tears well up in her eyes. She swallowed hard and managed to get her voice under control. "To be honest, she's not doing very well. She's been through so much in her life."

The image of Anna's first husband flashed through Erica's mind. There were so many things she couldn't explain, even though there was something about this woman that made her want to do so. And she suddenly found herself telling Vivianne the whole story. She usually never discussed Anna's life, but she instinctively felt that Vivianne would understand. When she was done, tears were spilling down her cheeks.

"She certainly hasn't had an easy time of it. She needed that child," said Vivianne quietly, putting into words exactly what Erica had thought so many times. Anna deserved that baby. She deserved to be happy.

"I don't know what to do. She doesn't seem to notice when I'm with her. It's as if she has gone away somewhere. And I'm afraid that she might not come back."

"She hasn't gone away." Vivianne bounced Anton on her knee. "She has sought shelter in a place where it doesn't hurt. She knows that you're there. The best thing you can do is to visit her and touch her. We've forgotten how important it is to be touched, yet we all need it in order to survive. So touch her, and tell her husband to do that too. We often make the mistake of not wanting to bother someone who is grieving. We think they need peace and quiet and to be left alone. Nothing could be further from the truth. Human beings are herd animals, and we need to feel the herd around us, we need the closeness, warmth, and touch of other people. So make sure that Anna is surrounded by her herd. Don't let her stay in her room all alone. Don't allow her to slip away to that place where there may not be any grief but there aren't any other emotions either. Force her to come out of there."

Erica sat in silence for a moment. She was thinking about what Vivianne had said and realized that she was right. They shouldn't have let Anna withdraw from them. They should have made a greater effort.

"And don't feel guilty," said Vivianne. "Her grief has nothing to do with your joy."

"But she must feel that . . ." said Erica, and now the tears were flowing harder than ever. "She must feel that I got everything while she got nothing."

"She knows that what happened to the two of you isn't connected. If anything is going to stand between you, it's your feeling of guilt rather than any envy or anger that Anna might feel because your babies survived. That's all in your own mind."

"How can you be so sure?" Erica wanted to believe Vivianne, but she didn't dare. This woman had never met her sister, so how could she tell what Anna was thinking or feeling? All the same, there was a ring of truth to what she'd said.

"I can't explain how I know. I just do. I understand people. You'll simply have to trust me," said Vivianne firmly. And to her surprise, Erica realized that she did. She trusted her.

A short time later, as she was headed toward the day care center, she felt more at ease than she had in a long time. She had let go of what had been stopping her from drawing close to Anna again. She had rid herself of that feeling of helplessness.

# Fjällbacka 1871

*F*inally the ice had set in. It had arrived late that winter, not appearing until February. In a sense it made Emelie feel freer. After a week the ice was thick enough to walk on, and for the first time since she'd come to the island, it would be possible for her to leave on her own, if she wished to do so. It would involve a long walk as well as a certain amount of risk, because it was said that no matter how thick the ice, treacherous cracks existed where the current flowed most swiftly. Yet it was possible.

In another sense it made her feel more confined, because Karl and Julian couldn't make their regular trips to Fjällbacka. She had come to dread their return, when they'd arrive drunk and spiteful, but at least their absence gave her some breathing space. Now they spent more time in her presence, and the atmosphere was oppressive. She tried to be pleasant and quietly went about her chores. Karl still hadn't touched her, and she hadn't tried to make any more advances. In utter silence she lay in bed, pressing her body against the cold wall of the room. But the damage was done. His loathing for her had not diminished, and she felt more and more lonely.

The voices were louder now, and she had begun to see more of what her common sense told her was impossible; yet she knew it wasn't just her imagination. The dead gave her a feeling of solace. They were her only company on this desolate island, and their sorrow resonated with her own. Their lives hadn't turned out as they'd planned. They understood each other, even though their fates were separated by the thickest of walls. Death.

Karl and Julian didn't notice them in the same way that she did. But once in a while the two men seemed filled with an uneasiness that they couldn't explain. On those occasions, she could see their fear, and it made her secretly happy. She no longer lived for the love she had felt for Karl; he wasn't the man she'd thought he was. However this was her life now, and there was nothing she could do about it. She could merely rejoice at his fear, and take comfort from the dead. They gave her a feeling of being specially chosen. She was the only one who knew that they existed. They were hers.

But after being icebound for a month, she began to realize that fear was also apparent in her own face. The atmosphere had grown more tense. Julian seized every opportunity to yell at her and vent his frustration at being confined to the island. Karl regarded her with a cold expression, and the two men were always whispering to each other. With their eyes fixed on her, they would sit on the kitchen bench and put their heads together, murmuring. She couldn't hear what they said, but she knew it wasn't good. Sometimes she would catch snatches of their conversation when they thought she was out of earshot. Lately they'd talked a lot about the letter that Karl had received from his parents shortly before the ice set in. Their voices were agitated whenever they discussed the letter, but she couldn't work out what it might have said. And truth be told, she didn't really want to know. The anger in Julian's words, and the resigned tone of Karl's voice made shivers run down her spine.

Nor did she understand why her parents-in-law never came to visit, or why she and Karl never went to see them. His childhood home was only an hour's journey from Fjällbacka. If they left early in the morning, they could have made it back well before darkness fell. But Emelie never dared broach the topic. Every time a letter arrived from his parents, Karl would be in a gloomy mood for days. The latest letter had prompted a reaction that was worse than ever. But as usual, Emelie was relegated to the sidelines, unable to comprehend what was happening around her.

# 9

**N**ice place," said Gösta. His eyes swept over the apartment. Even though he was pleased with himself for taking the initiative, his stomach churned at the thought of Hedström's reaction.

"Probably gay," said Mellberg.

Gösta sighed. "What exactly are you basing that assumption on?"

"Only gay guys have places as neat and tidy as this one. Real men always have a few piles of crap in the corners. And they definitely don't have curtains on the windows." He frowned as he pointed to the snow-white curtains. "Besides, everybody says that he never had any girlfriends."

"I know, but . . ." Gösta sighed again and gave up trying to argue. Mellberg may have been born with two ears, just like everyone else, but he seldom used them for listening.

"If you take the bedroom, I'll take the living room. Okay?" Mellberg began pulling books from the shelves.

Gösta nodded as he surveyed the room. It was a bit impersonal. A beige sofa, a coffee table made of dark wood with a
light-colored rug underneath, a TV on a stand, and a bookcase
with a small selection of books. At least half of them were non-
fiction works about economics and accounting.

"What a strange guy," said Mellberg. "He has hardly any
possessions."

"Maybe he liked living an uncluttered life," said Gösta and
then went into the bedroom.

It was as neat as the living room. A bed with a white head-
board, a bedside table, several white-painted wardrobes, and a
chest of drawers.

"There's a woman in the photograph in here," Gösta yelled
to Mellberg as he picked up a small picture that was leaning
against the lamp on the bedside table.

"Is she a hottie? Let me see." Mellberg came into the bedroom.

"Er, well, maybe pretty would be a better description."

Mellberg glanced at the photo and made a face to indicate
that he wasn't especially impressed. He went back to the living
room, leaving Gösta to stand there holding the picture. He
wondered who she was. She must have meant something to
Mats Sverin. It seemed to be the only photograph in the whole
apartment, and he'd kept it in the bedroom.

Gösta put the picture back on the table and began going
through the chest of drawers and wardrobes. He found only
clothing, nothing of a more personal nature. No diaries, no old
letters or photo albums. Though he meticulously searched every
nook and cranny, after a while he had to concede that there
was nothing of interest. It was almost as if Sverin had never
existed prior to moving into the apartment. The only thing that
contradicted this was the picture of the woman.

Gösta went back to the bedside table and picked up the photograph again. He thought her very pretty. Slender and petite,

with long blond hair, which the wind was ruffling around her face at the moment the picture was taken. He squinted and held the photo closer as he studied every detail. He was looking for some clue that might tell them who she was or at least where the photo was taken. Nothing had been written on the back, and the only thing to be seen behind the woman was a lot of greenery. But when he took another look, he suddenly noticed that on the right side of the photo a hand was visible. Someone was either on his way into or out of the picture. It was a small hand. The photo was too blurry for him to be a hundred percent sure, but he thought it was a child's hand. Gösta put the photo down. Even if he was right, that didn't really tell him much. He turned on his heel and started to leave the bedroom, but then changed his mind. Returning to the bedside table, he picked up the photo and tucked it in his pocket.

"This really wasn't worth the trouble," muttered Mellberg. He was on his knees, peering under the sofa. "Maybe it would have been better to let Hedström handle the search after all. It feels like a complete waste of our time."

"We haven't done the kitchen yet," said Gösta, pretending not to hear Mellberg's complaints.

He began pulling out drawers and opening cupboards in the kitchen, but he found nothing of interest. The dishes looked as if they came from IKEA, and neither the refrigerator nor the pantry was particularly well stocked.

Gösta turned and leaned against the counter. Suddenly he caught sight of something lying on the kitchen table. A cord ran down under the table and was plugged into a socket in the wall. He picked up the cord for a closer look. It was a computer cable.

"Do we know whether Sverin had a laptop?" he called.

He didn't get an answer, but he could hear footsteps trudging toward the kitchen.

"Why do you ask?" said Mellberg.

"Because there's a computer cable here, but nobody mentioned anything about a laptop."

"It's probably at his office."

"But wouldn't they have said so when Paula and I were over there? They must realize that we'd be interested in seeing his laptop."

"Did you ask them?" Mellberg raised an eyebrow.

Gösta had to admit that they hadn't. They'd completely forgotten to ask for permission to inspect Sverin's computer. Presumably it was still in the council offices. He suddenly felt like a fool, standing there with the cable in his hand, so he let it fall to the floor.

"I'll drop by the council offices later on," he said, and walked out of the kitchen.

⟨∞⟩

"God, I hate waiting. Why does everything have to take so long?" Patrik muttered with annoyance as he pulled into the parking lot in front of Göteborg police station.

"Getting the report by next Wednesday is actually quite fast," said Paula. She held her breath as Patrik barely missed hitting a lamppost.

"I suppose you're right," replied Patrik as he got out of the car. "But we have no idea how long it's going to take to get the results from the forensics lab. Especially the data on the bullet. If there's a match on record, we need that information now, not in two weeks' time."

"It can't be helped. Besides, there's nothing we can do," said Paula, heading toward the entrance.

They'd phoned to say they were coming, but the receptionist still asked them to take a seat and wait. Ten minutes later a muscular and unbelievably tall man appeared and came striding over to them. Patrik reckoned he must be well over six feet tall. When he stood up to shake hands, he felt like a midget in comparison. It was even more extreme for Paula, who was so short that she reached only to the man's waist.

"Welcome. I'm Walter Heed. We spoke on the phone."

Patrik and Paula introduced themselves and were duly escorted out of the reception area.

Those shoes must be special-order, thought Patrik, staring in fascination at Walter's feet. They were like small boats. Paula gave Patrik a poke in the side. Embarrassed, he made an effort to look straight ahead.

"Come in. This is my office. Would you like a cup of coffee?"

They both nodded and were immediately served coffee from the vending machine out in the hall.

"So, you need information on an assault case, is that right?"

Patrik merely nodded in reply.

"I have the file here, but I'm not sure I'll be able to tell you much."

"Could you give us a brief summary of the facts?" asked Paula.

"Of course. Now, let me see . . ." Walter opened the folder and swiftly scanned a few documents. He cleared his throat. "Mats Sverin returned home late to his apartment on Erik Dahlbergsgatan. He wasn't sure of the exact time, but he thought it was not long after midnight. He'd been out to dinner with some friends. The victim's memory was rather hazy afterward, because he suffered severe blows to the head, and there were gaps in what he could recall." Walter raised his eyes from the folder and continued his report without referring to the file again. "In the end, what we managed to get out of him was that a bunch of young thugs were standing outside his front door. When he told one of them off for taking a piss there, they attacked him. But he couldn't give us a clear description or even tell us how many there were. We interviewed Mats Sverin on several occasions after he regained consciousness, but unfortunately we learned very little." Walter sighed as he closed the file folder.

"And that's as far as you got with the investigation?" asked Patrik.

"Yes. There was too little to go on. And no witnesses. But . . ." He hesitated and then took a sip of his coffee.

"But what?"

"This is just speculation on my part . . ." Again he hesitated.

"We'd appreciate anything you can give us," said Paula.

"Well, the whole time I had the feeling that Sverin knew more than he was telling. I have no proof, but when we were talking to him, he seemed to be holding back."

"You mean he knew who attacked him?" asked Patrik.

"I have no idea whether he did or not." Walter threw out his hands. "As I said, it was just a sense that he was withholding information. But you know as well as I do that there are lots of reasons why a victim might choose to remain silent."

Patrik and Paula nodded.

"I wish I could have devoted more time to the case and dug up more information. But we just don't have the resources, and in the end we had to shelve the investigation. We realized that we weren't going to get any further unless some new lead turned up."

"You might say that's exactly what has happened now," said Patrik.

"Do you think there's a connection between the assault and the murder?"

Patrik crossed his legs and took a few seconds to consider the question before he answered.

"At this stage we're trying to keep an open mind. But that's certainly one possibility. It's certainly an interesting coincidence that Sverin was assaulted only a few months before he was found shot to death."

"True. Well, be sure to let us know if there's any way we can assist you." Walter stood up, unfolding his tall body. "Our investigation remains open, and we might be able to help each other out."

"Absolutely," said Patrik, shaking hands with him. "Could we have a copy of your file?"

"I've already had one made for you," said Walter, giving Patrik a stack of documents. "Can you find your way out?"

"Sure. By the way . . ." Patrik turned as they were about to leave the office. "We were thinking of paying a visit to the organization that Sverin used to work for. Can you tell us how to get there?" He took out a piece of paper on which he'd jotted down the address.

Walter gave them a few simple directions, and then they said goodbye.

"That wasn't very productive," said Paula when they were once again seated in the car.

"Don't say that. It took a lot for him to stick out his neck like that and admit that a crime victim was holding back information. We need to find out more about the attack on Sverin. Maybe his move to Fjällbacka was an unsuccessful attempt to flee from something in Göteborg."

"Oh, so that's why we're starting with his previous employer," Paula concluded as she fastened her seat belt.

Patrik backed out of the parking lot, and Paula closed her eyes when he almost ran into the side of a blue Volvo 740 which, for some inexplicable reason, he hadn't noticed in the rearview mirror. Next time she was going to insist on taking the wheel. Her nerves weren't going to stand much more of Patrik's driving.

The children were running around in the courtyard. Madeleine was chain-smoking, even though she knew that she ought to stop. But here in Denmark it seemed everybody smoked.

"Mamma, can I go over to Mette's?" Her daughter Vilda was standing in front of her with tousled hair and rosy cheeks from all the fresh air and activity.

"Of course you can," she said, kissing Vilda on the forehead.

One of the best things about this block of apartments was that the big courtyard was always filled with children, and they were constantly running in and out of each other's homes, like one big family. She smiled and lit another cigarette. It was strange to feel so safe. She hadn't felt this way in such a long time that she could hardly remember what it was like. They'd been living here in Copenhagen for four months now, and the days seemed to pass at a leisurely pace. She had even stopped flinching when she went past the windows. Now she walked past, standing tall, even when the curtains were open.

They'd taken care of everything. It wasn't the first time, but things were different now. She had spoken to them herself, explained why she and her children needed to disappear again. And they had listened. The next night she'd received word to pack a bag for herself and her kids, and go down to the car that was waiting, with the motor running.

She had made up her mind not to look back. Not for an instant had she doubted that she'd made the right decision, yet sometimes she couldn't push aside the pain. It appeared in her dreams, waking her, and she'd lie in bed staring into the darkness. There she would see him—the man she couldn't allow herself to think about.

The cigarette burned her fingers, and she swore and tossed the butt to the ground. Kevin gave her an intent look. She'd been so lost in her own thoughts that she hadn't noticed when he sat down next to her on the bench. She reached out to ruffle his hair, and he offered no objection. He was such a serious boy. Her big little boy. Even though he was only eight, he'd already been through so much.

All around them they heard happy shouts echoing between the buildings. She had already noticed some Danish words sneaking into her children's vocabulary. She was both amused and frightened. Letting go of what had once been, of the people they once were, involved a sense of loss. Over time, the children would lose their own language, lose their Swedish with the Göteborg accent. But she was willing to make that sacrifice. They were home now, and they wouldn't have to move anymore. They could stay here and forget everything that they'd left behind.

She stroked Kevin's cheek. In time he would become a child like the others again. And that would make it all worthwhile.

⌒∞⌐

Maja came running and threw herself into Erica's arms, which was what she always did when her mother came to pick her up. After giving Erica a hug and a wet kiss, she reached up her hands to try and pat her little brothers in the stroller.

"Looks like somebody is very fond of her brothers," said Ewa, who stood outside, ticking off the names of the children from her list as someone came to fetch each of them.

"Yes, most of the time, at least. But they do get a swat now and then." Erica patted Noel's cheek.

"It's not unusual for a child to react when younger siblings arrive and she's no longer getting her parents' full attention." Ewa leaned over the stroller to say hello to the twins.

"I agree. It's perfectly understandable, and things have actually been going amazingly well."

"Do they sleep through the night?" Ewa tickled the boys and received two toothless smiles in return.

"They're good sleepers. The only problem is that Maja thinks it's boring when they're asleep, so if she gets the chance she likes to slip upstairs and wake them."

"I can imagine! She's a very plucky and resourceful little girl."

"That's putting it mildly."

The twins started squirming in the stroller, and Erica glanced around to see what had become of her daughter.

"Go and have a look at the jungle gym." Ewa nodded toward the playground. "That's her favorite place."

And she was right. At that very moment Erica saw Maja come racing down the slide, a big smile on her face. She took some convincing, but eventually Maja agreed to stand on the running board so they could leave the day care center.

"Go home?" asked Maja. Erica had turned right instead of left as she usually did when they were walking home.

"No, we're going to visit Aunt Anna and Uncle Dan," she said, and was rewarded with a jubilant cry from her daughter.

"Play with Lisen. And Emma. Not Adrian," Maja firmly announced.

"Is that so? Why don't you want to play with Adrian?"

"Adrian is a boy."

Clearly no further explanation was necessary, because that was the extent of the information Erica was able to get out of her daughter. She sighed. Should the division between boys and girls really occur so early? Determining what a child should or should not do, what a child wore and who she played with? She felt guilty, wondering whether she had contributed to this by giving in to her daughter's demands that everything of hers should be pink and princess-like. Maja's entire wardrobe was now filled with pink clothes, because that was the only color she was willing to wear; otherwise she threw a fit. Was it wrong to allow her to make her own decisions?

Erica pushed those thoughts aside. She didn't have the energy
for that topic at the moment. Besides, it was taking all her strength
to push the heavy stroller. She paused for a moment at the traffic
circle before setting off again, heading left along Dinglevägen. She
could see Dan's and Anna's house on Falkeliden, but it suddenly
seemed much further away than usual. Finally she reached it, but
the last bit up the hill had nearly done her in, and for a long time
she simply stood at their front door, trying to catch her breath. Her
pulse finally slowed enough so that she could ring the bell, and
only a few seconds later the door was flung open.

"Maja!" shrieked Lisen. "And the babies!" She turned
around and shouted into the house:

"Erica's here. And Maja and the babies! They're so adorable!"

Erica couldn't help laughing at Lisen's enthusiasm. She
stepped aside to allow Maja to go in.

"Is your pappa home?"

"Pappa!" yelled Lisen in answer to Erica's question.

Dan came into the hall from the kitchen.

"Oh, it's great to see you," he said, holding out his arms to
give Maja a hug. She was very fond of Dan.

"Come in, come in." He put Maja down, and she quickly
ran off to see what the other kids were doing. By the sound of
things, they were watching a children's program on TV.

"Sorry that I keep popping over like this," said Erica as she
hung up her jacket. She lifted the bassinets out of the stroller
and followed Dan, who led the way into the kitchen.

"We're delighted to have some company," said Dan, rubbing
his face. He looked terribly tired and dejected.

"I've just made a fresh pot of coffee," he added, looking at
Erica to see if she'd like some.

"Since when do you even need to ask?" she said with a wry
smile. She put the twins down on a blanket that she'd taken
out of the babies' diaper bag.

Then she sat at the kitchen table, and Dan took a seat across from her after pouring two cups of coffee. Neither of them spoke for a while. They knew each other so well that silence never made them uncomfortable. Strangely enough, her sister's husband had been Erica's boyfriend once upon a time. But that was so long ago that they could hardly remember it. Their relationship had developed instead into a warm friendship, and Erica couldn't have wished for a better husband for her sister.

"I had an interesting conversation today," she said at last.

"Really?" said Dan, sipping his coffee. He was a man of few words, and he also knew that Erica didn't need much encouragement in order to continue.

She told him how she'd bumped into Vivianne and what she'd said about Anna.

"We've let Anna withdraw from everyone, when we should have done the opposite."

"I'm not so sure about that," said Dan, getting up to refill their cups. "It feels like whatever I do is the wrong thing."

"But I think she's right. I'm certain of it. We can't let Anna just lie in bed and quietly waste away. If necessary, we have to force her to pay attention to us."

"Maybe you've got a point," he said, although he sounded doubtful.

"It's at least worth a try," Erica insisted. She bent down to check on the twins. They were lying on the blanket on the floor, waving their little hands and feet in the air. They looked so content that she leaned back in her chair again.

"Anything is worth a try, but . . ." Dan fell silent, as if he didn't dare say out loud what he was thinking, for fear that it might become true. "But what if nothing helps? What if she's given up?"

"Anna doesn't give up," said Erica. "She's at a low ebb now, but she won't give up. You have to believe that. You have to believe in Anna."

She stared at Dan, forcing him to meet her gaze. Anna wouldn't give up, but she needed help taking those first steps. And they were going to give her that help.

"Could you watch the boys? I'm going to sit with her for a while."

"Sure, I'll take care of the little tykes." Dan smiled wanly. He stood up and then sat down on the floor next to Anton and Noel.

Erica was already on her way out of the kitchen. She went upstairs and quietly opened the door to the bedroom. Anna was lying in exactly the same position as before. On her side, with her face turned toward the window. Erica didn't say a word, just lay down on the bed and pressed her body against Anna's. She put her arm around her and pulled her close, feeling her own warmth enveloping her sister.

"I'm here, Anna," she whispered. "You're not alone. I'm here."

◦◦◦

The food that Gunnar had brought was starting to run out, but she hesitated to phone Matte's parents again. She didn't want to think about him, about how disappointed he must have felt.

Nathalie blinked away the tears and decided to wait to call them until the following day. They had enough to make do, she and Sam. He didn't eat much. She was still feeding him like a baby, forcing him to take each bite, only to see most of it spill out of his mouth again.

She shivered, wrapping her arms around her body. Even though it wasn't particularly cold outside, it felt as if the wind blowing across the island came straight through the walls of the house, through her thick clothing, through her skin, and into her bones. She put on yet another sweater, a heavy one that her father had always worn whenever he went out fishing, but it made no difference. It was as if the chill were coming from inside of her.

Her parents wouldn't have liked Fredrik. She had known that from the moment she met him, yet she had pushed the thought away. They had died and left her on her own, so why should they have the right to influence her life? That was how she had felt for a long time: that they had abandoned her.

Her father died first. One day he suffered a heart attack and collapsed at home, never to get up again. Death was instantaneous, the doctor had said, trying to console them. Three weeks later her mother had received her death sentence. Liver cancer. She lingered for another six months before she passed away in her sleep, for the first time in months with a peaceful, almost happy expression on her face. Nathalie sat beside her when she died, holding her hand and trying to feel what she ought to feel: grief and loss. Instead she was filled with anger. How could they leave her all alone? She needed them. With them she had felt safe; she had always been able to return to their embrace after doing something stupid, something that made them shake their heads and say gently: "But Nathalie, what were you thinking?" Who was going to keep an eye on her now? Who was going to rein in her wild side?

She sat at her mother's deathbed, and in a single moment she became an orphan. Only she was nothing like the orphan in *Annie*, a favorite film from her childhood. While that little girl had been adopted by a kindly millionaire, Nathalie was left to her own devices, with no one to stop her making impulsive and stupid decisions, or pushing the boundaries, even when she knew she shouldn't. And so Nathalie took up with Fredrik— something which would have prompted her parents to have a serious talk with her. They would have tried to persuade her to drop him, to turn away from the life that would lead straight into the abyss. But they weren't there. They had abandoned her, and deep in her heart she was furious about that.

She sat down on the sofa and drew her knees to her body, wrapping her arms around her legs. Matte had been able to soothe her anger. For a few hours, on one brief evening and night, she had not felt alone for the first time since her parents died. And now he was gone. She leaned her forehead on her knees and wept. She was still the little, abandoned Nathalie.

❧

"Is Erling in?"

"He's in his office. Go ahead and knock." Gunilla half-rose from her chair to point in the direction of Erling's closed door.

"Thanks." Gösta nodded and headed down the corridor. He was mortified at having to return on this errand. It wouldn't have been necessary if he'd only thought to ask about Mats's computer when he was here with Paula. But it hadn't occurred to either of them on their last visit.

"Come in!" Erling said at once when he heard the knock. Gösta opened the door and went in.

"If the police keep dropping in like this, we can stop worrying about security at the office." Erling put on his best politician's smile and enthusiastically shook Gösta's hand.

"Er, yes, well, there's one thing that I need to follow up on," muttered Gösta as he sat down.

"Ask away. We'll do whatever we can to help the police."

"It has to do with Mats Sverin's computer. We've just done a search of his apartment, and he seems to have had a laptop computer. Is it here at the office?"

"Mats's computer? I've no idea. Let me go and see."

Erling stood up and went out into the hall, turning immediately to enter the neighboring office. He came back almost at once.

"No, it's not here. Was it stolen?" He looked nervous as he again took his place behind the desk.

"We don't know. But we'd like to get hold of it."

"Have you found Mats's briefcase?" asked Erling. "It's brown leather. He always had it with him whenever he went to and from work, and I know that he often put his laptop inside."

"No, we haven't found a brown briefcase."

"That's not good. If the computer and briefcase have been stolen, sensitive information might fall into the wrong hands."

"What sort of information?"

"I just mean that of course we wouldn't want information about civic finances and the like to be spread willy-nilly without some sort of control being imposed. It's public information, so there's nothing secret about it, but we still want to know how and where the information is made available. And with the Internet, you never know where things end up."

"That's true," said Gösta.

He couldn't help feeling disappointed that the laptop wasn't here in the office. What could have happened to it? Was Erling right to fear that it had been stolen? Or could Mats have stowed it somewhere other than in his apartment?

"Well, thanks for your help, anyway," said Gösta, getting to his feet. "I'm sure we'll be in touch again. And if the laptop or briefcase should turn up, could you please phone us at once?"

"Of course," said Erling, following Gösta out into the corridor. "Would you mind doing the same? It's very worrisome to think that council property has disappeared like this. Especially now. Project Badis is the biggest venture we've ever embarked on." Erling stopped abruptly. "Wait a minute. When Mats left the office on Friday, he mentioned that there were some discrepancies that concerned him. He was going to take up the issue with Anders Berkelin, who is responsible for the Badis finances. You could ask him if he knows anything about the missing laptop. It may be a long shot, but as I said, we'd like to get it back most urgently."

"We'll have a talk with him, and we'll let you know as soon as we find the computer."

Gösta sighed to himself as he left the council building. It looked as if there was going to be a lot of work to do on this case—too much work. And the golf season was already well under way.

❧

The Refuge premises were discreetly located in an office park in Hisingen. Patrik missed the entrance at first but finally managed to find it after driving past a few times.

"Do they know we're coming?" asked Paula as she got out of the car.

"No. I decided not to give them any advance warning."

"What do you know about this organization?" She nodded at the name printed on the sign in the entryway.

"They help battered women, providing shelter when they need to escape. Hence the name of the group: the Refuge. They also offer support while the woman remains in the relationship, helping her and any children to leave the abusive situation. Annika said she couldn't find out much more than that. They seem to operate with maximum discretion."

"Perfectly understandable," said Paula, pressing the button next to the name on the plaque. "Even though this wasn't exactly an easy place to find, I assume that they don't receive the women here."

"No. They probably have space somewhere else."

"Hello? The Refuge." A voice crackled over the intercom, and Paula gave Patrik an inquiring look. He cleared his throat.

"My name is Patrik Hedström. My colleague and I are from the Tanum police. We'd like to come in and ask you a few questions." He paused. "It's about Mats Sverin."

Silence. Then they heard a buzzing sound and they were able to push open the door. The office was on the second floor, so they took the stairs. Patrik noted that the door to the Refuge offices was different from the other doors in the building. It was more solid, made of steel with a seven-lever deadbolt. They rang another bell, which prompted crackling over another intercom.

"It's Patrik Hedström."

After a few seconds the door was unlocked.

"Sorry. We always handle visitors with the greatest caution." A woman in her forties wearing worn jeans and a white sweater stood in the doorway. She held out her hand. "Leila Sundgren. I'm the director of the Refuge."

"Patrik Hedström. And this is my colleague Paula Morales." They greeted each other politely.

"Come in. We can sit in my office. You said this was about Matte?" There was a slight nervousness in her voice.

"Let's wait until we get to your office," said Patrik.

Leila nodded and led the way to a small but bright room. The walls were covered with children's drawings, and the desk was neat and tidy. Not at all like Patrik's. He and Paula sat down.

"How many women do you help each year?" asked Paula.

"About thirty come to live with us. There's a tremendous need. Sometimes it feels as if it's just a drop in the sea, but unfortunately it's a matter of limited resources."

"How is the organization financed?" Paula was genuinely interested, so Patrik leaned back and let her ask the questions.

"We get money from two sources: social services contributions and individual donations. But as I mentioned, money is in short supply, and we always wish we could do more."

"How many employees do you have?"

"We have three paid staff members, plus an ever-changing number of volunteers. The salaries aren't substantial; I want to emphasize that. All of us who work here have taken pay cuts, in comparison with our previous jobs. We're not in it for the money."

"Mats Sverin—was he one of the paid employees?" Patrik interjected.

"Yes. He was hired as the financial officer. He worked here for four years and did a fantastic job. In his case, the salary was laughable if you consider what he'd been earning before. He was a truly dedicated staff member. And it didn't take much to persuade him to participate in this experiment."

"Experiment?" said Patrik.

Leila paused, looking as if she needed a moment to formulate what she wanted to say.

"The Refuge is unique," she said at last. "Normally there are no men in women's crisis organizations. I'd go so far as to say that it's completely taboo for a man to work for this type of group. But when Mats worked here, we had an equal number of men and women on staff—two women and two men—and that was exactly what I had in mind when I started the Refuge. It hasn't always been easy though."

"What do you mean?" asked Paula. This was all new to her; she'd never had any real contact with crisis services for women.

"It's an extremely controversial issue, and each side of the argument has its staunch supporters. The ones who insist that men should be kept out are of the opinion that women need a male-free zone after everything they've endured. Others, like myself, think that's the wrong way to go. I believe that men have a role to play in women's groups. There are men in the world, after all, and keeping them out creates a false sense of security. Moreover there's tremendous value in showing that there are other kinds of men than the ones these women have had to deal with all their lives. It's important to show that good men do exist. That's why I've gone against the flow and chosen to be the first women's crisis group to have both male and female employees." She paused for a moment. "Of course this means that the men we take on must undergo a thorough background check. We need to have total confidence in them."

"And you had confidence in Mats?" asked Patrik.

"He was the good friend of my nephew. For a couple of years they spent a lot of time together, so I met Matte on many occasions. He told me he was dissatisfied with his job and that he was looking for something more. And when he heard about the work of the Refuge, he got all fired up and succeeded in convincing me that he was the right person for the job. He really wanted to help people, and he had that opportunity here."

"Why did he quit?" Patrik asked, looking at Leila. He registered a flicker in her eyes, but the next second it was gone.

"He wanted to move on. And after he was assaulted, he started thinking about returning home. That's not uncommon. He was badly injured. You know that, don't you?"

"Yes. We talked to the doctor at Sahlgrenska Hospital," said Patrik.

Leila took a deep breath. "Why have you come here to ask questions about Matte? It was months ago that he left."

"Has anyone been in touch with him since then?" asked Patrik, ignoring her question.

"No. We didn't socialize outside of work, so we lost touch after he left. But now I really want to know why you're asking all these questions." Her voice rose slightly, and her hands were clasped on top of her desk.

"Mats was found dead the day before yesterday. Shot."

Leila gasped. "That can't be true."

"I'm afraid it is," said Patrik. Leila's face had turned white, and he wondered whether he ought to go and get her a glass of water.

She swallowed hard, trying to pull herself together, but her voice shook as she asked, "Why? Do you have any idea why?"

"At this point we're dealing with an unknown perpetrator." Patrik heard himself, as usual, switch to dry police jargon, which he did whenever the situation became emotionally charged.

"Is there any connection to . . . ?" Leila was too shaken to complete the sentence.

"At the moment we don't know," Paula told her. "We're simply trying to find out more about Mats. To find out whether there was anyone in his life who had a motive for killing him."

"Running an organization of this kind," said Patrik, "I assume that you're accustomed to receiving threats."

"Yes, we are," said Leila. "Although the threats are usually directed at the women rather than at us. Besides, Mats dealt primarily with the financial side of things, so he was the contact staff member for only a handful of women. And as I said, he left more than three months ago. I have a hard time seeing why . . ."

"You don't recall any incidents from the time he was working here? Was there any situation that stands out, any threat directed specifically at him?"

Again Patrik thought he saw a flash in her eyes, but it vanished so swiftly that he assumed he must have imagined it.

"No, not really. Matte mostly worked in the background. He took care of the account books. Debits and credits."

"How much contact did he have with the women who sought help from your group?" asked Paula.

"Very little. He mainly dealt with administrative issues." Stunned by the news of Mats's death, Leila could only stare at Patrik and Paula in bewilderment.

"Then I don't think we have any further questions at this time," said Patrik. He put one of his business cards on Leila's orderly desk. "If you or anyone else happens to think of anything, don't hesitate to give me a call."

Leila nodded and picked up his card. "Absolutely."

After they said goodbye, the heavy steel door fell shut behind them.

"What do you think?" asked Patrik quietly as they went down the stairs.

"I think she's hiding something," said Paula.

"I do too."

Patrik had a grim expression on his face. They were going to have to take a closer look at the Refuge.

# Fjällbacka 1871

**A**strange mood had hovered over the house all day long. Karl and Julian took turns tending to the lighthouse, but the rest of the time they had been avoiding her. Neither of them would look her in the eye.

The others also seemed to sense something ominous in the air. They were more present than usual, suddenly turning up, only to vanish just as swiftly. Doors slammed, and she heard footsteps overhead that stopped as soon as she went upstairs. They wanted to tell her something, she realized that, but she couldn't work out what it might be. Several times she felt someone breathing against her cheek and someone touching her shoulder or arm. A feather-light touch on her skin, but as soon as it disappeared, she thought she must have imagined it. Yet she knew it was real—just as real as the feeling that she needed to flee.

Emelie stared at the ice with longing. Maybe she ought to venture out on it. As soon as that thought occurred to her, she felt a hand on her back that seemed to be nudging her toward the front door. Was that *what they wanted to say? That she should leave while she still could? But she lacked the courage. Aimlessly she wandered through the house. Cleaning, tidying up, and trying not to think. It felt as if the absence of those malevolent glances from the two men was more foreboding and frightening than their stares.*

*All around her the others were trying to catch her attention. They wanted to make her listen, but no matter how hard she tried, she couldn't understand. She felt hands touching her, she heard footsteps impatiently following her everywhere she went, but the agitated whisperings, all those words jumbled on top of each other, were impossible to decipher.*

*As dusk fell, she found herself shaking all over. She knew that Karl would soon take the first shift in the lighthouse, and she needed to hurry to get dinner ready. Without thinking, she prepared the salted fish. As she poured out the water from the potatoes, her hands shook so badly that she almost scalded herself.*

*They sat down at the table, and suddenly she heard a thudding sound overhead. The sound got louder, more insistent. Karl and Julian didn't seem to hear it, but they stirred uneasily as they sat on the kitchen bench.*

*"Get out the schnapps," said Karl, his voice cracking. He nodded at the cupboard where the liquor was kept.*

*She didn't know what to do. Even though they usually came back from Abela's tavern as drunk as skunks, they rarely drank at home.*

*"Schnapps, I said!" Karl growled, and Emelie quickly got up. She opened the cupboard and took out the bottle, which was nearly full. She set it on the table and then got out two glasses.*

*"A glass for you too," said Julian. His eyes glittered with a look that sent shivers down her spine.*

*"I'm not sure if I . . ." she stammered. She seldom drank spirits. On a few occasions she had tasted a tiny bit, just enough to know that she didn't care for it.*

*Annoyed, Karl got up and took another glass out of the cupboard, slamming it down on the table in front of Emelie. Then he filled it to the brim.*

"I don't want to . . ." Her voice broke, and she felt herself trembling more than ever. No one had touched the food. Slowly she raised the glass to her lips and took a sip.

"Drink it down," said Karl. He took his place again, and poured an equal amount for himself and for Julian. "Drink it all down. Now."

From upstairs the thudding sound was growing louder. She thought about the ice that stretched all the way to Fjällbacka. The ice would have been able to carry her to safety if only she had listened, if only she had dared. But now it was dark, and it was no longer possible to flee. Suddenly she felt a hand on her shoulder, a brief touch telling her that she was not alone.

Emelie lifted her glass and downed the schnapps. She had no choice; she was a captive here. She didn't know why, but that was the way it was. She was their prisoner.

Karl and Julian emptied their glasses when they saw that she had finished hers. Then Julian reached for the bottle and filled her glass again, all the way to the top. The liquid spilled over the side and onto the table. They didn't have to say a word; she knew what she had to do. As they filled their own glasses, they kept their eyes fixed on her, and she realized that no matter what else happened she would be forced to raise her glass, again and again.

After a while the whole room seemed to be spinning, and she felt them taking off her clothes. She let them do it. The alcohol had made her limbs heavy, and she was unable to offer any sort of resistance. And while the thudding overhead got so loud that the sound filled her head, Karl lay down on top of her. Then came the pain and the darkness. Julian gripped her by the arms, and the last thing she saw was his eyes. They were filled with hatred.

# 10

t was a brilliantly sunny Friday morning. Erica turned over in bed and put her arm around Patrik. He had come home late. By then she had already gone to bed and managed only to mutter a sleepy "Hi" before she fell asleep again. But now she was awake, and she felt such a longing for him, for his body and the sort of intimacy that had occurred far too seldom during the past few months. She sometimes wondered when they'd find their way back to it. These years were passing much too quickly. Everyone had told her that the early childhood years were especially tough, that they could be hard on a marriage, and that it might be difficult for a wife and husband to feel close to one another. Now that she was in the midst of it all, she agreed, but only partially. Of course things had been hard when Maja was a baby. But her relationship with Patrik hadn't changed for the worse since the twins were born. After the accident the bond between them had grown stronger than ever, and she knew that nothing could tear them apart. But she missed the intimacy. It was something they just didn't get around to, what with all the diapers that had to be changed, the meals that had to be cooked, and the constant chore of dropping off and picking up their daughter at day care.

Patrik lay with his back to her. She crept close to him. It was one of the rare mornings she had woken of her own accord rather than because a child was crying. She pressed closer, sliding her hand inside his underwear. Slowly she began stroking him, feeling his response. Patrik still hadn't moved, but she could hear his breathing change and knew that he was awake. He was breathing harder. She was enjoying the warm feeling that spread through her body. Patrik turned over to face her. As they looked into each other's eyes, she felt a tingling in her stomach. Gently he began kissing her throat. She uttered a faint moan as she stretched her neck so that he could reach the spot behind her ear that was so sensitive.

Their hands began wandering, and he slipped off his underwear. She quickly removed the T-shirt she slept in and with a giggle pulled off her panties.

"It's been a while," murmured Patrik as he continued to nibble the back of her neck, making her squirm.

"Mmmm, I think we need a little more practice." Erica ran her fingertips along his spine. Patrik turned her over on her back and was just about to lie down on top of her when a familiar sound issued from the room across the hall.

"Waaaaa!" A shrill voice followed by another, and then they heard feet padding along the hall. Maja was standing in the doorway with her thumb in her mouth and her favorite doll under her arm.

"The babies are crying," she said with a frown on her face. "Get up, Mamma. Get up, Pappa."

"Okay, okay, we're coming, you little munchkin." With a heavy sigh Patrik rolled out of bed. He quickly pulled on a pair of jeans and a T-shirt and headed for the nursery after casting an apologetic glance at Erica.

The lovemaking was over for the day. She pulled on her jogging suit, which lay on the floor next to the bed, and then followed Maja downstairs to the kitchen to make breakfast for them, and prepare bottles of formula for the twins. Her body was still warm, but the tingling feeling had vanished.

But when she looked up and saw Patrik coming down the stairs holding a newly awakened baby in each arm, she felt the tingling again. She really loved that husband of hers.

"We didn't come up with anything particularly useful," said Patrik when everyone was present. "On the other hand, there are some new questions that we need to answer."

"So you didn't find out any more about the assault?" asked Martin, looking disappointed.

"No, according to the police there were no witnesses to the attack. The only thing they had to go on was Mats Sverin's own statement that he didn't know the group of kids who assaulted him."

"You don't sound too convinced by that," said Martin.

"We discussed it on the way home," said Paula. "We both had the feeling that there's more to the story, so we need to do some digging."

"Are you sure that wouldn't be a waste of time?" asked Mellberg.

"I can't guarantee it, but we think it would be worth our while taking a closer look," said Patrik.

"What did you find out at Sverin's former workplace?" asked Gösta.

"Nothing much of interest there either. At least, not directly. But we plan to keep that avenue open too. We talked to the director of the organization, and she seemed upset to hear of Mats's death, but she wasn't . . . how should I put it?"

"She didn't seem terribly surprised," Paula interjected.

"Another of your feelings?" said Mellberg, sighing heavily. "Bear in mind that the station has limited resources. We can't be running off in all directions and doing whatever we like. Personally, I think it's a waste of effort to be sniffing around the victim's life in Göteborg. My long experience on the force has taught me that the answer is often to be found closer to home. For example, have we taken a good hard look at his parents? I take it you're all aware of the statistics—most murders are committed by a relative or someone close to the victim."

"Yes, well, in this case I don't consider Gunnar and Signe Sverin to be at the top of our list of candidates." Patrik restrained himself from rolling his eyes.

"I don't think that they should be ruled out so quickly. You never can tell what secrets a family might be hiding."

"True, but in this particular instance, I don't agree." Patrik crossed his arms as he leaned against the kitchen counter and swiftly changed the subject. "Martin and Annika, did you come up with anything?"

"No, everything seems in order. There's nothing out of the ordinary about Mats Sverin in the public records. He never married, and he's not listed as the father of any children. After he moved away from Fjällbacka, he was registered at three different addresses in Göteborg. The last one was on Erik Dahlbergsgatan. The lease on that apartment was still in his name, but he had sublet it to another tenant. He had taken out two loans: a student loan and a car loan. Nothing unusual about the payments. He'd owned a Toyota Corolla for the past four years." Martin paused to consult his notes. "His employment record matches the information we already have. He was never convicted of any sort of crime. That's as much as we've been able to find out. Judging by the public records, Sverin seems to have led a completely normal life with nothing remarkable to report."

Annika nodded her agreement. They had hoped to find more, but this was all they'd been able to track down.

"Okay, at least we know that much," said Patrik. "But we still need to search Sverin's apartment. Who knows what we might find there?"

Gösta cleared his throat. Patrik gave him an inquiring look. "Yes?"

"Er, well . . ." Gösta began.

Patrik frowned. It was never a good sign when Gösta cleared his throat.

"What are you trying to say?" Patrik wasn't sure he really wanted to know, since his colleague was obviously having a hard time spitting out the words. When Gösta cast an entreating glance at Mellberg, Patrik felt his stomach lurch. Gösta and Bertil did not make a good combination.

"The thing is . . . Torbjörn phoned yesterday while you were in Göteborg." Gösta fell silent, swallowing hard.

"Yes?" Patrik repeated. He had to stop himself from stepping forward to shake the words out of the man.

"Torbjörn turned over the apartment to us yesterday. And we know how you hate to waste time, so Bertil and I thought we might as well go over there and have a look around."

"You did what?" Patrik grabbed hold of the edge of the counter, forcing himself to breathe calmly. He remembered all too well the feeling of pressure in his chest, and he knew that under no circumstances should he allow himself to get upset.

"There's no reason to react that way," said Mellberg. "In case you've forgotten, I'm the boss of this station. Which means that I'm your superior officer, and I made the decision to go over to the apartment."

Though Patrik realized that Bertil was right, that didn't make it any easier to bear. Mellberg might be the official police chief, but in reality Patrik had undertaken that role ever since Mellberg had arrived at the station when he was transferred from Göteborg.

"What did you find?" he asked after a moment.

"Not much," Mellberg admitted.

"The apartment felt more like a temporary residence than somebody's home," said Gösta. "There were hardly any personal possessions. In fact, I'd say none."

"Seems a bit odd," said Patrik.

"His laptop is missing," Mellberg added, as he scratched Ernst behind the ear.

"His laptop?"

Patrik's irritation grew. Why hadn't he thought of that? Of course Mats Sverin would have a laptop, and it should have been one of the first things he asked the crime-scene techs about. He silently cursed himself.

"How can you be certain that it's missing?" he went on. "Maybe it's at the office. Maybe he didn't have a computer at home."

"Apparently he had only one computer," said Gösta. "And we found a cord for a laptop in the kitchen. Plus Erling has confirmed that Sverin had a laptop that he used for work and usually took home with him."

"So you've had another talk with Erling?"

Gösta nodded. "I went over there yesterday after we were done at the apartment. He seemed concerned that the computer is missing."

"I wonder if the killer took it. And if so, why?" said Martin. "By the way, has anyone found Sverin's cell phone? Has that disappeared too?"

Patrik swore again. Yet another thing that he'd missed.

"Maybe there's something on his computer that might reveal a motive for the murder or who the killer is," said Mellberg. "If we can just locate the computer, we'll have the whole case sewn up."

"Let's not get ahead of ourselves," said Patrik. "We have no idea where the laptop might be, or who could have taken it. But we definitely need to locate it, as well as his cell. Until then, let's not jump to conclusions."

"If we ever find it," said Gösta. Then his face lit up. "Erling said that Sverin was concerned about something in the accounts. He was going to meet with a man named Anders Berkelin, who's in charge of finances at Badis. Maybe he has the laptop. They were working together on the project, so it's possible that Sverin left the computer with him."

"Gösta, I want you and Paula to drive over there and have a talk with him. Martin and I will go to the apartment. I want to take a look around. And we're supposed to get Torbjörn's report sometime today, aren't we?"

"That's right," Annika told him.

"Okay, then. And Bertil, you'll take charge of things here?"

"Of course," said Mellberg. "That goes without saying. And you haven't forgotten what's happening tomorrow, have you?"

"Tomorrow?" Everyone turned to give him an inquiring look.

"It's the VIP event at Badis. We're invited, remember—and we have to be there at eleven o'clock."

"Do we really have time for that now?" said Patrik. "I assumed it had been canceled since we have more important matters to think about at the moment."

"What's best for the town and the surrounding area has always been our top priority." Mellberg stood up. "We are role models for the community, and our participation in local projects is of paramount importance. So I'll expect to see all of you at Badis tomorrow morning at eleven."

A resigned murmur passed through the room. They knew it was pointless arguing with Mellberg. And a couple of hours spent getting a massage and being pampered, body and soul, might do miracles for their energy level at work.

∞

"Goddamn stairs." Gösta stopped halfway up.

"We could have driven to the other side and parked in front of Badis instead," said Paula as she paused to wait for him.

"Why didn't you mention that earlier?" He took a couple of deep breaths before continuing. He hadn't managed to play enough rounds of golf this year to get himself in shape. Reluctantly he also had to acknowledge that age was beginning to take its toll.

"Patrik wasn't exactly thrilled that you went to the apartment." They had avoided the topic on the way over, but Paula could no longer resist bringing it up.

Gösta snorted. "If I remember correctly, Hedström is not head of the station."

Paula didn't reply, and after a moment of silence Gösta sighed.

"Okay, maybe it wasn't such a good idea to go there without first talking to Patrik. Sometimes it's hard for us old guys to accept that a new generation has taken over. We have experience and seniority on our side, but that doesn't seem to mean anything."

"I think you underestimate yourself. Patrik always has positive things to say about you. But as far as Mellberg is concerned, well . . ."

"He does?" Gösta sounded happily surprised, and Paula hoped that he wouldn't see through her white lie. Gösta didn't often contribute to their work, and Patrik didn't exactly shower him with praise. But he was nice enough, and he meant well. It wouldn't do any harm to give him a little encouragement.

"Mellberg is definitely in a class by himself," said Gösta, stopping again as they reached the top of the long flight of stairs. "So now let's see what these people are like. I've heard a lot about this project, but I reckon it takes a particular breed to be willing to team up with Erling." He shook his head and then turned his back to Badis and gazed out across the water. It was another beautiful early summer day, and there was barely a ripple in the bay near Fjällbacka. Here and there some sparse vegetation was visible, but the gray rocks dominated. "All I can say is this is a damned spectacular view," said Gösta, sounding unusually philosophical.

"Yes, it's great, isn't it? Badis certainly has an unbeatable location. It's strange that it was allowed to fall into such disrepair for so long."

"It was a matter of money. It must have cost millions to fix up the place, given the state of the building. And the renovation isn't half bad. Question is, how much of the bill are we going to be paying in taxes?"

"Now you sound more like your old self, Gösta. I was starting to worry." Paula smiled and headed toward the entrance. She was impatient to get to work.

"Hello?" Once inside, they called out several times and after a few minutes a tall, nondescript man came to greet them. His blond hair was cut in the appropriate style, his designer glasses were the appropriate type, and his handshake was firm. It occurred to Paula that she'd have trouble recognizing him again if she ran into him on the street.

"We spoke to you on the phone," she said as introductions were made. They sat down at one of the tables in the dining room where documents were spread out next to a laptop computer.

"Nice office," she said, looking around the room.

"I've also got a cubbyhole back there," said Anders Berkelin, gesturing vaguely with his hand. "But I work better in here. It seems less confining. As soon as the place opens for business, I'll probably have to crawl back into my hole." He smiled, and even his smile was perfectly appropriate. "I understand that you wanted to ask me some questions about Mats." He closed the laptop and looked at them. "It's just so awful."

"Yes, he seems to have been well-liked," said Paula, opening her notebook. "Did you work together on Project Badis from the very beginning?"

"No, only since he was hired by the local council a few months ago. Before that, things were a bit messy over there, so we had to take on a lot of the burden ourselves. Mats was like manna from heaven."

"Presumably it took him a while to get up to speed. A project like this must be very complicated."

"Well, it's not really all that complicated. There are two financial backers. The local council and the two of us—my sister and myself. We share the expenses equally and we'll also be sharing the profits."

"And how long do you estimate it will take before the place is profitable?" asked Paula.

"We've tried to be as realistic as possible with our calculations. There's no point in building castles in the air, so to speak. We estimate that it'll be about four years before we reach the 'break-even point,'" he said, using the English term.

"Break even?" said Gösta.

"The point when all the costs have been paid off," Paula clarified.

"Oh, right," Gösta muttered, embarrassed at his lack of familiarity with English. He'd picked up a lot of phrases from the golf tournaments he watched on the sports channel, but the terms he'd learned weren't much use outside of golf.

"What sort of things did you and Mats work on together?" asked Paula.

"My sister and I are in charge of all the practical matters here. We've coordinated the renovation work, hired the staff, and basically taken responsibility for creating the business. Then we've billed the local council for its share of the expenses. It was Mats's job to keep tabs on the account books and make sure the bills were paid. In addition, we've also had an ongoing discussion about project expenses and income. The council has also had a large say in things." Anders pushed his glasses up. It was hard to see his eyes behind the lenses.

"Did you have any disagreements?" Paula was taking notes as they talked, and one page was already nearly filled with illegible scrawls.

"That depends on what you mean by disagreement." Anders clasped his hands on the table. "We didn't agree on everything, but Mats and I enjoyed a good and constructive dialogue, even if we didn't always see eye to eye."

"And no one else had any problems with him?" asked Gösta.

"On the project?" Anders looked as if the idea was absurd. "No, absolutely not. Nothing beyond the differences of opinion that he and I had over certain details. Nothing that was so serious it would . . . No, definitely not." He shook his head vigorously.

"According to Erling Larson, Mats was going to drop by here last Friday to talk to you about something that was worrying him. Did he do that?" asked Paula.

"Yes. Mats was here for a short time. He stayed about half an hour. But I think it's an exaggeration to say that he was worried. There were a few numbers that didn't add up, and the projections needed to be adjusted slightly, but that's not so strange. We straightened it all out in no time."

"Is there anyone here who can confirm what you've just told us?"

"No, I was the only one here at the time. He arrived rather late. Around five o'clock. I think he came straight from work."

"Do you recall whether he had his laptop with him?"

"Mats always had his laptop with him, so I can be fairly sure that he did. Yes, that's right. I remember that he brought his briefcase along."

"And he didn't leave it here?" asked Paula.

"No. I would have noticed if he did. Why? Is his laptop missing?" Anders gave them a nervous look.

"We don't know yet," said Paula. "But if it should turn up, we'd be grateful if you'd contact us at once."

"Of course. But as I said, he didn't leave it here, at any rate. And we'd be quite concerned if his computer really has disappeared. It contains sensitive information about Project Badis." Again he pushed up his glasses.

"I understand." Paula got up, and Gösta took that as a signal to do the same. "Give us a call if anything else occurs to you." She handed Anders her card, which he put in a card holder that he took out of his pocket.

"I'll do that," he said. He kept his pale blue eyes fixed on the two officers as they headed for the door.

୶୦

What if they found her and Sam here? Strangely enough, the thought hadn't occurred to Nathalie until now. Gråskär had always been such a safe place, and only now did she realize that they could find her here if they wanted to.

The shots were still loud in her memory. They had echoed through the silence of the night, and then everything was quiet once again. And she had fled, taking Sam and leaving chaos and devastation behind. Leaving Fredrik.

The people he'd had dealings with could easily track her down. At the same time, she knew that she'd had no choice other than to come here and wait to be found or to be forgotten. They knew that she was weak. In their eyes she had been nothing more than Fredrik's accessory, a beautiful jewel, a shadow who discreetly made sure that their glasses were filled and the humidor was never empty. For them she hadn't been a real person, and now that might be to her advantage. There was no reason to chase down shadows.

Nathalie went out into the sunlight, trying to convince herself that she was safe. But the doubts lingered. She walked around the corner of the house, gazing out at the water, past the islands to the mainland. One day a boat might appear, and then she and Sam would be caught here like rats in a cage. She sat down on the bench, hearing how it creaked under her weight. The wind and the salt had taken a toll on the wood, and the old bench leaned wearily against the wall of the house. There were many things on the island that needed attention. On the other hand, some of the flowers kept coming up in the flowerbeds. The hollyhocks were the ones she remembered best. When she was little, and her mother tenderly tended the flowers, the hollyhocks had filled the entire back row. Now only a few lonely stocks had come up, and it remained to be seen what color they would be. The roses hadn't yet bloomed, but she was hoping it would be the ones that she loved most, the light pink variety, that had survived. But all of her mother's herbs had long since perished. Only a few strands of chives bore witness to the fact that at one time an herb garden had thrived there, so delightfully fragrant whenever she had run her hand through the plants.

She got up and looked in the window. Sam was lying on his side, with his face turned away from her. He slept for a long time in the mornings now, and she had no reason to make him get out of bed. Maybe he needed to sleep and dream in order to heal what had been damaged.

Quietly she sat back down. The restlessness in her body was slowly calmed by the steady sound of the water lapping against the rocks. They were on Gråskär Island, she was a shadow, and no one was going to find them. They were safe.

&sect;

"Couldn't Mamma do it today?" Patrik sounded disappointed. He was talking on his cell as he took the tight curve near Mörhult, driving too fast.

"Tomorrow afternoon? Well, I suppose it can't be helped. It'll have to wait until tomorrow then. Love you. See you later."

He ended the call, and Martin gave him an inquiring look.

"I was thinking of taking Erica with me to talk to Sverin's old girlfriend, Nathalie Wester. According to his parents, Mats was planning to go and see her, but they don't know if he ever did."

"Couldn't you just phone her and ask?"

"Yes, I suppose I could. But I usually get better results meeting someone face to face, and I want to talk to as many people as possible who knew Mats, even if it was long ago. He's a mystery. I need to know more."

"And why should Erica go with you?" Martin gratefully climbed out of the vehicle in the parking lot in front of the block of apartments.

"She went to school with Nathalie. And Mats."

"Oh, that's right. I heard about that. So it's probably a good idea if she goes with you. She might make Nathalie feel more at ease."

They walked up the stairs and stopped at the door to Mats Sverin's apartment.

"I hope Mellberg and Gösta haven't made too much of a mess," said Martin.

"We can always hope." Patrik had no illusions that his colleagues had been particularly careful. Not Mellberg, at any rate. Gösta could sometimes rise to the occasion and prove to be quite competent.

They stepped cautiously around the patches of dried blood in the hall.

"Somebody is going to have to deal with this eventually," said Martin.

"I'm afraid that's going to be the job of the victim's parents. I hope they can find someone to help them. No one should have to clean up their own child's blood."

Patrik went into the kitchen.

"Here's the computer cable that Gösta was talking about. I wonder whether Gösta and Paula have found the laptop by now. They probably would have phoned if they had." He was thinking aloud.

"Why would Sverin have left it at Badis?" said Martin. "No, I'll bet it was the person who shot him who took the computer."

"It looks as if Torbjörn and his team have taken fingerprints from the cable, at any rate. If they got some good prints, maybe that will give us a lead."

"A killer who was careless, you mean?"

"Luckily there seem to be plenty who fall into that category."

"But they seem to be getting more careful since TV started showing those forensics crime shows. Seems like every petty thief now knows the basics about fingerprints and DNA."

"That's true, but there will always be idiots in the world."

"Then let's hope that it's an idiot we're dealing with here." Martin went back to the hall and continued on to the living room. "I see what Gösta meant," he called.

Patrik stayed where he was, standing in the middle of the kitchen.

"About what?"

"About this place feeling like a temporary residence. It's very impersonal. Nothing that says anything about who he was. No photos, no knickknacks, and nothing but reference books on the shelf."

"Like I said: he's a mystery." Patrik came into the living room.

"Hmmm, maybe he was just a very private person. Why should that be so mysterious? Some people are more reserved than others, and I don't find it so strange that he didn't discuss girlfriends and personal matters at the office."

"That's not the only thing though," said Patrik, slowly walking around the room. "He doesn't seem to have had any friends. His apartment is extremely impersonal, as you said yourself. And he didn't tell anyone about the terrible beating he suffered . . ."

"You don't have proof of that last statement, do you?"

"No, I don't. But something's not right. Besides, he was found shot to death in his own front hall. I mean, your average person doesn't end up getting shot like that. The stereo and TV are still here, so if it was a burglary, we're dealing with a thief who was very stupid or very lazy."

"The laptop is missing," Martin reminded Patrik as he pulled out a drawer from the TV stand.

"Yes, but . . . I have a gut feeling about this." Patrik went into the bedroom and started looking around. Everything Martin had said was true. There was no evidence to support the churning feeling in his gut, the sense that below the surface there was another layer to Mats Sverin that needed to be brought to light.

They spent an hour meticulously going through everything, only to arrive at the same conclusion that Gösta and Mellberg had reached on the previous day. There was nothing here. The apartment might as well have been an IKEA room set. Except that even those were more personal than Mats Sverin's home.

"Shall we go?" said Patrik with a sigh.

"Yes. There's not much else we can do. Let's hope that Torbjörn's come up with something useful."

Patrik locked the door to the apartment. He'd been hoping to find a lead that they could pursue. So far all he had were vague suspicions, and not even he was prepared to act on those alone.

"Lunch at Lilla Berith?" asked Martin as they got in the car.

"That sounds good," replied Patrik without enthusiasm, backing the vehicle out of the parking lot.

✑

Vivianne quietly opened the door to the dining room and went over to Anders. He didn't look up. He was typing rapidly on the computer keyboard.

"What did they want?" She sat down across from him, on the chair where Paula had been sitting. It was still warm.

"They asked about Mats and the work we did together. They wondered whether his laptop was here." He didn't look up.

"What did you tell them?" She leaned across the table.

"As little as possible. I said we had a good working relationship, and that his laptop wasn't here."

"Is this . . ." She hesitated. "Is this going to affect us in any way?"

Anders shook his head and for the first time looked at his sister.

"Not if we don't let it. He was here last Friday. We talked for a while and resolved a few questions. When we were done, he left, and none of us has seen him since. That's all they need to know."

"You make it sound so simple," said Vivianne. She felt apprehension well up inside her. Apprehension and questions that she didn't dare ask.

"It *is* simple." He spoke tersely, not letting his voice reveal any emotion. But Vivianne knew her brother all too well. She knew that in spite of the steady gaze of his blue eyes behind his glasses, he was worried. However much he tried not to show it.

"Is this worth it?" she asked at last.

He looked at her in surprise.

"That's what I tried to talk to you about the other day, but you refused to listen."

"I know." She raised her hand and wrapped a lock of blond hair around her index finger. "I don't really have any doubts; I just wish that it was over so we could finally have some peace and quiet."

"Do you think we'll ever have that? Maybe we're so damaged that we'll never find what we're looking for."

"Don't say that," she told him fiercely.

He had spoken the forbidden words that sometimes came to her in weak moments, the words that crept in when she was lying in bed in the dark, on the verge of sleep.

"We're not going to say or think such a thing," she repeated firmly. "We've drawn all the short straws in life, we've had to fight for everything, nothing has ever been free. We deserve this." She stood up so abruptly that her chair fell over backward and landed on the floor with a bang. Leaving it there, she fled to the kitchen, needing to occupy her brain so it wouldn't start dwelling on other matters. With shaking hands she began rifling through the refrigerator and pantry to make sure they had everything they needed for tomorrow's pre-dedication events.

❦

Mette, who lived in the next apartment, had been nice enough to offer to look after the kids for a couple of hours. Madeleine didn't have any specific plans; unlike most people, her life wasn't filled with all the errands and chores that she so longed to make part of her days. She simply needed some time for herself.

She strolled along Strøget, Copenhagen's pedestrian street, heading toward Kongens Nytorv. All the shops were brimming with enticing summertime wares. Clothes, swimsuits, sunhats, sandals, jewelry, and beach toys. Everything that normal people, with normal lives, could buy without realizing how fortunate they were. That didn't mean she was ungrateful. On the contrary, she was extremely happy to find herself in a foreign city that was able to offer her something she hadn't experienced in so many years. Safety. Usually knowing they were safe was enough, but occasionally, like today, she longed so desperately just to be like everyone else. She didn't want to have luxuries or to buy lots of useless items that cluttered up the closets, but she would have liked to be able to afford little everyday things, to go into a shop and buy herself a swimsuit because she was going to take the children swimming for the weekend. Or to go to a toyshop and buy a Spiderman duvet cover for Kevin, because she thought he might sleep better if he shared his bed with his hero. Instead, she had to search her pockets for enough Danish kroner to catch the bus into town. There was nothing normal about that, but at least she was safe. Even though so far only her brain was certain of that—not her heart.

She went into the Illum department store and headed straight for the pastry shop with its wonderful aroma of baking and chocolate. She practically started drooling when she caught sight of the Wienerbrød with chocolate in the center. She and her children weren't starving, although the neighbors must have noticed what their situation was like, because sometimes they brought over dinner, with the excuse that they'd made too much food for their own families. She really couldn't complain, but she would have loved to walk up to the counter, point at the Wienerbrød, and say to the assistant: "Three of the ones with chocolate, please." Or even better: "Six pieces of Wienerbrød with chocolate, please." Then they could really gorge themselves, each of them greedily devouring two pastries and afterward, feeling a bit stuffed, they would lick the chocolate off their fingers. That would be a real treat, especially for Vilda. She'd always been such a chocoholic. She even liked the chocolates filled with cherry liqueur that came in boxes of Aladdin candies, the ones that everybody else refused to eat. Vilda would devour them with a delighted smile. He had always brought chocolates for Vilda and Kevin.

She pushed away these thoughts. She shouldn't be thinking about him. If she did, the anxiety would get so bad that she wouldn't be able to breathe. She hurried to the exit and continued on toward Nyhavn. As soon as she saw the water she could feel herself breathing easier. She fixed her gaze on the horizon as she passed the beautiful old harbor area, where the outdoor cafés were now filling with customers, and the proud owners of the boats lining the docks were busily sweeping and polishing their vessels. Across the water was Sweden and the city of Malmö. Boats left nearly every hour, but the trip could also be made by car or train across the bridge. Sweden was so close, and yet so far away. It was possible that they'd never go back. Her throat closed up at the thought. She'd been surprised by how much she missed her homeland. She hadn't really gone very far, and Denmark was deceptively similar to Sweden. But there were so many things that were different, and her friends and family weren't here. And there was no way of knowing whether she'd ever see them again.

She turned away from the water, hunched her shoulders, and slowly walked back to town. She was lost in her own thoughts when she felt a hand on her shoulder. Panic instantly overwhelmed her. Had they found her? Had he found her? With a scream she turned around, ready to hit, scratch, and bite—whatever it took. A man with an alarmed expression was looking at her.

"I didn't mean to startle you." The stout, elderly man was so taken aback by her reaction he looked as if he was going to have a heart attack. "You dropped your scarf, and you didn't hear me when I called."

"Sorry, I'm really sorry," she stammered. Then she began to sob, which alarmed the man even more.

Without another word, she fled, running for the nearest bus, which she knew would take her home. She had to get back to her kids. She had to feel their arms around her neck and their warm bodies pressed against her own. That was the one thing that made her feel safe.

❧

"Torbjörn's report is in," said Annika as soon as Patrik and Martin came in the door.

Patrik was so full that he could hardly breathe. He'd eaten way too much pasta for lunch at the Lilla Berith restaurant.

"Where is it?" he asked as he strode through the reception area and yanked open the door to the corridor.

"On your desk," Annika told him.

He hurried toward his office, with Martin in tow.

"Have a seat," Patrik said, pointing to the chair in front of his desk. He dropped onto his own chair and began reading the documents that Annika had left for him.

Martin looked as if he wanted to rip the pages from his colleague's hands.

"What does it say?" he asked after a couple of minutes, but Patrik merely waved his hand dismissively and continued reading. After what felt like an unbearably long time, he put down the report, looking disappointed.

"Nothing?" queried Martin.

"Well, nothing new, at any rate." Patrik sighed, leaned back, and clasped his hands behind his head.

For a moment neither of them spoke.

"No clues whatsoever?" Even as Martin asked the question, he knew what the answer would be.

"You can read the report yourself, but it doesn't seem like it. Strangely enough, the only fingerprints inside the apartment belonged to Mats Sverin. There were other prints on the front door handle and the bell outside. Presumably some of them belong to Signe and Gunnar. There was also a different set of prints on the door handle inside, so they might belong to the killer. If so, we can use them to link an eventual suspect to the crime scene, but since the fingerprints aren't on our database, they're of no use at the moment."

"Okay. So that's that. We'll just have to hope that Pedersen has something more for us in the postmortem report on Wednesday," said Martin.

"I don't really know what that could be. It appears to have been a simple matter of someone shooting Sverin in the back of the head and then leaving. The perpetrator doesn't even seem to have entered the apartment. Or if he did, he was careful to erase all traces."

"Did it say that in the report? Had the door handles been wiped clean?" Martin sounded a tad more hopeful.

"Good idea, but I don't think . . ." Patrik didn't finish his sentence as he leafed through the report again. After scanning the pages, he shook his head. "Apparently not. Sverin's fingerprints were on all the surfaces that you might expect: door handles, cupboard handles, the kitchen counter, and so on. Nothing seems to have been deliberately wiped clean."

"Which indicates that the murderer never went beyond the front hall."

"That's right. And unfortunately that means that we still can't establish whether Mats knew his killer. Whoever rang the bell could have been someone familiar to him, or a complete stranger."

"But he felt secure enough to turn his back on whoever it was that he'd let into the apartment."

"I'm not so sure about that. He may have been trying to flee from the person who was at the door."

"True," said Martin. He paused, then said, "So what do we do now?"

"That's the question, isn't it?" Patrik stretched his back and ran a hand through his hair. "The search of the apartment didn't produce any results. The interviews we've done haven't given us any leads. And the technical report hasn't either. What's more it's unlikely that Pedersen will come up with anything significant. So what do we do now?"

It was unlike Patrik to be so despondent, but the lack of leads in this case was stalling the investigation. There must be something in Mats Sverin's secret life that would account for his murder. Because not just anybody got himself shot in the head. Not just anybody got murdered in his own home. There had to be a motive, and Patrik refused to give up until he found out what it was.

"I'd like you to go with me to Göteborg on Monday. We need to pay another visit to the Refuge," he said.

Martin's face lit up.

"Sure. I'd be delighted," he said as he got up. Patrik was almost ashamed to see how happy his colleague looked at being asked to come along. He realized that he'd been ignoring Martin a bit.

"Take the report with you," he said before Martin headed for the door. "It's best if you read it yourself, in case I missed some important detail."

"Okay." And he eagerly reached for the report.

After Martin had left the room, Patrik smiled to himself. At least he'd made one person happy today.

~∞~

The hours passed so slowly. He and Signe moved about their home in silence. They had nothing to say to each other, hardly dared open their mouths for fear of releasing the scream hiding inside.

Gunnar had tried to get her to eat. It had always been Signe who fussed over him and Mats, saying that they weren't eating enough. Now he was the one who fixed sandwiches and cut them up into small pieces, trying to persuade her to taste them. She did her best, but he could see how the bites of food seemed to swell in her mouth, and she could hardly choke them down. Finally he couldn't take it any longer; he couldn't stand seeing his own expression mirrored on her face on the other side of the kitchen table.

"I'm going out to see to the boat. I won't be gone long," he told her. She didn't even seem to hear him.

Moving slowly, he put on his jacket. It was late afternoon, and the sun was low in the sky. He wondered whether he'd ever again find joy in a sunset. Whether he'd ever feel anything again.

The route he took through Fjällbacka was a familiar one, but at the same time it felt different. Nothing was the same. Even the mere act of walking seemed alien. Something that had previously felt so natural now seemed forced and contrived, as if he had to tell his brain to set one foot in front of the other. He regretted not taking the car. It was a relatively long walk from Mörhult, and he noticed that the people he encountered along the way were staring at him. Some even crossed to the opposite pavement if they thought he wasn't looking, so they wouldn't have to speak to him. They probably had no idea what to say. And Gunnar didn't know how to respond if they did speak, so maybe it was best that they treated him like a leper.

Their boat was docked way out by Badholmen. They'd had the berth for many years, and he automatically turned right to cross the small stone bridge. He was completely lost in his own world and didn't notice anything until he had almost reached the berth. The boat was gone. Gunnar glanced around in confusion. It should have been here. It was always here. A small wooden motorboat with a blue canopy. He walked along the dock, all the way out to the end of the pontoon wharf. Maybe it had been moored in the wrong place for some reason that he couldn't fathom. Or maybe it had gotten loose and drifted away among the other boats. Yet the sea had been calm, and Matte had always been so careful about tying up the boat properly. Gunnar walked back to the empty berth. Then he took out his cell.

⌒◯⌒

Patrik had just stepped in the door when Annika called him at home. He clamped the phone between his right ear and shoulder so he could talk as he picked up Maja, who was eagerly jumping around him with her arms outstretched.

"Sorry, what did you say? The boat is missing?" He frowned. "Yes, I'm at home, but I can drive down there and have a look. No, it's no problem. I'll handle it."

He set Maja down so he could press the button to end the call. Then he took her hand and led the way to the kitchen, where Erica was preparing two bottles, cheered on by the babies perched on the table in their bassinets. Patrik leaned down and gave each of his sons a kiss and then went over to kiss his wife too.

"Hi. Who was on the phone?" asked Erica, putting the bottles in the microwave.

"Annika. I have to go out again, but only for a little while. It seems that Gunnar and Signe's boat has been stolen."

"That's awful." Erica turned around to look at Patrik. "Who would be wicked enough to do a thing like that?"

"I have no idea. According to Gunnar, Mats was apparently the last person to use it, assuming he went out to visit Nathalie, that is. It seems odd that their boat would be the only one missing."

"Go on," she said, and then kissed him on the lips.

"I'll be back in no time," he told her, heading for the front door. Too late he realized that Maja would probably throw a minor fit if he rushed off immediately after coming home. Feeling guilty, he told himself that Erica would undoubtedly deal with the situation. And he'd be back soon.

Gunnar was waiting for him on Badholmen, standing on the other side of the stone bridge.

"I can't understand what could have happened to our boat," he said, lifting his cap to scratch his head.

"It couldn't have just drifted away, could it?" asked Patrik. He followed Gunnar to the empty berth.

"I can't say for sure what happened. All I know is that the boat isn't here," said Gunnar, shaking his head. "Matte was always so careful about tying it up. That was something I taught him when he was only a child. And we haven't had any stormy weather to speak of lately, so I can't believe that the boat tore away from its moorings." He shook his head again, even more emphatically. "Somebody must have stolen it. But I can't understand what they'd want with an old dinghy like that."

"Hmm, well, I suppose it'd be worth a few kroner." Patrik squatted down. He ran his eyes over the berth, and then stood up again. "I'll write up a report when I get back to the station.

But we can start by having a word with the Coast Guard service. They'll keep an eye out for it when they're out in their boats making their rounds."

Without another word Gunnar fell in behind Patrik as he set off across the bridge. In silence they walked the short distance around the boathouses to the Coast Guard offices. No one seemed to be there, and when Patrik tried the door, he found it locked. But then he noticed movement inside the *MinLouis,* the smallest of the Coast Guard vessels, and he went over and knocked on the window. A man appeared in the stern, and Patrik recognized Peter, who had helped them on that fateful day at sea when one of the female participants in the reality show *Sodding Tanum* was murdered.

"Hello there. How can I help you?" Peter smiled up at them, drying his hands on a towel.

"We're looking for a missing boat," said Patrik, pointing toward the empty berth. "It's Gunnar's boat. It's not where it's supposed to be, and we don't know what happened to it. We were wondering if you could keep an eye out for it?"

"Sure. I heard about what happened," said Peter quietly, giving Gunnar a nod. "Please accept my condolences. And of course we'd be happy to help. Do you think it might have gotten loose on its own? If so, it wouldn't have gone very far. And it would probably drift toward land and not out to sea."

"No, we think it was stolen," said Patrik.

"People can be vile sometimes." Peter shook his head. "It's a wooden motorboat, right, Gunnar? With a blue or green canopy?"

"Yes. It's blue. And it says *Sophia* on the stern." He turned to Patrik. "I was in love with Sophia Loren when I was young. And when I met Signe, I thought she looked exactly like her. So I named the boat *Sophia.*"

"Okay. At least now I know what to look for. I'll be making my rounds in a while, and I promise to take a look for *Sophia.*"

"Thanks," said Patrik. He looked at Gunnar and asked, "Are you sure that Mats was the last one to use the boat?"

"Well, I can't really be sure about that." Gunnar hesitated. "But he said that he wanted to go out and visit Nathalie, so I assumed that . . ."

"If he didn't borrow the boat, then when was the last time you saw it?"

Peter had gone back inside the cabin to continue working on his equipment, so Gunnar and Patrik were alone on the wharf.

"In that case, it would probably have been last Wednesday. But we should just ask Nathalie. Haven't you talked to her yet?"

"We were planning to go out there tomorrow. I'll ask her then."

"That'll be good," said Gunnar, tonelessly. Then he shuddered. "Good Lord, that means that she doesn't even know yet. We didn't think about phoning her. We didn't . . ."

Patrik placed a hand on his shoulder to calm him.

"You and Signe have had other things on your mind. I'll tell her when we go out to the island. Don't worry."

Gunnar nodded.

"Can I give you a ride home?" asked Patrik.

"Yes, I'd be very grateful," said Gunnar, sighing with relief. Then he followed Patrik to his car. Neither of them spoke all the way out to Mörhult.

# Fjällbacka 1871

The ice had started to break up. The April sun was slowly melting the snow, and on the island tiny tufts of green were venturing out of the crevices. She had only a vague memory of what had happened. She recalled the spinning ceiling, the pain, and glimpses of their faces. But sometimes the terror came back to her so vividly that it made her gasp for breath.

None of them had spoken of the incident. It wasn't necessary. She'd heard Julian tell Karl that maybe now his father would get his wish. It wasn't hard to understand that the whole episode had to do with the letter that had arrived, but that did nothing to diminish the shame and humiliation she felt. It had taken threats from her father-in-law to get her husband to fulfil his marital duties. No doubt the old man had begun to wonder why she and Karl had no children.

In the morning she had awakened feeling stiff and frozen. She was lying on the floor with her heavy black woollen dress and her white petticoats hitched up around her waist. Quickly she pulled them down, but the house was empty. No one else was there. With a pounding headache and dry mouth, she had hauled herself to her feet. She felt an ache between her legs, and when she later went out to the privy, she saw the blood that had dried on the inside of her thighs.

Many hours later Karl and Julian came back from the lighthouse, both of them acting as if nothing had happened. Emelie had spent the whole day frenetically scouring the house with soap and scrubbing-brush. Nothing had interrupted her work. Even the dead were keeping strangely quiet. Then she had started preparing the evening meal so that it would be ready by five o'clock, but she seemed hardly aware of her movements as she peeled the potatoes and fried the fish. Only a slight trembling in her hands when she heard the footsteps of the two men as they approached the front door betrayed the emotions churning inside her. Karl and Julian came in, hung their heavy jackets in the front hall, and sat down at the table without paying her any attention. And that was how the winter days had passed. With hazy memories of what had happened, and the cold spreading a frozen white carpet over the water.

But now the ice was beginning to crack, and occasionally Emelie would go outside and sit down on the bench next to the house, lifting her face to the sun. Sometimes she found herself smiling, because now she was certain. At first she wasn't sure, since she didn't know her own body very well, but finally there was no longer any doubt. She was with child. The night that she remembered as a bad dream had led to something good. She was going to have a baby. Someone she could take care of, someone she could share her life with here on the island.

She closed her eyes and placed her hand on her stomach as the sun continued to warm her cheeks. Someone came and sat down next to her, but when she opened her eyes, no one was sitting beside her. Emelie closed her eyes again and smiled. It felt so good not to be alone.

# 11

The morning sun was rising above the horizon, but Nathalie didn't notice as she stood on the dock and stared out across the islands toward Fjällbacka.

She didn't want any visitors. She didn't want them to force their way into the world that she and Sam had created here on the island. It belonged to them and no one else. But she couldn't say no when the police called. Besides, she had a problem and needed help. There was practically no food left, and she couldn't bring herself to phone Mats's parents. Since she was going to have visitors, she decided to ask them to bring her some groceries, just the essentials. It seemed a bit cheeky to ask someone she'd never met to do her grocery shopping, but she really had no choice. Sam wasn't yet well enough to make the trip to Fjällbacka, and if they didn't fill up the refrigerator and pantry, they'd soon starve to death. She wasn't planning to allow the officers to go any further than the dock. The island belonged to her; the island belonged to them.

Matte was the only person she'd been willing to invite here. She continued staring out at the water as her eyes filled with tears. She could still feel his arms wrapped around her, and his kisses on her skin. His smell, which had seemed so familiar and yet had changed—belonging to a grown man now, not a boy. She hadn't known what the future might bring, what their reunion might mean in terms of how they would live their lives. But for a brief time their encounter had carried with it a possibility. It had opened a window and let a little light into the darkness in which she had lived for so long.

Nathalie wiped away the tears with the back of her hand. She couldn't allow herself to surrender to the yearning and pain. She was already holding on to life with her bare knuckles, and she could not loosen her grip. Matte had gone, but Sam was still here. And she had to protect him. Nothing else—not even Matte—was more important. Protecting her son was her most important and sole task in life. Now that other people were on their way over here, she needed to focus on that.

❧

Something had changed. They never let her be in peace. Anna could still feel someone's body pressed close to hers. Someone was breathing next to her, radiating warmth and energy. She didn't want to be touched. All she wanted was to disappear into the desolate but safe shadowland where she had now dwelled for so long. Everything outside was too painful; her skin and her soul had grown too sensitive after all the blows she had suffered. She simply couldn't stand any more.

And they didn't need her. She brought nothing but misfortune down upon everyone around her. Emma and Adrian had been subjected to things that no child should ever have to go through, and she found it unbearable to see the sorrow in Dan's eyes over the loss of their son.

At first they seemed to understand. They had left her alone, allowed her to simply lie in bed. Sometimes they tried to talk to her, but they gave up so easily that she realized they felt the same way she did. That their grief had been caused by her, and that it would be best for everybody if she just stayed where she was.

With Erica's last visit, however, something had changed. Anna had felt her sister's body close to her own, felt Erica's warmth dragging her out of the shadows, pulling her closer to life, trying to make her come back. Erica hadn't said much. Her body spoke for her, making the warmth spread through joints that felt cold and frozen even though she was lying under a blanket. Anna had tried to resist it, concentrating on a dark point deep inside, a point that couldn't be touched by a warm body.

When the warmth from Erica's body disappeared, it was replaced by another. Dan's body was the easiest to resist. His energy was filled with so much sorrow that it practically reinforced her own, and she didn't have to make any real effort to stay in the shadows. The children's energy was the most difficult to hold at bay. Emma's soft little body pressed against her back, her arms reaching around her waist. Anna was forced to muster all her strength to fight against it. And then Adrian, smaller and less confident than Emma, but his energy was strongest of all. She didn't have to open her eyes to know who had come in to lie down next to her. Despite lying on her side, unmoving, with her eyes fixed on the sky outside of the window, she knew whose warmth was pressing against her.

She wanted them to leave her alone and allow her to lie in bed undisturbed. The thought that she might not have enough strength to fight back made terror rise up inside of her.

Now Emma was here. Her body stirred slightly. She must have fallen asleep, because from the shadowland Anna could tell that her daughter's breathing had changed, growing deeper. Then Emma changed position, pressed closer, like an animal seeking comfort. And Anna could feel herself being drawn from the shadows again, toward the energy that crept into every nook of her body. She needed to keep focusing on that point, the dark point inside of her.

The door to the room opened. Anna felt the bed sway as someone climbed onto it and curled up at her feet. Small arms wrapped tightly around her legs, as if they would never let go. Adrian's warmth seeped into her, and it got harder and harder to stay in the shadows. She could resist the children one at a time, but not when they were both here, not when their energies combined to get even stronger. Slowly she felt herself losing her grip as she was pulled back toward what was in the room and in life.

With a deep sigh Anna turned over. She looked at her daughter's slumbering face, those familiar features that she hadn't been able to look at for so long. And for the first time she fell into a sound sleep, with one hand cupped over her daughter's cheek, and with the tip of her nose pressed against Emma's. Adrian had also fallen asleep, curled up at Anna's feet like a puppy. His hold on her legs slowly loosened as he relaxed. And then they all slept.

⌒∞⌒

Erica laughed until the tears ran down her face as they stepped aboard the boat.

"Are you telling me that you took a bath in seaweed?" She wiped her eyes with the back of her hand and then laughed again, which prompted a fit of hiccupping when she saw the offended look on Patrik's face.

"So? Shouldn't men be allowed to pamper themselves once in a while? From what you've told me, you've tried out plenty of strange things. I distinctly remember you saying not so long ago that you were smeared with mud and then rolled up in plastic wrap at some spa you went to." He backed the boat away from the dock at Badholmen.

"Yes, but . . ." Erica succumbed to another fit of giggles.

"I think you're displaying some rather outmoded prejudices here," said Patrik, glaring at her. "A seaweed bath is actually super healthy for men. It draws the toxins out of the body, and since men obviously have a harder time getting rid of that sort of stuff, we have an even greater need for the treatment."

By now Erica was clutching her stomach, so helpless with laughter that she couldn't speak. Patrik decided to ignore his wife and concentrate on steering the boat out of the harbor. Of course he was laying it on a bit thick to wind Erica up, but the truth was that he and his colleagues had really enjoyed the spa treatments they'd received at Badis.

At first he'd been extremely skeptical about getting into a bathtub filled with seaweed. Then he realized that it actually didn't smell as bad as he'd imagined, and the water was nice and warm. When he sat in the tub and leaned forward while his back was massaged with bunches of seaweed that were rubbed against his skin, he was converted. And he couldn't deny that his skin felt like new when he got out of the tub. Softer, smoother, and with a new glow. But when he tried to tell Erica about it, she'd started laughing hysterically. Even his mother, who had come over to babysit for Maja and the twins, had snickered at his enthusiastic report.

The wind was picking up. He closed his eyes, feeling the gusts against his face. There weren't many other boats out on the sea, but in only a few weeks there would be dozens of them heading in and out of the harbor.

Erica had finally stopped laughing, and her expression had turned serious. She put her arms around Patrik as he sat at the helm and leaned her head against his shoulder.

"How did she sound when you phoned?"

"Not exactly overjoyed," said Patrik. "She didn't seem too keen on having visitors. But when I said that she was welcome to visit us on the mainland instead, if she preferred, she decided she'd rather have us come to the island."

"Did you tell her that I'd be coming with you?" A swell made the wooden boat rise, and Erica wrapped her arms more firmly around Patrik's waist.

"Yes. I told her that we were married and that you'd like to come along so you could see her. She didn't really react to that, although it sounded as if it would be okay."

"What are you hoping to learn by talking to Nathalie?" Erica let go of Patrik and sat down nearby on the thwart.

"To be honest, I really have no idea. We still don't know whether Mats went out to visit her on Friday. I suppose that's what I want to find out. And we also need to tell her what happened to him."

He corrected the course to make way for a motorboat that was heading toward them at high speed.

"Idiots," he snarled, glaring at the boat as it passed a bit too close.

"Couldn't you have asked her about it on the phone?" Erica was also staring at the boat as it sped away. She didn't recognize the occupants. A bunch of young guys in their late teens. Probably an early group of vacationers—the kind that would soon be filling Fjällbacka.

"Yes, I could have done that. But I prefer to ask my questions in person. I get more productive results that way. What I really want is to form a clearer picture of who Mats was. At the moment he seems like one of those life-size cardboard cut-outs, flat and one-dimensional. No one seems to know anything about him, not even his parents. His apartment looks like a hotel room. There are hardly any personal items. And then there's the matter of the assault . . . I need to find out more."

"But from what I understand, Mats and Nathalie haven't been in contact for years."

"That's what his parents say, but we don't really know that. At any rate, she seems to have been an important person in his life, and if he did go out to visit her, he might have told her something that we'd find useful. She may have been one of the last people to see him alive."

"Okay, I get it," said Erica, but she sounded doubtful. She'd come along out of sheer curiosity. She was curious as to how the years had changed Nathalie and what sort of person she'd become.

"So that must be Gråskär," said Patrik, squinting.

Erica craned her neck to peer at the island they were approaching.

"Yes, that's it, all right. The lighthouse is wonderful." She shaded her eyes with her hand to see better.

"I don't think I care for the looks of that island," said Patrik, though he had no idea what made him say that. Then he had to turn his attention to pulling the boat up next to the small pier.

A tall, slender woman was standing there, waiting for them. She reached for the line that Erica tossed up onto the dock.

"Hi," said Nathalie, giving them a helping hand as they climbed out of the boat.

She's beautiful but much too thin, thought Patrik as he took her hand. Her bones were clearly visible under her skin, and although she seemed to be a naturally slim person, she must have lost a good deal of weight recently, because her jeans were too big, needing to be held up with a belt cinched tight around her waist.

"My son isn't feeling well. He's asleep in bed up at the house, so I was thinking that we could have some coffee and talk out here on the dock." Nathalie pointed to a blanket that she had spread out on the wooden planks.

"Fine, that's no problem," said Patrik, sitting down. "I hope it's nothing serious."

"No, he has a slight cold, that's all. Do you have kids?" She sat down across from Patrik and Erica and started pouring coffee from a thermos. The pier was relatively sheltered from the wind, the sun was shining, and the air was warm. It was a lovely spot to have coffee.

"Oh yes, we certainly do," replied Erica with a laugh. "We have Maja, who will soon be two, and Noel and Anton, who are twins and almost four months old now."

"You must have your hands full." Nathalie smiled, but the smile didn't reach her eyes. She handed Erica a platter of rusks. "I'm afraid this is all I have to offer you."

"Oh, right," said Patrik, getting up. "I brought the groceries you asked for."

"Thanks. I hope it wasn't too much trouble. With Sam being sick, I'd prefer not to drag him into town to shop. Signe and Gunnar helped me out before, but I don't want to make a habit of asking them."

Patrik had hopped down into the boat and now set two full bags of groceries from the Konsum supermarket on the pier.

"What do I owe you?" Nathalie reached for her purse, which was lying next to her.

"I'm afraid it came to a thousand kronor," said Patrik apologetically.

Nathalie took two five-hundred-krona bills out of her wallet and handed them to him.

"Thank you," she said again.

Patrik merely nodded and sat back down on the blanket.

"It must feel rather isolated, staying out here." He gazed at the small island. The lighthouse towered above them, casting a long shadow over the rocks.

"No, it's great," said Nathalie, taking a sip of her coffee. "I haven't been here in years, and Sam has never seen the island before. I thought it was about time he did."

"Why now?" asked Erica, hoping she didn't sound too nosy.

Nathalie didn't look at her. Instead, she fixed her eyes on a distant point on the horizon. The small gusts of wind that reached them caught hold of her long hair, which she impatiently brushed out of her face.

"There are a few things that I need to think about, so it just seemed natural for us to come out here. There's really nothing here. Nothing but thoughts and time."

"And ghosts, from what I've heard," said Erica, reaching for a rusk.

Nathalie didn't laugh. "You're thinking about the fact that it's called Ghost Isle, right?"

"Yes. But you must have found out by now whether there's any truth to the rumors. I remember that we spent the night here once when I was in secondary school, and we were all really scared. Do you think it's an apt nickname for the place?"

"Maybe."

Nathalie clearly didn't want to discuss the subject further, so Patrik took a deep breath before broaching the topic that couldn't be put off any longer. As he calmly explained what had happened, Nathalie began to shake. She stared at him in disbelief. She didn't say a word, but she was shaking uncontrollably, as if she might break into a thousand pieces right before their eyes.

"We still don't know exactly when he was shot, so we're trying to find out as much as possible about his last days. Gunnar and Signe said that he was planning to come out here to see you last Friday."

"Yes, he was here." Nathalie turned around to look toward the house. Patrik had the feeling that she did that mostly so he wouldn't see her expression.

When she turned back to face them, she still looked dazed, but she had stopped shaking.

Erica impulsively leaned forward to put her hand on Nathalie's. There was something so fragile and vulnerable about her, and it roused Erica's protective instincts.

"You were always so nice," said Nathalie, and then pulled her hand away without looking at Erica.

"So last Friday . . ." said Patrik cautiously.

Nathalie shuddered, and a veil seemed to fall over her eyes.

"He came over in the evening. I didn't know that he was coming. I hadn't seen him in years."

"When was the last time you saw each other?" asked Erica, unable to resist glancing toward the house. She was afraid that Nathalie's son might wake up and slip out. Since having kids of her own, she felt as if she'd become the mother of all the children in the world.

"We said goodbye when I moved to Stockholm. I was nineteen, I think. A whole lifetime ago." She laughed. A brief, bitter laugh.

"Have you kept in touch over the years?"

"No. Well, maybe a few postcards in the beginning. But we both knew that it wasn't a good idea. Why prolong the pain by pretending things were otherwise?" Nathalie brushed a few strands of blond hair out of her face again.

"Whose decision was it to break up?" asked Erica. She just couldn't restrain her curiosity. She'd seen them together so many times, seen the golden light that seemed to radiate from the two of them. The golden couple.

"We never really used those words. But it was my decision to move away. I couldn't stay here. I needed to get out

213

into the world. See things, do things, meet new people." She laughed that same bitter laugh that neither Erica nor Patrik understood.

"So last Friday, when Mats came out here, how did you react?" asked Patrik, wanting to continue the questioning even though he wasn't sure it would lead to anything. Nathalie seemed so fragile. He felt as if he might break her in two if he said the wrong thing. And in the final analysis, this might have nothing at all to do with the case.

"I was surprised. But Signe had told me that he'd moved back home. So I thought he might turn up."

"Were you happily surprised?" asked Erica, reaching for the thermos to refill her cup.

"Not at first. Well, I don't know. I don't believe in looking back. Matte belonged to the past. At the same time . . ." She seemed to get lost in her own thoughts. "At the same time, maybe I never really left him. I don't know. At any rate, I let him come up to the house."

"Approximately what time was it when he arrived?" asked Patrik.

"Hmm . . . I think it was around six. I'm not really sure. Time isn't very important out here."

"How long did he stay?" Patrik shifted position, grimacing a bit. His body didn't like sitting on such a hard surface for very long. He found himself yearning for another nice, warm seaweed bath.

"He left sometime later that night." The pain was as clearly etched on her face as if she'd screamed it out loud.

Patrik suddenly felt uncomfortable. What right did he have to ask these questions? What right did he have to go snooping around in something that ought to be kept private, something that had taken place between two people who had once upon a time loved each other? But he forced himself to go on. In his mind he pictured the body lying on its stomach in the hall, with a big, gaping hole in the head, a pool of blood on the floor, and blood spattered over the wall. As long as the killer was on the loose, it was the job of the police to snoop. Murder and the right to privacy were two things that didn't go together.

"So you've no idea what time he left?" he asked gently.

Nathalie bit her lip. Her eyes were shiny with tears.

"No, he left while I was asleep. I thought that . . ." She swallowed several times, looking as if she were trying to keep her composure, as if she didn't want to lose control in front of them.

"Did you try calling him? Or did you phone Signe and Gunnar to ask them?" said Patrik.

The sun had slowly moved while they were talking, and the long shadows from the lighthouse were getting closer.

"No." She started trembling again.

"Did Mats say anything when he was here that might give us a lead? Something that might tell us who would have wanted him dead?"

Nathalie shook her head. "No, I can't believe that anyone would ever want to harm Matte. He was . . . Well, you know, Erica. He was exactly the same now as he used to be back then. Kind, thoughtful, loving. Exactly the same." She looked down, running her hand over the blanket.

"Yes, we understand that Mats was well-liked, a very nice person," said Patrik. "At the same time, there are parts of his life that we need to find out more about. For instance, he was the victim of an assault just before he moved back to Fjällbacka. Did he tell you anything about that?"

"Not much. I saw the scars and asked him about them. He just said that he was in the wrong place at the wrong time, and that it was a bunch of kids who attacked him."

"Did he mention his job in Göteborg?" Patrik had hoped to find out more about the assault that might explain the uneasy feeling he had inside. No such luck. Nothing but dead ends.

"He said that he'd loved the job, but found it exhausting. Meeting all those battered women who were so damaged . . ." Her voice broke, and again she turned away to look toward the house.

"Did he tell you anything else that we should know about? Was there any particular person that he felt threatened by?"

"No. He just talked about what the job had meant to him. In the end, though, it left him worn out. He didn't have the strength to keep doing that type of work. And after being in the hospital, he decided to come back here."

"Permanently, or only for a while?"

"I don't think he knew. He said that he was taking one day at a time. Trying to heal both his body and soul."

Patrik nodded and then hesitated before asking the next question.

"Did he tell you whether there was a woman in his life? Or more than one?"

"No, and I didn't ask. He didn't ask me about my husband either. Who we loved now or had loved in the past was of no importance that evening."

"I understand," said Patrik. "By the way, the boat is missing," he added, as if in passing.

Nathalie looked confused. "What boat?"

"Signe and Gunnar's boat. The one Mats used to come over here."

"It's gone? Stolen? Or what do you mean?"

"We don't know. It wasn't tied up at the dock when Gunnar went to look for it."

"Matte must have taken it to get home," said Nathalie. "How else could he have gotten to the mainland?"

"So he did come out here in the motorboat. Nobody gave him a ride, or anything like that?"

"Who would do that?" asked Nathalie.

"I don't know. All we can say for sure is that the boat is missing, and we have no idea where it might have gone."

"Well, he used it to come out here, and he must have gone home in it too." She ran her hand over the blanket again.

Patrik glanced at Erica, who was unusually quiet as she sat there, listening. "I think it's time for us to go," he said, getting up. "Thanks for agreeing to meet with us, Nathalie. And please accept our condolences."

Erica stood up too. "It was nice to see you again, Nathalie."

"It was nice to see you too." Nathalie gave Erica an awkward hug.

"Take care of Sam, and give us a call if you need anything, or if we can help in any other way. If his cold gets worse, we can arrange for the district doctor to come out here and have a look at him."

"I'll let you know." Nathalie followed them over to the boat.

Patrik started the engine and was about to pull the boat away from the dock when he stopped abruptly.

"Do you remember whether Mats had his briefcase with him?"

Nathalie frowned as she considered the question. Then her face lit up. "A brown briefcase? Made of leather?"

"Exactly," said Patrik. "That's gone missing too."

"Wait here." Nathalie turned on her heel and sprinted toward the house. A few minutes later she came out, holding something. When she got close to the dock, Patrik saw what it was. The briefcase. His heart skipped a beat.

"He forgot it. I haven't touched it. I hope I haven't caused any trouble." She knelt down on the pier so she could hand the briefcase to Patrik.

"We're just glad to find it. Thanks!" he said. He was already thinking about what the briefcase might contain.

After they had backed away from the dock and set off toward Fjällbacka, Patrik and Erica both turned to wave to Nathalie. She waved back. The shadow from the lighthouse was now stretching all the way to the pier. It looked as if it might swallow her whole.

# 12

**C**an we go out and search for a while?" Gunnar had a hard time keeping his voice steady as he stood on the wharf.

Peter looked up from what he was doing and seemed on the verge of saying no. Then he gave in.

"Okay, we can take a short trip around. But it's Sunday, and I need to get home soon."

Gunnar stood in silence, gazing straight ahead, his eyes like two dark holes. With a sigh, Peter went into the wheelhouse to start the engine. He helped Gunnar on board, gave him a life jacket, and with an expert hand steered the boat out of the harbor. After they'd gone some distance, he decreased the speed.

"Where do you want to start searching? We looked around this area when we were out here before, but we didn't see anything."

"I don't know." Gunnar peered out through the windshield. He couldn't just sit at home and wait. He couldn't bear to see

Signe sitting motionless on her chair in the kitchen. She had stopped cooking, baking, and sweeping, stopped doing all the things that made her the person she was. And what about him? Who was he, now that Matte was gone? He had no idea. The only thing he knew for sure was that he needed some sort of goal in a life that had lost all meaning for him.

He had to find the boat. That was something he could do, something that would take him away from home, away from the silence and everything that reminded him of his son, away from the house where Matte had grown up. The footprint in the cement in the driveway, which Gunnar had put in when Matte was five. The toothmark on the chest of drawers in the front hall, which happened when Matte came running too fast, slipped on the rug, and struck his front teeth so hard on the drawer that they left two visible dents in the wood. All those small things that showed that Matte had been there, that Matte had been theirs.

"Head toward Dannholmen," said Gunnar. He really had no idea where to look. There was nothing to indicate that the boat might be found in that direction. But it was as good a place as any to start their search.

"So how are things at home?" asked Peter cautiously as he focused his attention on steering. Occasionally he would cast a look around to see if the motorboat might have drifted ashore somewhere.

"Fine, thanks," said Gunnar.

That was a lie, because things weren't fine at all. But what was he supposed to say? How could he describe the emptiness that filled a home after losing a child? Sometimes he was amazed to find himself still breathing. How could he go on living and breathing when Matte was gone?

"Fine," he repeated.

Peter merely nodded. That's the way it was. People hadn't a clue what to say. They said the obligatory phrases, the words that were expected of them in such a situation, and they tried to be sympathetic. At the same time, they thanked their lucky stars that they were not the ones who had suffered such a loss. Grateful that their own children, their loved ones, were alive. That was just the way it was. They were only human.

"You don't think it could have come untied, do you?" Gunnar wasn't sure whether he was talking to Peter or to himself.

"I don't think so. If it had, it would have drifted in among the other boats. No, I think somebody must have taken it. Those old wooden boats have been going up in value, so maybe it was a work-for-hire. If that's the case, we're not going to find it out here. They usually take them someplace where they can be pulled out of the water and then carted off on a boat trailer."

Peter turned right and headed past Småsvinningarna. "Let's go out to Dannholmen. After that, we'll have to turn around and go back. Otherwise my family will start to worry."

"Okay," said Gunnar. "Could we go out again tomorrow?"

Peter looked at him.

"Sure. Come by around ten, and we'll go out looking. But only if there are no emergency call-outs for the Coast Guard."

"Good. I'll be there," Gunnar said as he continued to peer at the islands.

❦

Mette had invited them over for dinner, as she often did, pretending that it was her turn, even though Madeleine never reciprocated. Madeleine played along, although she felt a pang of humiliation because she was never able to return the invitation. She dreamed of casually saying to Mette: "Would you and your kids like to have dinner with us tonight? It won't be anything fancy." But she couldn't do that. She couldn't afford to invite Mette and her three children to dinner. She hardly had enough food for Kevin, Vilda, and herself.

"Are you sure it's okay?" she asked as she sat down at the table in Mette's bustling kitchen.

"Of course it is. I have to cook a big dinner for my three little pigs, so three more won't make any difference." Mette tenderly ruffled the hair of her middle son, Thomas.

"Cut it out, Mamma," he said, annoyed, but Madeleine could tell that he liked it.

"A little wine?" Without waiting for an answer, Mette poured her a glass from the red wine that came in a box.

She turned around and stirred the pots on the stove. Madeleine sipped her wine.

"Are you keeping an eye on the kiddies?" Mette called into the other room. Two voices said "yes" in reply. Her two youngest children, a ten-year-old girl and Thomas, who was thirteen, were watching Kevin and Vilda, who were drawn to them like magnets. Her oldest, a boy of seventeen, was seldom home anymore.

"It's more likely that my kids are bothering yours," said Madeleine, taking another sip of her wine.

"Not at all. They love them, and you know it." Mette wiped her hands on the tea towel, poured herself a glass of wine, and sat down across from Madeleine.

In terms of appearance, two women couldn't be less alike, thought Madeleine, briefly picturing the pair of them as if she were an impartial observer. She was short and blond, built more like a child than a woman. Mette looked like that famous stone statue depicting a voluptuous female, which Madeleine remembered from her art classes in school. Big and curvaceous, with thick red hair that seemed to have a life of its own. Green eyes that were always sparkling, even though she too had suffered setbacks in her life that ought to have stripped them of their gleam long ago. Mette seemed to have a fondness for choosing weak men who quickly became dependent on her and then mostly sat around, making demands, like baby birds with their mouths open wide. Eventually Mette would have enough, as she'd told Madeleine. But it wouldn't be long before the next baby bird would move into her bed. That was why the children each had a different father, and if it hadn't been for the fact that all three of them had inherited Mette's red hair, it would have been impossible to tell that they were siblings.

"So how's it going with you, my dear?" asked Mette, twirling her glass in her hands.

Madeleine felt herself freeze. Even though Mette had confided everything in her, openly sharing her life and her shortcomings, Madeleine had never dared do the same. She was so accustomed to living in fear, always scared to say too much. For that reason, she kept everybody at arm's length. Almost everybody.

But at this moment, on a Sunday evening in the kitchen with Mette, as the pots simmered on the stove and the wine warmed her from the inside, she could no longer hold herself back. She started telling her story. When the tears came, Mette moved her chair next to hers and put her arms around Madeleine. And in Mette's safe embrace, she told her everything. Even about him. Despite having moved to a foreign country, a foreign life, he was still so near.

# Fjällbacka 1871

**K**arl's hatred toward her seemed to get worse and worse as the baby inside of her grew. And now she realized that it truly was hatred, though she didn't understand why. What had she done? Whenever he looked at her, his eyes were filled with disgust. At the same time she thought she could see despair in his glance, like the look in the eyes of a captured animal. As if he was caught and couldn't get free, as if he was as much a prisoner as she was. But for some reason, he turned this against her, seemingly regarding her as his prison guard. Julian didn't make things any better. His dark outlook seemed to influence Karl, whose earlier indifference, which in the beginning could have been mistaken for a distracted friendliness, had now disappeared completely. She was the enemy.

Gradually, Emelie had grown used to their harsh words. Both Karl and Julian complained about everything she did. The food was either too hot or too cold. The portions were too small or too big. The house was never clean enough, and their clothes were never laundered or mended to their liking. Nothing ever met their approval. Yet their critical words she could handle; she'd developed an armor against them. It was the physical abuse that she had a harder time accepting. In the past, Karl had never hit her, but after she told him she was carrying a child, her life on the island changed. She was forced to learn to live with the pain of slaps and blows. And he also allowed Julian to raise his hand to her. She was stunned. Wasn't this the news they had both wanted to hear?

If not for the child she was expecting, she would have walked into the sea. The ice had been gone for a long time now, and the summer was waning. Without the kicks inside of her stomach urging her on and giving her strength, she would have gone straight into the water from the narrow shore and headed through the dangerous currents toward the horizon until the sea took her. But the child gave her such joy. After each stern word, each blow, she would retreat to the life that was growing inside her. The baby was her lifeline. The memory of that evening when the child was conceived was something that she'd pushed into a far corner of her mind. That was no longer of any importance. The child was moving inside her womb, and it was hers.

Having scrubbed the wooden floor with soap she laboriously hauled herself to her feet. All the rugs were hanging outside, getting an airing in the breeze. She ought to have given them a thorough wash in the spring. All winter long she had saved up ashes from the fireplace to use for scouring. But because of her pregnancy and the weariness she'd felt all spring and summer, she had settled for simply airing out the rugs. The child was due in November. Maybe she'd have the energy to wash the rugs around Christmastime, if all went well.

Emelie stretched her aching back and threw open the front door. She walked around the side of the house and then allowed herself to pause and rest for a moment. This was where she had her pride and joy: the garden that she'd so carefully cultivated in this stark and desolate setting. Dill, parsley, and chives were growing among the hollyhocks and bleeding hearts. The small garden was so heartbreakingly lovely in the midst of that gray and barren environ that she felt a pang every *time she rounded the corner and caught sight of it. This little plot was hers, she alone had created it. Everything else on the island belonged to Karl and Julian. They were always in motion. When they weren't working their shift at the lighthouse or sleeping, they were hammering, building, and sawing. They certainly weren't lazy—she had to grant them that—but there was something frenetic about all that activity, the way they resolutely battled the wind and salt water that mercilessly broke down whatever they had just repaired.*

*"The front door is open." Karl came around the corner, startling her so that she put her hand over her stomach. "How many times have I told you to close the door? Is that so hard to understand?"*

*He looked angry. She knew that he'd taken the night shift at the lighthouse, and fatigue made his eyes look darker than usual. Frightened, she cowered before his gaze.*

*"I'm sorry, I thought that . . ."*

*"You thought! You stupid woman. You can't even close the door. You do nothing but waste time instead of doing what you're supposed to do. Julian and I slave away, day and night, while you squander your time on things like this." He took a step forward, and before she could react, he yanked a budding hollyhock out by the roots.*

*"No, Karl! Don't!" She didn't stop to think. All she could see was the stalk hanging from his clenched fist, as if he were slowly throttling it. She grabbed his arm and tried to take the flower away from him.*

*"What do you think you're doing?" he snarled.*

*His face was pale, and she saw that strange mixture of hatred and despair in his eyes as he raised his hand to strike her. It was as if he were hoping that the blow would relieve his own torment, but each time he was disappointed. If only she knew the reason for his agony and why she seemed to be the cause of it.*

*This time instead of flinching she steeled herself and turned up her face to receive the slap that she knew would come. But his hand stopped in midair. She looked at him in surprise and then followed his gaze, which was directed out to sea, toward Fjällbacka.*

"*Someone is on their way over here . . .*" *she said.*

She had lived on this island for nearly a year now, and not once had they ever had a visitor. Aside from Karl and Julian, she hadn't seen a living soul since the day she climbed into the boat that would bring her out to Gråskär.

"It looks like the pastor." Karl slowly lowered the hand that was holding the hollyhock. He looked down at the flower, as if wondering how it had ended up in his grasp. Then he dropped it and nervously wiped his hands on his trouser legs.

"Why would the pastor be coming here?"

Emelie saw the fear in his eyes, and for a moment she couldn't help enjoying the sight, but then she cursed herself for feeling that way. Karl was her husband, and the Bible said that a woman should honor her spouse. No matter what he did, no matter how he treated her, she had to obey that dictate.

The boat carrying the pastor drew closer. When it was only a few hundred yards from the dock, Karl raised his hand in greeting and walked down to welcome their visitor. Emelie's heart was pounding hard. Was it a good thing or a bad thing that the pastor had turned up so unexpectedly? She placed her hand protectively over her stomach. She too felt fear stirring inside.

# 13

Patrik was annoyed that he hadn't managed to get much done the previous day. Even though it was Sunday, he'd gone to the station and written up a report about the missing boat, then checked to see whether it might have been advertised in *Blocket* or some other list of classified ads. But he didn't find anything. Later he had talked to Paula and asked her to go through the contents of Sverin's briefcase. He'd taken a quick look inside, just enough to see that the laptop was there, along with a handful of documents. For once they'd had luck on their side in this investigation. The briefcase also contained a cell phone.

Eager to make progress today, he summoned Martin and headed out to the car for the drive to Göteborg.

"Where do we start?" asked Martin. He was in the passenger seat, as usual, although he'd done his best to try to persuade Patrik to let him drive.

"At the social services office, I think. I talked to them on Friday and said we'd probably arrive around ten o'clock."

"And then the Refuge? Have you come up with any new questions for them?"

"I'm hoping that we'll find out a bit more about them from social services. Hopefully that might give us a lead."

"What about Severin's ex-girlfriend? Did he tell her anything?" Martin kept his eyes on the road ahead, instinctively grabbing hold of the handle above the door whenever Patrik made a risky maneuver to overtake a container truck.

"No. We didn't learn much from her. Except that she gave us the briefcase, of course. And that may turn out to be a productive discovery, but we won't know until Paula has examined everything. We're not going to mess with the laptop, since we have no idea how to crack the password. We'll have to send it on to the tech guys."

"How did Nathalie take the news of Severin's death?"

"She seemed very shaken. She came across as pretty fragile. Not an easy person to read."

"Isn't this where we're supposed to get off?" Martin pointed to an exit, and Patrik swore as he turned the wheel so hard that the vehicle behind almost ran straight into them.

"Bloody hell, Patrik," said Martin, his face pale.

Ten minutes later they reached the social services building and were immediately ushered into the office of the director, who introduced himself as Sven Barkman. After the usual courtesies, they all sat down at a round conference table. Barkman was a short, slight man with a narrow face. The sharpness of his chin was further emphasized by a goatee. An image of Professor Calculus from *The Adventures of Tintin* suddenly sprang into Patrik's mind; the likeness was striking. But the man's voice didn't match his appearance, which surprised both Martin and Patrik. Barkman had a deep, low voice that seemed to fill the room. It sounded as if he would be a good singer, and when Patrik looked around, this impression was confirmed. An array of photographs, certificates, and awards showed that Sven Barkman sang in a choir. Patrik didn't recognize the name of the group, but clearly it was very successful.

"I understand that you have some questions regarding the Refuge," said Sven, leaning forward. "May I ask why? We're very careful about keeping tabs on the groups that we liaise with on social welfare matters. So naturally we're a bit concerned when we receive inquiries from the police. Besides, the Refuge is somewhat unusual in its approach, as you may be aware. And to be honest, we scrutinize their work rather more than we do the activities of other groups."

"Are you referring to the fact that both men and women work on the crisis cases?"

"Yes. That's not the norm. Leila Sundgren has really put her neck on the line with this experiment of hers, but we support her."

"There's no reason for you to be alarmed. A former employee has been murdered, and we're trying to find out more about his life. Since he worked for the Refuge up until four months ago, and considering what sort of work is involved, we're taking a close look at the group. But we have no reason whatsoever to believe that there are any irregularities."

"That's good to hear. So, let's see now . . ." Sven began leafing through the papers on the table in front of him as he quietly hummed. "Yes, well . . . hmm . . . oh, that's right."

He continued to talk to himself as Patrik and Martin waited patiently.

"Okay, now I have everything clear in my mind. I just needed to refresh my memory. We've worked with the Refuge for the past five years, or five and a half, to be exact. And I assume that, since this is a homicide investigation, I should be as precise as possible." He laughed. It was a low, chuckling laugh. "The number of cases that we've referred to them has increased sharply. Naturally, we were cautious at first, because we had to make sure that our collaboration with the group was functioning properly. Over the past year, four women have been referred to them via our office. All in all, I would estimate that the Refuge takes care of some thirty women per year." He looked up, apparently waiting for a follow-up question.

"Can you talk us through the process? What sort of cases do you pass on to the Refuge? It seems rather an extreme measure to take, and I assume that you try other avenues first," said Martin.

"Quite right. We work extensively with a wide range of these cases, and organizations like the Refuge are a last resort. There are times when we find out early on that there are problems in a particular family. But there are other cases when it takes us quite a while to spot the warning signals."

"What would be a typical case?"

"It's difficult to answer that question. I'll give you an example. Say we get a call from the school about a child who seems to be in a bad way. Our next step is to follow up with various measures, including a visit to the family, to assess the situation. We would also check for any documentation that hasn't been brought to our attention earlier."

"Documentation?" asked Patrik.

"Yes. There may have been several visits to the hospital, and when these are combined with the reports from the school, a pattern starts to emerge. We simply gather as much information as we can. At first we try to work with the family in its current situation, but that's not always successful. As I said, helping the woman and any children to flee is a last resort. Unfortunately, it's not as infrequent as we might wish."

"How does it work, in practice, when you have to turn to groups like the Refuge?"

"We contact them directly rather than sending a written report," said Sven. "Leila Sundgren is our primary contact at the Refuge. We usually meet in person to provide background information and discuss the particular woman's situation."

"Does the Refuge ever turn you down?" asked Patrik, shifting position. The chair he was sitting on was extremely uncomfortable.

"That has never happened. Because there are children at the shelter, they won't accept women who are drug addicts or who have severe psychological problems. But we know that, so we don't refer those types of cases to them. We find other shelters for those women. So no, the group has never refused to take any of the women we've referred."

"What happens when the group takes over?" asked Patrik.

"First we talk to the woman and set up a contact for her. Naturally, we handle this as discreetly as possible. The point is to make sure that they're safe and that no one can find them."

"And later on? Do things ever get difficult for you at the social services office? I can imagine that some men get very angry when they discover that their wife and children have disappeared," said Martin.

"Yes, but they don't disappear for good. That would be illegal. We can't hide a child from its father, because he has a legal right to contest such actions. But we do receive our share of threats here at the office, and we regularly have to call the police. So far, nothing serious has happened, knock on wood."

"And what sort of follow-up do you do?" Martin persisted.

"The case remains with us, and we have ongoing contact with the relevant organization. Our objective is to arrive at a peaceful solution. In most instances, that's not possible, but we do have some success stories."

"I've heard of cases where women have received help from these sorts of organizations so that they can flee the country.

Do you know anything about that? Do any of the women ever disappear?" asked Patrik.

Sven fidgeted a bit. "I know what you're referring to. I read the newspapers too. There have been a few cases where women we worked with have disappeared, but we've no way of saying whether a particular group helped them to do that. We just have to assume that they found a way to leave on their own."

"Can we talk off the record for a moment?"

"Off the record, I do think they receive help from certain organizations. But since we have no proof, there's nothing we can do about it."

"Have any of the women that you've referred to the Refuge disappeared in this way?"

For a moment Sven didn't reply. Then he took a deep breath. "Yes."

Patrik decided to drop the subject. It would probably be more productive to ask staff at the Refuge directly. The social services office seemed to operate on the principle of: "the less we know, the better." And he was doubtful that Sven Barkman could help further.

"We'd like to thank you for your time. Unless there's anything else you'd like to ask?" Patrik glanced at Martin, who shook his head.

On their way back to the car, Patrik felt a sinking sensation in his chest. He'd had no idea that so many women were forced to flee their homes—and the only statistic he'd been given was for cases involving the Refuge, so that was just the tip of the iceberg.

∞

Erica couldn't stop thinking about Nathalie. She had been the same, and yet not. A paler copy of herself, and terribly preoccupied in some way. The golden shimmer that had surrounded her in school was now gone, even though she was just as beautiful, just as unreachable. It was as if something inside of her had vanished. Erica had a hard time describing it. All she knew was that she felt sad after the encounter with Nathalie.

She pushed the stroller, stopping several times on Galärbacken.

"Mamma tired?" asked Maja as she happily perched on the running board of the twins' stroller. The boys had just dozed off, and with luck they'd sleep for a good hour.

"Yes, Mamma's tired," Erica told her daughter. She was breathing hard, and a wheezing sound could be heard in her chest.

"Come on, Mamma," said Maja, giving a hop on the running board in order to help out.

"Thanks, sweetie." Erica gathered her strength to push the stroller the last part of the way past the fabric shop.

After delivering Maja safely to the day care center, Erica was on her way home when an idea occurred to her. Her curiosity had been roused by the visit to Gråskär. The long shadow of the lighthouse and Nathalie's expression when they talked about the island and its ghosts had set Erica wondering. Why not find out a bit more?

Turning the stroller around, she began walking toward the library. She had the whole day to kill and she might as well spend her time there while the twins were asleep. At least that felt more productive than sitting on the sofa and watching *Oprah* or *Rachael Ray*.

"Hi, good to see you!" May, the librarian, smiled as Erica parked the stroller inside the front door and off to the side so it wouldn't be in anyone's way. Fortunately the library was totally deserted, and there didn't seem to be much risk that she'd have to compete for space with anyone else.

"And you brought those adorable twins," said May, leaning down to look inside the stroller. "Are they as good as they are cute?"

"Like little angels," Erica told her truthfully. Because she really couldn't complain. The problems that she'd had when Maja was a baby had vanished, which was probably due to her own attitude this time around. When the boys woke in the night and started crying, she felt only gratitude instead of dread. Besides, they were seldom cranky, and they woke only once a night when they were hungry.

"Well, you know your way around the library, so I'll leave you to it. Give me a shout if you need any help. Are you working on a new book?" said May, peering at her.

To Erica's great joy, the whole town was proud of her achievements and followed her publications with great interest.

"No, I haven't started on another one yet. I was thinking of doing some research for my own amusement."

"Oh, really? What's the topic?"

Erica laughed. The people who lived in Fjällbacka were not known for being shy. Their guiding principle seemed to be: If you don't ask, you'll never find out. She had no objections to that attitude. She herself was more inquisitive than most, as Patrik never failed to point out.

"I was actually thinking of looking for books on the archipelago. I want to read up on the history of Gråskär."

"Ghost Isle?" said May. She headed for the shelves on the far side of the room. "So you're interested in ghost stories? In that case, you should have a talk with Stellan at Nolbotten. And Karl-Allen Nordblom knows a lot about the archipelago."

"Thanks. I'll start by seeing what I can find here. Ghosts, the history of lighthouses, and anything of that nature would interest me. Do you think you've got any books on those topics?"

"Hmm . . ." May was studying the shelves. She pulled out a volume, quickly leafed through it, and then set it back. She took out another, studied the table of contents, and tucked it under her arm. After a few minutes she'd found four books, which she handed to Erica.

"These might be useful. It won't be easy to find any published volumes specifically about Gråskär, but you could talk to the staff at the Bohuslän Museum," she said as she took her place behind the library counter.

"I'll start with these," said Erica, nodding toward the four books she was holding. After making sure that the twins were still asleep, she sat down and began to read.

⁖

"What is it?" Their classmates had gathered around them in the schoolyard, and Jon felt the thrill of being the center of attention.

"I found it. I think it's some kind of candy," he said, proudly holding out the bag.

Melker pushed him aside.

"What do you mean, you found it? We found it together."

"Did you take that out of a garbage can? Yuck, that's disgusting! Throw it away, Jon." Lisa wrinkled her nose and then moved on.

"But it's inside a bag." Carefully he opened the seal. "And by the way, it was in a litter basket, not in a garbage can."

Girls were so pathetic. When he was younger he'd played a lot with girls, but ever since starting school, things had changed, and the girls seemed totally different. As if aliens had taken them over. All they did was make a fuss and giggle.

"God, girls are so ludicrous," he said out loud, and all the other boys crowding around him agreed. They knew exactly what he meant. The candy was probably perfectly fine, since it had been tossed into a litter basket.

"And they're inside a bag," exclaimed Melker, echoing what Jon had said. All the boys nodded.

They had waited until the lunch break to retrieve the bag. Candy was forbidden at school, so what they'd found looked especially exciting—sort of like the powdered white licorice that came in a tin shaped like a hockey puck. The fact that they'd discovered the discarded candy all on their own made them feel like adventurers, like Indiana Jones. Jon—or rather Jon, Melker, and Jack—would be the heroes of the day. Now it was just a matter of working out how much they'd have to share with the others in order to maintain their hero status. The other boys would be mad if they didn't get any. But if they gave away too much, there wouldn't be enough left over for the three of them.

"You can all have a taste. Three dips with the finger each," Jon finally decided. "But we get to go first, since we found it."

Melker and Jack each solemnly licked an index finger and then reached for the bag. Their fingers came away covered with white powder, and with a delighted expression they stuck them in their mouths. Would it taste salty, like powdered licorice? Or sour, like the sherbert candies that came in those saucer shapes? They were greatly disappointed.

"It doesn't taste of anything. Do you think it's flour?" said Melker, and then he walked away.

Jon was crestfallen as he looked at the bag. He licked his finger as the others had done and stuck it deep inside the powder. Hoping that Melker was wrong, he stuck his finger in his mouth. It tasted of nothing. Absolutely nothing. Although he did feel a slight tingling on his tongue. Furious, he tossed the bag into a litter basket and headed for the school. He had a weird sensation in his mouth. He stuck out his tongue and wiped it on his shirt sleeve, but that didn't help. Now his heart began pounding very fast. He was sweating, and his legs didn't seem to want to obey him. Out of the corner of his eye he saw that Melker and Jack had fallen to the ground. They must have stumbled on something, or else they were just playing around. Then he felt the ground come rushing up toward him. Everything went black before he even hit the pavement.

✾

Paula wished Patrik had taken her with him to Göteborg instead of Martin. On the other hand, it gave her the opportunity to examine the contents of Mats Sverin's briefcase in peace and quiet. She had immediately sent the laptop over to the technical division; the personnel there were much more computer-savvy than she was and would know how to deal with it properly.

"I hear the briefcase has been found," said Gösta, sticking his head in the door to her office.

"Yup. I've got it here." She pointed to the brown leather briefcase lying on her desk.

"Have you had a chance to examine it?" Gösta came in, pulled up a chair, and sat down next to her.

"Well, I haven't done much yet, other than to remove the laptop and send it over to the tech guys."

"Good thinking. It's best to let them handle it. I expect it'll take a while before we hear back from them though," said Gösta with a sigh.

"There's not a lot we can do about that. I didn't want to risk wrecking the data by doing it myself. But I've had a look at the cell phone. It didn't take long. He had hardly any numbers stored on it, and the only calls seem to have been to and from his office and his parents' house. No pictures, no saved text messages."

"He was an odd fellow from the sounds of it," said Gösta. Then he pointed at the briefcase. "So, shall we take a look at the rest?"

Paula pulled over the briefcase and cautiously began emptying it. She spread out all the items on the desk in front of them. When she was sure that the briefcase was completely empty, she set it on the floor. They were looking at several pens, a pocket calculator, paper clips, a pack of Stimorol chewing gum, and a thick stack of documents.

"Shall we divide them up?" Paula picked up the papers, giving her colleague an inquiring look. "I'll take half, and you can take half. Okay?"

"Okay," said Gösta, reaching for his share. He set the papers on his lap and began leafing through them as he softly hummed to himself.

"Could you possibly take them to your office?"

"Oh, all right. Sure." Gösta got up and went to his own office, which was right next door.

As soon as she was alone, Paula started going through the documents lying on the desk in front of her. She frowned more and more for every page she turned. After half an hour of intense reading, she got up and went to Gösta's office.

"Do you understand any of this?"

"No, not a word. It's just a bunch of numbers and terms that I can't decipher. We're going to have to ask somebody for help with this. But who?"

"I don't know," said Paula. She'd been hoping to present to Patrik her findings by the time he got back from Göteborg. But the financial terms used in the documents meant nothing to her.

"We can't ask anyone at the council, since they probably have a vested interest in this. What we need is an outsider who's willing to take a look and explain what it all means. We could send the documents over to the financial division, of course, but then we'd have to wait for an answer."

"I'm afraid I don't know any economists."

"Me neither," said Paula, drumming her fingers on the doorframe.

"What about Lennart?" said Gösta suddenly, his face lighting up.

"Lennart who?"

"Annika's husband. Isn't he an economist?"

"You're right," she said, as she stopped drumming her fingers. "Come on. Let's go and ask her." She gathered up the papers and headed for the reception area with Gösta on her heels.

"Annika?" She tapped lightly on the open door.

Annika spun her chair around and smiled when she saw Paula.

"Yes? Can I help you with something?"

"Your husband's an economist, isn't he?"

"Yes, he is," said Annika, bemused. "He's head of finance at ExtraFilm."

"Do you think he could help us out? These were in Mats Sverin's briefcase." Paula waved the stack of papers. "They're financial documents. Gösta and I are completely clueless and need help to work out what they say and whether they're of any importance to the investigation. Do you think Lennart would be willing to take a look?"

"I can ask him. If he says yes, when do you need his help?"

"Today," said Gösta and Paula simultaneously, and Annika laughed.

"I'll give him a call. I'm sure there won't be a problem. You'll just need to get the documents over to his office."

"I can take them over right away," said Paula.

They waited while Annika talked to her husband. They'd met Lennart many times when he dropped by the station to see Annika, and it was impossible not to like the man. He was over six feet tall and the nicest person imaginable. After many years of trying unsuccessfully to have a child, he and Annika had found out that they could adopt a baby girl from China, so they both had a new sparkle in their eyes.

"Okay. He said you can bring the documents over. He's not too busy at the moment, so he promised to look at them immediately."

"Great! Thanks!" Paula gave her a big smile and even Gösta managed a faint smile, which totally transformed his usually gloomy face.

Paula rushed out and got in the car. It took her only a few minutes to drive over to Lennart's office and deliver the documents, and she whistled cheerfully all the way back. But she abruptly stopped whistling when she pulled up in front of the station. Gösta was standing outside, waiting for her. And judging by his expression, something had happened.

⁂

Leila opened the door wearing the same worn denims as before, with an equally baggy sweater, although this time it was gray instead of white. Around her neck hung a long silver chain with a heart-shaped charm.

"Come in," she said, leading the way to her office. It was as neat as on the previous occasion, and Patrik wondered how people managed to keep everything so tidy. Try as he might to be organized, it was as if gremlins snuck into his office and messed everything up the minute he looked away.

Leila shook hands with Martin and introduced herself before they all sat down. He cast an interested glance at the children's drawings on the walls.

"Have you found out who shot Matte?" asked Leila.

"We're pursuing various lines of inquiry, but we have nothing further to report at the moment," Patrik said evasively.

"But I assume that you think it has something to do with us, since you've come back here," she said. Her fingers toyed with the necklace, betraying her agitation.

"As I said, we haven't made a great deal of progress. We're working several potential leads." Patrik spoke calmly. He was accustomed to people acting nervous when he came to see them. It didn't necessarily mean that they had anything to hide. The mere presence of a police officer was enough to provoke anxiety. "We just wanted to ask you a few more questions and take a look at the documentation on the women who were offered shelter while Mats was working here."

"I'm not sure I can agree to that. It's sensitive information. If we release details, it might cause trouble for the women."

"I understand, but the information will be safe with us. And this is a homicide investigation. We have the legal right to see the documents."

Leila paused to consider this.

"Of course," she said at last. "But I'd prefer not to allow the documents out of the office. If we can agree that everything stays here, then I'll let you look through whatever we have."

"That's fine. Thanks very much," interjected Martin.

"We've just had a meeting with Sven Barkman," said Patrik.

Leila immediately began fiddling with her necklace again. She leaned toward them as she spoke.

"We're totally dependent on maintaining a good relationship with social services. I hope you didn't lead him to believe that there's anything fishy about our organization. We're already in a rather difficult position, and some people regard us as somewhat unorthodox."

"Don't worry, we made the purpose of our visit very clear, and we emphasized that there's nothing at all suspect about the Refuge."

"I'm glad to hear that," said Leila, but she still looked uneasy.

"Sven estimated that around thirty cases are referred to you from various social services offices every year. Does that sound right?"

"Yes, I think that's the number I gave you the last time you were here." Her voice took on a more professional tone, and she clasped her hands on the desk.

"How many of these cases would you estimate end up causing . . . how shall I put it? Problems?"

Martin had dived in with his question, and Patrik reminded himself that he needed to let him take the lead more often.

"I assume you mean men who turn up here?"

"Yes."

"As a matter of fact, none. Most men who beat their wives or children don't think they're doing anything wrong. In their eyes, it's the woman who's at fault. It's all a matter of power and control. And if they're going to threaten anyone, it's the woman and not the crisis center."

"But there is a type of man who might, isn't there?" asked Patrik.

"Indeed. A few every year. But mostly we hear about them from the social services staff."

Patrik's attention was caught by one of the drawings on the wall behind Leila, directly above her head. A gigantic figure next to two smaller ones. The big one had fangs and looked angry. He couldn't understand how anyone could hit a woman; and as for hitting a child . . . The very thought that someone would hurt Erica or his children made him grip the arms of his chair.

"How do you handle your cases? Let's start with that."

"We have a chat with the social worker, and they will summarize the case. Sometimes the woman comes to see us before moving in. Often she'll be accompanied by someone from social services. Otherwise she might arrive by cab or a friend might bring her here."

"Then what happens?" asked Martin.

"That depends. Sometimes it's enough that the woman stays with us for a while until the situation calms down, and then the problems get resolved. Sometimes, if we think it's too dangerous for the woman to remain in the area, we have to move her to another crisis facility. We might also offer legal help in arranging that her whereabouts are kept hidden within the system. Some of these women have spent years living in constant fear. They may exhibit many of the same symptoms as prisoners of war. For instance, they may be completely incapable of taking action. In that case, we step in and help them with the practical matters."

"And the psychological issues?" Patrik stared at the drawing of the big, dark figure with fangs. "Are you able to help with those too?"

"Not as much as we'd like. It's a question of resources. But we do have a good relationship with several psychologists who donate their services. Our primary concern is to get help for the children."

"Recently there's been a lot in the newspapers about women who have been given help to flee the country and are then charged with kidnapping their children. Are you familiar with any cases like that?" Patrik studied Leila closely, but she gave no indication that the question made her uncomfortable.

"As I said, we depend on maintaining a good working relationship with social services. We can't afford to take that sort of action. We offer the help that's permissible within the law. Of course there are women who take matters into their own hands and go underground. But that's not something the Refuge promotes or is willing to help with."

Patrik decided to drop the subject. She sounded convincing enough, and he sensed that he wasn't going to get any further by pressuring her.

"What about the few cases that give you extra trouble—are those the ones where you have to move the women to a different shelter?" asked Martin.

Leila nodded. "It happens."

"What sort of problems are we talking about?" Patrik felt his cell vibrating in his pocket. Whoever was trying to reach him would just have to wait.

"We've had cases where the men have found out where our shelter is located. For instance, by following our staff members. Each time we've learned something from the experience and improved our security measures. But you should never underestimate how obsessed these men can be."

Patrik's cell continued to vibrate, and he placed his hand over his pocket to mute the sound.

"Did Mats get specifically involved in any of these incidents?"

"No. We make a point of insisting that none of our staff gets too involved in individual cases. We have a system in place so that the woman has a different contact person after a while."

"Wouldn't that mean an even greater sense of insecurity for the women?" Patrik's cell had started up again, and he was getting annoyed. How hard was it to understand that he couldn't take the call at the moment?

"Maybe so, but it's important, because it allows us to keep our distance. Personal relationships and involvement would only increase the risk for the women. It's for their own good that we work this way."

"How safe is the new address when they're moved somewhere else?" Martin changed tack after casting an inquiring glance at Patrik.

Leila sighed. "Unfortunately, we simply don't have the resources in Sweden to provide the security that these women need. As I said, we usually move them to another crisis center in a different city and keep their personal information as secret as possible. We also provide the women with an emergency signal device, in cooperation with the police."

"This device, how does it operate? We've not come across this in Tanumshede."

"They're linked to the police emergency switchboard. If someone presses the button, the police are instantly notified. At the same time, the speaker on the telephone is activated, so the police can hear what's happening in the apartment."

"What about the legal issues? Custody of the children, and so on? Don't the women have to appear in court?" asked Patrik.

"It can be handled by an ombudsperson. So that's something we can resolve." Leila reached up to tuck a lock of hair behind her ear. Her hair was cut in a neat pageboy style.

"We'd like to take a closer look at the more problematic cases that you handled while Mats was working here," said Patrik.

"Okay. But the cases aren't sorted individually, and not everything is accessible. We send most of the paperwork to social services when the women move out, and we don't keep documents beyond a year. I'll get out what we have, and then you can go through everything and see what you can find." She held up an admonitory finger. "As I said, I don't want anything to leave this office, so you'll have to takes notes." She stood up and went over to the file cabinets.

"Here you are," said Leila, placing about twenty file folders in front of them. "I'm going out for lunch now, so you can sit here undisturbed. I'll be back in an hour, if you have any questions."

"Thanks," said Patrik. He gave the stack of files a discouraged look. This was going to take time. And they didn't even know what they were looking for.

Erica didn't manage to stay very long at the library as both twins decided to take only a short nap, but at least she made a start. When she wrote about true crime cases she had to spend long hours doing meticulous research, which she found just as interesting as the actual writing process. And now she wanted to continue looking into the legends of Ghost Isle.

She had to force herself to put all thought of Gråskär aside, because as soon as she turned the stroller onto the driveway in front of their house in Sälvik, the twins began crying loudly. They were hungry. She hurried inside and quickly prepared two bottles of formula, feeling guilty that she was so happy not to be breastfeeding them.

"Now, now. Slow down a bit, sweetie," she said to Noel.

He was always the greedier of the two. Sometimes he'd take such big gulps that he'd end up nearly choking. Anton, on the other hand, was slower, and it took him twice as long to drink a whole bottle. Erica felt like Super-Mamma as she sat there with a bottle in each hand, feeding the two babies simultaneously. Both boys had their gaze fixed on her, and she felt herself going cross-eyed from trying to look at both of them at once. So much love directed at her.

"All right then. Do you feel better? Do you think your mother could take off her coat now?" she said with a laugh when she discovered that she was still wearing both her coat and her shoes.

She placed each boy in his bassinet, hung her coat in the front hall, removed her shoes, and carried the babies into the living room. Then she sat down on the sofa and propped her feet up on the coffee table.

"Mamma will do something useful in a while. But first she needs to spend a little time with Oprah."

The boys seemed to ignore her.

"Is it boring when your big sister isn't home?"

At first Erica had let Maja stay home as much as possible, but after a while she noticed that her daughter was going stir-crazy. She needed to be with other children, and she missed the day care center. That was a big change from the awful period when leaving Maja at the center felt like initiating a minor world war.

"Why don't we pick her up early today? What do you boys think about that?" She interpreted their silence as agreement. "Mamma hasn't even had her coffee yet," she said, getting to her feet. "And you know how Mamma gets when she hasn't had coffee. 'Un poco loco,' as Pappa usually says. Not that we should pay too much attention to everything he says."

Erica laughed and went into the kitchen to make herself a pot of coffee. The light was blinking on the answering machine. She hadn't noticed before. Someone had actually taken the trouble to leave a message, so she pressed the button to play it back. When she heard the voice on the machine, she dropped the coffee scoop and pressed her hand to her mouth.

"Hi, sis. It's me. Anna. Provided you don't have any other sisters, that is. I'm a bit worse for wear, and I've got the world's lousiest hairdo. But I'm here. I think. Almost, at any rate. And I know that you've been here and that you've been worried. I can't promise that . . ." The voice rambled on. It was raspy and sounded different, with an underlying hint of pain. "I just wanted to say that I'm here now." Click.

Erica didn't move for a couple of seconds. Then she slowly sank to the floor and began to cry. She was still holding the coffee pot in a tight grip.

⌘

"Don't you have to leave for work soon?" Rita gave Mellberg a stern look as she changed Leo's diaper.

"I'm going to be working from home until after lunch."

"Oh, you're working at home . . ." said Rita, casting a glance at the TV, which was showing a program about people who built machines from scrap metal and then entered them in competitions.

"I'm gathering my strength. That's important too. As a police officer it's easy to get burned out, otherwise." Mellberg lifted up Leo and raised him high in the air, making the boy whoop with laughter.

Rita relented. She couldn't stay angry with Bertil. Of course she saw what others saw: that he was a boor, that he could be terribly loutish, and sometimes he couldn't see beyond his own nose. Plus he never wanted to do more than the bare minimum of work. But at the same time, she saw another side of him. How he beamed whenever Leo was near, how he never hesitated to change a diaper or get up in the middle of the night if the baby was crying. How he treated her like a queen and looked at her as if she were God's gift to humanity. He had even thrown himself with enthusiasm into learning to dance the salsa, which was her passion in life. He would never be king of the dance floor, but he was able to lead quite decently, without causing too much damage to her feet. She also knew that he loved his son Simon with all his heart. Simon, who would soon turn seventeen, had come into Mellberg's life only a few years back, but every time his name came up in conversation, pride shone in Bertil's eyes. And he was always eager to keep in touch with his son and make himself available. For all of these reasons, Rita loved Bertil Mellberg so much that sometimes it felt as if her heart would burst.

She went into the kitchen. As she began fixing lunch, her concern about the girls returned. She had noticed that something wasn't right between them. It made her sad to see the unhappy expression on Paula's face. She suspected that even Paula didn't really know what was wrong. Johanna had closed herself off, withdrawing from all of them, not just from Paula. Maybe she felt it was too much to live in such close quarters with others. Rita could understand if Johanna didn't find it exactly ideal to be sharing the apartment with Paula's mother and her boyfriend, not to mention the two dogs. At the same time, it was very practical to have Bertil and herself here, able to step in as babysitters for Leo during the day when the girls were at work.

It must be difficult though, and she realized she ought to encourage them to look for their own apartment. But as she stirred the stew, she felt a pang in her heart at the thought of not being able to lift Leo out of his crib in the morning when he sat there, wide awake and smiling up at her. Rita wiped away her tears. It must be the onions in the stew; she couldn't very well be standing here crying in the middle of the day. She swallowed hard and hoped that the girls would work things out on their own. After tasting the stew she added another pinch of chili powder. If it failed to send heat through her whole body, she knew she hadn't put in enough.

Bertil's cell, which was lying on the kitchen table, began ringing. She went over to look at the display. The station. They're probably wondering where he is, she thought as she carried the phone into the living room. Bertil was sitting on the sofa, sound asleep with his head tilted back and his mouth open. Leo was curled up on his big belly. His little fist was curved around his cheek, and he was sleeping with calm, deep breaths that made his chest rise and fall in time with his uncle Bertil's. Rita switched off the phone. The station would just have to wait. Bertil had more important things to do at the moment.

⌘

"So I take it that Saturday was a big hit," said Anders, giving Vivianne a searching look. She seemed tired, and he wondered whether she realized how great a toll this was taking on her. Maybe their past had finally caught up with them. But he knew better than to say anything; she didn't want to hear it. She was so stubborn and determined, which was the very reason why she, and possibly he too, had survived. He had always been dependent on her. His sister had taken care of him, done everything for him. But he wondered whether things had started to change, and they were slowly switching roles.

"How's it going with Erling?" he asked, prompting a grimace from Vivianne.

"Well, if it weren't for the fact that he sleeps so soundly at night, I don't think I could stand it," she said with a joyless laugh.

"We're almost there," he said in an attempt to console her, but he could see that she wasn't really listening. Vivianne had always possessed a special sort of inner light, and even though no one else had noticed, he could see that it was fading.

"Do you think they'll find the laptop?"

Vivianne gave a start.

"No. They would have found it by now if it was going to turn up."

"I suppose you're right."

Neither of them spoke for a moment.

"I tried to call you yesterday," Vivianne said hesitantly.

Anders felt his body tense.

"Really?"

"You didn't pick up all evening."

"I must have switched off my cell," he said evasively.

"All evening?"

"I was tired, so I took a bath and read for a while. I also spent some time going over the reports."

"Oh. Right," she said, but he could hear that she didn't believe him.

In the past they'd never kept secrets from one another, but that too had changed. At the same time, they felt closer to each other than ever before. He was having a hard time working out what he wanted. Now that the goal was within reach, things suddenly didn't seem as clear as they had, and his thoughts were keeping him awake at night, making him toss and turn in bed. Things no longer seemed as simple as they once had.

How was he going to tell her this? The words had been on the tip of his tongue so many times, but when he opened his mouth, nothing came out. He couldn't do it. There was so much that he owed her. He could still smell the stink of cigarettes and liquor, hear the clinking of glasses and the sound of people moaning like animals. He and Vivianne had lain curled up together in her bed. She had held him close, and even though she wasn't much bigger than him, she had felt like a giant emanating a sense of security that would protect him from all evil.

"I hear that Saturday was a big success!" exclaimed Erling as he came out of the toilet, wiping his wet hands on his trouser legs. "I just talked to Bertil, and he practically waxed poetic about the whole experience. You're amazing. Do you know that?"

He sat down next to Vivianne and put his arm around her shoulders with a possessive look. Then he delivered a wet kiss to her cheek, and Anders saw how she had to struggle not to pull away. Instead, she smiled sweetly and took a sip of tea from the mug on the table.

"The only complaint was about the food." A deep furrow appeared on Erling's forehead. "Bertil wasn't particularly thrilled with what was served. I don't know whether the others shared his opinion, but he's the one who takes the lead, of course, and we ought to listen to our customers."

"Exactly what was wrong with the food?" asked Vivianne. She spoke in an icy tone, but Erling didn't notice.

"Apparently there were far too many vegetables, and also a few strange items, from what I understood. And there wasn't much gravy either. So Bertil suggested that we offer a more traditional menu that would appeal to a wider range of people. Good, plain food, in other words." Erling's face lit up with enthusiasm, as if he anticipated a standing ovation.

Vivianne, however, had reached her limit. She stood up, fixing her eyes on Erling.

"It sounds as though their time at the spa was completely wasted. I thought you understood my philosophy, my view of what's important for both the body and soul. We're concerned with health here, and we serve food that will provide positive energy and strength, not junk that will lead to heart attacks and cancer." She turned on her heel and walked swiftly away. Her long plait swayed in time with her footsteps.

"Oh dear," said Erling, clearly taken aback at the reception to his suggestion. "Looks like I really put my foot in it this time."

"You might say that," replied Anders drily. Erling could behave however he liked. Soon it wouldn't make any difference. Then worry overwhelmed him again. He was going to have to talk to Vivianne. He was going to have to tell her.

⁓

"So what exactly are we looking for?" asked Martin. He looked up at Patrik, who merely shook his head.

"I don't really know. I think we need to follow our gut feelings, read through all the material in the folders, and see if there's anything that we should follow up."

They leafed through the documents in silence.

"Bloody hell," said Patrik after a while, and Martin nodded.

"And this is just for the past year. Or not even that long. And the Refuge is only one of many women's crisis centers. We really have no clue about the sort of things that go on in some women's lives." Martin carefully closed up one folder, set it aside, and opened another.

"I can't understand . . ." said Patrik, voicing the thought that had been occupying his mind ever since they arrived at the Refuge.

"What fucking bastards," Martin agreed. "And it seems like it can happen to anyone. I don't know Anna very well, but she seems like a strong-minded person who would never end up in the clutches of somebody like her ex-husband."

"I know what you mean." Patrik scowled at the thought of Lucas. Thank God all that was behind them now, but that man had managed to cause so much pain for his family before he died. "It's hard to understand why a woman would stay with a man who beats her."

Martin set another folder on the desk and took a deep breath.

"I wonder what it's like for the people who work here and have to deal with this on a daily basis. Maybe it's not so strange that Sverin would decide that he'd had enough and wanted to move back home."

"I can see why they have that rule about staff not getting too involved, and why they're constantly changing the individual in contact with each woman. Otherwise it would be practically impossible not to get personally involved."

"Do you think that might have been what happened to Mats?" asked Martin. "Could the assault be connected with someone here? Leila used the word 'obsessed.' Maybe one of the men decided that Sverin was more than just a contact person and decided to give him a warning."

Patrik nodded. "I've been thinking along the same lines. But in that case, who would it be?" He pointed to the stack of folders on the desk. "Leila claims to know nothing about it, and I don't think there's any point trying to pressure her for more information at this stage."

"We could talk to the other staff members. Maybe we could even talk to a couple of the women. I can imagine that a lot of gossiping goes on, and if what we're theorizing really happened then that sort of news would spread fast."

"Hmm . . . could be," said Patrik. "But I'd like to have more facts before we do any real digging here."

"How are we going to find out more?" Martin impatiently ran his hands through his short red hair, making it stand on end.

"I think we should talk to the neighbors in the block of apartments where Mats was living. The assault took place right outside the front door, so maybe somebody saw something but never reported it. And now we have the names of the women that Mats was the contact for, so hopefully we'll have a reason to come back."

"Okay." Martin bowed his head and went on reading.

They closed up the last folder just as Leila came dashing into the office. She hung her jacket and handbag on a hanger.

"Did you find anything interesting?"

"We're not sure yet. But at least we have the names of the women that Mats dealt with. Thanks for letting us look at the files." Patrik gathered up the folders in a neat pile, and then Leila put them back in the file cabinet.

"You're welcome. I do hope you realize that we're willing to do whatever we can to cooperate with you." She leaned against the shelf that held three-ring binders.

"We appreciate that," said Patrik. Then he and Martin stood up.

"We were very fond of Matte. He was the kind of person who didn't have a bad bone in his body. Keep that in mind as you work on the case."

"We'll do that," said Patrik, shaking hands. "Believe me, we'll do that."

༄

"Why doesn't a single person answer their damn phone?" snapped Paula.

"Not even Mellberg?" said Gösta.

"No. Nor Patrik. And Martin's cell goes straight to his voicemail, so he must have switched it off."

"I'm not too surprised about Mellberg. He's probably home asleep. But we can usually get hold of Hedström."

"He must be tied up. In the meantime we'll have to deal with this ourselves and bring them up to date later." She drove into the parking lot at Uddevalla Hospital and stopped the car.

"I assume they're in intensive care," she said, leading the way to the entrance.

They made straight for the elevator and waited impatiently for it to carry them up to the correct floor.

"A nasty business," said Gösta.

"Yes, I can imagine how worried their parents must be. Where could they have gotten hold of shit like that? They're only seven years old."

Gösta shook his head. "I have no idea."

"We'll just have to see what they say."

When they reached the ward, Paula stopped the first doctor they saw.

"Excuse me. We're police officers, and we're here regarding the boys from Fjällbacka school."

The tall man in the white coat nodded.

"They're my patients. Come with me." He set off, taking long strides, and both Paula and Gösta had to jog to keep up with him.

Paula tried to breathe through her mouth. She hated hospitals and all the smells. It was the sort of place that she did her best to avoid, but given her chosen profession, she had to visit hospitals much more often that she would have liked.

"They're going to be fine," said the tall doctor over his shoulder. "The school reacted quickly, and there was an ambulance in the neighborhood, so they were brought in relatively fast, and we were able to get the situation under control."

"Are they awake?" asked Paula. She panted a bit as she ran along the corridor, enough to remind herself that she ought to go back to working out at the gym. She hadn't done much of that lately. Plus she'd been eating too much of Rita's good food.

"They're awake, and the parents have all agreed to let you talk to the boys." The doctor stopped outside a room that was almost at the end of the corridor.

"Let me go in first and speak to the parents. From a medical perspective, there's nothing to prevent you talking to the boys. I expect you'll want to know where they found the cocaine."

"Are you sure it was cocaine?" asked Paula.

"Yes. We did some blood tests that confirmed it." The doctor pushed open the door and went in.

Paula and Gösta paced up and down the corridor as they waited. After a few minutes the door opened and a number of somber-looking adults came out, their faces flushed from crying.

"We're from the Tanum police," said Paula, shaking hands with everyone. Gösta did the same; he seemed to be acquainted with several of the parents.

"Do you know where the boys found the drugs?" asked one of the mothers, wiping her eyes with a handkerchief. "We think our children are safe at school and then . . ." Her voice started quavering, and she leaned against her husband, who put his arm around her.

"So the boys haven't told you anything?"

"No, I think they're too ashamed. We've told them that they won't get in trouble, but we haven't been able to get any information out of them yet, and we haven't wanted to pressure them too much," said one of the fathers. Though he seemed composed, his eyes were red-rimmed.

"Would it be okay if we talked to them alone? We promise not to frighten them," said Paula, giving them a wry smile. She suspected that she didn't seem particularly threatening, and Gösta looked like a nice, sad old dog. She had a hard time imagining that anyone would be scared of them, and apparently the parents agreed because they nodded their assent.

"Why don't we all have a cup of coffee in the meantime?" said the father with the red-rimmed eyes. The others seemed to think this was a good idea. He turned to Paula and Gösta and said, "We'll be in the waiting room over there. And we'd appreciate it if you'd let us know what you find out."

"Of course," said Gösta, patting the man on the shoulder.

They went into the room. The boys were lying in beds that had been placed side by side. Three pitiful little creatures tucked into their hospital beds.

"Hi," said Paula, and all three faintly answered her greeting. She wondered which boy they should begin with. When two of them cast hasty glances at the third boy, who had dark curly hair, she decided to start with him.

"My name is Paula." She pulled a chair over to his bed and motioned for Gösta to do the same. "What's your name?"

"Jon," said the boy weakly, but he didn't dare look her in the eye.

"How are you feeling?"

"Okay." He was nervously plucking at the blanket.

"What an awful thing to happen, huh?" She was totally focused on Jon, but out of the corner of her eye she saw that the other two boys were listening intently.

"Uh-huh . . ." He looked up at her. "Are you really from the police?"

Paula laughed. "Yes, I am. Don't I look like a police officer?"

"Er, not really. I know that girls can be policemen, but you're so small." He smiled shyly.

"We need small police officers on the force too. What if we need to get into a very tiny space, for example?" she said. Jon nodded, as if that was a perfectly reasonable explanation.

"Would you like to see my police ID?"

He nodded eagerly, and the other boys craned their necks to see better.

"Maybe you could take out your ID too, Gösta, so the other boys could see it."

Gösta smiled, got up, and went over to the next bed.

"Wow. Your ID looks exactly like on TV," said Jon. He studied it for a moment and then handed it back.

"That was pretty dangerous stuff you found. I hope you understand that," said Paula, trying not to sound too stern.

"Hmm . . ." Jon again lowered his gaze and began plucking at the blanket.

"But nobody is angry with you. Not your parents or your teachers. We're not angry either."

"We thought it was a bag of candy."

"It does look a bit like the powder from those flying-saucer candies, doesn't it?" she said. "I probably would have made the same mistake."

Gösta had sat down again, and Paula waited for him to interject a few questions, but he seemed happy to let her carry out the interview. She'd always been good with children.

"Pappa says that it was drugs," said Jon, tugging at a thread from the blanket.

"Yes, that's right. Do you know what drugs are?"

"Poison. Except that you don't die from it."

"Drugs can actually kill you. But you're right that they're poison. That's why it's important for you to help us find out where that powder came from, so we can prevent anybody else from being poisoned." She spoke in a calm, friendly voice, and Jon began to relax.

"Are you sure you're not angry?" He looked her in the eye. His lower lip was quivering.

"Very, very sure. Cross my heart," she told him, hoping the expression wasn't hopelessly out-of-date. "And your mamma and pappa aren't angry either. They're worried, that's all."

"We were over near the block of apartments yesterday," said Jon. "We were hitting tennis balls against the wall. There's a factory there. At least, that's what I think it is. With high walls and no windows, so we can't break any glass. That's why we usually play over there. Then on our way home we were looking for bottles that we could turn in for money. In the litter baskets outside the apartments, and that's when we found the bag. We thought it was a bag of candy." The thread came loose from the blanket, leaving a tiny hole in the weave.

"Why didn't you taste the candy yesterday?" asked Gösta.

"We thought it was cool to find so much of it, so we wanted to take the bag to school and show everybody. It seemed more exciting to taste it when everyone had some too. But we were going to keep most of it for ourselves, of course. We thought we'd just share a little."

"Which litter basket was it in?" asked Paula. She knew the industrial building that Jon was talking about, but she wanted to be one hundred percent sure.

"Over by the parking lot. You see it when you come through the gate where we were playing tennis."

"Where the woods and hill are off to the right?"

"Yes, that's the one."

Paula glanced at Gösta. The litter basket where the boys had found the cocaine was outside Mats Sverin's front door.

"Thank you, boys. You've been a huge help," she said as she got to her feet. She felt a churning in her stomach. Maybe this was finally the breakthrough that they'd been waiting for in the investigation.

# Fjällbacka 1871

*T*he pastor was big and fat and gratefully grabbed hold of Karl's hand so he could climb up onto the dock. Emelie curtseyed modestly. She'd never been to a church service in town. Here she stood now, blushing and hoping that the pastor wouldn't think her failure to attend had to do with a lack of will or faith on her part.

"It's certainly an isolated place, isn't it? Beautiful, though," the pastor added. "But isn't there someone else who lives here?"

"Julian," said Karl. "He's tending to the lighthouse at the moment. I can fetch him if you like."

"Yes, please. That would be good." Without waiting to be invited, the pastor started walking toward the house. "Since I've finally made it out to this island, I might as well meet all of the inhabitants." He laughed and held the door open for Emelie while Karl set off for the lighthouse.

"What a nice, tidy house you have here," said the pastor, looking around.

"*Our humble home isn't much to look at.*" Emelie discovered that she was hiding her hands under her apron. They looked so rough after all the scrubbing she did, but she couldn't deny that the pastor's words of praise made her happy.

"There's no reason to scorn what's humble and simple. From what I can see, Karl should consider himself lucky to have such a clever wife." He sat down on the kitchen bench.

Emelie was so embarrassed that she didn't know what to say, so she began making coffee.

"May I offer you some coffee?" She wondered if she had anything to serve with it. Then she realized they had only the plain rusks that she'd baked, but they would just have to do, since his visit was unexpected.

"I never turn down a cup of coffee," replied the pastor, smiling.

Emelie was starting to feel less nervous. He didn't seem to be a stern sort of pastor—not like Preacher Berg, in her former church. The mere thought of having to sit at the same table with Berg made her knees wobble.

The door opened and Karl came in. Right behind him was Julian, with a wary expression on his face. He avoided looking the pastor in the eye.

"So this is Julian?" The pastor was still smiling, but Julian merely nodded as they briefly shook hands. Karl and Julian sat down across from the pastor while Emelie set the table.

"I hope you're taking care that your wife doesn't work too hard, now that she's in this blessed condition. I can see that she's a splendid housekeeper. You must be very proud of her."

At first Karl didn't answer. Then he said, "Yes, Emelie is very efficient."

"All right. Come and sit down now," said the pastor to Emelie, patting the seat next to him.

Emelie did as he said, but she couldn't help staring at his black coat and white collar. She had never been so close to a preacher before. It would have been unthinkable to sit down with old Berg and converse *over a cup of coffee. Her hands shook as she poured the coffee, filling her own cup last.*

"It's quite a surprise that you've come out here to see us," said Karl. He was clearly wondering what the purpose of the pastor's visit could be.

"Yes, well, you haven't exactly been regular churchgoers," said the pastor, sipping his coffee. He'd put three lumps of sugar in his cup, and Emelie thought his coffee must taste awfully sweet.

Karl suddenly looked small and awkward, and at that moment Emelie couldn't understand why she was so afraid of him. Then she remembered that evening and placed her hand over her stomach.

"It's true that we haven't been to church as often as we should," said Julian, bowing his head. He still hadn't looked the pastor in the eye. "But Emelie reads the Bible to us every night, so this is not an un-Christian home."

Emelie looked at him in alarm. Was he actually going to sit here and lie to the pastor? It was true that passages from the Bible were read in this house, but she was the only one who did that, whenever she had a spare moment. Neither Julian nor Karl had ever shown any interest in the Holy Scriptures. In fact, on several occasions they had scoffed at her for reading the Bible.

The pastor nodded. "That's good to hear. Especially in a place like this, so barren and inaccessible and far from the house of the Lord. Here one has to seek solace and guidance in the Bible on one's own. So I'm happy to hear that you do. It would please me even more to see you in church. Especially you, my dear Emelie." He patted her knee, making Emelie jump. It was nerve-wracking enough to be sitting so close to a preacher. The fact that he had also touched her was almost more than she could bear. She had to restrain herself from leaping to her feet out of sheer fright.

"I've had a talk with your aunt. She was a bit worried since she hasn't heard from you. And now that Emelie is with child, it would be good if the doctor had a look at her to make sure that everything *is progressing as it should." He cast a stern glance at Karl, who also avoided meeting his gaze.*

*"Of course," he muttered, staring down at the table.*

*"Good. Then that's settled. The next time you come to Fjäll-backa, you'll bring Emelie along and let the doctor examine her. Your dear aunt would also appreciate a visit from you, Karl." He winked and then reached for a rusk. "Very tasty," he said as the crumbs spilled from his lips.*

*"Thank you." Emelie was not just thanking him for the compliment. Thanks to him, she was going to have a chance to go into town and see other people. Maybe Karl would also let her go to church once in a while. That would make it so much easier to tolerate her life on the island.*

*"Well, I think Karlsson is probably getting tired of waiting for me. He was kind enough to bring me over here in his boat, but I'm sure he's eager to get back home. I want to thank you for the coffee and the delicious rusks." The pastor stood up, and Emelie quickly got up to allow him to slip past.*

*"How about that? Our stomachs are almost the same size," said the pastor.*

*Emelie felt herself turning bright red with embarrassment. Then she couldn't help smiling. She liked this preacher, and she could have fallen to her knees and kissed his feet out of gratitude because he realized that she needed to go to Fjällbacka.*

*"I suppose you've heard what people say about this island, haven't you?" said the pastor with a laugh as Karl and Emelie accompanied him down to the dock. Julian had mumbled a hasty goodbye and returned to the lighthouse.*

*"What do you mean?" asked Karl, helping the pastor into the boat.*

*"It's said that there are ghosts out here. But it's just talk, of course. Or maybe you've actually seen something?" He laughed again, making his fat cheeks quiver.*

*"We don't believe in such things,"* said Karl, tossing in the mooring line that he'd just untied.

Emelie didn't say a word. But as she waved goodbye, she thought about those who were her only real companions on the island. It wouldn't do to discuss them with the pastor. And besides, no one would ever believe her.

As she walked back to the house, she saw them out of the corner of her eye. She wasn't afraid of them. Not even after they had started showing themselves to her. She knew they wished her no harm.

# 14

H i, Annika. Paula has been trying to get hold of me, but now she's not answering her phone." Patrik was standing outside the front door of the Refuge, pressing one finger to his left ear as he held the cell to his right. The roar of the traffic was so loud that he had trouble hearing what Annika was saying.

"What was that? The school? Wait, I couldn't hear you. Cocaine? Okay, I got it. At the Uddevalla Hospital."

"What's all that about?" asked Martin.

"Three second graders in Fjällbacka found a bag of cocaine and ate some of the stuff." Patrik's expression was grim as they walked toward the car.

"Bloody hell. How are they doing?"

"They're in the hospital, but apparently they're going to be fine. Gösta and Paula are over there right now."

Patrik got behind the wheel, and Martin took the passenger seat. They drove off, with Martin staring pensively out of the window.

"Second graders. We always think the kids are safe in school, especially in Fjällbacka, which doesn't have the problems of a big city. And then it turns out that they're not safe after all. This'll scare the shit out of everybody."

"Yes, it's not like when we were kids. Or at least, when I was a kid," Patrik said with a crooked smile. There really wasn't much of an age difference between him and his colleague.

"I think you could say the same about my school days," replied Martin. "Although by then we did have calculators instead of an abacus."

"Ha ha, very funny."

"Things were so uncomplicated back then. We had fun in the playground kicking a ball around. We got to be kids. Nowadays it feels as though everybody is in such a hurry to grow up. They all want to smoke and fuck and drink and do everything else between heaven and earth before they even start secondary school."

"I know what you mean," said Patrik, feeling a surge of anxiety in his chest. In the blink of an eye, it would be time for Maja to start school. And Martin was right: things weren't the same as in their day. He didn't even want to think about that. He wanted his daughter to remain a child as long as possible, and preferably live at home until she was forty. "But I don't think cocaine is all that common," he said, mostly in an attempt to reassure himself.

"No, it must have been a case of really bad luck. I'm glad they're going to be okay. It could have turned out much, much worse."

Patrik nodded.

"Shall we drive over to the hospital?" asked Martin, but Patrik turned the car toward the center of Göteborg instead of heading for the E6.

"I reckon Paula and Gösta can handle things on their own. I'll give Paula a call to make sure, but while we're here I'd like to have a talk with Mats's tenant and the other neighbors in the building. It seems a waste of time to drive all the way back later when we can do it now."

Patrik called Paula. After a few minutes he ended the call.

"They've got the situation under control, so we'll stick to our plans here. We can stop at the hospital on our way home, if they're still there."

"Good. Did she find out where the kids found the stuff?"

"In a litter basket outside the block of apartments where Mats Sverin lived."

Martin didn't say a word for a moment. Then he asked, "Do you think it's related to the case?"

"Who knows?" Patrik shrugged. "The cocaine could belong to any number of people who live in that building. But it's definitely interesting that it was found outside Sverin's front door."

Martin leaned forward to read the street signs. "Turn here. Erik Dahlbergsgatan. What number are we looking for?"

"Forty-eight." Patrik slammed on the brakes to avoid hitting an old woman who was taking her time to cross the street. He waited impatiently for her to pass before he stepped on the accelerator again.

"Take it easy," said Martin, leaning against the door.

"There it is," replied Patrik, ignoring his comment. "Number forty-eight."

"I hope somebody's home. Maybe we should have phoned ahead."

"We'll ring the bell and hope we're in luck."

It was a lovely old brick building. The apartments probably all had old-fashioned stucco work and hardwood floors.

"What's the name of the tenant?" asked Martin when they reached the door.

Patrik took a slip of paper out of his pocket. "Jonsson. Rasmus Jonsson. And the apartment is on the first floor."

Martin nodded and pressed a button on the intercom. The nameplate next to it still said *Sverin*. He was rewarded almost immediately with a crackling sound.

"Yes?"

"We're from the police. We'd like to talk to you. Would you mind letting us in?" Martin spoke as distinctly as he could into the intercom.

"What's this about?"

"We'll explain when you'll let us in. Would you please unlock the door?"

There was a click on the intercom, and then the buzzing of the front door.

They walked up a flight of stairs, studying the nameplates on the doors.

"Here it is," said Martin, pointing to the one on the left.

He rang the bell. When they heard footsteps approaching from inside, they both took a step back. The door opened, but the safety chain was still on. A young man in his twenties peered at them suspiciously.

"Are you Rasmus Jonsson?" asked Patrik.

"Who wants to know?"

"As we said, we're from the police. We want to talk to you about Mats Sverin, the person who sublet you this apartment."

"Is that so?" His tone of voice bordered on impudence, and he still hadn't removed the safety chain.

Patrik felt annoyance creeping over him, and he glared at the young man.

"Either you let us in so we can have a quiet, friendly conversation. Or I make a few calls, and you'll end up having your entire apartment searched while you spend the rest of the day and maybe part of tomorrow down at the station."

Martin glanced at his colleague. It wasn't like Patrik to issue empty threats. They had no reason to search this apartment or to take Jonsson in for questioning.

For several seconds no one spoke. Then the man unhooked the safety chain.

"Fucking fascists," said Rasmus Jonsson, backing into the hall.

"Wise decision," said Patrik.

There was a heavy scent of hash hovering over the apartment, which explained why the young man had shown such reluctance to allow the police in. When they entered the living room they saw piles of anarchist literature and antiestablishment posters tacked up on the walls. Clearly they were in enemy territory.

"Don't get too comfortable. I'm studying, and I don't have time for shit like this." Rasmus sat down at a small desk, which was cluttered with books and notepads.

"What are you studying?" asked Martin. They didn't run into many anarchists in Tanumshede, and he was genuinely curious.

"Political science," said Rasmus. "In order to get a better understanding of how we've ended up in this bloody mess, and how we can change society." He sounded as if he were lecturing first graders, and Patrik stared at him in amusement. He wondered whether life and the passage of time would eventually alter this young man's ideals.

"Are you subletting this apartment from Mats Sverin?"

"Why are you asking?" said Rasmus. The sun shone through the living-room window, and Patrik realized that he was looking at someone who had the exact same shade of red hair as Martin. But Rasmus had chosen to grow a beard, so the impression was even more intense than with Martin.

"I repeat: Are you subletting this apartment from Mats Sverin?" Patrik spoke calmly, though he was beginning to lose patience.

"Yes, that's correct," Rasmus admitted reluctantly.

"I'm sorry to tell you that Mats Sverin is dead. Murdered." Rasmus stared at him.

"Murdered? What the hell do you mean? And what does this have to do with me?"

"Nothing, hopefully. But we're trying to find out more about Mats and his life."

"I don't really know him, so I can't be much help."

"Let us decide that," said Patrik. "Did you sublet the place furnished?"

"Yes. Everything in the apartment belongs to him."

"He didn't take anything with him?"

Rasmus shrugged. "I don't think so. He packed up anything that was personal in nature, like photographs and so on. But then he drove all of it to the garbage dump. He said he wanted to get rid of the old junk."

Patrik glanced around. There seemed to be as few personal belongings here as in the apartment in Fjällbacka. They still had no idea why, but apparently Mats Sverin had wanted to make a fresh start. Patrik turned again to Rasmus.

"How'd you get the apartment?"

"Through an ad. He needed to rent it out fast. Apparently he'd been assaulted and he wanted to leave town."

"Did he tell you anything about it?" Martin interjected.

"About what?"

"The assault," said Martin patiently. The source of the sweet smell in the apartment was obviously making the young student a bit foggy.

"No, not really." Rasmus hesitated, which roused Patrik's interest.

"But . . . ?"

"But what?" Rasmus began rocking the desk chair from side to side.

"If you know anything about the attack on Mats, we'd appreciate hearing about it."

"I don't cooperate with cops." His eyes narrowed.

Patrik took a couple of deep breaths to calm himself down. This guy was really getting on his nerves.

"My offer stands. A nice, calm conversation with us, or else we call in the troops—and that means the apartment will be searched while you take a trip down to the station."

Rasmus stopped rocking the chair. He sighed. "I didn't see anything personally, so you've got nothing on me. But you should have a talk with old man Pettersson upstairs. He seems to have seen a lot."

"Why hasn't he told the police?"

"You'll have to ask him. All I know is that there's been talk in the building that the old guy knows something." Rasmus pressed his lips together, and they realized they'd had all they were going to get out of him.

"Thanks for your help," said Patrik. "Here's my card, in case you happen to think of anything else."

Rasmus glanced at the card Patrik held out, then took it, holding it between his thumb and index finger, as if it smelled bad. Then he deliberately dropped it into the wastepaper basket.

Patrik and Martin were both relieved to go back out to the landing and leave the cloying smell of hash behind.

"What a nasty piece of work." Martin shook his head.

"I'm sure life will catch up with him some day," said Patrik, hoping that he wasn't getting as cynical as he sounded.

They went upstairs and rang the bell next to the nameplate that said *F. Pettersson*. An elderly man opened the door.

"What do you want?" He sounded as cross as Rasmus. Patrik silently wondered if there was something in the water that was affecting the mood in this building. Everybody seemed to have gotten out on the wrong side of the bed.

"We're from the police, and we'd like to ask you a few questions about a previous tenant named Mats Sverin. He lived in the apartment below." What with sullen anarchists and grumpy old men, Patrik's patience was at breaking point. It took a real effort to stay calm.

"Mats? Now that was a strange boy," said the man without showing any intention of letting them in.

"He was assaulted outside the building before he moved away."

"The police have already been here to ask about that."

The man leaned on his cane. Sensing indecision, Patrik moved a step closer.

"We have reason to believe that you know more than you've told the police."

Pettersson looked down and then motioned them inside with his head.

"Come in," he said, shuffling along the hall to lead the way.

This apartment was not only much brighter than the apartment below, it was also much more pleasantly decorated, with classic furniture and paintings on the walls.

"Have a seat," said the old man, pointing his cane at a sofa in the living room.

Patrik and Martin did as he said and then introduced themselves. They learned that the man's first name was Folke.

"I'm afraid I have nothing to offer in the way of refreshments," said Folke, his tone much less belligerent than before.

"That's okay. We're actually in a bit of a hurry," said Martin.

"As I was saying . . ." Patrik cleared his throat. "From what we understand, you have information regarding what happened to Mats Sverin the night he was assaulted."

"Hmm . . . I'm not so sure about that," said Folke.

"It's important that you tell the truth this time. Because Mats has been murdered." The old man's startled expression gave Patrik a moment's petty satisfaction.

"That can't be right."

"Unfortunately, it is. And if you have anything to tell us about the assault, I'd appreciate hearing it now."

"It's not good to get involved. There's no knowing what those types might do," said Folke, placing his cane on the floor in front of him. He clasped his hands on his lap, suddenly looking very old and fragile.

"What do you mean by 'those types'? According to Mats's own statement to the police, it was a bunch of young thugs who attacked him."

"Young thugs," snorted Folke. "Those weren't young thugs! No, those were the sort of guys that you should never get mixed up with. I don't understand how a nice boy like Mats would end up in their company."

"What do you mean by that, sir?" asked Patrik. He suddenly found himself taking a more formal tone with the elderly gentleman.

"Motorcyclists."

"Motorcyclists?" Martin looked at Patrik in surprise.

"The kind you read about in the papers. Like Hells Angels and the Bandits, or whatever they're called."

"Bandidos," Patrik automatically corrected him as all sorts of thoughts began whirling through his mind. "If I understand you correctly, it wasn't kids who assaulted Mats, it was a motorcycle gang?"

"Yes, that's what I said. Are you deaf, son?"

"Why did you lie to the police and tell them that you hadn't seen anything? I was told there were no witnesses to the incident." Patrik couldn't hide his frustration. If only they'd known about this from the beginning.

"It's best to stay out of the way of those types," Folke stubbornly insisted. "It had nothing to do with me. I don't like to get involved in other people's business."

"So that's why you said that you hadn't seen anything?" It was one of the things Patrik found hardest to accept: people who stood by and watched, then threw up their hands and said it wasn't their concern.

"It's best to stay out of the way of those types," Folke repeated, but he couldn't look them in the eye.

"Did you see anything that might give us a lead as to who these guys were?" asked Martin.

"They had an eagle on their backs. A big, yellow eagle."

"Thank you," said Martin, and got up to shake the old man's hand. After a moment's hesitation, Patrik did the same.

A short time later they were on their way to Uddevalla. Both of them were deeply engrossed in their own thoughts.

⌘

Erica couldn't wait any longer. After pulling herself together, she called Kristina and asked her to babysit. And as soon as she heard her mother-in-law's car door slam, she threw on her jacket, rushed outside, and drove toward Falkeliden. When she got there she remained sitting in the car for a long time. Maybe she ought to stay away for a while and leave them in peace. Anna's brief phone message was a bit confusing. She might have misinterpreted what her sister had said.

Erica gripped the steering wheel as she sat there with the engine switched off. She didn't want to make a mess of things.

There had been occasions in the past when Anna had accused her of barging in and trying to meddle in her affairs. And often she was right. When they were growing up, Erica had wanted to compensate for what she thought was a lack of love from their mother. Now she knew better, and Anna did too. Elsy had loved them, but she hadn't been capable of showing it. And the two sisters had grown close over the past few years, especially after all the trouble with Lucas.

At this moment, Erica wasn't at all sure what to do. Anna had her own family, after all. Dan and the children. Maybe they needed to have her to themselves. Suddenly Erica caught sight of her sister in the kitchen window. She fluttered past like a ghost, then turned and peered at Erica's car. She raised her hand and motioned for her to come inside.

Erica flung open the car door and hurried up the steps. Dan opened the door before she could ring the bell.

"Come in," he said, and she saw a thousand different emotions flit across his face.

"Thanks." Hesitantly she stepped inside, hung up her jacket, and with a strange feeling of reverence went into the kitchen.

Anna was sitting on a chair at the kitchen table. She hadn't spent the entire time in bed, so Erica had seen her downstairs before. But since the accident, Anna hadn't seemed truly present. Now she did.

"I listened to your phone message," said Erica, sitting down across from Anna.

Dan poured each of them a cup of coffee and then discreetly left to join the noisy kids in the living room so the two sisters could talk in peace.

Anna's hand shook slightly as she raised the cup to her lips. She looked almost transparent. Fragile. But her gaze was steady.

"I was so scared," said Erica, feeling the tears begin to fall.

"I know. I was scared too. Scared to come back."

"But why? I mean, I understand. I get that . . ." She struggled to find the right thing to say. How could she put words to Anna's grief when the truth was that she really didn't understand the first thing about it?

"It was dark. And it hurt less to stay in the dark than to be out here with all of you."

"But now?" Erica's voice quavered. "Now you're here."

Anna nodded gently and took another sip of coffee.

"Where are the twins?"

Erica didn't know what to say, but Anna seemed to understand her hesitation. She smiled.

"I'm so anxious to meet them. Who do they take after? Are they very much alike?"

Erica looked at her, still cautious about how to react.

"They're actually not much alike. Not at all. Noel is louder. He makes it very clear when he wants something, and he's so determined. Stubborn as could be. Anton is almost the exact opposite. He never screams for anything, and he seems to think that life is great. He's very content, in other words. But I don't really know who they take after."

Anna's smile grew wider. "You're kidding me, right? You've just described yourself and Patrik. And you're not the one who's content, if I may say so."

"No, but . . ." Erica began, then fell silent as she realized that what Anna had said was true. She had, in fact, described herself and Patrik, though she knew that he wasn't always as calm at work as he was at home.

"I'd like to meet them," Anna said again, looking steadily at Erica. "There's no connection to what happened to me, and you know it. It wasn't the twins' fault that my son died."

Now Erica couldn't hold back her tears. She wasn't yet convinced that Anna was right about there being no connection—it would take time for her to believe that—but the guilt that she'd carried during the past months slowly began seeping away.

"I can bring them over any time you like. As soon as you feel up to it."

"Why don't you go get them now? If it's not too much trouble, that is," said Anna. Some color had returned to her cheeks.

"I could phone Kristina and ask her to drive over with them."

Anna nodded. A couple of minutes later Erica had arranged for her mother-in-law to bring the boys to the house.

"It's hard," said Anna. "I feel like the darkness is there even now, hovering on the edge of things."

"At least you're here now." Erica put her hand over her sister's. "I came over to see you while you were lying in bed upstairs, and it was so awful. It felt like only a shell of you was there."

"I suppose that's true. It almost makes me panic when I realize that I'm still partially that way. I feel like a fragile shell, and I don't know how I'm going to fill myself up again. It's so empty. In here." She placed her hand over her stomach, stroking it gently.

"Do you remember anything about the funeral?"

"No." Anna shook her head. "I remember it was important for us to have a funeral, that it seemed necessary. But I can't recall the actual service."

"That's okay," said Erica, getting up to refill their cups.

"Dan said that it was your idea to take turns lying next to me in bed."

"Well, it wasn't really my idea." Erica sat down again and told her sister about Vivianne.

"Give her my best wishes and thank her. I'd still be lying upstairs in the dark otherwise, and I might have gone even deeper into myself. So deep that I might not have been able to come back at all."

"I'll tell her hello when I see her."

The doorbell rang, and Erica leaned back, craning her neck so she could look into the front hall.

"That's probably Kristina and the twins."

She was right. Dan opened the front door to Erica's mother-in-law. She got up and went out to the hall to help, noticing happily that both of her sons were awake.

"They're such little angels," said Kristina, casting a glance toward the kitchen.

"Would you like to come in?" asked Dan, but Kristina shook her head.

"No, I think I'll go on home now. It's best if you have some time to yourselves."

"Thank you," said Erica, giving her a hug. As much as she'd come to like her mother-in-law, consideration for others wasn't really Kristina's strong suit.

"It was no problem. I'm happy to help out. You know that." Then she hurried off.

Erica picked up a bassinet in each hand and took the twins into the kitchen.

"This is your aunt Anna," she said as she carefully placed them on the floor next to Anna's chair. "And this is Noel and Anton."

"There's certainly no question who the father is, at any rate." Anna sat down on the floor next to the babies, and Erica did the same.

"A lot of people have said they're the spitting image of Patrik. But we can't really see it ourselves."

"They're wonderful," said Anna. Her voice quavered, and Erica was suddenly worried that she might have done the wrong thing by arranging for Anna to meet her sons. Maybe it was too soon. Maybe she should have said no.

"It's fine," said Anna, as if she could read Erica's thoughts. "Can I hold them?"

"Of course you can," said Erica. She sensed Dan's presence behind them. He was undoubtedly holding his breath, just as she was. He too was uncertain as to whether this was the right thing to be doing.

"Let's take little Erica first," said Anna with a smile as she picked up Noel. "So you're stubborn like your mamma. Is that right? Your mother is going to have her hands full with you, isn't she?"

She held him close, nuzzling the hollow of his neck. She put Noel down and picked up Anton, repeating the same process with him. Then she rocked him in her arms.

"They're lovely, Erica." Anna looked at her sister over Anton's little bald head. "They're simply lovely."

"Thank you," said Erica. "Thank you."

∽∞∾

"What have you found out?" Patrik asked eagerly as he and Martin came into the hospital waiting room.

"Well, I told you most of it on the phone," replied Paula. "The boys found a bag containing white powder in a litter basket near the block of apartments. The ones that face the Tetra Pak building."

"Okay. Do we have the bag?" asked Patrik as he sat down.

"It's right here." Paula pointed to a brown paper sack on the table. "And before you ask: yes, we've handled it with the appropriate caution. But unfortunately, a lot of people touched it before it came to us. The kids, teachers, and hospital staff."

"We'll have to do a careful analysis. Could you arrange to have it sent over to the forensics lab? Then we'll have to get fingerprints from everyone who might have touched it. Start by getting the parents' permission to fingerprint the boys."

"Of course," said Gösta, nodding.

"How are the kids?" asked Martin.

"According to the doctors, they've been through a helluva time. It could have ended very badly, but luckily they didn't ingest much of the powder, only a small taste of it. Otherwise we'd be down at the morgue instead of sitting here."

That thought was so awful that no one spoke for a few moments.

Patrik cast a glance at the paper bag. "We should also check whether Mats Sverin's prints are on it."

"Do you think his murder could be drug-related?" Paula frowned, leaning back on the hard sofa. She was having trouble finding a comfortable position, so she ended up leaning forward again. "Did you find out something in Göteborg that might indicate that?"

"No, I can't say that we did. We do have some more information to work on, but I thought we'd discuss it at our usual meeting back at the station later on." He stood up. "Martin and I are going to Fjällbacka to have a word with some of the teachers. Could you make sure the bag gets sent to the lab, Paula? Tell them it's urgent."

She smiled. "They'll probably make that assumption, since it's coming from you."

Nathalie had felt slightly uneasy ever since Erica and Patrik had visited. Should she ask the doctor to come over? Sam still hadn't uttered a sound since they'd arrived on the island. At the same time, she trusted her instincts. All he really needed was time. Time to heal his soul, not his body, which was the only thing a doctor would bother to examine.

She hardly dared think about that night. It felt as if her brain shut down every time those horrific memories started to worm their way into her mind. So how could she expect Sam's little soul to handle it? They had shared the same terror. And she wondered whether they now shared the same fear that it might all catch up with them out here. She tried to soothe him, telling him that they were safe on the island. That nothing horrid could find them here. But she wasn't sure her tone of voice matched her words. Because she herself didn't quite believe what she was saying.

If only Matte . . . Her hand shook at the thought of him. He would have been able to protect them. She hadn't wanted to tell him everything when they spent that evening and night together. But she had told him a little, enough so that he'd know why she was no longer the same person. She knew that she should have told him the whole story. If only they'd had more time, she would have confided everything in him.

She sobbed, then took a deep breath, trying to regain her composure. She didn't want Sam to see her despair. He needed to feel secure. That was the only thing that would erase from his memory the sound of the shots, the only thing that would take away the images of blood and his pappa. It was her job to make everything right again. Matte couldn't help her.

⁂

It took a while to collect all the fingerprints they needed. Two sets were still missing: the ambulance medics were out on their rounds and wouldn't be back until later. But Paula had a feeling that they were wasting time gathering all these fingerprints. Her instincts told her that it was more important to determine whether Sverin's prints were on the bag. And they needed to know soon.

Paula knocked on the office door.

"Come in." Torbjörn Ruud looked up as she entered.

"Hi. I'm Paula Morales from the Tanum police. We've met a few times before." She suddenly came off all self-conscious. Usually Paula was a stickler when it came to the proper procedures; after all, rules existed for a reason. Yet she'd come here to ask Torbjörn to disregard all the protocols. In her opinion, this was one of those times when the rules needed to be bent a little.

"Oh yes, I remember you." Torbjörn motioned for her to take a seat. "How's the investigation coming along? Have you heard from Pedersen yet?"

"No, we're expecting the ME's report on Wednesday. Otherwise we don't really have much to go on, and we haven't made as much progress as we'd hoped . . ."

She fell silent, wondering how to formulate her request.

"Something happened today," she said at last. "We don't yet know whether it has anything to do with the murder . . ." She set the paper bag on the desk.

"What's in there?" asked Torbjörn, reaching for it, but drawing back his hand before he touched it.

"Cocaine," Paula told him.

"Where did you find it?"

Paula quickly briefed him on what had taken place, and what the boys had told them.

"It's not often that I have a bag of cocaine dropped on my desk," said Torbjörn, studying Paula.

"I realize that," she said, feeling her face turn red. "But you know how things will go. If we send the bag to the forensics lab, it will take forever to get the results. And I have a feeling this could be very important. So I was wondering if we could be a bit flexible in this situation. If you could help me find out just one thing, I'll handle all the formalities afterward. And I'll take full responsibility, of course."

Torbjörn was silent for a few moments.

"What exactly do you want me to do?" he asked finally, but he still looked dubious.

Paula told him what she wanted, and Torbjörn nodded.

"Okay, we'll make an exception this once. But if anything happens, you'll have to take responsibility, as you said. And you need to make sure that everything looks above board."

"You have my word," said Paula, feeling a surge of excitement. She was right, she was convinced of that. Now all that remained was to prove it.

"Okay, come with me," said Torbjörn, getting to his feet. Paula hurried after him. She was going to owe him big-time after this.

∽

"I hope I didn't offend you today," said Erling. He didn't dare look her in the eye.

Vivianne was poking at her food and didn't answer. As always when he found himself in disfavor, he felt his whole body knotting with discomfort. He really shouldn't have passed on what Bertil had said about the food served at Badis. What had he been thinking? Vivianne knew what she was doing, and he shouldn't have interfered.

"Darling, you're not cross with me, are you?" He stroked the back of her hand.

She didn't respond, and he had no idea what to do next. He could usually coax her out of a bad mood, but today she seemed in no mood to be placated.

"It looks as if a lot of people have accepted the invitation to the dedication festivities on Saturday. All the Göteborg celebrities are coming. Real celebrities, not just those B-list personalities like Robinson-Martin. And I've managed to book the band Arvingarna."

Vivianne frowned. "But I thought Garage was going to play."

"They'll just have to settle for being the opening act. We can't very well turn down Arvingarna, can we? They'll bring in a big crowd." He was starting to forget his worries. Project Badis usually had that effect on him.

"But we won't receive our money until next Wednesday. I hope you realize that." Vivianne raised her eyes from her plate and seemed to be thawing a bit.

Delighted, Erling continued on the same track.

"That's no problem. The council will cover the bills until then, and most of the suppliers have agreed to wait for payment, since we've guaranteed the money. So you don't need to worry."

"That's good to know. Of course, Anders is the one who's in charge of all those matters, so I assume he's been informed."

Now a little smile had begun to play over her lips, and Erling suddenly had butterflies in his stomach. After lunch, when he was filled with anxiety because of his faux pas, a plan had begun to take shape in his mind. He couldn't understand why he hadn't thought of it earlier. Fortunately, he was a man of action, and he knew how to get things done without too much advance preparation.

"Sweetheart," he said.

"Hmm," said Vivianne, taking another bite of the quorn casserole she'd made.

"There's something that I want to ask you . . ."

Vivianne stopped chewing and raised her eyes to look at him. For a moment Erling thought he saw a flash of fear, but it disappeared at once, and he assumed he was imagining things. It was probably just nervousness.

With an effort he knelt down next to her chair and took a small box out of his jacket pocket. The label on the lid said

*Nordholms Gold & Watches.* It didn't take a genius to guess what was inside.

Erling cleared his throat. This was a big moment. He took Vivianne's hand, and in a solemn voice he said:

"I would like to take this occasion to ask if you would do me the great honor of marrying me." What had sounded so elegant in his mind now sounded merely pompous. He tried again: "Er, that is, I was thinking that we should get married."

That wasn't much better, and he could hear his heart pounding in his chest as he waited for her answer. In truth he was pretty certain what she would say, but he couldn't be absolutely sure. Women could be so capricious.

Vivianne was silent a little too long, and Erling's knees started to hurt. The box was trembling in his hand, and he felt tension gathering along his spine.

At last she took a deep breath and said, "Yes, of course, we should get married, Erling."

Relieved, he took the ring out of the box and slipped it on her finger. It wasn't expensive, but Vivianne didn't care much about material things, so why should he spend a lot of money on a ring? And he'd gotten it for an excellent price, he thought happily. Tonight he counted on getting good value for his money. It had been a disturbingly long time since they'd made love, but this evening they were going to celebrate.

He got up, his back creaking, and took his seat again. With a triumphant expression he raised his glass to Vivianne in a toast, and she replied in kind. For a second he thought he saw that strange look in her eyes again, but he pushed the notion aside and took another sip of his wine. Tonight he had no intention of falling asleep on the sofa.

⌾

"Is everyone here?" said Patrik. The question was purely rhetorical. He could see exactly who was present; he was merely trying to cut through the buzz of voices in the kitchen.

"Everybody's here," said Annika.

"Then there are a few things we need to discuss." Patrik brought out the big flip-chart that they used for jotting down notes at their meetings.

"First of all: the boys are continuing to improve, and they don't seem to have suffered any permanent injury."

"Thank God for that," said Annika, relieved.

"Before we discuss the cocaine discovery, I'd like to run through what else happened today. Paula, how did you do with your examination of the briefcase?"

"So far we haven't come up with anything specific," said Paula briskly. "But we're hoping to know more very soon."

"There was a load of financial documents inside the briefcase," Gösta clarified, after glancing at Paula. "We couldn't make much sense of them, so we gave them to Lennart, Annika's husband. He's going to take a look before we send them on."

"Good," said Patrik. "When does Lennart think he can get back to us?"

"Day after tomorrow," said Paula. "As for the cell phone, there was nothing of interest on it. I sent the laptop over to the tech division, but God only knows when we'll get a report from them."

"It's frustrating, I know, but there's nothing we can do about that." Patrik crossed his arms. He'd started writing notes on the flip-chart. In big letters it now said: *Lennart, Wednesday.*

"What did Sverin's old girlfriend say? Did she have anything to tell us?" asked Mellberg. Everyone was startled, and Patrik looked at his boss in astonishment. He hadn't thought Mellberg paid the slightest attention to what was happening with the investigation.

"Mats went out to see her on Friday evening, but he left sometime during the night," he said, adding the information to the chart. "That narrows down the time frame for the murder. The earliest it could have happened is in the wee hours of Saturday morning, which also fits with the sound that the neighbor heard. I'm hoping that Pedersen's report will help us to pinpoint the time of death even further."

"Did she strike you as fishy? Maybe this was all a lovers' quarrel?" Mellberg went on. Ernst, who was lying at Mellberg's feet, reacted to his master's tone of voice by lifting his head inquisitively.

"'Fishy' isn't exactly the word that I'd use to describe Nathalie, but she did seem a bit distracted. She and her son are living out there on the island at the moment. Apparently she and Mats hadn't been in contact for many years, which tallies with what his parents told us. The pair of them were probably reliving old memories that evening."

"Why did he leave in the middle of the night?" asked Annika, turning automatically to Martin, who looked insulted. He was a steady family man these days, but there had been a time when he'd had quite an active love life. The object of his affections had a tendency to change from week to week, and sometimes his colleagues still teased him about that. He'd turned his back on that sort of life the minute Pia came into the picture, and he'd never regretted his decision.

Now he reluctantly thought back to the old days.

"I don't see anything strange about that. Sometimes a guy just wants to avoid all that chatter the morning after." Everyone looked at him in amusement, and he shrugged. "What? Boys will be boys." He blushed, making his freckles turn bright red.

Patrik couldn't help grinning, but then he forced himself to turn serious again.

"No matter what his reason, we now know that Mats went home in the early hours of Saturday morning. But the question is, what has happened to his boat? He must have gone home in it."

"Have you checked the ads in *Blocket*?" Gösta reached for a biscuit and dipped it in his coffee.

"I checked all the classified ads yesterday, but so far nothing," said Patrik. "There's an alert posted for the boat, and I've talked to the Coast Guard, so they'll keep an eye out for it."

"It seems like a strange coincidence for the boat to go missing right now."

"Yes, it does. Has anyone searched his car?" Paula sat up straighter and looked at Patrik.

He nodded. "Torbjörn and his team went over Sverin's car. It was parked outside the building where he lived. But they didn't find anything."

"I see," said Paula, leaning back in her chair again. She thought they might have missed something, but Patrik clearly had the situation under control.

"What did you find out in Göteborg?" asked Mellberg as he slipped a biscuit to Ernst.

Patrik and Martin exchanged glances.

"Well, it turned out to be a very productive trip. Would you like to tell everybody about our meeting with social services, Martin?"

Patrik's decision to let his youngest colleague take the lead a bit more often had an immediate effect. Martin's face lit up. He delivered a clear and concise report on their meeting with Sven Barkman and the information he'd given them about the Refuge and its collaboration with social services. After casting an inquiring glance at Patrik, he went on to describe their visit to the Refuge office.

"As far as we know, there were no threats directed at Mats because of his work with the organization. At least, the director of the Refuge claims to be unaware of any such threats. She did, however, allow us to look through the documents pertaining to the women who received help from the Refuge during the last year that Sverin worked there. We're talking about approximately twenty cases."

Patrik nodded, and then Martin continued:

"Without more to go on, it's impossible to determine whether one or more of the cases might be of interest and warrant further investigation. We took notes and wrote down the names of those women that Mats was the contact person for. So we can follow up on that. I have to say, though, it was bloody depressing to sit there and read through those files. Many of the women were living in a hell that we can't even begin to imagine . . . It's really hard to describe." Embarrassed, Martin fell silent, but Patrik understood exactly what he meant. He too had been affected by the hellish lives that they had glimpsed in those files.

"We're considering talking to the other staff members," said Patrik. "And maybe also some of the women who received help from the Refuge while Mats worked there. But that might not be necessary. We now have a statement from a witness that could give us a potential lead." He paused for effect, noting that he had everyone's full attention. "From the start I've felt there was something odd about the assault on Mats. So Martin and I took a chance and went over to the building where Mats used to live in Göteborg. As you know, the attack took place right outside the front entrance, and we managed to speak with a neighbor. We wanted to confirm what Sverin had reported about the teenagers who beat him up. But according to the neighbor, who actually witnessed the incident, the assault was carried out by a much older gang. 'Motorcyclists' was the term he used."

"Oh, shit," said Gösta. "Why would Sverin lie about that? And why didn't the neighbor say anything before?"

"As far as the neighbor is concerned, it's the usual story. He was scared and didn't want to get involved. A lack of civic courage, in other words."

"And Sverin? Why didn't he tell the truth?" Gösta persisted.

Patrik shook his head. "Maybe he was scared too. Maybe it's as simple as that. But these biker gangs aren't known for attacking random people on the street, so there must be a reason for the assault."

"Did the neighbor recall any identifying marks?" asked Paula.

"An eagle," said Martin. "The neighbor said that he saw an eagle on their jackets. So it should be easy enough to find out which gang it was."

"Get in touch with our colleagues in Göteborg. I'm sure they can help you with that," said Mellberg. "That's what I've been saying all along. An ugly customer, that Sverin. If he was mixed up with those types, it's no surprise that he ended up in the morgue with a bullet in his skull."

"I wouldn't go that far," said Patrik. "We have no idea whether Mats was mixed up with them, and so far there's no indication that he was involved with any sort of criminal activity. I thought we should start by asking the director of Refuge whether she recognizes this particular biker gang, and whether her organization has had any contact with them. And, as Bertil suggested, we should also talk to our colleagues in Göteborg. Yes, Paula?"

Paula had raised her hand.

"Well, the thing is," she began hesitantly. "I decided to speed things up a bit today. Instead of sending the paper bag to the lab, I took it straight to Torbjörn Ruud. You know how long it can take to get lab results. Things end up at the bottom of the pile, and . . ."

"Yes, we know. Go on," said Patrik.

"I had a chat with Torbjörn, and I sort of asked him for a favor . . ." Paula shifted uncomfortably, not sure how Patrik was going to react. "To be blunt, I asked him to do a quick comparison between the fingerprints on the bag and Sverin's prints." She took a deep breath.

"Go on," Patrik said again.

"He found a match. Mats's fingerprints were on the paper bag containing the cocaine."

"I knew it!" Mellberg pumped his arm in triumph. "Narcotics and associating with a criminal gang. I knew all along he had something to hide."

"I still say that we should proceed with caution," said Patrik, although he didn't sound as sure of himself as before.

Thoughts were whirling through his mind, and he was trying to make sense of them. To a certain extent, he had to agree with Mellberg. But the image that he'd formed of Mats Sverin after talking to his parents, his coworkers, and Nathalie did not fit with this new information. For all that Patrik had consistently had a feeling that something wasn't quite right, he couldn't accept Bertil's assessment of Mats.

"Was Torbjörn quite sure?"

"Yes, one hundred percent sure. The bag will now be sent on, and his conclusion will be formally confirmed. But Torbjörn is positive that Mats Sverin held that bag in his hands."

"That changes things. We need to find out from the known local drug dealers whether they had anything to do with Mats. But I have to say this doesn't seem . . ." Patrik shook his head.

"Rubbish," Mellberg snorted. "I'm convinced that once we start nosing around, we'll soon have our killer. A good old-fashioned drug-related murder. That shouldn't take much effort to solve. He probably owed somebody money."

"Hmm . . ." said Patrik. "In that case, why would he toss the bag in a litter basket near his apartment? Or maybe somebody else did that? Either way, we need to check this out. Martin and Paula, could you have a talk with the usual suspects tomorrow?"

Paula nodded as Patrik began writing on the flip-chart. He knew that Annika always took notes at their meetings, but writing on the chart gave him a feel for the big picture.

"Gösta and I will talk to Mats's colleagues, and this time we'll ask more specific questions."

"Specific?"

"Such as whether they heard or observed anything that might explain why Mats would be holding a bag of cocaine."

"You mean we're going to ask them whether he was a drug addict?" Gösta didn't seem too enthusiastic.

"We don't know that yet," said Patrik. "We won't have Pedersen's report until the day after tomorrow. Until then, we have no idea what kind of substances may have been found in Mats's body."

"We could ask his parents," suggested Paula.

Patrik swallowed hard. It wasn't a task he relished, but he knew she was right.

"Yes, we need to talk to them too. Gösta and I will handle it."

"What about me?" asked Mellberg.

"I'd really appreciate it if you, as the chief of police, could hold down the fort here," said Patrik.

"Right. That's probably best." Mellberg stood up, visibly relieved, and Ernst followed close on his heels. "We all need to get our beauty sleep now. It's going to be a busy day tomorrow, but we'll solve this case soon. I can feel it in my bones." Mellberg rubbed his hands together but didn't receive much of a response from his subordinates.

"Okay, you heard what Bertil said. Go home and get some sleep. We'll start fresh in the morning."

"What about the Göteborg lead?" asked Martin.

"We'll start at this end first. Then we'll review it when we have more information. Not tomorrow, though. That means we'll probably make another trip to Göteborg on Wednesday."

They ended the meeting, and Patrik went out to his car. He spent the whole drive home lost in thought.

# Fjällbacka 1871

*I*t was early autumn before she was allowed to leave Gråskär for the first time. The boat pitched alarmingly, just as it had when she came to the island, but this time she didn't feel panicked. She had been living so close to the sea and had become familiar with the sounds and shiftings of the water. If it hadn't been for the fact that the sea had kept her imprisoned on the island, she would probably have learned to appreciate it. And now the waves were carrying her to the harbor.

The surface of the sea was as smooth as a mirror, and she couldn't resist the temptation to lower her hand and trail her fingers alongside the boat. She had to lean over the railing to reach the water as she held her other hand protectively over her stomach. Karl stood at the helm. He seemed so different now that he was away from Gråskär and the shadow of the lighthouse. He looked so handsome. She hadn't thought about that in a long time. The spiteful glint in his eyes had made him seem ugly. But if she looked at him now, as he stood facing forward, she was able to recall what she had once found so attractive. Maybe *it's the island that has changed him, thought Emelie. Maybe there's something about the island that has unleashed the evil inside of him. She immediately pushed any such thoughts away. What a fool she was. But Edith's words of warning still echoed in her mind.*

*For today, at least, they were leaving the island behind, if only for a few hours. She was going to see other people, help to buy the groceries they needed, and have coffee with Karl's aunt, who had invited them to her home. She also had an appointment to see the doctor. She wasn't worried. She knew that everything was as it should be with the child, who kicked so eagerly inside of her stomach. Nevertheless, it would be a blessing to have this confirmed.*

*She closed her eyes and smiled. The wind felt lovely against her skin.*

*"Sit down properly," said Karl, making her jump.*

*She remembered again that first boat trip. She had been newly married and filled with anticipation. Karl had still treated her kindly back then.*

*"I'm sorry," she said, lowering her gaze. She didn't really know why she was apologizing.*

*"And no unnecessary chatter." His voice was cold. He was once again the same Karl as on the island. The ugly man with the malevolent eyes.*

*"Yes, Karl." She kept her eyes lowered, staring at the deck of the boat. The child inside of her kicked so hard that she gasped for breath.*

*Suddenly Julian got up from where he was seated across from her and sat down next to her. A little too close. Then he grabbed hold of her arm.*

*"You heard what Karl said. No talking. No talking about the island or anything that is no one else's concern." His fingers dug deeper into her arm, and she grimaced.*

*"All right," she said, the pain making her eyes fill with tears.*

*"Now sit quietly in the boat. It's easy to fall overboard," said Julian in a low voice. Then he let go of her arm and stood up. He went back to his seat and turned to look in the direction of Fjällbacka, which was now visible up ahead.*

*Trembling, Emelie placed her hands over her stomach. She suddenly found herself missing those she had left behind on the island. Those who were forced to stay there, unable ever to leave. She promised herself that she would pray for them. Maybe God would hear her prayer and show mercy to those poor lost souls.*

*When the boat docked near the marketplace, she blinked away her tears and felt a smile spread across her lips. Finally she was among other people again. She was still able to leave Gråskär.*

# 15

**M**ellberg was whistling as he walked to work. He could tell that it was going to be a good day. He'd made a few phone calls the previous night, and he now had half an hour to get everything ready.

"Annika!" he called as soon as he stepped into the reception area.

"I'm sitting right here. No need to shout."

"Would you mind getting the conference room ready?"

"The conference room? I didn't know we had a fancy place like that here at the station." She took off her computer glasses, letting them dangle from the cord around her neck.

"Okay, okay. You know what I'm talking about. The only room that has space for lots of chairs."

"Lots of chairs?" Annika was starting to feel uneasy. It didn't bode well that Mellberg had turned up so early in the morning, and in such high spirits.

"Yes. Rows of chairs. For the press."

"The press?" said Annika, feeling her uneasiness settle into a hard lump in her stomach. What was he up to now?

"Yes, the press. I'm holding a press conference here, and the reporters need someplace to sit." He was prattling like a child.

"Does Patrik know about this?" Annika glanced at her phone.

"Hedström will find out about it soon enough if he ever decides to come in to work. It's already two minutes past eight," said Mellberg, ignoring the fact that he himself rarely turned up at the station before ten. "The press conference is scheduled for eight thirty. In less than half an hour. And as I was saying, we need a room."

Annika again glanced at her phone, but then she realized that Mellberg wasn't going to leave her alone until she got up off her ass and began arranging chairs in the only room that was suitable. She was hoping that then he'd go into his office and she'd have a chance to call Patrik, to warn him what was about to happen.

"What's going on?" Gösta asked from the doorway as Annika began setting up chairs.

"Mellberg is apparently going to hold a press conference here."

Gösta scratched the back of his head and looked around the room.

"Does Hedström know?"

"That's exactly what I asked Bertil. And no, evidently he doesn't. This is one of Mellberg's bright ideas, and I haven't been able to get hold of Patrik to warn him."

"Warn me about what?" Patrik appeared in the doorway behind Gösta. "What's going on?"

"We're to have a press conference in . . ." Annika looked at her watch. "Ten minutes."

"You're kidding, right?" said Patrik, but he could see from Annika's expression that this was no joke.

"That bloody . . ." Patrik turned on his heel and headed straight for Mellberg's office. Then they heard a door open, followed by the sound of agitated voices before the door closed.

"Ay ay ay," said Gösta, again scratching the back of his head. "I think I'll go to my office." He disappeared so fast that Annika wondered whether he'd actually been standing there at all, or if he was just a mirage.

Muttering to herself, she continued setting up chairs, though she'd have given anything to be a fly on the wall in Mellberg's office. She could hear voices rising and falling behind his door, but she couldn't make out any of the words. Then the bell rang, and she hurried to open the front door.

Fifteen minutes later, the journalists had all gathered. There was a muted hum of voices in the room. Some of them knew each other, but some didn't. Reporters had arrived from *Bohus-läningen*, *Strömstads Tidning*, and the other local newspapers. Even the local radio station was represented, as well as the evening papers—the "big guns," who were not frequent visitors to the area. Annika bit her lip nervously. Mellberg and Patrik still hadn't appeared, and she wondered whether she should say something or just wait to see what happened. She chose to do the latter, although she kept casting glances at Mellberg's office door. Finally it was flung open, and Mellberg came rushing out, bright red in the face and with his hair in disarray. Patrik stood in the doorway with his hands on his hips, and in spite of the distance, Annika could see his angry expression. As Mellberg came toward her at top speed, Patrik went into his own office and slammed the door, rattling the pictures hanging on the wall of the corridor.

"Young whippersnapper," muttered Mellberg as he pushed past Annika. "Who does he think he is, coming here and telling me how to run things?" He stopped, took a deep breath, and fixed his comb-over. Then he went into the room.

"Is everyone here?" he asked, smiling broadly as the crowd murmured affirmatively.

"Good. Then let's get started. As I told you last night, the investigation into the murder of Mats Sverin has taken a new direction." He paused, but no one seemed to have any questions yet. "Those of you from the local press have probably already heard that we had a serious incident occur here yesterday. Three little boys were taken to emergency at Uddevalla Hospital."

A few of the reporters nodded.

"The boys had found a bag containing white powder. They thought it was candy, so they tasted it. But the powder turned out to be cocaine, and it made them sick. They were taken to the hospital by ambulance." He paused again, straightening his back. He was in his element. He loved press conferences.

The reporter from *Bohusläningen* raised his hand, and Mellberg nodded brusquely.

"Where did the boys find the bag?"

"In Fjällbacka, in a litter basket outside the block of apartments near Tetra Pak."

"Have they suffered any permanent injury?" A journalist from one of the evening papers asked the question without waiting his turn.

"The doctors say that they'll make a full recovery. Luckily, they didn't ingest very much of it."

"Do you think that a known addict tossed away the bag? Or is there a connection to the murder? You implied something of the sort in your opening remarks," interjected the reporter from *Strömstads Tidning*.

Mellberg was enjoying the way the tension was building in the audience. They could all see that he had a scoop for them, and he planned to make the most of it. After a moment of silence, he said:

"The bag was in a litter basket right outside Mats Sverin's front door." He slowly looked from one person to the next. Everyone's eyes were fixed on him. "And we've identified his fingerprints on the bag."

A murmur started up in the room.

"Holy shit," said the guy from *Bohusläningen*. Several hands shot up.

"So do you think it was a drug deal that went bad?" The journalist from *GT* was swiftly taking notes as his photographer snapped one picture after another. Mellberg reminded himself to suck in his stomach.

"We don't want to say too much at this stage, but that's one of the theories we're working on, yes."

He enjoyed hearing his own voice. If he'd made different choices in life, maybe he could have been the spokesman for the Stockholm police department. He could have been the one appearing on TV when the Swedish politician Anna Lindh was murdered, or sitting on a morning talk show sofa to discuss the Palme assassination.

"Is there any suggestion that drugs were involved in the murder?" asked the reporter from *GT*.

"I'm not at liberty to say," replied Mellberg. It was all a matter of throwing the press titbits. Not too many, not too few.

"Have you looked into Sverin's background? Did you find any evidence of drugs?" Now it was the guy from *Bohusläningen* who managed to get in a question.

"I can't discuss that either."

"Have you received the report from the postmortem?" the *GT* reporter continued. The more tactful journalists were starting to give him angry looks.

"No. We're expecting the results sometime this week."

"Do you have any suspects?" The *Göteborgs-Posten* journalist managed to get a word in edgewise.

"Not at the present moment. Okay, I think that's as much as we can say for the time being. You have all the information we're able to give you, and we'll keep you posted as the investigation progresses. But in my opinion, we're on the verge of a major breakthrough in the case."

His words prompted a flood of questions, but Mellberg merely shook his head. They'd have to be satisfied with the few scraps he'd given them. Practically floating on air as he returned to his office, he congratulated himself on a job well done. Patrik's door was closed. What a sourpuss, Mellberg thought, his face clouding over. Hedström ought to realize who was in charge here at the station and who had the most experience with these matters. And if that didn't suit him, he could just look for a job elsewhere.

Mellberg sat down in his chair, propped his feet up on the desk, and clasped his hands behind his head. He had definitely earned a little nap.

<hr/>

"Who should we start with?" asked Martin as he emerged from the vehicle. They were in the parking lot next to the block of apartments.

"How about Rolle?"

Martin nodded. "Sure. It's been a while since we had a chat with him. It won't hurt to pay him a little attention."

"I just hope he's coherent."

They walked up the stairs, and when they were standing outside Rolle's apartment, Paula rang the doorbell. No one answered, so she pressed the bell again, harder this time. A dog started barking.

"Shit. That's his German shepherd. I forgot about the dog."
Martin shook his head uneasily. He didn't like big dogs, especially dogs owned by drug addicts.

"That dog's not dangerous. I've met her several times." Paula
rang the bell again, and now they heard footsteps approaching.
The door opened a crack.

"Yes?" Rolle said suspiciously. Paula took a step back so
he could see her properly. Standing at the man's feet, the
dog was barking loudly and looking as if she wanted to leap
through the narrow door opening. Martin moved over to
the staircase leading to the floor above and took two steps
up, even though he couldn't have explained why that should
be any safer.

"Paula. From the Tanum police. We've met a few times
before."

"Right. I recognize you," the man said, but he made no
move to remove the safety chain and let them in.

"We'd like to come in for a moment. Just have a little talk
with you."

"A little talk? Oh sure. I've heard that before." Rolle didn't
budge.

"I mean what I say. We're not here to arrest you." Paula
spoke calmly.

"Okay, okay, come in." He opened the door.

Martin stared at the German shepherd. Rolle was holding
the dog by the collar.

"Hi, doggie." Paula knelt down to scratch her behind the
ears. The dog finally stopped barking and allowed herself to
be petted. "What a good girl you are. All right now. You like
that, don't you?" She kept on scratching the big ears, to the
dog's obvious delight.

"She's a good dog, my Nikki," said Rolle, letting go of
her collar.

"Come on, Martin." Paula motioned for him to come closer. Still not entirely convinced, Martin came down from the stairs to join Paula and Nikki. "Let her say hello to you. She's really sweet."

Martin reluctantly obeyed. He began petting the big dog and was rewarded with a lick on his hand.

"See? She likes you," said Paula.

"Hmm," said Martin, a bit embarrassed. The dog really didn't seem so dangerous up close.

"Now we need to have a chat with your master," said Paula, standing up. Nikki looked up at her for a moment before dashing inside.

"I like your decor," said Paula, looking around as they entered the apartment.

Rolle rented a one-room place, and it was clear that neatness was not a high priority. The furnishings consisted of a narrow wood-framed bed with mismatched linens, an old TV console that stood in the middle of the room, a scruffy-looking sofa, and a rickety coffee table. Everything looked as if it had been pulled out of a Dumpster, which was very likely the case.

"Let's sit in the kitchen." Rolle led the way.

Martin knew that, according to police records, the man was thirty-one, but he looked at least ten years older. Tall, slightly stooped, greasy hair that reached to the collar of his faded, checked shirt. His jeans were covered with stains and torn in several places—the result of long-time wear and not a fashion statement.

"I haven't got any refreshments," said Rolle sarcastically, snapping his fingers at Nikki to make her lie down on the floor at his feet.

"That's not necessary," said Paula. Judging by all the plates and cups piled up in the sink and on the bench, there wouldn't be any clean china even if they'd been offered coffee.

"So what do you want?" He sighed heavily and then began gnawing on his right thumbnail. He'd already chewed some of his nails down so far that the fingertips looked inflamed.

"What do you know about the guy across the hall?" asked Paula, looking at him steadily.

"What guy?"

"Who do you think?" said Martin. He found himself motioning for Nikki to come over and lie down next to him instead.

"The guy who was shot in the head? Is that who you mean?" Rolle calmly met Paula's gaze.

"Good guess. Well?"

"Well what? I don't know anything about it. I told you that before."

Paula cast an inquiring glance at Martin, who nodded. He was the one who had talked to Rolle when the police were knocking on doors after the murder.

"Since then, a number of things have come to our attention." Paula's voice had suddenly grown cold. Martin thought to himself that he wouldn't want to get on her bad side. She might be small, but she was tougher than most guys he knew.

"Really?" Rolle's tone was nonchalant, but Martin could see that he was listening.

"Did you hear about the boys who found a bag of cocaine outside?" asked Paula. Rolle stopped chewing on his thumbnail.

"Cocaine? Where?"

"In a paper bag, right there in that bin." She nodded toward the green litter basket that was visible through the kitchen window.

"Cocaine in a paper bag?" Rolle repeated, with a gleam in his eye.

That must be the ultimate fantasy for a drug addict, thought Martin. To find a bagful of drugs in a litter basket. It'd be like winning the lottery.

"Yes. And the little boys tasted it. They ended up in the ER. It could have killed them," said Paula.

Rolle nervously ran his hand over his greasy hair.

"What a fucking mess. Kids shouldn't touch stuff like that."

"They're seven years old. They thought it was a bag of candy."

"But you said they're going to be okay, right?"

"Yes, they'll be okay. And hopefully they'll never go near that sort of shit again. The kind of shit you deal in."

"I'd never sell to kids. You know me, for Christ's sake. I'd never give any to kids."

"We don't think you would, either. As I said, they found it in the litter basket." Paula allowed her voice to soften a bit. "But there's a connection between the guy who was murdered and that bag of cocaine."

"What connection?"

"That's not important." Paula waved her hand dismissively. "What we want to know is whether you had any contact with him, whether you know anything. And no, we're not going to arrest you for it if you did," she went on before Rolle had time to speak. "We're investigating a murder, and that's much more important. But it could be to your benefit in the future if you decide to help us now."

Rolle seemed to ponder what she'd said. Then he shrugged and sighed.

"Unfortunately, I've got nothing for you. I saw the guy in passing now and then, but I never talked to him. It didn't look like we'd have much to talk about. Although, if what you say is true, maybe we had more in common than I thought." He laughed.

"And his name never cropped up among your other contacts?" Martin interjected. Nikki had moved over near him, and he was scratching her neck.

"No," said Rolle reluctantly. He probably would have liked to earn some extra points with them, but evidently he knew nothing.

"If you should hear anything, give us a call, okay?" Paula took out a business card and handed it to Rolle, who shrugged again and then stuffed the card in the back pocket of his stained jeans.

"Sure. You can find your own way out, can't you?" He grinned as he reached for a container of snuff lying on the table. When his shirt sleeve hitched up, they could see the needle tracks in the crook of his arm. Rolle was addicted to heroin, not cocaine.

Nikki saw them to the door, and Martin patted her before they closed the door behind them.

"One down. Three more to go." Paula started down the stairs.

"It's so much fun spending the day with a bunch of druggies," said Martin, as he followed.

"If you're lucky, you might meet some more dogs. I've never seen anybody switch so fast from sheer terror to total infatuation."

"She was nice," muttered Martin. "But I really don't care for big dogs."

⁂

Erica felt as if a weight had been lifted from her shoulders. In her heart she knew that there was a long road ahead, and that Anna might suddenly slip back into the darkness. Nothing was certain. At the same time, Anna was a fighter. She had proved that in the past, pulling herself up through sheer willpower, and Erica was convinced that she'd be able to do it this time too.

Patrik was also pleased to hear about Anna's progress when she'd told him. This morning he'd been whistling when he left for work and she hoped that his good mood would last. Ever since he'd collapsed and been taken to the hospital, she had kept a close watch on his moods—maybe too close. She was terrified that something might happen to Patrik. He was her best friend, her beloved husband, and the father of her wonderful children. She didn't want him to put all that at risk by working himself to death. She refused to allow him to do that.

"Hi. We're back," she said as she pushed the stroller into the library.

"Hi," said May cheerfully. "You didn't finish what you were working on yesterday, did you?"

"No. There are a few more reference books that I'd like to look at. I'd thought I'd do it now, while the boys are asleep."

"Okay. I'm here if you need anything."

"Thanks," said Erica, sitting down at a table.

It was a complicated business, trying to find what she was looking for. She pulled out a notepad so she could write down references to other sources that turned up along the way. Usually they turned out to be no help, leading her to information about other islands and areas in Sweden. Occasionally, however, she found a few helpful nuggets, just as with any other research project.

She leaned forward to peer into the stroller. The twins were sleeping peacefully. Stretching out her legs, she returned to her reading. It had been a long time since she read any ghost stories. When she was a kid, she'd devoured all the scariest tales she could find. Everything from Edgar Allan Poe to Nordic folktales. Maybe that was why, as an adult, she'd started writing books about real murder cases. They were almost like an extension of the creepy tales from her childhood.

"You can make copies of anything you want to take with you," said May, helpfully.

Erica nodded and got up. She'd found a number of pages that she wanted to read more closely at home. There was a familiar tingling sensation in her stomach. She loved delving for information and assembling the puzzle, piece by piece. After spending several months thinking about nothing but babies, she was thoroughly enjoying having a more grown-up project to occupy her mind. She'd told her publisher that she wouldn't begin work on her next book for at least six months, and that was a decision that she intended to stick to. Nevertheless, she needed to keep her brain busy until then, and this felt like a good start.

Having stuffed a stack of photocopies in the babies' diaper bag, she headed for home at a leisurely pace. The twins were still asleep. Life was good.

⸎

"That fucking bastard, that damn shitty . . ." Patrik's language wasn't usually so coarse, but Gösta could certainly understand his mood. This time Mellberg had really outdone himself.

Patrik pounded his hand on the dashboard so hard that Gösta jumped.

"Remember your heart. You're not supposed to get stressed."

"Okay, okay," said Patrik, forcing himself to take a couple of deep breaths to calm down.

"Over there." Gösta pointed to a parking place. "So how are we going to approach this?" he asked as they sat in the car for a moment.

"There's no reason to beat around the bush," said Patrik. "It's all going to be in the newspapers, anyway."

"Yes, but we need to focus on this, regardless of what Mellberg has done."

Patrik looked both surprised and chastened as he cast a glance at Gösta.

"You're right. What's done is done, and we need to get on with the job at hand. I suggest that we start with Erling and then talk to Mats's other coworkers. We need to find out whether any of them noticed any signs of narcotics or drug use."

"Like what?" Gösta hoped that he didn't sound too stupid, but he really didn't know what Patrik was getting at.

"Well, for instance, if Mats was behaving strangely or exhibiting any other unusual signs. He seems to have been such a proper sort, but maybe they can think of something that doesn't fit the pattern."

Patrik got out of the car and Gösta followed. They hadn't phoned ahead to find out who might be at work in the council offices, but when they spoke to the receptionist, they found they were in luck. Everyone was present.

"Could we see Erling first?" Patrik asked, making it sound more like a command than a request.

The young receptionist nodded, looking slightly alarmed. "He doesn't have any meetings scheduled," she told them as she pointed down the corridor. Gösta already knew where to find Erling's office.

"Hello there," said Patrik as they stood in the doorway.

"Well, hello!" Erling stood up and came forward to shake hands. "Come in, come in. How's it going? Have you made any progress? I heard about those little boys yesterday. Good Lord, what's the world coming to these days?" He took his seat behind the desk.

Patrik and Gösta exchanged glances and then Patrik began.

"The thing is, there seems to be a connection." He cleared his throat, uncertain how to proceed. "We have reason to believe that there's a connection between Mats Sverin and the cocaine that the boys found."

There was utter silence in the room as Erling stared at them and they waited calmly for his response. His surprise seemed genuine.

"I . . . but . . . how . . ." he stammered, and then merely shook his head.

"You didn't suspect anything of this kind?" asked Gösta to help him along.

"No, absolutely not. We'd never have thought . . . never in a million years." For once he seemed at a loss for words.

"So there was no sign that things weren't as they should be with Mats? Mood swings, turning up late for work, or difficulties keeping appointments? Maybe a change in his appearance?" Patrik studied him closely, but Erling seemed truly stunned.

"No. As I said before, Mats was the epitome of a stable person. Maybe a bit reserved when it came to certain topics, but that's all." He shuddered. "Could that be the reason? Because of drugs? Maybe it wasn't so strange after all that he never discussed his personal life."

"We don't know for sure. But it's possible that was the reason."

"This is terrible. If it comes out that we had somebody like that on the staff, somebody working here, it'll be disastrous."

"I'm sorry to tell you this," said Patrik, again cursing to himself, "but the fact is that this morning Bertil Mellberg held a press conference regarding this matter, so it's bound to be made public sometime today."

As if on cue, the receptionist appeared in the doorway with flushed cheeks and a worried expression.

"I don't know what it's about, Erling, but the phones have gone crazy. A lot of reporters are trying to reach you, and both *Aftonbladet* and *GT* want to speak to you urgently."

"Dear God," said Erling, wiping his brow where beads of sweat had gathered.

"The only advice we can give you is to say as little as possible," said Patrik. "I'm very sorry that the press has become involved at such an early stage in the investigation. Unfortunately, there was nothing I could do to prevent it." His tone was bitter, but Erling seemed oblivious to anything but his own crisis situation.

"Of course I'll have to take the calls," he said, nervously rocking his chair back and forth. "I'll deal with the situation, but a drug addict working for the town . . . How on earth am I going to explain that?"

Patrik and Gösta realized that they weren't going to get another sensible word out of Erling, so they stood up.

"We'd like to talk to the rest of the staff," said Patrik.

Erling glanced up, although he wasn't really focusing on them.

"Yes, of course. Go ahead and talk to them. Now, if you'll excuse me, I need to take these calls." He wiped his forehead with a handkerchief.

They slipped out and knocked on the door of the next office.

"Come in," chirped Gunilla, apparently blissfully unaware of what was going on.

"Could we have a few words with you?" said Patrik.

Gunilla nodded cheerfully. Then her expression changed.

"Oh dear. Here I am, merrily laughing. But I assume you're here about Mats, right? Have you found out anything?"

Patrik and Gösta exchanged glances, uncertain how to tell her what they wanted to know. They sat down.

"We have a few more questions," Gösta began. He was feeling nervous. They really didn't know enough to ask sensible questions.

"All right. Go ahead and ask," said Gunilla, smiling again.

Evidently she's the kind of person who's always upbeat and positive, thought Gösta. The sort that he wouldn't want to have around at seven in the morning before he'd had his first cup of coffee. He was grateful that his late wife had shared his own sour mood in the morning, so they'd been able to grumble to themselves in peace and quiet.

"Yesterday several schoolkids ended up in the hospital after tasting some cocaine that they'd found," said Patrik. "Maybe you heard about it?"

"Yes, it was awful. But I heard the incident was going to have a happy ending."

"That's right. The boys are okay. But it turns out that there are certain connections between the incident and our investigation."

"Connections?" said Gunilla, shifting her perky chipmunk eyes from Patrik to Gösta and back again.

"Yes. We've found a link between Mats Sverin and the cocaine." He could hear that he sounded a tad formal, which always happened when he was feeling uncomfortable. And this was not a pleasant situation. But it was better for Mats's coworkers to hear about it now instead of reading it in the newspapers.

"I don't understand."

"Well, we think that Mats may have used cocaine." Gösta looked down at the floor.

"Mats?" Gunilla's voice sounded a bit shrill. "You can't be serious. Not Mats."

"We know nothing of the circumstances," Patrik explained. "And that's why we're here. To find out if anyone noticed anything strange about him."

"Anything strange?" repeated Gunilla. Patrik could see that she was starting to get upset. "Mats was the nicest man you could ever meet. I just can't imagine that he . . . no, I just can't."

"So there was nothing about his behavior that struck you as odd? Nothing that you noticed?" Patrik was clutching at straws now.

"Mats was an exceptionally wonderful person. It's unthinkable that he would ever have been involved with drugs." She tapped her pen on the desk to emphasize each syllable.

"I'm sorry, but we have to ask these questions," Gösta apologized. Patrik nodded and stood up. Gunilla stared after them angrily as they left her office.

An hour later they were finally able to leave the council building. They had talked to the other staff members, and they had all reacted in the same way. Not one of them could imagine Mats Sverin being mixed up in drugs.

"That confirms my own feeling. And I never even met the man," said Patrik when they were once again sitting in the car.

"I agree, and we still have the worst ahead of us."

"I know," said Patrik as he drove out of the parking lot and headed for Fjällbacka.

⌘

He had found them. She knew it. Just as she knew that she had nowhere else to go. She had used up all possible avenues of escape. It had been so easy to shatter everything once again. All it took was a postcard—without any message or the name of the sender, postmarked in Sweden—to destroy her hopes for the future.

Madeleine's hand shook as she turned over the postcard after studying the side that was blank except for her name and new address. No words were necessary; the picture on the card said everything. The message couldn't be more clear.

Slowly she walked over to the window. Down in the courtyard Kevin and Vilda were playing, unaware that their lives were about to change again. She clutched the postcard in her hand until it was damp with sweat from her fingers. She was trying to gather her thoughts to make a decision. The children looked so happy as they played with the other kids. The desperate look in their eyes had gradually disappeared, though a hint of fear still remained. They had seen too much, and that was something she could never undo, no matter how much love she showered upon them. And now everything was wrecked. This had seemed like the only option, one last chance at a normal life. Leaving behind Sweden and him and everything else. How could she give them a sense of security when her last lifeline had been cut?

Madeleine leaned her forehead against the windowpane. It felt cold on her skin. She watched as Kevin helped his sister up the ladder of the slide. He placed his hands on Vilda's rear end, both supporting her and giving her a little push. Maybe she'd done the wrong thing by making him the man in the family. He was only eight. But he had so naturally assumed the role and taken care of his girls, as he called them. He had grown with the responsibility, finding security in his role. Kevin raised his hand to push a lock of hair out of his eyes. He looked so much like his father, but he had her heart. Her weakness, as *he* used to call it as the blows fell.

Slowly she began beating her forehead against the window. Hopelessness filled her body. Now nothing was left of the future she had planned. Harder and harder she pounded her head on the glass, noticing how the familiar feeling of pain brought with it a strange sense of calm. She dropped the postcard and the picture of the eagle with outspread wings slid along the floor. Outside, Vilda came down the slide with a delighted smile.

# Fjällbacka 1871

So how are things going for you out there on the island? It must be terribly lonely." Dagmar gave Emelie and Karl a piercing look as they sat stiffly on the loveseat across from her. The delicate little coffee cup looked so out of place in Karl's rough hand, but Emelie managed to hold it with a certain elegance as she sipped at the hot drink.

"How could it be otherwise?" replied Karl, without looking at Emelie. "Lighthouses are always in isolated locations. But we're doing fine. And I'm sure you know that, don't you?"

Emelie was embarrassed. She thought Karl was speaking too brusquely to Dagmar, who was his aunt, after all. Emelie had been taught to show respect for her elders, and the minute she met Dagmar, she instinctively liked this woman. And besides, of all people, Dagmar ought to understand her situation, because she too had been married to a lighthouse keeper. Her husband, Karl's uncle, had held that job for many years. While Karl's father had been expected to inherit and run the family farm, his younger brother had been given free rein to choose *his own path. Karl's uncle had been his hero and the one who inspired him to turn to the sea and to lighthouses for his living. During the period when he was still talking to her, Karl had once told Emelie about this. But now Karl's uncle Allan was dead, and Dagmar lived alone in a little house next to Brand Park in Fjällbacka.*

*"Of course I know what it's like," said Dagmar. "And you knew what you were getting into after hearing Allan's stories. The question is whether Emelie knew."*

*"She's my wife, so she has no say in the matter."*

*Emelie again felt embarrassed by her husband's behavior, and tears began welling up in her eyes. But Dagmar merely raised her eyebrows in response to Karl's remark.*

*"I heard from the pastor that you're a very good housekeeper," she said, turning to Emelie.*

*"Thank you. I'm glad he thinks so," said Emelie quietly, bowing her head to hide her blush. She took another sip of coffee, savoring the taste of it. It was seldom that she could enjoy a good, strong cup of coffee. Karl and Julian usually bought very little of that particular staple when they were in Fjällbacka. They'd rather spend their money at Abela's tavern, she thought bitterly.*

*"How's it going with the man who is helping you out? Is he a good worker who does a decent job? We had all sorts of different types helping us, Allan and I. Some of them weren't much good."*

*"He does a fine job," said Karl, setting his cup down on the saucer so hard that it rattled. "Isn't that so, Emelie?"*

*"Yes," she murmured, although she didn't dare look at Dagmar.*

*"How did you happen to find him, Karl? I hope he was recommended to you, because you can never trust adverts in the newspapers."*

*"Julian came with excellent references, and he quickly proved himself worthy of the praise."*

*Emelie looked at her husband in surprise. Karl and Julian had worked together for years on a lightship. That was something she'd learned when she overheard them talking about it. Why didn't he mention that now? She pictured Julian's glowering eyes. His hatred that had grown worse and worse, and she shuddered at the thought of it. All of a sudden she noticed that Dagmar was looking at her.*

*"So you have an appointment to see Dr. Albrektson today, is that right?" she said.*

*Emelie nodded. "I'm going to see him a little later. So he can make sure that everything is fine with the baby boy. Or girl."*

*"Looks to me like it's a boy," said Dagmar, and there was genuine warmth in her eyes as she gazed at the rounded swell of Emelie's stomach.*

*"Do you have any children? Karl didn't tell me," said Emelie. She wasn't shy about the attention her pregnancy attracted, and she was eager to talk about the miracle happening inside of her body, especially with someone who had been through the same experience. But she instantly received a sharp poke in the side.*

*"Don't be so nosy," Karl snapped.*

*Dagmar waved aside his admonishment. But her eyes were sad as she replied. "Three times I carried the same joy that you now carry. But each time the good Lord had other plans. All of my babies are up there in heaven." She looked up, and in spite of her sorrow, she seemed confident in her belief that God knew best.*

*"I'm sorry, I . . ." Emelie didn't know what to say. She was dismayed that she hadn't known.*

*"That's all right, my dear," said Dagmar. Impulsively she leaned forward and placed her hand on Emelie's.*

*This kind gesture, the first in such a long time, almost made Emelie burst into tears. But because of Karl's blatantly scornful stare she controlled herself. The three of them sat in silence for a while. Emelie could feel the elderly woman's gaze boring into her, as if she could see the chaos and darkness. Dagmar didn't remove her hand, which was thin and sinewy and marked by years of hard work. But Emelie thought it was beautiful—just as beautiful as the woman's narrow face, with all its furrows and wrinkles, revealing a well-lived life that had been filled with love. Emelie suspected that Dagmar's gray hair, which was pulled back in a tight bun, would still fall in lovely, thick tresses to her waist when she took out the hairpins.*

*"Since you don't know your way around here, I was thinking of going with you to see the doctor," said Dagmar at last, lifting her hand from Emelie's.*

*Karl immediately voiced his objection.*

*"I can do that. I know where his office is. There's no need for you to trouble yourself."*

*"It's no trouble." Dagmar gave Karl a stern look. Emelie saw that some sort of power struggle was playing out between them, and finally Karl gave in.*

*"All right, if you insist," he said, setting down the dainty china cup. "I can take care of some more important matters in the meantime."*

*"Yes, you do that," said Dagmar, continuing to stare at him without blinking. "We'll be gone about an hour, and then you can meet us back here. Because I assume you don't intend to do the grocery shopping without your wife, do you?"*

*It was formulated as a question, but Karl correctly took it to be an order, and he replied with a slight shake of his head.*

*"All right then." Dagmar got up and motioned for Emelie to follow her. "Let's go, you and I, so we won't be late. And we'll let Karl tend to his own business."*

*Emelie didn't dare look at her husband. He had lost the tug-of-war, and she knew that she would pay for it later. But as she followed Dagmar out to the street and headed toward the marketplace, she pushed all such thoughts aside. She wanted to enjoy the moment, no matter how high the price might be. She stumbled on a cobblestone, and Dagmar's hand instantly gripped her arm. Feeling safe, Emelie leaned on her for support.*

# 16

A ny word from Patrik and Gösta?" Paula asked as she paused outside Annika's door.

"No, not yet," said Annika. She started to say something else, but Paula was already on her way to the kitchen, eager for some coffee in a clean cup after spending all morning in the filthy homes of drug addicts. Just to be safe, she nipped into the toilet to wash her hands thoroughly. When she turned around, Martin was waiting his turn.

"Great minds think alike," he said with a laugh.

Paula dried her hands and stepped aside to make room for him at the sink.

"Shall I pour you a cup too?" she asked over her shoulder as she headed for the kitchen.

"Sure, thanks," he shouted over the sound of the water gushing from the tap.

The coffee pot was empty, but the hotplate underneath was red-hot. Paula swore, switched off the coffeemaker, and began scrubbing the black residue in the bottom of the pot.

"It smells like something's burning in here," said Martin as he came in.

"Some idiot took the last drop of coffee and then forgot to turn off the machine. Wait a few minutes and I'll make a fresh pot."

"I wouldn't mind a cup myself," said Annika behind them. She went over to the kitchen table and sat down.

"How's it going?" asked Martin as he sat down next to Annika and put his arm around her.

"I assume you haven't heard the news?"

"What news?" Paula was scooping coffee into the filter.

"There was quite a commotion here this morning."

Paula turned around to give her an inquiring look.

"What happened?"

"Mellberg held a press conference."

Martin and Paula exchanged glances, as if to see if they'd really heard the same thing.

"A press conference?" said Martin, leaning back in his chair. "You're kidding!"

"No. Apparently he got this brilliant idea last night and called the newspapers and the radio stations. And they all took the bait. We had a full house here. Even *GT* and *Aftonbladet* turned up."

Paula set down the holder for the coffee filter with a bang.

"Is he out of his mind? What the hell was he thinking?" She could feel her pulse quicken and forced herself to take a deep breath. "Does Patrik know about this?"

"Oh yes, he certainly does. They were locked in Mellberg's office for some time. I couldn't hear much, but the language they were using wasn't exactly child-friendly."

"I'm not surprised," said Martin. "Why on earth would Mellberg do a thing like that? I assume he talked about the cocaine angle, right?"

Annika nodded.

"It's really premature to do that. We don't know anything yet," said Paula, sounding discouraged.

"I'm sure that's what Patrik tried to point out," said Annika.

"How did the press conference go?" Paula finally pressed the button on the coffeemaker and sat down as the coffee began dripping into the pot.

"Well, it was the usual Mellberg circus. I wouldn't be surprised if the newspapers put the story on the front page tomorrow."

"Bloody hell," said Martin.

For a few moments none of them spoke.

"So how'd it go for you?" asked Annika, deciding to change the subject. She'd had more than enough of Bertil Mellberg for one day.

"Nothing much to report." Paula got up and poured coffee into three mugs. "We talked to some of the usual suspects who are involved with drug dealing around here, but we didn't find any links to Mats."

"I can't really picture him hanging out with the likes of Rolle and his pals." Martin gratefully took the mug of steaming black coffee that Paula handed him.

"I have a hard time picturing that myself," she said. "Still, it was worth a try. Not that there's much cocaine being bought and sold around here. It's mostly heroin and amphetamines."

"Have you heard from Lennart?" asked Martin.

Annika shook her head.

"No. I'll tell you as soon as he gets back to me. I know that he spent a couple of hours going through the documents last night, so at least he's making progress. And he said he'd have something for you by Wednesday."

"Good," said Paula, sipping her coffee.

"When will Patrik and Gösta be back?" asked Martin.

"No idea," said Annika. "They were heading for the council offices first. After that, they wanted to see Mats's parents in Fjällbacka. So it might take a while."

"I hope they talk to the parents before the newspapers start phoning them," said Paula.

"I wouldn't count on it," said Martin, looking gloomy.

"Damn Mellberg," said Annika.

"Yes, damn Mellberg," muttered Paula.

The three of them sat there in silence, staring down at the table.

⁊◌⁊

After a couple of hours spent reading and looking up things on the Internet, Erica could tell that she had been sitting too long. Still, her research had turned out to be quite productive. She'd found out a lot about Gråskär, its history, and the people who had lived there. And those who, according to legend, had never left the island. It made no difference that she didn't believe in ghosts. The tales fascinated her, and part of her really did want to believe.

"We need some fresh air, don't you think?" she said to the twins, who were lying close together on the blanket on the floor.

It was always quite a job to get the two babies and herself dressed to go out, but it was starting to get easier now that they could make do with lighter coats. Sometimes there was a cold wind blowing, so she decided it was better to be safe than sorry and put a warm cap on each boy. A short time later they were off. She was looking forward to the day when she could get rid of the ungainly stroller. It was heavy and hard to maneuver, even though it did provide her with plenty of much-needed exercise. Though she knew it was ridiculous to worry about the extra pounds she'd put on during her pregnancy, she'd never learned to be satisfied with her own body. She hated the fact that she was so shallow, so predictably like a girl, but that little voice inside her head kept whispering that she wasn't good enough. And it seemed harder to get rid of that negative self-image than anything else.

She picked up the pace and felt herself starting to sweat. Not many people were out, but she nodded at everyone she met, exchanging a few words here and there. Many asked after Anna, but Erica gave only brief replies. It seemed too personal to talk about how her sister was doing—or not doing. She didn't yet want to share the warm feeling that she carried in her heart. It still felt much too fragile.

After passing the row of boathouses, looking like a string of red beads, she paused to look up toward Badis. She wanted to have a brief talk with Vivianne, to thank her for the advice she'd offered regarding Anna, but climbing the steep flight of stairs seemed an insurmountable task. After a moment's thought she realized that she could take the alternative path. It would be an easier climb than taking the stairs. Having made up her mind, she turned the heavy stroller around and steered it toward the next street. When she finally reached the top of the steep hill, she was panting so hard that she thought her lungs would explode. But at least she'd made it, and now she could take the upper road to Badis.

"Hello?" She took a couple of steps inside. The twins were still in the stroller, which she had parked just outside the front entrance. She wasn't about to go to the trouble of lifting them out until she knew whether Vivianne was there.

"Hi!" Vivianne came around the corner, and her face lit up when she saw Erica. "Were you passing through the neighborhood?"

"I'm not disturbing you, am I? If I am, please say so. We're just out for a walk, me and the boys."

"You're not disturbing me in the least. Come on in. Would you like something to drink? Where are the twins?" Vivianne glanced around, and Erica pointed toward the stroller.

"I left them in the stroller because I wasn't sure that you'd be here."

"It feels like I'm here twenty-four/seven lately," said Vivianne, laughing. "Can you manage on your own to bring the babies inside while I go get us some refreshments?"

"Of course I can manage. I don't have much choice," said Erica with a smile as she went outside to get her sons. There was something about Vivianne that made other people feel good in her presence. Erica wasn't sure what it was, but she seemed to feel stronger around Vivianne.

She set the bassinets on the table and sat down.

"I didn't think that you'd be interested in green tea, so I brewed some more of that special rot-gut that you like."

Vivianne winked and put a cup in front of Erica, who gratefully accepted the pitch-black coffee. She cast a suspicious glance at the pale contents of Vivianne's cup.

"You get used to it, believe me," said Vivianne, taking a sip. "Green tea has tons of antioxidants. They help the body prevent cancer. Among other things."

"Oh, really?" said Erica, sipping her coffee. No matter how healthy the tea was, she couldn't do without caffeine.

"How's your sister doing?" asked Vivianne as she patted Noel on the cheek.

"Better, thanks." Erica smiled. "That was why I dropped by. I wanted to thank you for the advice you gave me. I think it helped."

"Good. There are lots of studies showing the healing effect of human touch."

Noel started whimpering. After giving Erica an inquiring look, Vivianne lifted him out and held him in her arms.

"He likes you," said Erica when her son instantly settled down. "He's not always that easy to please."

"They're both wonderful." Vivianne nuzzled her nose against Noel's and he tried to grab her hair with his chubby little fists. "So now you're probably sitting there wondering if you dare ask me why I've never had any kids of my own."

Erica nodded with embarrassment.

"I've just never been that lucky," said Vivianne, rubbing Noel's back.

Something flashed, and Erica looked at Vivianne's hand. "Wait a minute. Are you engaged? That's fantastic! Congratulations!"

"Thank you. Yes, it's great." Vivianne smiled faintly and then averted her eyes.

"Forgive me for saying this, but you don't sound very enthusiastic."

"I'm just tired," said Vivianne, pushing her plait over her shoulder so Noel couldn't reach it. "We've been working night and day, so it's hard to muster much enthusiasm for anything. But of course I'm very happy."

"So maybe now . . ." Erica motioned toward Noel and then realized she was being a little too pushy. At the same time, she couldn't help herself. She could see so much longing in Vivianne's face when she looked at the babies.

"We'll have to wait and see," said Vivianne. "Why don't you tell me about your work. I realize that you're on maternity leave right now and fully occupied with these two, but have you started thinking about a new book?"

"Not yet. But I'm enjoying doing some research of my own in the meantime. Just to keep on my toes, so I don't fill up my whole brain with baby prattle."

"Research on what?" Vivianne was gently bouncing Noel up and down on her knee, and he appeared to be enjoying the motion. Erica told her about the trip out to Gråskär, about Nathalie, and about the local nickname for the island.

"Ghost Isle," said Vivianne pensively. "There's usually a grain of truth in those kinds of old legends."

"Well, I don't know if I really believe in ghosts and spirits," laughed Erica.

"There are plenty of things that we may not see but that still exist," said Vivianne, staring at her with a solemn expression.

"Are you saying that you believe in ghosts?"

"I think that's the wrong word to use. But after working with health issues for so many years, it's my experience that there's more to us than the physical body. A person consists of energies, and energy never disappears; it just becomes transformed."

"Have you personal experience? Of ghosts, or whatever you want to call them?"

Vivianne nodded. "Many times. It's a natural part of our existence. So if that's the rumor about Gråskär, then there's probably some truth to it. You should talk to Nathalie. I'm sure she's seen manifestations out there. Provided she's receptive to that sort of thing, of course."

"What do you mean by that?" Erica was fascinated by this subject, hanging on Vivianne's every word.

"Some people are more receptive to such things—things that we can't perceive with our normal senses. Just as some people can hear or see better than others, some of us are more perceptive than others. But everyone has the potential for developing that ability."

"I'm skeptical about that. But I'd love to be proven wrong."

"So go back out to Gråskär." Vivianne winked. "There seem to be plenty of them out there."

"All that aside, the island has an interesting history. I'd like to discuss it with Nathalie and find out what she knows. If nothing else, maybe she's curious about the island's past. And I could at least tell her what I've found out so far."

"I can see that you're not very good at putting aside all other interests while you're on maternity leave," said Vivianne with a smile.

Erica had to agree. It wasn't her strong suit, playing the role of a full-time mother. She reached out for Anton. No doubt Nathalie would enjoy hearing more about the island and its history. Not to mention the ghosts.

⁂

Gunnar looked at the ringing telephone. It was the old-fashioned kind, with a number dial and a heavy receiver sitting on the cradle. Matte had tried to get them to replace it with a wireless phone. He had even given them one as a Christmas present a couple of years back, but it was still in its box somewhere down in the basement. They liked the old phone, he and Signe. Now it made no difference.

He continued to stare at the phone. Slowly his brain worked out that the shrill tone meant that he was supposed to pick up the receiver and answer.

"Hello?" He listened carefully to what the voice on the other end was saying. "That can't be right. What kind of idiot are you? How can you even say such—" Unable to bring himself to continue the conversation, he slammed down the receiver.

A moment later the doorbell rang. Still shaking from the phone call, Gunnar went to the front hall and opened the door. A camera flashed, and a flood of questions was hurled at him. He quickly slammed the door, turned the lock, and leaned his back against the wooden paneling. What was going on? He looked up at the stairs. Signe was resting in the bedroom. He wondered if she'd been awakened by all the commotion. What was he going to say to her if she came downstairs? He didn't understand a word of what they'd told him. It was so preposterous.

The doorbell rang again. He shut his eyes, exhaustion flooding over him. Some sort of conversation was going on outside, but he couldn't make out any of the words. All he could distinguish was the loud and angry tone of the exchange. Then he heard a familiar voice.

"Gunnar, it's Patrik and Gösta from the police. Could you let us in?"

Gunnar pictured Matte in his mind. First alive, then lying on the hall floor in a pool of blood and with the back of his head blown apart. He opened his eyes, turned around, and unlocked the door. Patrik and Gösta slipped inside.

"What's happening?" asked Gunnar. Even to him his voice sounded strange and far away.

"Could we sit down somewhere?" Without waiting for an answer, Patrik turned toward the kitchen.

The doorbell rang again, along with the phone. The two sounds were piercing. Patrik lifted up the receiver, put it down, and then removed it from the cradle.

"I can't switch off the doorbell," said Gunnar in confusion.

Gösta and Patrik exchanged a look over his head, and then Gösta went back to the front door. He stepped outside, hastily pulling the door closed behind him. Once again Gunnar could hear angry voices flinging words at each other. A moment later Gösta returned.

"That should keep them quiet for a while." Then he gently steered Gunnar toward the kitchen.

"We need to speak to Signe too," said Patrik, his expression taking on a hint of embarrassment.

Now Gunnar was truly nervous. If only he knew what this was all about.

"I'll go get her," he said, turning around.

"I'm right here." Signe was coming down the stairs, looking as if she'd just gotten out of bed. She wore a bathrobe wrapped tightly around her, and on one side of her head, her hair was standing on end. "Who keeps ringing the doorbell? And what are you doing here? Have you found out anything?" She fixed her gaze on Patrik and Gösta.

"Let's all go into the kitchen and sit down," said Patrik.

Signe now looked just as uneasy as Gunnar.

"What's happened?" She came down the last steps and followed them to the kitchen.

"Have a seat," said Patrik.

Gösta pulled out a chair for Signe, and then everyone else sat down too. Patrik cleared his throat. Gunnar wanted to cover his ears with his hands; he couldn't bear to hear more about what the voice on the phone had insinuated. As Patrik began speaking, Gunnar looked down at the table. It was all lies—incomprehensible lies. But he realized what was going to happen. The lies would be printed in black and white and become truths. He glanced at Signe and saw that she too understood. The more the police officer talked, the emptier her expression became. He had never seen anyone die before, but that's what he was seeing right now. And there was nothing he could do. Just as he'd been unable to protect Matte, he was now paralyzed as he watched his wife disappear.

He felt a rushing inside of his head. A roaring sound filled his ears, and he thought it strange that none of the others reacted. The sound got louder with the passing of every minute, until he could no longer hear what the policemen were saying. He was merely aware of their lips moving. He felt his own lips move, forming the words to tell them that he needed to use the toilet. He felt his legs standing up and then carrying him toward the hall. It was as if someone else had taken over and was manipulating his body. And he obeyed in order not to listen to the words that he didn't want to hear, in order to get away from that empty look in Signe's eyes.

Behind him they continued to talk as he staggered along the hall, past the toilet, and over to the door that was next to the front entrance. His hand moved of its own accord, pressing down on the handle to open the door. He stumbled but then regained his balance, and slowly, step by step, made his way downstairs.

The basement was shrouded in darkness, but he had no intention of turning on the light. The darkness suited the roaring sound, and it propelled him forward. Fumbling, he opened the cupboard next to the furnace. It wasn't locked, as it should have been, but that didn't matter. If he'd found it locked, he would have smashed it open.

The butt was a familiar shape in his hand after all the elk hunts earlier in the year. Without thinking, he took a bullet out of the box. He wouldn't need more than one, so there was no need to waste time by putting in more. He loaded the bullet, hearing the click, which was strangely audible through the roaring noise that kept getting louder and louder.

Then he sat down on the chair near the workbench. Without hesitation, his finger located the trigger. He gave a start when he felt the steel scrape against his teeth, but after that his only thought was how right this was, how necessary.

Gunnar pulled the trigger. The roaring stopped.

⌘

Mellberg had an unfamiliar pressure in his chest. It was unlike anything he'd ever felt before, and it had started the moment that Patrik phoned from Fjällbacka. An uncomfortable pressure that refused to go away.

Ernst was whimpering in his basket. In his own doglike way, he seemed to sense his master's depressed mood. He got up, shook his huge body for a moment, and then padded over to Mellberg and lay down at his feet. That helped a little, but the unpleasant feeling remained. How could he have known that this would happen? That the man would go down to the basement, stick his hunting rifle in his mouth, and blow his head off? Surely no one could expect him to have foreseen that?

Try as he might to cling to such thoughts, they refused to take hold.

Mellberg stood up abruptly, and Ernst scrambled as his pillow suddenly vanished.

"Come on, old boy, let's go home." Mellberg took the dog's leash from its hook on the wall and fastened it to Ernst's collar.

It was eerily quiet as they stepped out into the corridor. Everyone was holed up in their offices behind closed doors, but he could sense their reproach through the walls. He'd seen it in their eyes. And for perhaps the first time in his life, he was forced to do some soul-searching. A voice inside of him was saying that they might be right.

Ernst was tugging on the leash, so Mellberg hurried out into the fresh air. He pushed away the image of Gunnar lying on a cold gurney, waiting for the postmortem. He also tried not to think about the wife—or rather, the widow, since that was her status now. Hedström had said that she had seemed totally out of it, and she hadn't uttered a sound when the shot was fired in the basement. Patrik and Gösta had rushed downstairs, and when they came back to the kitchen, they found that Signe hadn't moved. She'd been taken to the hospital for observation, but the look in her eyes told Hedström that she would never really be alive again. He'd seen it happen a few times in the course of his career. People who looked as if they were alive, who were breathing and moving about, and yet they were completely empty inside.

Mellberg took a deep breath before opening the door to the apartment. He was on the verge of panic. He wished he could get rid of the pressure in his chest, he wished everything would return to normal. He didn't want to think about what he'd done or not done. He'd never been very good at dealing with the consequences of his actions, nor had it ever bothered him very much when things went wrong. Until now.

"Hello?" Suddenly he longed desperately to hear Rita's voice and feel enveloped by her calm, which always made him feel so good.

"Hi, sweetheart! I'm in the kitchen."

Mellberg unfastened Ernst's leash and kicked off his shoes. Then he followed the dog, who ran toward the kitchen, wagging his tail. Rita's dog Señorita came to meet Ernst, wagging her tail just as happily as they sniffed at each other.

"Dinner in an hour," said Rita, her back turned to him.

Something on the stove smelled delicious. Bertil pushed his way past the dogs, who always seemed to take up as much space as possible, and went to wrap his arms around Rita. Her plump body felt warm and familiar, and he hugged her hard.

"Wow, what brought that on?" laughed Rita, turning around to put her arms around his neck. Bertil closed his eyes, realizing how fortunate he was and how rarely he thought about that. This woman in his arms was everything he'd dreamed of, and he couldn't understand even for a second why he'd ever thought that life as a bachelor was the best way to live.

"So what's going on?" She pulled out of his arms so she could get a proper look at him. "Tell me what's happened."

He sat down at the kitchen table and let the words spill from his mouth. He didn't dare look at her.

"But, Bertil," said Rita, squatting down next to him. "That sounds like it wasn't such a great move on your part."

Oddly enough, it felt good that she didn't try to offer platitudes to comfort him. She was right, after all. It hadn't been a good idea to contact the press. But he could never have imagined anything like this would happen.

"What do you see in me?" he asked at last. He looked her in the eye, as if he wanted to see what Rita's answer would be, and not just hear the words. It wasn't often that he made the effort to see himself through someone else's eyes. Finding it uncomfortable and embarrassing, he'd always tried his best not to do so, but he couldn't avoid it any longer. And right now he didn't want to avoid it. For Rita's sake, he wanted to be a better person, a better man.

She looked at him without moving for a long time. Then she caressed his cheek.

"I see someone looking at me as if I were the eighth wonder of the world. A man who is so full of love that he'd do anything for me. I see someone who helped bring my grandson into the world, and who is always willing to help when needed. Someone who would sacrifice his own life for a little boy who thinks that his grandpa Bertil is the best thing on earth. I see someone who has more prejudices than anybody I've ever met, but who is always ready to let them go when life proves that he's wrong. And I see a man who has his flaws and faults, and perhaps thinks a little too highly of himself, but who is suffering in his soul right now because he knows that he did something stupid." Rita took his hand and squeezed it. "No matter what, you're the one that I want to wake up next to every morning, and to me you're as perfect as you could be."

The pot on the stove had started to boil over, but Rita paid it no mind. Mellberg could feel the pressure in his chest starting to ease. And in its place there was now room for an entirely new sensation. A feeling of deep gratitude.

ᴄ◌◌ᵕ

The sinking feeling was still there. She wondered if she'd ever be free from that insistent longing for what she knew she'd never be able to touch again. Nathalie shifted uneasily under the covers. It was early evening, too early to be in bed, but Sam was asleep, and she'd been trying to read for a while. After half an hour, though, she'd managed to turn the page only once, and she could hardly even remember what book she was holding in her hands.

Fredrik hadn't liked the fact that she enjoyed reading. He considered it a waste of time, and whenever he found her with her nose in a book, he would yank it out of her grasp and throw it across the room. She knew what was behind his actions. He'd never read a book in his life, and he couldn't stand the thought that she was better educated and knew more than he did, or that she had access to other worlds. He was the smart and worldly one; her role in the relationship was to be pretty and keep her mouth shut, asking no questions and voicing no opinions. At a dinner party they'd once hosted at their home, she'd made the mistake of getting involved in the men's discussion of American foreign policy. The views she expressed made it clear that she knew what she was talking about, and that was more than Fredrik could bear. He'd kept his temper until the guests left. Then she'd paid a high price for speaking up. At the time she'd been in the third month of her pregnancy.

There was so much that he'd stolen from her. Slowly but surely he had taken over her thoughts, her body, her self-esteem. She couldn't allow him to take Sam too. He was her life, and without him she was nothing.

She put the book down on the bed and turned over with her face to the wall. Almost at once it felt as if someone had sat down on the edge of the bed and placed a hand on her shoulder. She smiled and closed her eyes. Somebody was humming a lullaby; the voice was lovely, but faint, hardly more than a whisper. She heard a child laugh. A boy was playing on the floor at his mother's feet and listening to the song, just as Nathalie was. She wished that she could stay here forever. Here they were safe—she and Sam. The hand on her shoulder was soft and consoling. The voice kept on singing, and she wanted to turn over to look at the child. Instead she felt her eyelids grow heavy.

The last thing she saw in the borderland between dream and reality was the blood on her hands.

⌒◯◯⌒

"You mean Erling let you go of his own free will?" Anders kissed Vivianne on the cheek as she came in the door.

"Crisis at his office," said Vivianne, gratefully accepting the glass of wine that her brother handed to her. "Besides, he knows that we have a lot to do before the opening."

"Right. Should we go through all of that first?" said Anders. He sat down at the kitchen table, which was covered with papers.

"Sometimes it all seems so meaningless," said Vivianne, sitting down across from him.

"But you know why we're doing this."

"Yes, I know," she said, looking at the wine in her glass.

Anders suddenly noticed the ring she was wearing.

"What's that?"

"Erling proposed." Vivianne raised her glass and took a big gulp of the wine.

"Really?"

"Yes," she said. What was she supposed to say?

"Have we received all the RSVPs?" Sensing it was time to change the subject, Anders pulled out several lists of names that had been clipped together.

"Yes. Last Friday was the deadline."

"Good. Then at least that part is under control. What about the food?"

"We've already bought everything. The cook seems good, and we have enough waiters on staff."

"Isn't this a little absurd?" said Anders suddenly, setting the guest lists back on the table.

"What do you mean?" said Vivianne. A smile tugged at her lips. "What's wrong with having a bit of fun?"

"Yes, but there's an awful lot of work involved." Anders pointed at all the papers on the table.

"Which will result in a fabulous evening. A grand finale." She raised her glass in a toast to her brother and downed the rest of her wine. Suddenly the taste and smell made her feel sick. The images in her mind were so clear and distinct, despite the fact they'd come so far since then.

"Have you given any thought to what I said?" asked Anders, giving her a searching look.

"About what?" She pretended not to understand.

"About Olof."

"I told you: I don't want to talk about him."

"We can't go on like this." His voice was pleading, and she couldn't understand why. What was it he wanted? This was the only thing they knew. To keep going on. That was how they'd lived ever since they were free of him—free from the stench of red wine, cigarette smoke, and the strange odors of the men. She and Anders had done everything together, and she couldn't grasp what he meant when he said they couldn't go on.

"Did you hear the news today?"

"Yes." Anders stood up and began setting the table for their dinner. He gathered all the papers into a neat stack, which he placed on one of the kitchen stairs.

"What do you think?"

"I don't think anything," he said, putting two plates on the table.

"I went over to your place late that Friday after Matte came to Badis. Erling was asleep, and I needed to talk to you. But you weren't home." Now she'd said it, now she'd given voice to what had been nagging at her. She looked at Anders, praying for some reaction that might relieve her mind. But he didn't want to look at her. He didn't move, but carried on standing there with his eyes fixed on the table.

"I don't really remember what I was doing. Maybe I went for a late-night walk."

"It was after midnight. Who goes out for a walk at that hour?"

"You were out."

Vivianne felt tears pricking at her eyes. Anders had never had any secrets from her. They'd never had secrets from each other. Not until now. And that made her more afraid than she'd ever been before.

⌘

Patrik buried his face in her hair. For a few long minutes they simply stood like that in the front hall.

"I heard," said Erica at last.

The phones had started ringing in Fjällbacka as soon as the news had leaked out, and by now everybody knew. Gunnar Sverin had gone down to the basement and shot himself.

"Sweetheart." Erica could feel Patrik's breaths coming in a strange, choppy fashion, and when he finally pulled away from her, she saw the tears in his eyes. "What happened?" she asked.

She took his hand and led him into the kitchen. The children were asleep; the only sound was the muted voices from the TV in the living room. She gently pushed him onto a chair at the kitchen table and began fixing his favorite sandwich: crispbread with butter, cheese, and caviar, which he liked to dip in hot cocoa.

"I'm not hungry," mumbled Patrik.

"You have to eat," she said, using her best maternal voice as she continued making the food.

"Fucking Mellberg. He was the one who started the whole thing," he said at last, wiping his eyes on his shirt sleeve.

"I watched the news today. Was it Mellberg who . . . ?"

"Yes."

"He's really outdone himself this time." Erica stirred the O'boy cocoa into a saucepan of milk. Then she added an extra teaspoon of sugar.

"As soon as we heard the shot from the basement, we knew what had happened. Both Gösta and I. Gunnar said he was going to the toilet, but we didn't check to make sure. We should have thought . . ." The words seemed to get stuck in his throat, and again he had to wipe his eyes on his sleeve.

"Here," said Erica, handing her husband a piece of paper towel.

It hurt her to see Patrik cry, because it happened so seldom. Right now she would have given anything to see him happy again. She fixed two sandwiches and poured him a big, steaming hot cup of cocoa.

"All right, eat your food," she said firmly, setting everything on the table in front of him.

Patrik knew there was no point resisting. Reluctantly he dipped one of the sandwiches in the cocoa until the crispbread began to soften. Then he took a big bite.

"How's Signe?" asked Erica, sitting down next to him.

"I was already worried about her before this happened." Patrik was having a hard time getting down a second bite of the food. "And now . . . I don't know. They gave her a sedative, and she was admitted to the hospital for observation. But I don't think she'll ever really be herself again. She has nothing left." More tears began pouring down his face, and Erica got up to fetch another piece of paper towel.

"What are you going to do now?"

"We'll just keep on going with the case. Tomorrow Gösta and I are driving to Göteborg to follow up on a lead. And the ME's report from the postmortem is due in. We have to carry on working as usual. Or rather, we need to work even harder."

"And the newspapers?"

"We can't stop them from writing whatever they want to write. But I can tell you that nobody at the station is going to have anything to say to them. Not even Mellberg. If he does talk to any reporters, I swear that I'll bring up the matter with the police authorities in Göteborg. There are plenty of other things I could tell them too."

"I'm sure that's true," said Erica. "Would you like to stay up for a while, or should we go to bed?"

"Let's go to bed. I'd like to crawl under the covers with you and hold you close. Could I do that?" He put his arm around her waist.

"Absolutely."

# Fjällbacka 1871

*I*t had felt strange to be examined by the doctor. Emelie had never been ill in her life, and she wasn't used to the touch of a stranger's hands on her body. But Dagmar's presence had a calming effect on her, and after his examination, the doctor had assured her that everything looked good. It seemed certain that Emelie would give birth to a healthy child.

As they left the doctor's consulting room, she felt overwhelmed with happiness.

"Do you think it's going to be a girl or a boy?" asked Dagmar. They paused for a moment to catch their breath, and she placed her hand gently on Emelie's stomach.

"A boy," said Emelie. And she was as certain as she sounded. She couldn't explain why she knew that it was a boy kicking so hard inside of her. She simply knew.

"A little boy. I think you're right."

"I just hope that he's not . . ." Emelie caught herself and stopped in mid-sentence.

"You hope he doesn't take after his father. Is that it?"

"Yes," whispered Emelie, feeling all of her joy disappear. The thought of sitting in the boat with Karl and Julian to go back to the island made her want to flee.

"Karl hasn't had an easy time of it. His father has been very hard on him."

Emelie wanted to ask Dagmar what she meant, but she didn't dare. Instead, tears began spilling down her cheeks, and she felt ashamed as she hastily wiped them away on her sleeve. Dagmar looked at her with a solemn expression.

"Your appointment with the doctor didn't go well," she said.

Emelie looked at her in confusion.

"But I thought he said everything was as it should be."

"No, it didn't go well at all. In fact, things are so serious that you'll have to stay in bed for the rest of the pregnancy. And you need to be close to the doctor in case you need help. There's no question of you getting into a boat."

"Oh. But . . ." Emelie started to understand what Dagmar was saying, though she hardly dared believe her ears. "No, things didn't go well at all. But where should I . . . ?"

"I have a spare room. The doctor thought it would be a good idea if you moved in with me so that someone could look after you."

"Oh, yes," said Emelie, and tears welled up in her eyes again. "But won't that be too much trouble? We can't possibly pay you."

"That's not necessary. I'm an old woman living alone in a big house, and I'd be grateful for some company. And it would be a great joy for me to help bring a baby into the world."

"It didn't go well at the doctor's office," Emelie repeated hesitantly as they approached the marketplace.

"No, not well at all. He said you need to go straight to bed. Otherwise things could end very badly."

"Yes, that's what he said," replied Emelie, but she could feel her heart pounding when she saw Karl in the distance.

He caught sight of them and hurried toward them with an impatient look on his face.

"That certainly took a long time. We still have a lot to do, and we need to be heading home soon."

He's not usually in such a hurry, thought Emelie. Not all those times he and Julian stopped at Abela's tavern. It didn't matter then if they got home late. Suddenly Julian appeared behind Karl, and for a moment she was seized with such panic that she thought she might drop dead on the spot. Then she felt Dagmar link arms with her.

"That's out of the question," said Dagmar, her voice calm and steady. "The doctor has ordered bed rest for little Emelie. And he was quite insistent."

Karl looked bewildered. He stared at Emelie, and she could tell the thoughts were racing inside of his head like rats. She knew that he wasn't the least concerned about her; he was merely trying to weigh the consequences of what his aunt had just told them. Emelie didn't say a word. She rocked back and forth a bit because her feet and back ached after so much walking.

"But that simply won't do," said Karl at last, and she knew the rats were still racing around and around in his mind. "Who's going to take care of the housework?"

"Oh, I'm sure the two of you can handle that," said Dagmar. "Boil a few potatoes and fry up some herring, and you'll manage just fine on your own. I doubt very much that you'll starve to death."

"But where is Emelie supposed to go? We need to tend the lighthouse, so I can't stay on the mainland. And we can't afford to rent a room over here for her. Where are we going to find money for that?" His face was turning bright red, and Julian was staring at him angrily.

"Emelie can stay with me," said Dagmar. "I'll be very happy to have company, and I refuse to accept so much as an öre in payment. I'm *certain that your father would think this is an excellent arrangement, but I can speak to him, if you'd like."*

Karl stared at her for several seconds. Then he looked away.

*"No, that should work out fine," he muttered. "Thank you. It's very kind of you."*

*"It's my pleasure. Now I'm sure you can make your own way home in the boat."*

Emelie didn't dare so much as glance at her husband. She couldn't help feeling a smile tugging at her lips. Thank God she didn't need to go back to the island.

# 17

L ooks like you couldn't sleep last night either," said Gösta, noticing the dark circles under Patrik's eyes. He had shadows under his own eyes.

"No, I couldn't," said Patrik.

"This road must seem awfully familiar to you by now." He glanced in the direction of Torp as they once again headed for Göteborg.

"Uh-huh."

Gösta took the hint and leaned over to switch on the radio instead of trying to carry on a conversation with his colleague. An hour later, having listened to far too much pointless pop music, they finally reached the city.

"When you spoke to him on the phone, did he sound as if he'd be willing to help us?" asked Gösta. He knew from experience that cooperation between police districts often depended on the particular individual they happened to be dealing with.

If they ended up with a surly type, it would be almost impossible to find out any information.

"He sounded friendly," said Patrik as he led the way to the reception area. "Patrik Hedström and Gösta Flygare. We're here to see Ulf Karlgren."

"That's me," boomed a voice behind them, and a big man wearing a black leather jacket and cowboy boots stepped forward. "I was thinking we could sit in the cafeteria. My office is too cramped, and the coffee is better down here."

"Sure," said Patrik. He couldn't help looking this unlikely police officer up and down. Regulation attire clearly held no appeal for Ulf Karlgren, and that became even more apparent when Patrik glimpsed the faded T-shirt the man was wearing under his jacket. It said *AC/DC* across the chest.

"This way."

Ulf took long strides as he headed for the cafeteria. Patrik and Gösta did their best to keep up. From behind they noticed that the man had a long ponytail that compensated for the thinning hair on top of his head. And they could clearly see the outline of a snuff container in his back pocket.

"Hello, girls! You're more beautiful today than ever." Ulf winked at the women behind the counter, and they giggled happily. "So what have you got to tempt me today? I need to watch my figure, you know!" Ulf patted the stomach that was stretching his T-shirt tight, and Patrik found himself thinking about Mellberg. But that was as far as the similarities went. Ulf was a significantly more appealing type of person.

"We'll take a princess pastry each," said Ulf, pointing to a tray of enormous pastries covered with green marzipan.

Patrik started to protest, but Ulf waved aside his objections.

"You could use a bit of meat on those bones," he said, loading the pastries onto a tray. "And three cups of coffee. That will do it."

"You don't need to . . ." said Patrik as Ulf took a credit card out of his well-worn wallet.

"Don't worry about it. It's my treat. Come on, let's sit down."

They followed him to a table and sat down. Ulf's cheerful expression suddenly turned serious.

"I hear that you've got some questions about one of the biker gangs."

Patrik nodded. He briefly summarized what had happened and what they'd found out so far. Then he explained that a witness had seen Mats Sverin being assaulted by several guys who looked like bikers with eagles on their backs.

Ulf nodded. "That sounds credible. From your description, we could be talking about the IE."

"IE?" Gösta had already finished off his pastry. Patrik couldn't understand where his colleague put all the food that he ate. He was as gaunt as a greyhound.

"Illegal Eagles." Ulf had dropped four sugar cubes in his cup and was slowly stirring his coffee. "They're the number one gang in the area. Meaner, uglier, and more ruthless than all the others."

"Shit."

"If they're the ones involved, I'd advise you to proceed cautiously. We've had some rather unfortunate confrontations with that gang."

"What are they mixed up in?" asked Patrik.

"Drugs, prostitution, protection rackets, extortion—you name it. It'd be easier to tell you what they're *not* mixed up in."

"Cocaine?"

"Definitely. But also heroin, amphetamines, and, to a certain degree, anabolic steroids."

"Have you had a chance to check out whether Mats Sverin was ever part of any police investigations here?" asked Patrik.

"His name has never come up." Ulf shook his head. "That doesn't necessarily mean he wasn't involved, only that he never came to our attention."

"He doesn't exactly fit the profile. As a gang member, I mean," said Gösta, leaning back with a sated look on his face.

"The core group is made up of bikers, but there are all sorts of other types on the fringes, especially when it comes to narcotics. Some of our investigations have taken us right to the upper levels of society."

"Would it be possible to get in contact with this gang?" Patrik downed the last of his coffee.

Ulf immediately got up to get him some more.

"The second cup is free," he said when he came back and sat down. "As I was saying, I wouldn't recommend making direct contact with these gentlemen. We've had a number of unpleasant experiences with them. So if you could start from some other angle, maybe talk to people connected to this guy Sverin, I'd advise you to do that instead."

"I understand," said Patrik. "Who's the head of IE?"

"Stefan Ljungberg. A Nazi sympathizer who started the gang ten years ago. He's been in the slammer countless times, ever since he was eighteen. Before that, he was in a locked juvenile facility. You know the type."

Patrik nodded, though in truth it was a type he hadn't really encountered before. The criminals back home seemed awfully tame by comparison.

"What would make them come to Fjällbacka to put a bullet in somebody's head?" asked Gösta.

"I can think of a number of likely scenarios. Trying to leave the gang is usually the best way to end up with a bullet in your skull. Although that doesn't seem to be the case in this instance, so we have to consider other possibilities. Maybe they were cheated in a drug deal, maybe they were worried that somebody was going to talk. If so, maybe we should interpret the assault as a warning. But this is all pure speculation. I'll ask my colleagues if they've heard anything more concrete. I'd also recommend that you talk to people who were close to Sverin. Often they know more than they think."

Patrik was doubtful. This had proved the biggest problem in their investigation so far. No one seemed to know very much about Mats Sverin.

"Thank you for your time," he said, getting up.

Ulf shook hands with Patrik and smiled.

"No problem. We're only glad to be of help. Give me a shout if you have any other questions."

"I'm sure we will," said Patrik. There was so much that seemed logical about this particular lead. At the same time, it didn't feel right. He simply couldn't figure out this case. And he still had no idea who Mats really was. It was hard to get his head around the case when, over and over in his mind, Patrik kept hearing the shot from yesterday.

∽∞∽

"What shall we do now?" Martin was standing in the doorway to Paula's office.

"I don't know." She felt as discouraged as Martin looked.

The events of the previous day had taken a toll on all of them. No one had seen Mellberg. He'd locked himself in his office, and that was probably just as well. The way things stood at the moment, his colleagues would have had a hard time hiding their contempt. Fortunately for Paula, she hadn't seen him at home either. By the time she got home last night, he had already gone to bed. And when she left this morning, he was still asleep. At breakfast Rita had tried to talk to Paula about what had happened, but she had let it be known that she was in no mood to discuss the matter. And Johanna hadn't even tried to talk about it. She had simply turned away when Paula crawled into bed. The wall between them was getting higher. Paula felt her mouth go dry, as if from panic, at the thought. She had to take a sip of water from the glass on her desk. She didn't have the energy to think about Johanna right now.

"Isn't there anything we can do while they're in Göteborg?" Martin came in and sat down.

"Lennart is supposed to get back to us today," said Paula. She hadn't slept well, and no matter how much she sympathized with Martin's impatience, she was too tired to take the initiative herself. But Martin continued to sit there, fixing her with an inquiring look.

"Shall we phone Lennart to find out if he's done yet?" He took out his cell.

"No, no. He'll call as soon as he's finished looking at the documents. I'm sure he will."

"Okay." Martin put his cell back in his pocket. "So what shall we do while we wait? Patrik didn't leave any instructions. We can't just sit here doing nothing, can we?"

"I don't know." Paula could feel herself growing annoyed. Why was she the one who was supposed to decide? She wasn't much older than Martin and, besides, he'd been working at the station several years longer than she had, although she did have experience on the Stockholm police force. She took a deep breath. It wasn't fair to take out her frustration on Martin.

"Pedersen is supposed to deliver his report from the post-mortem today. I think we should start with that. I can call him and find out if he has any results for us."

"Okay. Then maybe we'll have something to work with." Martin looked like a happy puppy who had just received a pat on the head, and Paula couldn't help smiling. It was impossible to stay annoyed with Martin for very long.

"I'll phone him now."

Martin watched as she tapped in the number. Pedersen must have been sitting next to his phone, because he picked up on the first ring.

"Hi. This is Paula Morales in Tanumshede . . . You have it? Oh, good." She gave Martin a thumbs-up. "Of course. Just fax over the report. But could you give me a brief summary over the phone?" She nodded and made a few notes on the pad of paper on her desk.

Martin craned his neck, trying to read what she'd written, but then gave up.

"Hmm . . . I see . . . Okay." She listened some more and made a few more notes. Then she slowly put down the phone. Martin stared at her.

"What did he say? Anything we can use?"

"Not exactly. Mostly he just confirmed what we already knew." She looked down at her notes. "He said that Mats Sverin was shot in the back of the head with a nine-millimeter gun. One shot. He probably died instantly."

"What about the time of death?"

"That was the good news. He was able to determine that Mats died sometime after midnight, meaning in the early hours of Saturday morning."

"That's good. What else?"

"There was no trace of any narcotic substances in his blood."

"Nothing?"

Paula shook her head. "No. Not even nicotine."

"He could still have been a dealer."

"True. But it does make you wonder . . ." She looked at her notes again. "The most interesting part is going to be seeing whether the bullet matches any gun that we have on record. If there's a link to some other crime, it will make it much easier to find the weapon. And hopefully the murderer."

Suddenly Annika was standing in the doorway.

"The Coast Guard just called. They found the boat."

Paula and Martin exchanged glances. They didn't need to ask Annika which boat she was talking about.

⸎

Everything was packed. The instant Madeleine received the postcard, she knew what she had to do. There was no longer any use trying to flee. She was aware of the danger that awaited them, but it was just as dangerous to stay here. Maybe she and her children would have a better chance if they went back voluntarily.

Madeleine had to sit down on the suitcase to close it. One suitcase was all she'd been able to bring. She'd had to pack an entire lifetime into it. And yet she'd been filled with hope as she boarded the train for Copenhagen with the children and that one suitcase. She had felt pain and sorrow about what she was leaving behind, but happiness about what might be ahead.

She glanced around the small one-room apartment. A dreary place with only one bed where the kids had slept and a mattress on the floor for her. The apartment didn't look like much, but for a brief time it had been paradise. A safe place that was all their own. Until it had been transformed into a trap. They couldn't stay here. Mette had lent her money for the tickets without asking any questions. Maybe she had bought them a death sentence, but what choice did she have?

Slowly she got to her feet, picked up the postcard, and stuffed it in her worn purse. She wanted to rip it into a thousand pieces and flush them down the toilet, watching them disappear. But she knew that she needed to keep the card as a reminder. So she wouldn't change her mind.

The children were at Mette's. They had gone over there after playing in the courtyard, and Madeleine was grateful to have a little more time to herself before she had to break the news that they were going home. That word did not have a positive meaning for them. Scars, both internal and external, were the only things they had ever received from their so-called "home." She hoped they knew that she loved them, that she would never willingly do anything to harm them, but that she had no other option. If they were found here, trapped in this rabbit hole, none of them would be spared. She knew that for a fact. The only chance the rabbits had was to go back to the fox of their own free will.

It was time to leave. She could no longer put off the inevitable. Telling herself that the children would understand, Madeleine picked up the suitcase. She only wished that she really believed that.

⌒∞⌒

"I heard about Gunnar," said Anna.

She still looked like a fragile little bird, and Erica did her best to smile. "Don't think about things like that right now. You have enough on your mind."

Anna frowned. "I don't know. Strangely enough, it's good to feel sorry for someone other than myself."

"And it must be awful for Signe. She's all alone now."

"How is Patrik doing?" Anna tucked her legs under her as she sat on the sofa. The children were in school and the day care center, and the twins were taking their mid-morning nap in the stroller just outside the front door.

"He was pretty upset yesterday," said Erica, reaching for a cinnamon bun.

Belinda, Dan's eldest daughter, had baked the buns. She had started baking when she had a boyfriend who liked the domestic type. He was now history, but she still enjoyed baking, and she certainly seemed to have a natural talent for it.

"God, this is delicious." Erica rolled her eyes.

"I know. Belinda is a great baker. And Dan says that she's been wonderful with the other kids."

"Yes, she stepped in when she was really needed."

Belinda looked quite fierce with her dyed black hair, black fingernail polish, and heavy makeup. But when Anna retreated from everyone, she had taken her younger siblings under her wing, including Adrian and Emma.

"What happened wasn't Patrik's fault," said Anna.

"No, I know that. And I tried to tell him that. It's really Mellberg who should be blamed, but for some reason Patrik always feels responsible. He and Gösta were at Gunnar's house when he shot himself. Patrik thinks that he should have seen the warning signs and tried to stop him."

"What warning signs?" snorted Anna. "Nobody announces in advance that they're planning to kill themselves. There were several times when I . . ." She came to a halt and glanced at Erica.

"You would never do anything like that, Anna." Erica leaned closer and looked her sister in the eye. "You've been through so much, more than most people, and if you were going to kill yourself, you would have done it long ago. You don't have it in you."

"How can you be so sure?"

"I know because you haven't gone down in the basement to stick a gun in your mouth and pull the trigger."

"We don't have any guns," said Anna.

"Don't play dumb. You know what I mean. You've never thrown yourself in front of a car or slit your wrists or taken a load of sleeping pills or anything like that. You've never done any of those things because you're such a strong person."

"I'm not sure it's strength," murmured Anna. "I think it would take a lot of courage to pull that trigger."

"Not really. It only requires a moment of courage. After that, it's all over, and everybody else has to clean up the mess, if you'll pardon the expression. In my opinion, that's not courage. That's cowardice. Gunnar wasn't thinking about Signe at that moment. If he had, he wouldn't have done it. He would have shown more courage by staying with her so they could help each other. Anything rather than choosing the coward's way out. And that's something you have never chosen."

"Well, according to that woman there, you can solve all your problems by doing yoga, not eating meat, and taking five deep breaths a day." Anna was pointing at the TV where an enthusiastic health guru was expounding on the only way to happiness and good health.

"How can anyone find happiness without meat?" asked Erica.

Anna couldn't help laughing.

"You're such an idiot," she said, giving Erica a poke with her elbow.

"You can talk! You're the one who looks like a patient just released from the loony bin."

"That's so mean." Anna threw a pillow at Erica with all her might.

"Whatever it takes to get you to laugh," said Erica quietly.

◌∽◌

"I suppose it was only a matter of time," said Petra Janssen. Bile was threatening to rise in her throat, but as the mother of five children, she had developed a greater tolerance for disgusting smells over the years.

"Yes, it's no big surprise." Konrad Spetz, Petra's long-term partner, seemed to be having more trouble quelling the nausea he felt.

"The Narcotics guys will probably be here any minute."

They left the bedroom. The stench followed them, but in the living room on the floor below, it was easier to breathe. A woman in her fifties was sitting on a chair, sobbing as one of their younger colleagues tried to comfort her.

"Was she the one who found him?" Petra nodded toward the woman.

"Yes. She's the cleaning woman for the Westers. She usually comes in to clean once a week, but since they were away, she only needed to come in every other week. When she arrived today, she found . . . well . . ." Konrad cleared his throat.

"Have we located the wife and child?" Petra had been the last one to arrive on the scene. Today should have been her day off, and she and her family had been out at Gröna Lund amusement park when she received the phone call.

"No. According to the cleaning woman, the family had packed their bags to go to Italy. They were supposed to be gone all summer."

"We need to check with the airlines. If we're lucky, we'll find them on the beach, soaking up the sun," said Petra, but her expression was grim. She was all too aware of who was lying in that bed upstairs, and what sort of people he associated with. It seemed highly improbable that his wife and child were enjoying the sunshine. It was much more likely that they were lying dead in the woods somewhere. Or at the bottom of the bay at Nybroviken.

"I've already got someone looking into it."

Petra nodded with satisfaction. She and Konrad had worked together for over fifteen years, and their relationship functioned better than many marriages. But in terms of appearance, they were an odd couple, and that was putting it mildly. At five foot ten, and with a solid build that had been shaped by her five pregnancies, Petra towered over Konrad, who was not only short but slight in stature. He had a strangely asexual air about him that made Petra wonder whether he even knew how babies were made. At any rate, in all their years together, she'd never once heard him mention any sort of love life, with either a man or a woman. And she'd never asked. What they had in common was an acute intellect, a dry sense of humor, and a commitment to their job, which they'd managed to retain in spite of all the reorganizations inflicted on them by bosses who were political appointees with no understanding of what constituted good policework.

"We need to put out an alert for them and talk to the boys in narcotics," he added.

"Boys and girls," Petra corrected him.

Konrad sighed. "All right, Petra. Boys *and* girls."

Petra's five children were all daughters, so women's rights were a sensitive subject. He knew that Petra thought women were superior to men, but he'd never been foolish enough to ask her whether that wasn't reverse discrimination. He was smart enough to keep his thoughts on that subject to himself.

"What a mess it is up there." Petra shook her head.

"Looks like a number of shots were fired. The bed is full of bullet holes, and Wester is too."

"What made them think it would be worth it?" She let her gaze sweep over the bright living room and then shook her head again. "Sure, this is one of the most gorgeous houses I've ever seen, and no doubt they were living the good life, but they must have known that sooner or later everything would go to hell. And then he ends up rotting in his own bed, lying on the silk sheets with his body full of bullet holes."

"That's something wage-slaves like you and me will never understand." Konrad got up from the deep white cushions of the sofa and headed for the front hall. "It sounds like the Narcotics team is at the door."

"Good," said Petra. "Now we'll get to hear what the boys have to say."

"And the girls," said Konrad, and he couldn't help smiling.

⚬≫

"What should we do?" asked Gösta, sounding resigned. "It doesn't sound as if it's a good idea, talking to those guys."

"No," admitted Patrik. "We should probably leave that as a last resort."

"So what next? We suspect the IE carried out the assault, and possibly the murder, but we don't dare talk to them. Fine police officers we are." Gösta shook his head.

"Let's head back to the place where Mats was working when the assault occurred. So far we've only talked to Leila, but I think we should find out what the other staff members have to say. As I see it, that's the only way to move forward at the moment." He turned on the ignition and started driving toward Hisingen.

They were ushered inside at once, but Leila was looking a bit exasperated when they were shown to her office.

"Look, we do want to help, but I don't know what you're expecting to gain by coming here again." She threw out her hands. "We've shared the documents that we have, and we've answered all your questions. We simply don't know anything else."

"I'd like to talk to your staff. There are two others here in the office, aren't there?" Patrik's voice was friendly but firm. He realized that it was a nuisance, them turning up like this, but at the same time the Refuge was the only place where they might find out more information. Mats had obviously been dedicated to this organization and its mission, so maybe it was here that they'd learn more about him.

"Okay, you can sit in the break room," said Leila with a sigh, motioning to the door to the right of her office. "I'll send in Thomas, and then he can get Marie when you're done talking to him." She tucked a lock of hair behind her ear. "After that, I'd appreciate it if we could go back to working in peace. We understand that the police need to investigate the murder, and we feel for Matte's family, but we have important work of our own and there's nothing else we can tell you. In the four years that Matte worked here, he never said much about his personal life, and no one here has any idea who would want to kill him. Besides, that happened after he moved away."

Patrik nodded. "I understand. Once we've talked to the other staff members, we'll try to leave you alone."

"I don't mean to sound uncooperative, but I'm delighted to hear that." She left to speak to her staff while Patrik and Gösta installed themselves in the break room.

A moment later a tall, dark-haired man in his thirties came in. Patrik had seen him hurry past on their previous visits, but they hadn't exchanged more than a few words.

"So you worked with Mats?" Patrik leaned forward, resting his elbows on his knees and with his hands clasped.

"Yes, I started here soon after Mats did, so it's been almost four years now."

"Did the two of you spend any time together outside of work?" asked Patrik.

Thomas shook his head. He had brown eyes and a calm manner. He answered without hesitation.

"No, Matte was a very private person. I've no idea who his friends were, except for Leila's nephew. Even they seem to have lost contact."

Patrik sighed. It was the same thing everyone had said about Mats.

"Were you aware of any problems he might have had? Either personal or on the job?" interjected Gösta.

"No, nothing like that," replied Thomas at once. "Matte was always just . . . Matte. Incredibly calm and stable. He never got upset. I would have noticed if anything was wrong." He met Patrik's eye without blinking.

"How did he handle the situations that you deal with here?"

"All of us who work here end up being deeply affected by the lives that we come in contact with. At the same time, it's important to keep our distance; otherwise we'd never be able to keep doing this kind of work. Matte handled it all extremely well. He was warm and compassionate without getting too involved."

"How did you end up working here? From what I understand, the Refuge is the only women's crisis center that employs men. And Leila said that both male employees had to go through a careful screening process," said Patrik.

"Yes, Leila has taken a lot of shit because of me and Matte. Maybe you heard that Matte got the job through Leila's nephew. My mother is one of her best friends, and I've known Leila since I was a kid. When I came back to Sweden after doing volunteer work in Tanzania, she asked me whether I would consider working here. I've never regretted my decision even for a second. But it's a big responsibility. If I make any mistakes, it will just add more grist for the mill for those people who are opposed to men working at women's crisis centers."

"Did Mats have more contact than usual with any particular client?" Patrik studied Thomas's face to see if he might be holding back, but his expression remained as calm as ever.

"No, that's strictly forbidden, especially because of what I just told you. We have to maintain a professional relationship with the women and their families. That's rule number one."

"And Mats followed that rule?" asked Gösta.

"We all do," said Thomas, looking offended. "An organization like this depends on its good reputation. The slightest misstep could be disastrous. For example, the social services offices might stop working with us. And in the long run, that would hurt the very people that we're trying to help. As I've been trying to explain, we men have an even greater responsibility." His tone was growing sharper.

"These are questions that we have to ask," said Patrik, trying to smooth things over.

Thomas nodded.

"I know. I'm sorry for sounding upset. It's just so important not to have any shadows cast on our work, and I know that Leila is deeply worried about the effect all this might have on the organization. Sooner or later, someone is going to think that there's no smoke without fire, and then everything could start to fall apart. She has risked so much to set up the Refuge, and to run it in her own way."

"We understand. At the same time, we have to ask some uncomfortable questions. For example, this one." Patrik paused and then went on. "Did you see any sign that Mats was either using or dealing drugs?"

"Drugs?" Thomas stared at him. "I read the papers this morning. We were outraged by the bullshit they wrote. It's completely insane. The idea that Matte would be mixed up in that sort of thing is absurd."

"Have you come across IE?" Patrik forced himself to go on, though it felt more and more as if he was picking at an open wound.

"The Illegal Eagles, you mean? Yes, I'm sorry to say that I have come across them."

"We have a witness who says that it was members of that biker gang who put Mats in the hospital. And not a bunch of kids, as Mats claimed."

"You're saying it was IE who beat him up?"

"That's what we've been told," said Gösta. "Have you ever had any dealings with them?"

Thomas shrugged. "We have offered help to some women connected with members of that gang. But we've never had more problems with them than with other idiotic boyfriends and husbands."

"Was Mats the contact person for any of those women?"

"No, not as far as I'm aware. The assault must have been a case of unprovoked violence. He was probably just in the wrong place at the wrong time."

"That was his version of the incident too. The wrong place at the wrong time."

Patrik could hear how skeptical he sounded. Thomas ought to realize that this type of criminal gang didn't target people for no reason. Why was he trying to make out it was random?

"Well, that's all for now. Do you have a phone number where we can reach you if we have any other questions? Then we won't have to keep running over here," said Patrik with a wry smile.

"Of course." Thomas scrawled his phone number on a piece of paper and handed it to him. "Did you want to talk to Marie too?"

"Yes, please."

The two officers had a brief conversation as they waited. Gösta seemed to have accepted everything Thomas said as the truth and found him to be completely trustworthy. Patrik had his doubts. Thomas had certainly seemed honest and forthright, and he had answered all of their questions. Yet several times Patrik thought he detected some hesitation, although it was more a feeling that he had rather than anything he'd actually observed.

"Hi." A young woman came into the break room and shook hands with them. Her palms felt slightly clammy and sweaty, and she had red patches on her neck. Unlike Thomas, she seemed very nervous.

"How long have you worked here?" Patrik began.

Marie was fidgeting with her skirt. She was pretty in a doll-like way. A small, turned-up nose, long blond hair that kept falling into her eyes, a heart-shaped face, and blue eyes. Patrik judged her to be about twenty-five, but he wasn't sure. The older he got, the harder it was to estimate the age of people who were younger than him. Maybe that was a form of self-preservation, so that he could continue to picture himself as twenty-five.

"I started here about a year ago." The red patches on her neck grew brighter, and Patrik noticed that every once in a while she swallowed hard.

"Do you like the job?" He wanted her to relax, to let down her defenses. Gösta was leaning back in his chair, listening. He seemed to have decided to leave the interview to Patrik.

"Yes, I love working here. It's such important work. Of course, it's tough too, but in an important way, if you know what I mean." She was stumbling over her words and seemed to be having trouble formulating her thoughts.

"What did you think of Mats as a colleague?"

"Matte was just so sweet. Everyone liked him—everyone on staff, and the women too. They felt safe with him."

"Did Mats ever get too involved with any of the women?"

"No, no, that's rule number one. Never get personally involved." Marie shook her head vigorously, making her blond hair fly.

Patrik cast a quick look at Gösta to see whether he too thought this seemed to be a sensitive topic for her. But Gösta's face had suddenly gone rigid. Patrik took another look at him. What on earth was wrong?

"Er . . . I need to . . . Could I have a word with you? In private?" He reached out to tug on Patrik's sleeve.

"Of course. Should we . . . ?" He motioned toward the door, and Gösta nodded.

"Would you excuse us for a moment?" Patrik said. Marie looked relieved by this interruption in the conversation.

"What's wrong? We were just starting to get somewhere," snapped Patrik when they stepped out into the corridor.

Gösta studied his shoes. After clearing his throat a couple of times, he looked up at Patrik with a distraught expression on his face.

"I think I've done something really stupid."

# Fjällbacka 1871

*T*hat turned out to be the most marvelous time of her life. It was only when the boat carrying Karl and Julian had left Fjällbacka and headed for Gråskär that Emelie realized what life on the island had done to her. Now she felt as if she could breathe for the first time in ages.

And Dagmar insisted on pampering her. Emelie was sometimes embarrassed by how much fuss the old woman made of her, and how little she was expected to do. She tried to help with the cleaning, dishwashing, and cooking, because she wanted to be useful and not a burden. But Dagmar merely chased her away, saying that she ought to rest. Finally Emelie had to surrender to a will stronger than her own. And she had to admit that it was wonderful just to rest. Her back and joints ached, and the child was constantly kicking inside of her. Above all, she felt so tired. At night she could sleep for twelve hours straight and then take a nap after the midday meal, and still not feel fully awake during the daytime.

*It was lovely to have someone taking care of her. Dagmar made her tea and strange brews that were supposed to increase her strength. She also persuaded Emelie to eat the oddest things in order to fortify her body. None of them seemed to help much, because she still felt so tired, but she realized that it made Dagmar happy to feel needed. So Emelie cheerfully ate and drank everything that was placed in front of her.*

*What she enjoyed most was the evenings they spent together. Then they would sit in the parlor and converse as they knitted, crocheted, and sewed garments for the baby. Emelie had never devoted much time to such things until she came to stay with Dagmar. As a maid on a farm, she'd had other chores to tend to. But Dagmar was skilled with needle and thread, and she taught Emelie everything she knew. The piles of baby clothes and blankets grew to include little caps, gowns, socks, and everything else a newborn might need. Loveliest of all was the patchwork quilt that they both worked on for a while each evening. On one square after another they embroidered whatever pattern occurred to them. Emelie's favorite were the squares with hollyhocks. The sight of them always tugged at her heartstrings. Because no matter how strange it seemed, she sometimes missed Gråskär. Not Karl or Julian—she didn't miss them for an instant. But the island had become part of her.*

*One evening she'd tried to tell Dagmar about Gråskär and those who inhabited it and why she had never felt alone. But that was the one topic that she and Dagmar couldn't discuss. Dagmar's expression had grown stern, and she averted her eyes so that Emelie realized that the elderly woman didn't want to hear what she was saying. Maybe that wasn't really so strange. Even she thought it sounded odd when she tried to describe what she'd experienced, although it all seemed so natural when she was on the island. When she was among them.*

*There was one other topic that they never discussed. Emelie had tried to ask questions about Karl, about his father and his childhood. But then the same stern expression appeared on Dagmar's face. The only thing she would say was that Karl's father had always demanded a great deal from his sons, and that Karl had disappointed him. Dagmar* said that she didn't know all the details, and for that reason she didn't want to talk about it. So Emelie had stopped asking. Instead she allowed herself to sink into the calm embrace of Dagmar's home, and in the evenings she knitted little socks for the child whose arrival was rapidly approaching. Gråskär and Karl would have to wait. They belonged to another world, another time. Right now the only things that existed were the sound of her knitting needles and the yarn that shone so white in the glow from the paraffin lamps. She would return to life on the island soon enough. This was all just part of a brief and happy dream.

# 18

**W**here did you find it?" Paula shook hands with Peter and stepped on board the Coast Guard vessel.

"We had a call about a stranded boat in a cove."

"How come you didn't find it before? Haven't you been out looking for it?" asked Martin. He was enthusiastically surveying the Coast Guard vessel. He knew that she was capable of doing almost thirty knots. Maybe he could persuade Peter to increase their speed after they got further out.

"There are so many coves out here in the archipelago," said Peter, steering the boat away from the dock with a sure hand. "It's pure luck that anyone found it at all."

"And you're positive it's the right boat?"

"Not yet, but when I see it I'll recognize Gunnar's boat."

"How do we get it back home?" Paula was peering through the window. She'd spent far too little time on the water. It was astonishingly beautiful. She turned around and looked at

Fjällbacka, which was now behind them and quickly receding into the distance.

"We'll tow it back. I thought we should first go out there and make sure it's the right boat. Then I realized that you might want to examine the place where it was found."

"There's probably not much to see," replied Martin. "But it's nice to be out on the water for a while." He cast a glance at the throttle but didn't dare ask. More boats were appearing, and it might be foolish to go any faster, even though he wished they could.

"You should come out with me again sometime, and I can show you what kind of horsepower she's got," said Peter with an amused smile, as if he could read Martin's mind.

"That'd be great!" Martin's pale face lit up, and Paula shook her head. Boys and their toys.

"Over there," said Peter, turning the boat starboard. And there it was. A wooden motorboat, wedged into a small crevice. It didn't look damaged, but it seemed to be stuck.

"That's Gunnar's boat all right. I'm sure of it," said Peter. "Who wants to be the first ashore?"

Martin looked at Paula, who pretended not to have heard the question. She was a city girl from Stockholm. Wading ashore on sharp rocks was something she would leave to Martin. He climbed up on the bow, grabbed the mooring line, and waited for the right moment. Peter turned off the engine and then helped Paula out of the boat. She almost fell in after slipping on some algae, but she managed to keep her balance. Martin would never stop teasing her if she fell in the water.

Moving cautiously, they made their way over to the motorboat. On closer inspection they could see that it was undamaged.

"How the hell did it end up here?" Martin scratched his head.

"It looks like it just drifted," said Peter.

"Could it have drifted here all the way from the harbor?" asked Paula, but from the look on Peter's face she could tell that she'd asked a silly question.

"No," he said.

"She's from Stockholm," Martin explained, and Paula glared at him.

"Stockholm has an archipelago too."

Martin and Paula both looked skeptical.

"A flooded forest," they said in unison.

Paula walked around the boat. Sometimes people who lived on the west coast were so narrow-minded. If she heard anybody say one more time: "Ohhhh, you're from the backside of Sweden," she was going to slug the individual in question.

Peter climbed back on board *MinLouis*, and Martin tied a towline to Gunnar's motorboat. Then he motioned for Paula to come closer.

"Come and help me push," he said, as he started shoving the boat out of the crevice.

Paula carefully made her way over the sharp rocks to lend a hand. After a good deal of effort, they managed to get the boat loose, and it slipped smoothly away from the shore.

"All right then," said Paula and headed back to the Coast Guard vessel. Suddenly she felt her feet slip out from under her, and she fell. She was instantly soaking wet. Shit. Her colleagues were going to make fun of her for a long time to come.

⌒∞⌒

They were constantly with her now. They made her feel safe, even though she saw them only out of the corner of her eye. Sometimes she thought the boy looked a little like Sam, with his curly hair and that mischievous glint in his eye, except that he was blond, while Sam had dark hair. But like Sam, the boy kept his gaze fixed on his mother.

Nathalie sensed rather than saw the woman. And she heard her. The hem of her dress sweeping along the floor, the small admonitions directed at the boy, the warnings whenever she saw something that might be dangerous. She was a rather overprotective mother, just as Nathalie was. Occasionally the woman had tried to speak to her. There was something she wanted to say, but Nathalie refused to hear it.

The boy liked being in Sam's room. Sometimes it sounded as if Sam was talking to him, but she couldn't be sure. She didn't dare move closer to listen, because she didn't want to disturb them if they really were having a conversation. It gave her hope. In time, Sam would talk to her too. Even though she represented safety for him, she understood that Sam also associated her with all the terrible things he'd experienced in his life.

It was warm inside the house, but she found herself suddenly shivering. What if they weren't safe here after all? Maybe one day they'd see a boat approaching the island, just as she'd feared. A boat filled with the same evil that they'd tried to leave behind.

She heard voices coming from Sam's room. Her fear vanished as swiftly as it had appeared. The little blond boy was talking to Sam, and it sounded as if Sam was replying. Her heart leaped with happiness. It was so hard to know what was right. All she could do was follow her instinct, which was based on her love for Sam—and it kept telling her to give him more time. Let him heal here, in peace and quiet.

No boat was going to come. She repeated that to herself like a mantra as she sat at the kitchen table and looked out of the window. No boat was going to come. Sam was talking, and that must mean that he was on his way back to her. She heard the little boy's voice again. She smiled. She was glad that Sam had a friend.

⌐∞⌐

Patrik was watching Gösta rummage in his jacket pocket.

"Could you please tell me what this is all about?"

After a moment Gösta seemed to find what he was looking for. He pulled something out of his pocket and handed it to Patrik.

"What's this? Or rather, who is this?" Patrik was looking at the photograph he held in his hand.

"I don't really know. But I found it in Sverin's apartment."

"Where?"

Gösta swallowed hard. "In his bedroom."

"Can you explain to me how it happened to end up in your jacket pocket?"

"I thought it might be of interest, so I took it along. But then I forgot about it," said Gösta in a subdued voice.

"You forgot about it?" Patrik was so angry that for a second everything went black before his eyes. "How could you possibly forget something like this? All we've talked about lately is how little we know about Mats, and how hard it's been to find out who he knew."

Gösta seemed to shrink as they stood there in the corridor. "I realize that, but at least I'm showing it to you now. Better late than never, right?" He attempted a smile.

"And you have no idea who this is?" asked Patrik, now taking a moment to study the picture properly.

"Not a clue. But it must have been someone who was important to Sverin. And it occurred to me that . . . I thought about it when we were . . ." He nodded toward the room where Marie was waiting for them.

"It's worth a try," said Patrik. "But we're not done talking about this, you and I. Just so you know."

"I know." Gösta looked down at the floor, but he seemed relieved at the reprieve, no matter how temporary.

They went back into the break room. Marie looked as nervous as she had before.

Patrik got straight to the point.

"Who is this?" he said, placing the photo on the table in front of Marie. He saw her eyes open wide.

"Madeleine," she said, looking scared. She covered her mouth with her hand.

"Who's Madeleine?"

Patrik tapped his finger on the photo in order to force Marie to keep looking at it. She didn't answer as she uneasily shifted position on her chair.

"This is a murder investigation, and any information you have may help us to find out who killed Mats. That's what you want too, isn't it?"

Marie looked at them with an unhappy expression. Her hands were shaking, and her voice faltered as she finally began to tell them what she knew. About Madeleine.

⌒∞⌒

When the tech team arrived to carry out a thorough examination of the boat, Paula and Martin drove back to the station. Paula had borrowed a huge pair of waterproof trousers and an orange fleece shirt from the Coast Guard office. She glared at anyone who might even consider making some sort of sarcastic remark. Once seated inside the car, she turned up the heat. The sea water had been icy cold, and she was still freezing.

The volume on the radio was up as high as it would go, so they almost didn't hear Martin's cell when it rang. He turned down the music before answering his phone.

"That's great! Can we go over there now? We're headed back, so we can stop off there on the way." He ended the conversation and turned to Paula. "That was Annika. Lennart has finished going through the documents, so we can go see him any time we like."

"Perfect," said Paula, looking a bit happier.

Fifteen minutes later they parked in front of the ExtraFilm office. Lennart was eating lunch at his desk when they came in, but he set aside his sandwich and wiped his hands on a napkin. He cast a surprised look at what Paula was wearing, but wisely decided not to comment.

"I'm glad you're here," he said.

Lennart radiated warmth, just as his wife did. Paula thought that their adoptive daughter had no idea how lucky she was to end up with Annika and Lennart as her parents.

"She's so cute," said Paula, pointing at the photo of the little girl that Lennart had pinned up on his bulletin board.

"Yes, she certainly is." He smiled broadly, then motioned for them to sit down in the visitors' chairs in front of his desk. "I don't know whether it's really worth your time to sit down. I've looked through everything as carefully as I could, but there's really not much to tell you. The finances seem to be in order, and I didn't find anything that leaped out at me. I wasn't exactly sure what I was supposed to be looking for. From what I can tell, the town has invested a lot of money in the project and also negotiated extended payment clauses. But there's nothing that set off any alarm bells in here—my best financial instrument." Lennart patted himself on the stomach.

Martin started to say something, but Lennart went on:

"The Berkelins—Vivianne and Anders—are responsible for a large part of the expenses, and according to the documents, the financing that they've arranged is due to arrive on Monday. I'm afraid I haven't been much help."

"Yes, you have. At least it's good to hear that the town is doing a good job of handling our money." Martin stood up.

"Well, so far, so good. But everything depends on whether they're able to bring in customers. Otherwise it's going to be expensive for the taxpayers."

"We thought it was really nice, at any rate."

"Yes, Annika told me that all of you had a good time at the spa. And that Mellberg was apparently pampered like royalty."

Paula and Martin laughed. "We wish we could have seen it. Rumor has it that they gave him an oyster treatment. But we'll just have to imagine Mellberg covered with oyster shells," said Paula.

"Well, here's everything." Lennart handed them the stack of papers. "As I said, I'm sorry that I couldn't be of more help."

"It's not your fault. We'll have to keep looking, that's all," said Paula, but she couldn't hide how discouraged she felt. The discovery of Gunnar's boat had given them a little boost, but the euphoria hadn't lasted long. It seemed very unlikely that the boat would provide any new leads in the investigation.

"I'll drop you off and then go home to change my clothes," she told Martin as they neared the station. Then she gave him a warning look.

He nodded, but she knew that the minute he stepped in the door, he would be gleefully embellishing the story of how she'd taken an involuntary dip in the water.

Paula parked outside her building and dashed upstairs to the apartment. She was still feeling chilled, as if the cold water had seeped right into her bones. Her hands shook as she put the key in the lock, but finally she got the door open.

"Hello?" she called, expecting to hear her mother's cheerful voice from the kitchen.

"Hi," she heard. It was Johanna's voice, coming from the bedroom. She went in, surprised to find her home from work at this time of day.

Something was going on. Something that had kept Paula awake at night, listening to Johanna breathing. Even though

Paula could tell that she too was wide awake, she hadn't dared say anything. She wasn't sure that she really wanted to know what was troubling her. Now Johanna was sitting on their bed with such a dejected look on her face that Paula wanted to turn around and run away. All sorts of thoughts raced through her mind. All kinds of potential scenarios popped up, and she didn't want to see how any of them played out. But now they were both here, face to face, in an empty flat without all the usual commotion to hide behind. No dogs running around. No Rita singing loudly in the kitchen and playing with Leo. No Mellberg shouting obscenities at the TV. Nothing but silence. And the two of them.

"What on earth are you wearing?" asked Johanna at last, looking Paula up and down.

"I fell in the water," said Paula, glancing down at the ugly fleece shirt that was so big that it reached almost to her knees. "I just came home to change."

"Why don't you do that. Then we'll talk. I can't have a serious conversation with you dressed like that." She smiled wryly, which made Paula's stomach lurch. She loved Johanna's smile, but she hadn't seen it much lately.

"Could you make some tea while I get changed? Then we can sit in the kitchen."

Johanna nodded and left the room. Paula's fingers were stiff with cold and fear as she changed into jeans and a white T-shirt. Then she took a deep breath and went out to the kitchen. This was not a conversation that she wanted to have, but she had no choice. All she could do was close her eyes and dive in.

⌘

He hated lying to her. She had been everything to him for so long, and it frightened him that for the first time he was prepared to sacrifice what they had together. Anders was breathing hard as he headed up the steep, narrow slope toward Mörhult. He had to get out in the fresh air for a while, and away from Vivianne. There was no other way to view it.

Sometimes the past seemed so close. Sometimes he was still five years old, lying under the bed next to Vivianne, with his hands over his ears and his sister's arm wrapped tightly around him. Under that bed they had learned so much about surviving. But he was no longer content simply to survive. He wanted to live, and he didn't know whether Vivianne was helping or hindering him.

A car came rushing past at high speed, and he had to jump onto the shoulder. Badis was behind him. Their big project, and their last. Erling was the one who was making it all possible. And now the poor devil had actually proposed to Vivianne.

Erling had phoned to invite Anders to dinner tonight to cel-ebrate the engagement. Somehow Anders doubted that his sister was aware of these plans. Especially since that fat little police chief and his live-in girlfriend had been invited as well. Anders had declined the invitation, offering some feeble excuse. The combination of Erling and Bertil Mellberg didn't sound like a recipe for a pleasant evening. And under the circumstances, it would feel strange to be celebrating.

The road started to slope downward. He didn't really know where he was going; it didn't matter which direction he chose. Anders kicked at a stone that rolled down the hill until it disap-peared in a ditch. That was exactly how he was feeling at the moment. As if he was rolling faster and faster down a slope. The only question was, which ditch would he wind up in? It was bound to end badly, because there was no good option. He'd lain awake all night, trying to work out a solution, a compro-mise. But there was none to be found. Just as there had never been no middle road in the days when they lay under the bed with their heads pressed against the wooden slats.

He stood on the dock in front of the little stone bridge. There were no swans in sight. He'd been told that they usually built their nests to the right of the bridge, and every year they had a new flock of babies, who lived precariously close to the road. Apparently swans mated for life. That was what he wanted too. So far the only woman in his life was his sister. Not as a lover, of course, but she had always been his partner, the one he was supposed to spend his life with.

Now everything had changed. He needed to make a decision, but he had no idea how he was going to do that. Not when he could still feel the wooden slats against his head and Vivianne's protective arm holding him. Not when he knew that she had always been his defender and his best friend.

They had almost lost the battle for survival. The alcohol and the smells had been present even when their mother was still alive. But at the same time there had been small islands of love—moments that they had clung to. When she chose to escape, when Olof found her in the bedroom with an empty pill bottle on the floor, the last remnants of their childhood vanished. He blamed them, and they were severely punished. Every time the ladies from social services dropped by, he would pull himself together and charm them with his blue eyes, showing off his home and Vivianne and Anders, who silently stared at their feet as the ladies fussed over him. Somehow he always found out in advance when they were planning to come over, so the apartment would be clean and tidy when they showed up for their supposedly impromptu visits. Why hadn't he just given them up if he hated them so much? Anders and Vivianne had spent so many hours imagining the new mother and father they could have had if only Olof would let them go.

Presumably he wanted to keep them close so he could watch them suffer. But in the end they were determined to win.

Though he'd been dead for years now, he continued to serve as their incentive. They were determined to prove to him that they could be successful. And success was now within their reach. They couldn't simply give up and admit that Olof had been right when he said that they were worthless and would never amount to anything.

Off in the distance Anders could see the swan family approaching. The baby swans were bobbing along after their stately parents. They looked so sweet, with their downy gray feathers, but they were nothing like the stylish birds they would eventually become. Had he and Vivianne grown up to be big, beautiful birds? Or were they still little gray cygnets, hoping to be something else?

Anders turned around and slowly walked back up the hill. No matter what he decided, he had to do it soon.

⸎

"We know about Madeleine," said Patrik as he sat down in front of Leila without waiting for an invitation.

"I'm sorry?"

"We know about Madeleine," Patrik repeated calmly. Gösta had taken the chair next to him, but he was staring at the floor.

"I see. But what . . ." said Leila, looking nervous.

"You said that you were willing to cooperate with us, and that you'd told us everything. We now know that's not entirely true, and we'd like an explanation." He made his voice sound as stern as he could, and it seemed to work.

"I didn't think . . ." Leila swallowed hard. "I didn't think it was relevant."

"I don't believe that. Besides, it's not your job to decide what might be relevant or not." Patrik paused, then said, "What can you tell us about Madeleine?"

For a moment Leila sat in silence. Then she abruptly stood up and went over to the bookcase. She stuck her hand behind a row of books and took out a key. Taking her seat behind her desk again, she bent down and unlocked the bottom drawer.

"Here," she said curtly, placing a folder in front of them.

"What's that?" asked Patrik. Gösta leaned forward, equally curious.

"That's Madeleine's file. She's one of the women who needed the kind of help that goes beyond what society can offer."

"What does that mean?" Patrik began leafing through the documents.

"It means that we gave her help that isn't considered legal." Leila stared at them resolutely. All sign of nervousness was gone, and it looked as if she were challenging them to object. "Some of the women who come to us have tried everything. And then we try everything. But these women and their children are threatened by men who don't give a damn about the law, leaving us helpless. We have no way of protecting these women legally, so we help them to escape. To leave the country."

"What was the relationship between Madeleine and Mats?"

"I didn't know about it at the time, but afterward I found out that they were having an affair. We spent a long time trying to resolve the situation for Madeleine and her kids. During that time, they must have fallen in love, which was strictly forbidden, of course. But as I said, I wasn't aware of it then . . ." She threw out her hands. "When I found out, I was terribly disappointed. Matte knew how important it was for me to prove that men are needed in this type of organization. And he knew that everyone's eyes were on the Refuge, and that a lot of people hoped that we'd fail. I couldn't understand why he'd betray the Refuge like that."

"What happened?" asked Gösta. He took the file from Patrik.

The air seemed to go out of Leila. "Things got worse and worse. Madeleine's ex-husband kept finding out where she and the kids were staying. The police got involved, but that didn't help matters. Finally Madeleine couldn't take it anymore, and we realized that the situation was intolerable. If she and her children were going to stay alive, they would have to leave Sweden. Leave their home, their family, their friends, everything."

"When did you make this decision?" asked Patrik.

"Madeleine came to see me right after Matte was attacked and asked us to help her. We had already come to more or less the same conclusion."

"What did Mats think about this?"

Leila looked down at her desk. "We didn't tell him. Everything was arranged while he was in the hospital. When he came back to work, she was gone."

"Was that when you found out that they were having an affair?" Gösta placed the file back on the desk.

"Yes. Matte was inconsolable. He begged and pleaded for me to tell him where they'd gone. But I couldn't do that. It would have put her and the children in danger if anyone found out where they were."

"Did you ever suspect that there was a connection between this and the assault on Mats?" Patrik opened the folder and pointed to something written on one of the pages.

Leila fidgeted with a paper clip before answering.

"Of course the thought occurred to me. But Matte claimed there was no connection. And there wasn't much we could do."

"We need to talk to her."

"That's impossible," said Leila, shaking her head. "That would be much too dangerous."

"We'll take all necessary precautions. But we have to talk to her."

"I'm telling you that's impossible."

"I understand that you want to protect Madeleine, and I promise not to do anything that might put her at risk. I'm hoping that we can resolve this easily and quickly so that this"— he pointed at the folder on the desk—"can remain just between us. If not, we'll have to take up the matter with someone else."

Leila clenched her teeth, but she knew that she had no choice. With a single phone call Patrik and Gösta could bring down all the work that the Refuge was trying to accomplish.

"I'll see what I can do. But it will take time. Maybe until tomorrow."

"That's all right. Just give us a call as soon as you know anything."

"Okay. On one condition: we do things my way. The lives of many other people are involved here—not just Madeleine and her children."

"We realize that," said Patrik. He and Gösta stood up and once again left the building to drive back to Fjällbacka.

⁂

"Welcome, welcome!" exclaimed Erling, beaming as he stood in the doorway. He was glad that Bertil Mellberg and his girlfriend, Rita, were able to come over to celebrate the occasion. He really did like Mellberg, whose pragmatic attitude toward life was very close to his own. The man was such a reasonable person to deal with.

Having enthusiastically shaken Mellberg's hand, he kissed Rita on the cheek. Then, just to be safe, he kissed her on the other cheek too. He wasn't quite sure what the custom was in the southern lands, but surely he couldn't go wrong with a double kiss. Vivianne came to greet their guests and help them hang up their coats. Mellberg handed their hostess a bouquet of flowers and a bottle of wine, and she thanked him as effusively as courtesy required, and carried both out to the kitchen.

"Come in," said Erling, motioning them forward. As always, he was looking forward to showing off his home. He'd been forced to fight hard to keep the house after his divorce, but it had been worth all the trouble.

"What a lovely home," said Rita, looking around.

"You've certainly done well for yourself." Mellberg slapped Erling on the back.

"I can't complain," said Erling, handing a glass of wine to each of his guests.

"So what's for dinner?" asked Mellberg. The lunch he'd had at Badis was still fresh in his mind, so if a meal of seeds and nuts was in store for them, they could always stop at the sausage stand on the way home.

"Don't worry, Bertil." Vivianne winked at Rita. "I've made an exception this evening and planned a high-carb meal just for your sake. But a few vegetables may have slipped in as well."

"I suppose I'll survive," said Bertil, his laugh a little too hearty.

"Shall we sit down?" Erling put his arm around Rita and ushered her into the big, bright dining room. He couldn't deny that his ex-wife had had good taste when it came to the decor. On the other hand, he was the one who had paid for everything, so the result could be considered his doing—which was what he often claimed.

The appetizer was quickly dispatched, and Mellberg's face lit up when he saw that the main course was a sizable portion of lasagne. Not until they were having dessert, and after a few pokes under the table from Erling, did Vivianne show off the ring on her left hand.

"Oh my, is that what I think it is?" exclaimed Rita.

Mellberg squinted in an attempt to see what all the fuss was about. He finally noticed the shiny object on Vivianne's ring finger.

"Are the two of you engaged?" Mellberg took Vivianne's hand and studied the ring carefully. "Erling, you old rascal, you must have coughed up a small fortune for this."

"You can't get something for nothing. But she's definitely worth it."

"How splendid," said Rita, smiling warmly. "Congratulations to both of you."

"Yes, we need to celebrate. Don't you have anything stronger so we could drink a toast in your honor?" Mellberg looked with distaste at the glass of Baileys that Erling had poured him to accompany the dessert.

"Hmm . . . I could probably find us some whiskey." Erling got up and opened the large liquor cabinet. He set two bottles on the table and then took out four whiskey glasses, which he placed next to them.

"That one's a real gem." Erling pointed to one of the bottles. "A Macallan, twenty-five years old. And it wasn't cheap, I'll tell you that."

He poured a shot in two of the glasses, then reached across the table and set one glass at his own place and the other at Vivianne's. Then he put the cork back in and carefully returned the bottle with the expensive whiskey to the liquor cabinet.

Mellberg stared at him in astonishment.

"What about us?" he couldn't help asking. Rita seemed to be thinking the same thing, even though she didn't say it out loud.

Erling came back to the table and blithely opened the second bottle. A Johnnie Walker Red Label, which Mellberg knew cost 249 kronor at the State Liquor Store.

"It would be a waste to serve you the expensive whiskey," said Erling. "You wouldn't be able to really appreciate it."

With a cheerful smile, he poured the drinks and handed Mellberg and Rita each a glass. They stared in silence at their Johnnie Walker and then at the contents of Erling's and

Vivianne's glasses. It was a completely different color. Vivianne looked like she wanted to crawl under the rug.

"*Skål!* And *skål* for us, darling!" Erling raised his glass in a toast. Still mute with surprise, Mellberg and Rita did the same.

A short time later they made their apologies and left. What a stingy bastard, thought Mellberg as they rode home in the taxi. That was a big blow to a promising friendship.

⁓

The platform was deserted when they disembarked from the train. Nobody knew they were coming. Her mother would be in for a shock when they turned up, but Madeleine couldn't warn her of their arrival. It was going to be risky enough for them to stay with her parents. She would have preferred not to involve her parents at all, but they had nowhere else to go. Eventually she was going to have to talk to certain people and try to explain things, and she promised herself that she would pay Mette back for the train tickets. She hated being indebted to anyone, but that was the only way they could come back to Sweden. Everything else would just have to wait.

She didn't dare think about what was going to happen next. At the same time, a sense of calm had come over her. It felt strangely comforting to be trapped in a corner, with no possibility of going anywhere. She had given up, and that was actually a relief. It took so much energy to flee and to fight, and she was no longer afraid for herself. It was only the children that caused her to hesitate, but she was going to do everything in her power to make him under-stand and forgive. He had never touched the children, and they would be fine, no matter what happened. At least that was what she had to tell herself. Otherwise she was doomed.

They caught the number three tram at Drottningtorget. Everything was very familiar. The kids were so tired that they could hardly keep their eyes open, but they still pressed their noses against the window and stared out.

"There's the prison. Isn't that the prison, Mamma?" said Kevin.

She nodded. Yes, they had just passed Härlunda Prison. After that she ran through the next tram stops in her mind: Solrosgatan, Sanatoriegatan, and then they would get out at Kålltorp. They almost missed their stop because she forgot to press the button. At the last second she remembered, and the tram slowed and then came to a halt to let them get off. The summer sky was still light at this hour of the evening, but the streetlamps had just come on. There were lights on in most of the windows, including her parents' apartment. Her heart pounded harder and harder the closer she came. She was going to see her mother again. And her father. Feel their arms around her and see their faces when they caught sight of their grandchildren. Faster and faster she walked, with the kids running valiantly after her, eager to visit their grandparents, whom they hadn't seen in so long.

At last they stood outside their door. Madeleine's hand shook as she pressed the bell.

# Fjällbacka 1871

H e was such a beautiful baby, and the birth had been surprisingly easy. Even the midwife had said as much when she wrapped him in a blanket and placed him at Emelie's breast. A week later, she was still overwhelmed with happiness, and it felt as if her joy grew stronger with every minute.

Dagmar was just as happy as she was. If Emelie needed anything, she was instantly there, and she tended to the baby with the same expression of reverence as when she went to church on Sunday. He was a miracle that the two of them shared.

The baby slept in a basket next to Emelie's bed. She could sit there for hours just looking at him as he slept with one tiny fist pressed against his cheek. Whenever his lips twitched, she imagined it was a smile, an expression of joy to be in this world.

The clothes and blankets, which she and Dagmar had spent so many hours making, were now put to good use. They had to change the baby several times a day, and he was always clean and well fed. Emelie felt *as if she and Dagmar and the boy were living in their own little world, without sorrows or worries. And she had decided on a name. He would be called Gustav, after her father. She didn't even consider asking Karl first. Gustav was her son, hers alone.*

*Karl hadn't visited her even once during the time she had lived with Dagmar. But she knew that he must have been in Fjällbacka, because he and Julian had come to town as they always did. Although it was a relief not to have to see him, it hurt that she didn't mean more to him.*

*She had tried to talk to Dagmar about this, but she had shut down, as she always did whenever the conversation turned to Karl. She had again murmured that he hadn't had an easy time of it, and that she didn't want to get involved in the family's affairs. Finally Emelie had given up. She would never understand her husband, but no matter what, she was going to have to endure the consequences. The pastor had said "until death do you part," and that was how it would have to be. At least now she had something more than the others who had been her solace on the island. Now she had something real.*

*Three weeks after Gustav's birth, Karl came to fetch her. He hardly even glanced at his son. He merely stood in the front hall, looking impatient, and told her to pack her things. As soon as he and Julian were done buying supplies, they would be leaving for the island. And she and the baby would be coming with them.*

*"Have you heard anything from my father about the boy? I wrote to him, but I haven't received a reply," said Karl, looking at Dagmar. He sounded both anxious and eager, like a schoolboy wanting to please. Emelie's heart softened a bit when she saw Karl looking so uncertain. She wished that she knew more and could understand what he was feeling.*

*"He received your letter, and he is both pleased and satisfied." Dagmar hesitated. "He's been worried, you know."*

*They exchanged a glance that Emelie couldn't read as she stood there, holding Gustav in her arms.*

"*Father has no reason to worry,*" *said Karl hostilely.* "*Please give him my greetings.*"

"*I'll do that. But you must promise to take good care of your family.*"
*Karl looked down at the floor.*

"*Of course I will,*" *he said, and then turned on his heel.* "*Be ready to leave in a hour,*" *he added, speaking to Emelie over his shoulder.*

*She nodded, but she could feel her throat closing up. Soon she would be back on Gråskär. She hugged Gustav close.*

# 19

**D**id she get hold of her?" asked Gösta. He was still looking half-asleep.

"She didn't say. She just asked us to come to the office as soon as possible."

Patrik swore. There was a lot of traffic, and he had to keep changing lanes. When they reached the Refuge offices in Hisingen, he got out of the car and tugged at his shirt. It was soaked with sweat.

"Come in," said Leila quietly when she met them at the door. "We'll sit in the break room. It's more comfortable than my office. I've made some coffee and sandwiches, in case you didn't have time for breakfast."

They'd barely had time to eat anything before leaving for Göteborg, so Patrik and Gösta each reached for a roll after they sat down.

"I hope Marie isn't going to get into any sort of trouble over this," Patrik said. He'd forgotten to say anything yesterday, but when he'd gone to bed he couldn't sleep because he was worrying that the poor, nervous young woman might lose her job after telling them about Madeleine.

"Absolutely not. I take full responsibility. I should have told you myself, but my primary concern was for Madeleine's safety."

"I understand," said Patrik. It still bothered him that they'd lost so much time, but he could see why Leila had acted as she did. And he never stayed angry for long.

"Have you managed to get hold of her?" he asked, finishing his sandwich.

Leila hesitated. "I'm afraid we seem to have lost track of Madeleine."

"Lost track?"

"Yes. We helped her to escape abroad. I probably don't need to go into all the details, but it's done in a way that will guarantee maximum security. At any rate, she and the children were installed in an apartment. And now . . . now they seem to have left it."

"Left it?" Patrik repeated.

"Yes. According to our colleague who's on the scene, the apartment is empty, and the neighbor says that Madeleine and the children left yesterday. And they didn't seem to have any plans to return."

"Where could they have gone?"

"I suspect that they've come back to Sweden."

"Why would they do that?" asked Gösta. He reached for another roll.

"She borrowed some money from the neighbor to buy train tickets. And she has nowhere else to go."

"But why come back, considering what's waiting for her here?" Gösta was talking with his mouth full, sending a shower of crumbs onto his lap.

"I have no idea." Leila shook her head, and they saw the look of dismay on her face. She was clearly very upset. "You have to understand that it's a matter of an extremely complex psychology. You might wonder why a woman doesn't leave the first time she gets hit, but it's more complicated than that. In the end, a form of interdependency exists between the batterer and the victim, and sometimes the woman doesn't behave in a very rational way."

"Do you think she has gone back to her husband?" asked Patrik in disbelief.

"I don't know. Maybe she couldn't take the isolation any longer and she was missing her family. Even though we've worked with these issues for years here at the crisis center, we still don't always understand how the women think. And they have to make their own decisions about their lives. They're free to do as they wish."

"How do we go about finding her?" Patrik was feeling quite helpless. Yet another door had slammed in their faces. He had to talk to Madeleine. She might be the key to everything.

For a moment Leila didn't reply. Then she said, "I'd start with her parents. They live in Kålltorp. She may have gone there."

"Do you have their address?" asked Gösta.

"Yes, I do. But . . ." She paused. "You're dealing with extremely dangerous people. Madeleine and her family may not be the only ones at risk. You may be too."

Patrik nodded. "We'll be discreet."

"Are you planning to talk to him too?" asked Leila.

"Yes. I'm afraid it's unavoidable. But first we'd better talk to our colleagues here in Göteborg and find out what's the best approach to take."

"Be careful." She handed Patrik a piece of paper with an address written on it.

"We will," he said, but he wasn't as confident as he tried to sound. They were heading into deep water now, and the only thing to do was to swim as best they could.

"Nothing from the airlines?" said Konrad.

"No," said Petra. "They didn't leave the country. At least not under their own names."

"There are plenty of ways to get false passports and identities."

"If that's the case, it's going to take a while for us to find them. We should investigate all the other possibilities first. Then we'll know what the most likely scenario might be." Petra exchanged a glance with Konrad as they sat at their desks across from each other. Neither of them needed to be any more specific than that. The images they were both envisioning were clear enough.

"It would be pretty vicious if they killed a five-year-old," said Konrad. At the same time he knew that these individuals moved in circles where a human life meant nothing. Killing a child might be unthinkable for some of them, but not for all. Money and drugs had a way of transforming people into animals.

"I've talked to some of her women friends. She didn't have many, from what I understand, and none of them claim to have been very close to her. But they all say the same thing. Nathalie and Fredrik and their son were supposed to go to their house in Tuscany for the summer. And nobody had any reason to think they hadn't gone." Petra took a sip from the water bottle she always kept on her desk.

"Where's she from?" asked Konrad. "Are there any relatives she might be staying with? Something might have happened to prevent her and the boy going to Italy. Marital problems. Or maybe she was the one who shot him."

"Some of her friends hinted that it wasn't a particularly happy marriage, but I don't think we should jump to any conclusions at this stage. Do you know whether the bullets have been sent over to the lab?" She took another sip of water.

"Yes, and they're being given top priority. The narcotics division has been working for a long time on this guy and the organization behind him, so the case is at the top of their list."

"Good," said Petra, getting to her feet. "I'll check on Nathalie's family while you lean on the techs. Let me know as soon as they have anything we can work with."

"Okay," said Konrad, sounding amused. He had long since grown accustomed to Petra acting as if she was the one in charge, even though they held the same rank. But he didn't mind, since he'd never been interested in competing for status. He knew that she listened to him, and she respected his judgement and opinions, and that was what mattered most. He picked up the phone to call the technical team.

∞

"Are you sure this is the right address?" Gösta glanced over at Patrik.

"Yes, I'm sure. And I heard somebody moving around inside."

"Then I guess she's here," whispered Gösta. "Otherwise they would open the door."

Patrik nodded. "But the question is, what do we do now. We need to get them to let us in voluntarily." He paused to think. Then he took out his notebook and pen. He wrote down a few lines and tore out the page. Then he leaned down and slipped it under the door along with his business card.

"What did you write?"

"I suggested a place where we could meet. I hope she agrees," said Patrik as he started down the stairs.

"Do you think she might run instead?" Gösta had to hurry to keep up.

"I don't think so. I wrote that we wanted to talk to her about Mats."

"I hope you're right," said Gösta as they got into the car. "Where are we going?"

"The Delsjön nature reserve," said Patrik, and drove off with a lurch.

They left the vehicle in the parking lot and walked over to a picnic area at the edge of the woods. Then they waited. It felt great to be out in the country for a change, and the early summer day was as beautiful as could be. Pleasantly warm and sunny with not a cloud in the sky. Birds were chirping, and there was a quiet rustling in the trees.

It took about twenty minutes before they saw a slender woman walking toward them. Her shoulders were hunched, and she kept glancing around anxiously.

"Has something happened to Matte?" She had a surprisingly girlish-sounding voice.

"Why don't we sit down?" Patrik pointed to the bench they were standing next to.

"Tell me what's happened," she said, as she sank onto the bench. Patrik sat down next to her. Gösta chose to stand off to the side and let Patrik handle the conversation.

"We're from the Tanumshede police," Patrik told her. The expression on Madeleine's face made his stomach start to churn. He felt like an idiot for not having realized that they would have to deliver the news of Mats's death. He was going to have to tell this woman that someone who had clearly meant a great deal to her was now dead.

"Tanumshede? But why?" Her hands, which were lying on her lap, clenched into fists, and she gave him a pleading look. "Matte is from that area, but . . ."

"Mats moved home to Fjällbacka after you disappeared. He got a job there and sublet his apartment here in Göteborg. But he . . ." Patrik hesitated, but then went on. "He was shot almost two weeks ago. I'm sorry, but Mats is dead."

Madeleine gasped for breath. Her big blue eyes filled with tears.

"I thought they would leave him alone." She buried her face in her hands and sobbed.

Patrik patted her awkwardly on the back.

"Did you know that your ex-husband and his friends had assaulted Mats?"

"Of course I knew. I didn't believe for a minute that story about a gang of teenagers attacking him."

"And that was why you decided to flee?" said Patrik gently.

"I thought they would leave Mats in peace once we were gone. Before that happened, I was hoping that things could be worked out. That we could hide somewhere in Sweden. But when I saw Mats in the hospital . . . I realized that no one connected to us would be safe as long as we stayed here. We had to disappear."

"Why did you come back? What happened?"

Madeleine pressed her lips together, and Patrik could tell that she wasn't going to answer that question.

"It doesn't do any good to flee. If Matte is dead . . . That just proves that I'm right," she said, standing up.

"Is there anything we can do to help you?" asked Patrik, also getting to his feet.

She turned around. Her eyes were still filled with tears, but her expression was stony.

"No, there's nothing you can do. Nothing."

"How long were you and Mats together?"

"That depends on how you look at it," she said, her voice quavering. "But about a year. It wasn't allowed, so we kept it secret. We also had to be careful because of . . ." She didn't finish her sentence, but Patrik understood. "Matte was so different compared to what I was used to. So gentle and warm. He would never dream of hurting anyone. And that was . . . new for me." She laughed bitterly.

"There's something else that I have to ask you," said Patrik. He could hardly look at her. "Do you know whether Mats was mixed up in anything to do with drugs? Cocaine?"

Madeleine stared at him. "Why would you ask that?"

"A bag of cocaine was found in a litter basket outside the building where Mats lived in Fjällbacka. With his fingerprints on it."

"There must be some mistake. Matte would never touch drugs. But you know as well as I do who has access to such things," said Madeleine in a low voice. The tears began spilling down her face again. "I'm sorry, but I have to go home to my children now."

"Keep my card, and call if there's anything we can do, anything at all."

"Okay," she said, though they both knew that she would never call. "What you can do for me is catch the person who murdered Matte. I should never have . . ." She rushed off, sobbing.

Patrik and Gösta stood there, watching her leave.

"You didn't ask her very many questions," said Gösta.

"It's clear who she thinks killed Mats."

"Yes. And I'm not looking forward to what we have to do now."

"I know," said Patrik, taking his cell out of his pocket. "But we'd better phone Ulf. We're going to need help."

"That's the understatement of the year," muttered Gösta.

As the phone rang, Patrik had a nagging sense of uneasiness. For a fraction of a second he saw in his mind a crystal clear image of Erica and his children. Then Ulf came on the line.

∽∾

"Did you two have a nice time last night?" asked Paula. For a change she and Johanna were both home at the same time for lunch. Since Bertil had also arrived for a home-cooked meal, they were all gathered around the kitchen table.

"Well, that depends on how you look at it," said Rita with a smile, which clearly showed the dimples on her round cheeks. In spite of all the dancing she did, her body was still quite curvaceous. In Paula's eyes, her mother was extremely beautiful, and by all accounts, Bertil felt the same way.

"That stingy bastard served us cheap whiskey," muttered Mellberg. Normally he would have enjoyed drinking Johnnie Walker, and he'd never dream of spending his own money on an expensive bottle of whiskey. But why would Erling bring out the good stuff if he wasn't going to offer any to his guests?

"Yuck," said Johanna. "Drinking cheap whiskey would do anyone in."

"Erling poured glasses of expensive whiskey for himself and for Vivianne, and then he gave us the cheap kind," Rita clarified.

"How rude," said Paula in astonishment. "I didn't think Vivianne was like that."

"I don't think she is. She seemed very nice, and she looked thoroughly embarrassed. But there must be something about Erling that she finds attractive, because they surprised us by announcing their engagement."

"Wow." Paula tried in vain to imagine Erling and Vivianne together, but she couldn't. It would be hard to find a more mismatched couple. Well, her mother and Bertil might fit the bill. But oddly enough, she'd started viewing them as a perfect combination. She'd never seen her mother happier, and that was the only thing that mattered. For that reason, it was even more difficult to tell Rita what she and Johanna needed to say.

"How nice to have you both home," said Rita as she served the steaming hot soup from a big pot that she'd set on the table.

"Yes, especially since it seems like the two of you haven't been getting along lately." Mellberg stuck out his tongue at Leo, making the boy whoop with laughter.

"Be careful he doesn't choke on his food," said Rita, which made Mellberg immediately stop clowning around. He was deathly afraid of anything happening to Leo, who was the apple of his eye.

"Chew your food properly for Grandpa Bertil," he said.

Paula couldn't help smiling. Mellberg could be the most annoying man she'd ever met, yet she forgave him everything when she saw the way he looked at her son. Then she cleared her throat, fully aware that what she was about to say would be like a bomb exploding.

"Well, you're right that things have been a bit chilly between us lately. But yesterday Johanna and I had a chance to talk things over, and . . ."

"You're not going to split up, are you?" asked Mellberg. "It would be impossible to find somebody new. There aren't many dykes around here, and you'd probably never meet anyone else."

Paula rolled her eyes and prayed for patience. She counted backward from ten and then said:

"We're not breaking up. But we . . ." She cast a glance at Johanna for support.

"We just can't live here anymore," Johanna said.

"You can't live here?" Rita looked at Leo as her eyes filled with tears. "But where are you going to move? How are you . . . and the boy . . . ?" Her voice broke and the words didn't seem to want to come out in the right order.

"You can't move back to Stockholm. I hope you're not even considering that," said Mellberg. "Leo can't grow up in a big city like that. You understand that, don't you? He might grow up to be a delinquent or a drug addict or something equally bad."

Paula refrained from pointing out that both she and Johanna had grown up in Stockholm without suffering any damage. She realized that certain topics weren't worth arguing over.

"No, we're not going to move back to Stockholm," Johanna hastened to say. "We're happy here. But it might be hard to find an apartment in the area, so we're going to have to look in Grebbestad and Fjällbacka too. Of course the best thing would be if we could find one nearby. But at the same time . . ."

"At the same time, we do need to move," said Paula. "You've both been incredibly helpful, and it has been fantastic for Leo, but we need to have our own place." She squeezed Johanna's hand under the table. "So we'll just have to take whatever we can find."

"But Leo needs to see his grandpa and grandma every day. That's what he's used to." Mellberg looked as if he wanted to pull the boy out of his high chair and hold him close, never to let him go.

"We'll do what we can, but we need to move as soon as possible. Then we'll see what happens after that."

Silence descended over the table, and only Leo was his usual cheerful self. Rita and Mellberg exchanged worried glances. The girls were going to move and take the boy with them. That might not be the end of the world, but it certainly felt like it.

It was impossible to forget the blood. The red color had looked so garish against the white silk. She was filled with a terror that was worse than anything she'd ever felt. And yet the years she'd lived with Fredrik had been filled with frightening moments—episodes that even now she refused to think about, pushing them instead to the very back of her mind. Instead, she tried to focus on Sam and his love.

On that night she had stood there, frozen in place, staring at the blood. Then she had sprung into action, moving with a determination that she hadn't known she possessed. Their suitcases were already packed. She was wearing her nightgown, and in spite of the fear she felt, she took the time to pull on a pair of jeans and a sweater. Sam could wear his pajamas. She picked him up and carried him out to the car after loading everything else into the vehicle. He wasn't asleep, but he didn't say a word.

Everything had seemed so quiet. The only sound was a faint rumbling from the sparse nighttime traffic. She hadn't dared think about what Sam might have seen, or how it had affected him, or what his silence meant. He usually loved to chatter, but he hadn't said a word. Not one word.

Nathalie drew up her legs and wrapped her arms around her knees as she sat on the dock. She was surprised that she didn't feel restless after two weeks on the island. But the days seemed to have raced by. She hadn't yet decided what to do next, or what the future might hold for Sam and herself. Who knew if they even had a future? She had no way of knowing whether she and her son would be targeted by the people Fredrik was associated with, or whether they would be safe hiding out here. She would have preferred to withdraw from the world entirely and stay on Gråskär forever. That was easy enough to do in the summertime, but when winter arrived, they wouldn't be able to live here. And Sam needed friends and other people. Real people.

But he had to get well before she could make any decisions. Right now the sun was shining, and the sound of the sea lapping against the bare rocks lulled them to sleep at night. They were safe in the shadow of the lighthouse. Everything else could wait. And with time, the memory of the blood would fade.

"How are you feeling, sweetheart?" She felt Dan wrap his arms around her from behind, and she had to fight not to pull out of his embrace. She had emerged from the darkness and was able to see her children again, to spend time with them and feel the love she had for them. But she still felt dead inside whenever Dan touched her or gave her that entreating look.

"I'm okay," she said, wriggling out of his arms. "Just a little tired, but I'll try to stay up for a while. I need to retrain my muscles."

"Which muscles?"

She tried to smile at his joke, the way she always used to whenever he teased her. But she managed only a grimace.

"Could you go and get the children?" she asked him, wincing as she bent down to pick up a toy car lying on the kitchen floor.

"Let me get that," said Dan, quickly reaching down to get the toy.

"I could have done it," she snapped, immediately regretting her tone of voice when she saw his hurt expression. What was wrong with her? Why did she have this empty hole in her chest where all her feelings for Dan used to be?

"I don't want you to overdo it, that's all." Dan stroked her cheek. His hand felt cold against her skin, and she forced herself not to push it away. Why was she reacting like this to him, when she knew that he loved her so much and he was the father of the child she had wanted so badly? Had her feelings for Dan vanished when their son took his last breath?

Anna suddenly felt overwhelmed with fatigue. She couldn't bear to think about this right now. She wanted to be left alone so she could rest until the children came home and her heart would fill with the love she felt for them. A love that had survived.

"Will you go and pick them up?" she murmured, and Dan nodded. She didn't dare look at him, because she knew that his eyes would be filled with pain. "I need to lie down and rest for a while." She turned away and slowly went upstairs.

"I love you, Anna," he called after her.

She didn't reply.

∞

"Hello?" Madeleine called out as she came in the door.

The apartment was abnormally quiet. Were the kids asleep? It wouldn't be so strange if they were. They'd arrived late last night, and Kevin and Vilda had both gotten up early this morning, excited to be visiting their grandparents.

"Mamma? Pappa?" Madeleine said, lowering her voice. She took off her shoes and hung up her thin coat. For a moment she paused in front of the hall mirror. She didn't want them to see that she'd been crying. They were worried enough as it was. But it was such a joy to see her parents. Last night, dressed for bed and looking bewildered, they had opened the door. Then the wary expression on their faces had given way to big smiles. It had felt so good to be home again, even though she knew that the sense of security she felt was both an illusion and only temporary.

Everything was chaos. Matte was dead, and she realized that deep in her heart she had been hoping and praying that somehow they would find a way to be together.

She stood in front of the mirror, tucked her hair behind her ear, and tried to see herself as Matte had seen her. He'd told her that she was beautiful. She couldn't understand it, but she knew that he'd meant it. She could see it in his eyes every time he looked at her, and he'd had so many plans for what their future together could be. Even though she was the one who had made the decision to flee, she had still believed that one day his plans would be realized. Tears welled up in her eyes again. She looked up at the ceiling to prevent them from running down her cheeks. With an effort she blinked the tears away and took a deep breath. For the sake of her children, she needed to pull herself together and do what needed to be done. There was no time for grieving right now.

She turned and headed for the kitchen. That was where her parents spent most of their time. Her mother liked to knit, while her father sat at the table doing crossword puzzles, although lately he'd switched to sudoku.

"Mamma?" said Madeleine from the doorway. She stopped abruptly.

"Hi, honey." That voice, so gentle yet laced with contempt. She would never be able to escape from it.

Her mother's eyes were filled with fear. She was sitting on a chair facing Madeleine, with the muzzle of a gun pressed to her right temple. Her knitting was on her lap. Madeleine's father sat in his usual place near the window; a muscular arm wrapped around his neck made sure that he didn't move.

"We've been talking about the old days, my parents-in-law and I," said Stefan calmly. Madeleine saw how he pressed the gun even harder against her mother's temple. "It's nice to see you again. It's been a long time."

"Where are the children?" asked Madeleine, her voice little more than a croak. Her mouth had gone dry.

"They're in a safe place. Those poor kids. It must have been traumatic for them to be in the hands of a psychotic woman and not be allowed to see their father. But we'll make up for lost time now." He grinned, and his teeth flashed between his lips.

"Where are they?" She had almost forgotten how much she hated him. And how scared she was of him.

"I told you, they're safe." He pressed the gun even harder, and her mother winced with pain.

"I was thinking of coming to see you. That's why we came home," she pleaded. "I realized that I'd made a mistake. I came back to make things right."

"Did you get the postcard?"

It was as if Stefan hadn't heard a word she said. Madeleine couldn't understand how she'd ever found him attractive. She'd been so in love with him, convinced that he looked like a movie star with his blond hair, blue eyes, and chiseled features. She was flattered that he'd chosen her, when he could have had any woman he wanted. She was only seventeen and not very worldly. Stefan had courted her, showering her with compliments. The other side of him—his jealousy and need to control—hadn't come out until later. And by then it was too late. She was already pregnant with Kevin, and her self-esteem was so dependent on Stefan's opinion and attention that she couldn't leave him.

"The postcard arrived," she said, feeling suddenly very calm. She was no longer seventeen years old, and she had met a man who loved her. She pictured Matte's face and knew that she owed it to him to be strong. "I'll go with you. Just leave my parents alone." She shook her head at her father, who was trying to get up. "I need to work this out. I shouldn't have left. That was the wrong thing to do. We're going to be a family now."

Stefan suddenly took a step forward and struck her across the face with the gun. She felt the steel slam against her cheek and dropped to her knees. Out of the corner of her eye, she saw Stefan's thug force her father back down onto his chair. She wished with all her heart that her parents didn't have to get involved in this.

"We'll see about that, you whore." Stefan grabbed her by the hair and began dragging her away. She struggled to stand up. The pain was horrible; it felt as if her whole scalp was being torn off. Still gripping her hair, he turned around and aimed his gun toward the kitchen.

"You're not going to say a word about this. You're not going to do a fucking thing. Or else this will be the last time you'll see your daughter. Understand?" He pressed the gun against Madeleine's temple and looked first at her mother, then her father.

They nodded mutely. Madeleine didn't dare look at them. If she did, she'd lose all courage, lose the picture of Matte that she held in her mind, the image that was telling her to be strong, no matter what. She kept her eyes fixed on the floor as she felt a burning sensation at the roots of her hair. The gun was cold against her skin, and for a moment she wondered whether she'd feel the bullet boring into her brain or whether the light would simply go out.

"The children need me. They need us. We can be a family again," she said, trying to keep her voice steady.

"We'll see about that," Stefan said. His tone of voice scared her more than his grip on her hair, more than the gun pressed to her head. "We'll see about that."

Then he dragged her toward the front door.

∽∾∾

"Everything points to Stefan Ljungberg and his pals," said Patrik.

"So his wife is back in town?" asked Ulf.

"Yes, and his kids too."

"That's not good. She should have stayed as far away from that guy as possible."

"She didn't want to tell us why she came back."

"There could be a thousand different reasons. I've seen it happen so many times before. They get homesick, they miss their family and friends, or their life after running away doesn't turn out the way they'd imagined. Or the guy finds them and threatens them, so they decide they might as well come back."

"Are you aware that organizations like the Refuge some-times provide help that's not necessarily legal?" asked Gösta.

"Yes, but we choose to turn a blind eye to that sort of thing. Or rather, we choose not to waste any resources on it. They step in when society fails. We can't protect these women and children the way we should, so . . . Well, what can we do?" He threw out his hands. "So she thinks that her ex might be responsible for the murder you're investigating?"

"Yes, that's what she seemed to think," said Patrik. "And we have enough evidence pointing in that direction that we'd like to have a talk with him."

"As I told you before, that's not going to be easy. Partly because we don't want to jeopardize the ongoing police investigations regarding IE and their activities. And partly because it's best to stay out of the way of these guys, if at all possible."

"I'm aware of that," said Patrik. "But since the leads we're following all point to Stefan Ljungberg, I'd consider it a dereliction of duty not to talk to him."

"I knew you were going to say that." Ulf sighed. "Here's what we'll do. I'll bring along one of my best officers, and then the four of us will have a talk with Stefan. Not an interrogation, nothing aggressive that might provoke him. Just a little conversation. We'll take it nice and easy and see what we can find out. What do you say to that?"

"Okay. We don't really have much choice."

"Good. But we'll have to wait until tomorrow morning. Do you have a place to stay tonight?"

"I suppose we can stay with my brother-in-law." Patrik cast an inquiring glance at Gösta, who nodded. Then he took out his cell to call Erica's brother Göran.

Erica was disappointed when Patrik phoned to say that he wouldn't be home until the following day, but she quickly got over it. What a difference that was from when Maja was the twins' age. Back then, if he had called to say he was going to be delayed, she would have been seized with panic at the thought of spending a whole night alone with the baby. Now she would miss not having Patrik next to her in bed, but she wasn't worried about taking care of three children on her own. Things seemed to have settled down, and she was glad that this time she was able to enjoy her babies in a way that had never been possible with Maja. That didn't mean that she loved her daughter any less—not at all. She just felt calmer and more confident with the twins.

"Pappa will be home tomorrow," Erica told Maja, who didn't answer. She was watching *Bolibompa* on TV, and wouldn't have noticed if bombs were falling outside the window.

Erica had fed the twins and changed their diapers. Content and full, they had fallen asleep in the crib that they shared. And for once the rooms downstairs were reasonably tidy. She'd had a burst of energy and done some cleaning after coming home from the day care center. Even now enough energy remained that she was feeling a bit restless.

Erica went into the kitchen, made herself a cup of tea, and thawed out a few buns in the microwave. After pondering what to do, she fetched the stack of papers about Gråskär and sat down next to Maja with her tea, buns, and ghost stories. Soon she was deeply immersed in the world of phantoms. She longed to show all of this to Nathalie.

⚭

"Shouldn't you be going home to your girls?" said Konrad, looking up at Petra. He could see that outside their office windows in Stockholm's police headquarters on Kungsholmen, the streetlamps had come on.

"Pelle is taking care of the kids tonight. He's worked such long hours lately that it will do him good to spend a bit of time at home."

Petra's husband ran a café in Söder, and it was a constant juggling act for the two of them to coordinate their daily schedules. Sometimes Konrad wondered how she and Pelle had ever managed to have five children, since they were so rarely at home at the same time.

"Have you made any progress?" He stretched out his back. It had been a long work day, and his muscles were starting to ache.

"Her parents are dead, and she has no siblings. I'll keep looking, but she doesn't seem to have any relatives to speak of."

"I can't help wondering how she ended up with a guy like that," said Konrad. He turned his head from side to side to release the tension in his neck.

"I don't think it's hard to work out, considering the sort of person she is," said Petra drily. "One of those women who lives off her good looks and whose only goal in life is to find a man to support her. She doesn't give a damn where the money comes from and she spends her days shopping and getting beauty treatments and having long lunches with her women friends at Sturehof."

"Oh dear," said Konrad. "Sounds like someone is slightly biased."

"I will personally strangle any of my daughters who turn out that way. If you ask me, anyone who gets mixed up in that world has only themselves to blame. It's the price you pay when you choose to close your eyes and ignore the fact that the money smells."

"Don't forget, there's a child involved here too," Konrad reminded his colleague. Her expression softened at once. Petra was tough, but she was also more warmhearted than most, especially when it came to children who were threatened in some way.

"Yes, I know." She frowned. "That's why I'm sitting here even though it's ten o'clock at night and Pelle is probably living through a reenactment of the mutiny on the *Bounty* at home. It's certainly not because I'm worried about some rich guy's wife, at any rate."

She continued tapping the computer keys for a few moments and then logged out.

"Okay, that's enough. I sent off some queries, but I don't think we'll make any further progress tonight. We've got a meeting with the narcotics team at eight in the morning, so we can all go over the case together. Right now it's better for us to get a few hours' sleep so we'll be awake and alert."

"Makes sense." Konrad got up. "I hope tomorrow will be more productive."

"Otherwise we'll have to call on the media for help," said Petra with a look of disgust.

"I'm sure they've already gotten wind of the story." Konrad was past getting upset over newspaper reporters meddling in the work the police were doing. And he didn't have such a black-and-white view of journalists as Petra did. Sometimes they helped, sometimes they interfered. Either way, they weren't about to disappear, and he didn't think it did any good to keep tilting at windmills.

"Good night, Konrad," said Petra as she strode down the corridor.

"Good night," he said and switched off the light.

# Fjällbacka 1873

L ife on the island had changed, though much remained the same. Karl and Julian still had that same malicious glint in their eyes whenever they looked at her, and once in a while they would let drop some hurtful remark. But Emelie didn't care, because now she had Gustav. She devoted all her attention to her wonderful son; as long as she had him, she could stand anything. She could live on Gråskär until the day she died, if only she was allowed to keep Gustav with her. Nothing else mattered. That knowledge gave her a sense of calm, as did her belief in God. With every day that she spent on that desolate island, she heard God's word more and more clearly. She spent all of her free time studying the Bible, and its message filled her heart so full that she was able to shut everything else out.

To Emelie's great sorrow Dagmar passed away only two months after she returned to the island. She had died in such a terrible way that Emelie could hardly bear to think about it. One night someone *had broken into her house, no doubt to steal what little the old lady owned. The next day one of Dagmar's friends had found her murdered. Emelie's eyes filled with tears whenever she thought about her cruel fate. Sometimes it seemed more than she could bear. Who could be so evil and harbor such hatred that he would kill an old woman who had never done anyone any harm?*

*At night the dead whispered a name. They knew, and they wanted her to hear what they were saying. But Emelie didn't want to know, she didn't want to listen. She missed Dagmar with all her heart. It would have been comforting to know that she was over there in Fjällbacka, even though Emelie wouldn't have had a chance to visit, since she was not allowed to accompany the two men when they took the boat over to pick up supplies. But now Dagmar was gone, and Emelie and Gustav were once more alone.*

*Yet that wasn't entirely true. When she returned to Gråskär with Gustav in her arms, the dead were standing on the rocks, waiting. They had welcomed her back to the island. Nowadays she could see them without making any effort. Gustav was eighteen months old. At first she wasn't sure whether he could see them too, but now she was convinced that he could. Sometimes he would laugh loudly and wave his hands about. Their presence made him happy, and his joy was the only thing that mattered in Emelie's world.*

*Her life on the island might have seemed very monotonous, since all the days were so alike, but she had never felt more content. The pastor had come out to pay them another visit. She had the feeling that he was concerned and wanted to see how things were going. But he didn't need to worry. The isolation, which had previously made her skin crawl, no longer bothered her. She had all the company she needed, and her life had a purpose. Who could ask for more? The pastor had gone back home with a sense of relief. He had seen the calm in her face, seen the much-read Bible that lay open on the kitchen table. He had patted Gustav on the cheek as he slipped him a cough drop. "What a splendid little chap," he said, making Emelie beam with pride.*

Karl, on the other hand, ignored the boy completely. It was as if his son didn't exist. He had also moved out of the bedroom for good. He now slept in a room downstairs, while Julian slept on the kitchen bench. Karl claimed that the boy cried too much, but Emelie suspected he just used that as an excuse so he wouldn't have to share a bed with her. She didn't care in the least. She slept next to Gustav, with his chubby little arm around her neck and his face pressed against her cheek. That was all she needed. And God.

# 20

They had a pleasant evening with Göran. For most of their lives, Erica and Anna hadn't known that they had a brother, but he had soon grown close to his younger sisters. Both Patrik and Dan thought very highly of their brother-in-law. His adoptive mother, Märta, who had eaten dinner with them, was a wonderful old woman who had quickly become part of the extended family.

"Are you ready to go?" said Ulf as they stood in the parking lot outside police headquarters.

Without waiting for a reply, he introduced his colleague, Javier. He was even bigger than Ulf, if that was possible, and in considerably better shape. Apparently he wasn't the talkative type, and he shook their hands in silence.

"Do you want to follow us?" Ulf squeezed in behind the steering wheel of an unmarked police car.

"Sure, as long as you don't go too fast. I don't know my way around here," said Patrik. He and Gösta headed for their own vehicle.

"I'll drive as cautiously as a driving instructor," laughed Ulf.

They headed through town and then entered an area with fewer buildings. After another twenty minutes, there were almost no buildings at all.

"We're really out in the country," said Gösta, glancing around. "Do they live out in the woods?"

"Maybe it's not so strange that they live way out here. There are probably a lot of things they don't want the neighbors to see."

"True enough."

Ulf slowed and turned into a driveway in front of a big house. Several dogs came running out to the cars, barking loudly.

"Shit. I don't like dogs," said Gösta, staring out of the windshield. He jumped when one of the big dogs, a Rottweiler, began barking outside his door.

"Their bark is worse than their bite," said Patrik, switching off the engine.

"That's what you think," replied Gösta, making no motion to open the door.

"Come on." Patrik got out of the car but froze when three dogs surrounded him, baring their teeth and growling.

"Call off the dogs," shouted Ulf. After a minute a man came out of the front door.

"Why should I do that? They're doing their job. Keeping uninvited visitors away." He crossed his arms with an amused smile.

"Come on, Stefan. We're just here to have a little talk. Call off the damn dogs."

Stefan laughed, raised his hand to his lips, and whistled. The dogs stopped barking at once. They ran over to their master and lay down at his feet.

"Satisfied?"

Patrik couldn't help noticing that the leader of the IE was quite good looking. If it hadn't been for the coldness in his eyes, he might even have been called handsome. His clothes detracted from that impression: worn jeans, a stained T-shirt, and black motorcycle vest. On his feet he wore wooden clogs.

More men began appearing, all of them with the same wary and hostile expression.

"So what do you want? You're on private property," said Stefan. He was following their every move.

"We want to have a chat, that's all," Ulf repeated, holding up his hands in the air. "We're not here to make trouble."

There was a moment's pause while Stefan considered this. Nobody moved a muscle.

"Okay, come in," Stefan told them at last, shrugging as if to say that he didn't really care. He turned on his heel and walked toward the house.

Ulf, Javier, and Gösta took him at his word. His heart pounding in his chest, Patrik followed the others.

"Have a seat." Stefan pointed to several armchairs standing next to a dirty glass coffee table. He sat down on an ostentatious leather sofa, stretching out his arms along the back. The table was covered with beer cans, pizza boxes, and cigarette butts, only some of them in the ashtray.

"We didn't have time to clean up," said Stefan with a grin. Then he turned serious. "What do you want?"

Ulf glanced at Patrik, who cleared his throat. He was feeling nervous, and that was putting it mildly, to find himself in the headquarters of a biker gang. But there was no turning back now.

"We're from the Tanumshede police," he said, noticing to his dismay that his voice was shaking. Not a lot, but enough to bring an amused glint to Stefan's eyes. "We have a few questions with regard to an assault that took place back in February. On Erik Dahlbergsgatan. The man who was attacked was named Mats Sverin."

Patrik paused while Stefan continued to stare at him.

"And?"

"According to a witness, he was assaulted by some men who wore your emblem on their backs."

Stefan laughed scornfully and glanced at his men, who were keeping a close eye on the police officers from the far side of the room. They started laughing too.

"So what does the guy have to say about it? What was his name? Max?"

"Mats," said Patrik. It was obvious that the bikers were putting on a show, but he didn't yet know enough to be able to puncture Stefan Ljungberg's smug façade.

"Oh, excuse me. So what does Mats have to say? Did he say it was us?" Stefan stretched his arms out even further. It looked like he was taking up the whole sofa. One of the dogs came over and lay down at his feet.

"No," Patrik said reluctantly. "No, he didn't."

"All right then." Stefan grinned.

"It seems a little strange that you haven't asked who this man is that we're talking about," said Ulf, trying to entice the dog to come over. Gösta stared at him as if he were crazy, but the dog got up and padded over to Ulf to have his ears scratched.

"Lolita hasn't learned to hate the smell of a cop," said Stefan. "But she will. And as far as this Mats is concerned, I can't keep tabs on everybody. I'm a businessman and have contact with lots of people."

"He worked for an organization called the Refuge. Does that sound familiar?"

The longer they sat there, the more Patrik's loathing for this man grew. He was finding this charade frustrating. Stefan knew exactly what they were talking about. It would have been better if they could have taken him down to the station so that the witness from Erik Dahlbergsgatan could identify him. Though they had no proof that Stefan had participated in the beating of Mats Sverin, Patrik was convinced that he had. Considering how personal the situation was, he didn't think Stefan would have turned over the task to his thugs.

"Refuge? No, never heard of it."

"That's odd. Because they know you. Quite well, in fact." Patrik could feel himself boiling inside.

"Is that so?" said Stefan, feigning ignorance.

"How's Madeleine?" asked Ulf. Lolita was now lying on her back so he could scratch her stomach.

"You know what chicks are like. Things are a bit dodgy at the moment, but nothing that can't be resolved."

"Dodgy?" said Patrik tersely, and Ulf gave him a warning look.

"Is she home?" he asked.

Javier hadn't said a word. He radiated sheer muscle power, and Patrik understood why Ulf had decided to bring him along.

"Not at the moment," said Stefan. "But I'm sure she'll be sorry to have missed you. Chicks love having visitors."

He seemed totally calm, and Patrik had to restrain himself from punching the guy in the face.

Stefan got to his feet. Lolita instantly jumped up and crept over to her master. She pressed close to his legs, as if to apologize for leaving his side. Stefan leaned down to pat her.

"If that's all, I've got other things to do."

Patrik still had a thousand questions to ask. About the cocaine, about Madeleine, about the Refuge, and about the murder. But Ulf gave him another warning glance and nodded toward the door. Patrik realized the other questions would have to wait.

"I hope that guy's okay. The one who was attacked, I mean. That sort of thing can be a bad business." Stefan stood in the doorway, waiting for them to leave.

Patrik stared at him. "He's dead. Shot to death," he said, his face so close to Stefan's that he could smell stale beer and cigarettes on his breath.

"Shot?"

The grin was gone, and for a fraction of a second, Patrik saw a look of genuine surprise in Stefan's eyes.

⁂

"So was the house still standing when you got home last night?" Konrad looked at Petra through the small, round lenses of his glasses.

"Yeah, it was," said Petra, but she didn't really seem to be listening. Her attention was focused on the computer screen. After a moment she rolled back her chair and turned to Konrad. "I've found something in the records. Wester's wife owns property in Bohuslän, in the archipelago outside of . . ." She leaned forward to read what it said. "Fjällbacka."

"That's a great place. I've spent a couple of summer vacations out there."

Petra looked at Konrad in amazement. For some reason, she'd never really pictured him going on vacation. She had to bite her tongue to prevent herself asking who he'd gone there with.

"Where is this place?" asked Petra. "It looks like she owns a whole island. Called Gråskär."

"Between Uddevalla and Strömstad," said Konrad. He was going through Fredrik Wester's phone records—both outgoing and incoming calls. It was tedious work, but it had to be done, and phones could be gold mines for criminal investigations. He doubted that they would find anything in this instance. These boys were too shrewd to leave any traces behind. They probably used a phone card that they threw away the minute anything risky took place. But it was worth a shot, and Konrad was known for his tenacity. If a clue was lurking in these endless lists of phone calls, he would find it.

"I haven't managed to find a cell number for her yet," said Petra. "So it would probably be faster to contact the police up there. If they have a police force, that is. It's not exactly a big town. Maybe Göteborg is the closest station?"

"Tanumshede," said Konrad as he continued to type in phone numbers to compare with the list. "The closest police station is in Tanumshede."

"Tanumshede? How come you know that?"

"There was a big story in the papers a couple of days ago about a drug-related murder out that way." Konrad took off his glasses and rubbed the bridge of his nose. After staring too long at the small type on the lists, his eyes had begun to hurt.

"Oh, so that sort of shit doesn't only happen here in the big city."

"No, believe it or not there's a whole world outside of Stockholm. I realize that may seem strange, but it's a fact," said Konrad.

Petra had been born in Stockholm and she'd lived her whole life in the city. She rarely ventured north of Uppsala or south of Södertälje. "Is that so?" she said. "And where do you come from?" she added sarcastically. At the same time she realized it was odd that she didn't know, given that they'd worked together for fifteen years. But it had never come up in conversation.

"Gnosjö," replied Konrad, without taking his eyes off the phone lists.

Petra stared at him. "In Småland? But you don't have an accent."

Konrad shrugged. Petra was about to ask another question but stopped herself. She had just learned where Konrad was from and where he'd spent his vacations. That was more than enough information for one day.

"Gnosjö," she repeated with astonishment. Then she picked up the phone. "I'm going to call our colleagues in Tanumshede."

Konrad merely nodded. He was deeply immersed in the world of numbers.

⌘

"You look tired, sweetheart," Erica told Patrik, giving him a kiss. She was holding a baby in each arm, and he kissed his sons on the top of their heads.

"Yes, I'm feeling a bit worn out. How are things with you?" he asked, looking guilty.

"Everything's fine, as a matter of fact." She was surprised to hear herself say that, but she really meant it. Everything had gone smoothly. Maja was at the day care center, and the twins had just had their bottles, so they were both content.

"Was it worth the trip? How are Göran and Märta doing?" she asked as she lay the twins down on a blanket. "There's coffee if you'd like some."

"Thanks. That would be great." Patrik followed her to the kitchen. "I can only stay a short time. I have to get back to the station."

"Sit down for a few minutes and unwind," Erica said, practically shoving him down onto a kitchen chair. She set a cup of coffee in front of him, and he gratefully took a sip.

"Look, I've even baked buns." She set a plate of buns, still warm from the oven, on the table.

"Wow, I can't believe it. Looks like you're turning into a real homemaker, in spite of everything," said Patrik, but from the look on Erica's face, he realized the joke wasn't appreciated.

"Okay, tell me what you found out," she said, joining him at the table.

Patrik gave her a summary of what had happened in Göteborg. A hint of resignation was evident in his voice.

"And Göran and Märta are fine. They're thinking of coming to visit us some weekend in the near future."

Erica's face lit up. "That would be wonderful! I'll phone Göran this afternoon and we can agree on the date." Then she turned serious. "Something just occurred to me. Has anyone told Nathalie what happened to Gunnar?"

Patrik looked at Erica, realizing that she had a good point. "No, I don't think so. Unless she phoned Signe."

"Signe is still in the hospital. Apparently she's not doing well at all."

Patrik nodded. "Okay, I'll call Nathalie as soon as I get a chance."

"Good." Erica smiled. Then she got up, moved his coffee cup out of the way, and sat astride his lap. She ran her fingers through his hair and kissed him gently on the lips.

"I missed you."

"Mmm, I missed you too," he said, wrapping his arms around her waist.

From the living room they could hear the twins prattling happily, and Patrik saw a familiar gleam in Erica's eyes.

"Is my sweet wife in the mood to accompany me upstairs for a while?"

"Yes, please, dear sir. I would like that."

"So, what are we waiting for?" Patrik stood up so abruptly that Erica almost fell off his lap. He took her hand and led her toward the stairs. But the moment he set his foot on the bottom step, his cell rang. He fully intended to ignore it, but Erica stopped him.

"Sweetheart, you need to take that call. It might be the station."

"They can wait," he said. "Because believe me, this isn't going to take very long." He tugged at her hand again, yet she held back.

"I'm not sure that's much of a selling point," she said with a smile. "And you do have to answer the phone. You know that."

Patrik sighed. He knew she was right, no matter how disappointed he was.

"Will you give me a rain check?" He went out to the front hall to get his cell out of his jacket pocket.

"With pleasure, dear sir," said Erica and curtseyed.

Patrik laughed as he answered the phone. He truly loved this crazy wife of his.

∞

Mellberg was worried. It felt as if his whole life depended on resolving this matter. Rita was out taking a walk with Leo, and the girls were at work. He'd run home for a while to watch the sports program. But for the first time ever, he was unable to concentrate on what was happening on TV. Instead, he found himself paying attention to all the thoughts racing through his mind.

Suddenly he sat up. By God, he had the solution. It was right in front of his nose. He rushed out of the apartment and down the stairs to the office on the ground floor. Alvar Nilsson was sitting behind his desk.

"Hi, Mellberg!"

"Hi." Mellberg gave him a big smile.

"What's going on? Are you here to keep me company?" Alvar opened the top drawer of his desk and took out a bottle of whiskey.

Mellberg fought a silent battle with himself, but it ended as it always did.

"Sure, what the hell," he said, sitting down.

Alvar handed him a glass.

"There's something I want to talk to you about." Mellberg swirled the whiskey in his glass, taking a moment to savor the sight before sipping it.

"Is that so? What can I do for you?"

"The girls have decided that they want an apartment of their own."

Alvar looked amused. The "girls" were both over thirty.

"That usually happens in these situations." He leaned back and clasped his hands behind his head.

"The thing is, Rita and I don't want them to move too far away."

"I can understand that. But it's hard to find apartments in Tanumshede at the moment."

"That's exactly why I thought you might be able to help." Mellberg leaned forward and fixed his eyes on Alvar.

"Me? You know what the situation is here. All the apartments in the building are occupied. There's not so much as a cubbyhole that I could offer you."

"But there's a very nice three-room apartment immediately below ours."

Alvar gave him a surprised look.

"But the only three-room apartment in the building is . . ." He fell silent. Then he shook his head. "Not on your life. No, that's impossible. Bente would never agree." Alvar craned his neck and glanced nervously in the direction of the next room, where his Norwegian secretary and secret mistress was usually sitting at the desk.

"That's not my problem. But it might be yours." Mellberg lowered his voice. "I don't think your wife Kerstin would appreciate this little . . . arrangement of yours."

Alvar glared at Mellberg, who experienced a momentary discomfort. If he'd made a mistake, Alvar could throw him out of the office head first. He held his breath. Then Alvar started to laugh.

"My God, Mellberg. You drive a hard bargain. But let's not allow a woman to get in the way of our friendship. We'll solve this thing. I have a few contacts, and I'm sure I can fix Bente up somewhere else. Shall we set the move-in date for a month from now? But I don't intend paying for any sort of painting or repairs. You'll have to handle that yourselves. Agreed?" He held out his hand.

Mellberg breathed a sigh of relief and shook hands with Alvar.

"I knew I could count on you," he said. His stomach was bubbling with joy. Leo might be moving out, but only one floor down. He'd be able to run downstairs and see the boy as often as he liked.

"I think we should celebrate with another drink. What do you say?"

Mellberg held out his glass.

⌦

A frenzy of activity was going on at Badis, but Vivianne felt as if she were moving in slow motion. So many things had to be finished, so much had to be decided. But she couldn't stop thinking about Anders's evasive answers. He was keeping something from her, and that had opened up an abyss between them, so wide and deep that she could hardly see to the other side.

"Where should we put the buffet tables?" A waitress was giving her an inquiring look, and she was forced to pay attention.

"Over there on the left. In one long row so people can walk on both sides."

Everything had to be arranged properly. The place servings, the food, the spa rooms, the treatments. All the rooms had to look perfect, with flowers and fruit baskets for the guests of honor. And the stage needed to be set up for the band. Nothing could be left to chance.

Vivianne's voice was beginning to go as she answered questions coming from all directions. Every once in a while she would notice the sparkling ring on her finger, and she had to fight an urge to tear off that ring and hurl it against the wall. She couldn't lose control now, not when they were so close to their goal and life was finally about to take a new turn.

"Hi. What can I do to help?"

Anders looked terrible, as if he hadn't slept a wink all night. His hair was disheveled, and he had dark circles under his eyes.

"I've been trying to reach you all morning. Where have you been?" She was filled with dread. The thought that had crept into her mind refused to leave her alone. She didn't really believe that Anders was capable of such a thing, but she wasn't a hundred percent sure. How could anyone truly know what went on inside someone else's mind?

"I turned off my cell. I needed to sleep," he said, keeping his eyes averted.

"But . . ." She stopped herself. It was pointless. After everything they'd shared, Anders had chosen to shut her out. No words could express how hurt she felt.

"You could make sure that there's enough to drink," she said instead. "And enough glasses. I'd be grateful if you'd take care of that."

"Sure. I'll do anything for you. You know that," said Anders. For a moment he was his usual self. Then he turned around and headed for the kitchen.

I knew it, Vivianne thought. Tears ran down her cheeks. She wiped them off on her sleeve and started walking toward the spa rooms. She couldn't fall apart. That would have to wait until later. Right now she had to see to it that they had enough massage oil and oyster scrub.

∞

"We've had a phone call from our colleagues in the violent crimes division in Stockholm. They're trying to locate Nathalie." Patrik saw the astonishment on his colleagues' faces. He must have had the same expression when he answered his cell at home less than half an hour ago and Annika told him the very same thing.

"Why is that?" asked Gösta.

"Her husband was found murdered, and they've been worried that Nathalie and her son might also be dead. Fredrik Wester was apparently one of the big guns in the Swedish narcotics trade."

"You're kidding," said Martin.

"I had a hard time believing it myself. But apparently the narcotics division has had him under investigation for a long time, and recently he was found dead, shot in his own bed. He seems to have been there for a while, possibly a couple of weeks."

"But why didn't anyone find him sooner?" asked Paula.

"Evidently the family had packed their bags and were due to leave for their house in Italy. They were going to be gone all summer. So everyone assumed that they'd left."

"What about Nathalie?" said Gösta.

"As I said, at first they were afraid that Nathalie and Sam would be found in some wooded area with bullets in their foreheads. When I confirmed that they're both here, the Stockholm police concluded she must have fled with her son, trying to escape from whoever killed her husband. She might even have witnessed the murder, and in that case, it was smart to run away. But they can't rule out the possibility that she was the one who pulled the trigger."

"What's going to happen now?" Annika looked upset.

"Two of the officers handling the investigation will be arriving here tomorrow. They want to talk to her as soon as possible. We'll wait until they get here."

"What if Nathalie and Sam are in danger?" said Martin.

"Nothing has happened so far, and tomorrow we'll have reinforcements. I'm hoping that our colleagues will know how to handle the situation."

"Yes, it's probably best to allow Stockholm to deal with this," Paula agreed. "But am I the only one who thinks . . ."

"That there's a connection between the murder of Fredrik Wester and the murder of Mats Sverin? Yes, that thought occurred to me too," said Patrik. He had been almost convinced who the perpetrator was, but this new information changed everything.

"So how did it go in Göteborg?" asked Martin, as if he could read Patrik's mind.

"Good and bad." He told them what had happened during the two days that he and Gösta had been away. When he was done, silence settled over everyone in the kitchen, except for Mellberg, who snickered at whatever scene was playing out in his mind. He smelled suspiciously of whiskey.

"After having no leads, we now have two plausible leads," Paula concluded.

"Yes, and that's why it's extremely important not to get locked into any particular theory. We need to keep working. Tomorrow the officers from Stockholm will be here, and then we can talk to Nathalie. I'm also waiting for Ulf in Göteborg to advise how we can best proceed with IE. And then there's the technical evidence to consider. Still no match for the bullet?" asked Patrik.

Paula shook her head.

"It'll probably take time. The boat is also being examined, but we haven't heard back yet."

"What about the cocaine bag?"

"There are still some fingerprints that haven't been identified."

"I was thinking about the boat. We need to consult an expert on the currents out there, someone who can tell us what direction the boat would have drifted, how far, and so on." Patrik looked around and finally fixed his gaze on Gösta.

"I'll take care of it." Gösta sounded tired.

"Good."

Martin raised his hand.

"Yes?"

"Paula and I talked to Lennart about the documents that were found in Mats's briefcase."

"What did he say?"

"Unfortunately, everything seems to be in order. Although I suppose that's actually good news, depending on how you look at it." Martin blushed.

"Lennart couldn't find any irregularities," Paula clarified. "That doesn't necessarily mean that there aren't any, but according to the documents in Mats's possession, everything seems to be above board."

"Okay. What do we know about the laptop?"

"That's going to take another week," said Paula.

Patrik sighed. "It looks as though we're going to do a lot of waiting, but we need to continue working on what we have. I'm going to sit down and go over everything that we've learned so far. Then I'll have a feel for where we stand and whether we've overlooked anything. Gösta, you deal with the boat. Martin and Paula . . ." He paused for a moment. "I'd like both of you to start digging up whatever information you can find on IE's activities, and also Fredrik Wester. Our colleagues in Göteborg and Stockholm have promised to help. You can get the contact information from me, then you can request all the background material that they're able to share. The two of you can divide the workload however you see fit."

"Okay," said Paula.

Martin nodded agreement and then raised his hand again.

"What about the Refuge? Are we going to report them?"

"No," said Patrik. "We've decided not to. As we see it, there's no reason to do so."

Martin looked relieved. "By the way, how did you find out about Sverin's girlfriend?"

Patrik cast a glance at Gösta, who looked down at the floor.

"Meticulous police work. And a gut feeling." Then he clapped his hands. "Okay, let's get to work."

# Fjällbacka 1875

**D**ays became weeks, and months became years. Emelie had settled in, adapting to the calm rhythms of Gråskär. She felt as if she were living in harmony with the island. She knew exactly when the hollyhocks would bloom, when the heat of summer would change to the chill of autumn, when the ice would form, and when it would break up. The island was her world, and in that world Gustav was king. He was a happy child, and every day she was amazed at how much joy he found in the restricted setting that framed his life.

Karl and Julian hardly spoke to her anymore. They lived separate lives, even though they all shared such a confined space. The harsh words had also diminished. It was as if she was no longer a person, and subsequently there was no use harboring any rancor toward her. Instead, they seemed to regard her as an invisible being. She took care of everything that needed tending, but otherwise she required none of their attention. Even Gustav accepted this strange arrangement. He never tried to approach Karl or Julian. They were less real to him than *the dead. And Karl never called his son by name. On those few occasions when he mentioned him, he always referred to him as "the boy."*

*Emelie knew precisely when the hatred in their eyes had become indifference. It was just after Gustav turned two. Karl had come back from a trip to Fjällbacka with an expression on his face that she had a hard time deciphering. He was completely sober. For once he and Julian hadn't gone to Abela's—and that in itself was unusual. Several hours passed with not a word out of Karl, and Emelie had tried to guess what was going on. Finally he placed a letter on the kitchen table.*

*"My father died," he said. And it was as if in that moment Karl was finally free. Emelie wished that Dagmar had told her more about Karl and his father, but now it was too late. There was nothing to be done about it, and she was grateful that Karl at least left her and Gustav in peace.*

*As each year passed, it became clearer to her that God was present in everything on Gråskär. She was filled with gratitude that she and Gustav were allowed to live in this place where they could feel God's spirit in the movement of the water and hear His voice in the rushing of the wind. Each day on the island was a gift, and Gustav was such a lively boy. She knew that it bordered on sinful pride to hold such a high opinion of her son, who was made in her own image. But according to the Bible, he was also made in God's image, so she hoped that she might be forgiven this sin. Gustav was so lovely, with his fair, curly hair, his blue eyes, and those long lashes that rested on his cheeks when he slept beside her at night. He talked all the time, both with her and with the dead. Sometimes she would eavesdrop on him, a smile on her face. He said so many wise things, and they were so patient with him.*

*"Can I go outside, Mamma?"*

*He tugged at her dress and peered up at her.*

*"Yes, all right. You go ahead." She leaned down and kissed his cheek. "But be careful not to fall into the water."*

*Emelie watched as he raced out the door. She wasn't really worried. She knew that he wasn't alone. Both the dead and God were keeping watch over him.*

# 21

Saturday arrived with the most beautiful weather imaginable. Radiant sunshine, a clear blue sky, and only a slight breeze. All of Fjällbacka bubbled with anticipation. Those who were fortunate enough to have received an invitation to the evening's dedication festivities had spent a large part of the week agonizing over their attire and hair. Everyone who was anyone in the local community was going to be there, and rumor had it that several celebrities would be coming from Göteborg.

But Erica had other things on her mind. That very morning she had decided that it would be better if someone told Nathalie about Gunnar in person rather than over the phone. And she'd already been thinking of going out to see Nathalie to give her the information that she'd unearthed about Gråskär's history, as a little surprise. Now that she had a babysitter, she decided to make the trip out to the island.

"Are you sure that you can manage for such a long time?" she asked her mother-in-law.

Kristina snorted.

"With these little angels? No problem." She was holding Maja in her arms, and the twins were asleep in their bassinets.

"I'll be gone for quite a while. First I'm going to see Anna, and then I'm going out to Gråskär."

"You'll be careful, won't you? I'm not sure I like the idea of you going out there in the boat alone." Maja was starting to squirm, so Kristina set her down. Maja gave her baby brothers a couple of wet kisses and then ran off to play.

"You don't need to worry. I know how to handle a boat," laughed Erica. "As opposed to your son."

"You have a point there," said Kristina, but she was still looking concerned. "By the way, are you sure that Anna is strong enough for this?"

The same thought had occurred to Erica when Anna phoned and asked her to accompany her out to the grave. But she realized that she needed to let her sister make her own decisions.

"Yes, I think so," she said, sounding more confident than she felt.

"I really think it's a bit too soon," said Kristina, picking up Noel, who had started whimpering. "But I hope you're right."

I do too, thought Erica as she went out to the car to drive to the cemetery. But no matter what reservations she might have, she'd promised to go with Anna, and she couldn't very well back out now.

Anna was waiting at the big iron gate near the fire station. She looked so small. Her cropped hair made her seem even more fragile, and Erica had to stop herself from taking her sister in her arms and rocking her like a baby.

"Are you sure you're ready for this?" she asked gently. "We can go out there some other day if you like."

Anna shook her head. "No, I'm fine. And I want to go. I was so out of it at the time that I can hardly even remember the funeral. I need to see where his grave is."

"Okay." Erica took Anna's arm and they walked along the gravel path.

They couldn't have chosen a more beautiful day. A muted rushing sound came from the traffic moving past, but otherwise everything was calm and peaceful. The sun shone on the headstones, and many of the graves were well tended with fresh flowers that family members had left. Anna suddenly paused, and Erica nodded in the direction of the grave.

"He's next to Jens." Erica pointed to a round boulder made of granite, with the name Jens Läckberg etched into the surface. Jens had been their father's good friend, and they remembered him from their childhood as a man with an impressive paunch who had always been cheerful, sociable, and witty.

"How lovely it is," said Anna. Her voice was devoid of emotion, but grief was evident in her expression. They had chosen a similar headstone, a naturally rounded piece of granite. And the etching had been done in the same manner. It said "Little One" and the year. Just one year.

Erica felt her throat close up, but she forced herself to hold back the tears. For Anna's sake she needed to be strong. Her sister swayed a bit as she stared at the stone, which was all that she had left of the child she had wanted so badly. She grabbed Erica's hand and squeezed it hard. Tears ran down her face. Then she turned to face her sister.

"What's going to happen? How is it all going to work out?"

Without a word, Erica wrapped her arms around her and held her tight.

༓

"Rita and I have a suggestion." Mellberg put his arm around Rita and pulled her closer.

Paula and Johanna looked at them, wondering what this was all about.

"Well, we don't really know what your plans are," said Rita, looking a bit more hesitant than Mellberg. "You said that you need a place of your own . . . And, well, the question is, how far away you'd like to move."

"What are you two talking about?" asked Paula, staring at her mother.

"What we're wondering is whether it would be enough if you moved to the floor below." Mellberg looked at them expectantly.

"But there aren't any vacant apartments in the building," said Paula.

"There is one. At least, there will be next month. The three-room apartment below could be yours as soon as the ink dries on the lease agreement."

Rita studied the girls carefully to see whether she could work out what they were thinking. She had been overjoyed when Bertil told her about the apartment, but she wasn't sure how much distance the girls felt they needed.

"Of course we wouldn't be running in and out of your place all the time," she assured them.

Mellberg looked at Rita in surprise. Wouldn't they be allowed to come and go as they pleased? But he decided not to comment. The most important thing was for the girls to accept the offer.

Paula and Johanna looked at each other. Then they both smiled and began talking at once.

"That three-room apartment is great. It's filled with light, and there are windows facing in two directions. And the kitchen was recently remodeled. And that little room that Bente uses as a dressing room could be Leo's room, and . . ." They suddenly stopped talking.

"But where is Bente going to live?" asked Paula. "I didn't know that she was planning to move."

Mellberg shrugged. "I have no idea. I assume that she's found another place. Alvar didn't mention it when I talked to him. But he did say that you'll have to paint it and make any other changes yourselves."

"No problem," said Johanna. "That'll be fun. We'll fix it up really nice, won't we, sweetheart?" Her eyes were sparkling, and Paula leaned forward to kiss her on the lips.

"And we can still help out with Leo," Rita interjected. "As much as you want us to, that is. We don't want to intrude."

"We're going to need plenty of help," said Paula, wanting to reassure her. "And we think it's wonderful that Leo will have you and Grandpa Bertil so close. As long as we have our own apartment, everything will work out fine."

Paula turned to Mellberg, who had lifted Leo onto his lap.

"Thank you, Bertil," she said.

To his surprise, Mellberg felt a bit embarrassed.

"Oh, it was nothing." He pressed his face against the back of Leo's neck, which always made the boy giggle. Then he looked up and glanced around the kitchen table. Once again Bertil Mellberg felt deeply grateful for this new family of his.

᠗

He was wandering aimlessly through the building. People were running around, taking care of all the last-minute preparations. Anders knew that he ought to lend a hand, but the knowledge of what he was about to undertake left him feeling paralyzed. He wanted to do it, and yet he didn't. The question was whether he was brave enough to handle the consequences of his actions.

He still wasn't convinced, but soon he wouldn't be able to spend any more time mulling it over. Soon he would have to decide.

"Have you seen Vivianne?" asked a female staff member as she rushed past. Anders pointed to the next room. "Thanks. Everything's going to be so great tonight."

Everybody was scurrying and bustling. But Anders felt as if he were moving under water.

"There you are, my future brother-in-law," said Erling, putting his arm around his shoulders. Anders had to fight the impulse to shrug him off. "It's going to be terrific. The celebrities will be here around four, so they'll have time to get settled in their rooms. At six o'clock we open to the other guests."

"I hear the whole town is talking about the event."

"I'm not surprised. This is the biggest thing to happen in the area since . . ." He didn't finish his sentence, but Anders knew what he had planned to say. He'd heard about the reality show *Sodding Tanum* and what a disaster it had turned out to be for Erling.

"So where's my little turtledove?" Erling craned his neck and looked around.

Again Anders pointed to the next room, and Erling raced off in that direction. Vivianne was certainly in demand today. He went out to the kitchen, sat down on a chair in the corner, and rubbed his temples. He could feel a bad headache coming on. He found the first-aid box and took two aspirin. Soon, he thought. Soon he would make up his mind.

c◌৹

Erica could still feel the lump in her throat as she steered the motorboat out of the harbor. The engine had started up immediately, and she was enjoying listening to the familiar sound of the motor. The boat had been her father's baby. Even though she and Patrik weren't nearly as conscientious as her father had been, they tried to keep it in good repair. This year the wooden deck needed to be sanded down and revarnished. It was starting to peel in places. If she could persuade Patrik to babysit the children, she had a mind to do the work herself. Since writing books was such a sedentary job, she loved to do work that required more muscle-power once in a while. And she was better at practical things than Patrik, although that didn't really say very much.

She glanced to the right to catch a glimpse of Badis. She was hoping that they could go to the dedication event, at least for a little while, but they hadn't yet decided. Patrik had looked very tired this morning, and Erica didn't know whether Kristina would feel like babysitting all evening.

At any rate, she was looking forward to this visit to Gråskär. When she and Patrik had gone out there before, she had felt captivated by the atmosphere. Now that she'd read about the island, she was even more fascinated. She had looked at a lot of pictures of the archipelago, and there was no doubt that the Gråskär lighthouse was one of the most beautiful. Erica wasn't surprised that Nathalie liked being out there, although she thought that personally she'd go crazy after a few days without seeing any other people. Then she thought about Nathalie's son, and hoped he was feeling better. Presumably he was on the mend, since Nathalie hadn't phoned to ask for help.

A short time later Gråskär appeared on the horizon. Nathalie hadn't sounded very enthusiastic when Erica called, but after a little coaxing, she'd agreed to the visit. Erica was convinced that she would enjoy hearing more about the island's past.

"Can you manage to bring the boat in on your own?" Nathalie shouted from the dock.

"No problem. As long as you're not worried about the pier." She smiled to show she was joking and smoothly brought the boat alongside. She switched off the motor and tossed the mooring line to Nathalie, who carefully fastened it.

"Hi," Erica said as she climbed out of the boat.

"Hi." Nathalie smiled but didn't meet her eye.

"How's Sam?" Erica looked up toward the house.

"Better," said Nathalie. She looked thinner than the last time Erica saw her, and the outline of her collarbone was visible through her T-shirt.

"I brought you some freshly baked buns," said Erica, taking out a bag. "Oh no, I forgot to ask if you needed any groceries." She was annoyed with herself. She should have asked when she phoned. Nathalie probably hadn't wanted to bother her with such a request again, since they didn't know each other very well.

"No, don't worry. You brought over so much last time, and I can always ask Gunnar and Signe. But I don't know if I should trouble them right now."

Erica hesitated, but she couldn't bring herself to tell Nathalie the news just yet. She would wait until they sat down.

"I thought we could have coffee in the boathouse. It's such beautiful weather."

"Yes, it's not the kind of day to spend indoors." Erica followed Nathalie to the open-sided boathouse where coffee cups were set on a weather-beaten table with benches on either side. Fishing gear hung on the walls, along with the gleaming blue and green glass balls that were used as floats. Nathalie filled their cups with coffee from a thermos.

"How do you handle living so isolated like this?" asked Erica.

"You get used to it," said Nathalie quietly, gazing out at the water. "And I'm not totally alone out here."

Erica flinched and looked at her inquisitively.

"I mean, I do have Sam, you know," Nathalie said.

Erica had to laugh at herself. She'd immersed herself so deeply in the stories about Gråskär that she'd actually started to believe them.

"So there's no truth behind the nickname Ghost Isle?"

"I don't think anybody believes those old ghost stories," said Nathalie, again looking out at the water.

"Well, the name does give the island a certain allure."

Erica had put all the information she'd collected about Gråskär in a folder, which she now took out of her purse and slid across the table toward Nathalie.

"It may be a small island, but it has quite a colorful past. With a few highly dramatic events."

"Yes, I've heard a little about that. Mamma and Pappa knew a lot about the island, but I'm afraid I never paid much attention to what they said about it." Nathalie opened the folder. A light breeze riffled the pages.

"I put everything in chronological order," said Erica. Then she fell silent as Nathalie leafed through the photocopies.

"I can't believe all the information you've found," said Nathalie, crimson patches appearing on her cheeks.

"It was fun doing the research. I need to do something other than change diapers and feed crying babies." She pointed at an article that Nathalie was looking at. "That's the most mysterious incident in the island's history. A whole family disappeared without a trace from Gråskär. Nobody knows what happened to them or where they went. The house looked as if they'd got up and walked out the door, leaving everything just as it was."

Erica could hear that she sounded a bit too enthusiastic, but she found the incident so intriguing. Mysteries had always sparked her imagination, and this one was a true-life suspense story.

"Look what it says there," she said, her voice calmer now. "The lighthouse keeper, Karl Jacobsson, his wife, Emelie, their son, Gustav, and the lighthouse assistant, Julian Sontag, lived here on the island for several years. Then they simply vanished, as if they'd gone up in smoke. Their bodies were never found, and there wasn't a single clue as to what might have happened to them. Nor was there any reason to believe that they'd left voluntarily. There was nothing. Isn't that strange?"

Nathalie glanced at the article with an odd expression on her face.

"Yes," she said. "Very."

"You haven't seen them lurking about, have you?" asked Erica jokingly, but Nathalie didn't respond. She merely continued to stare at the article. "I wonder what happened," Erica went on. "Maybe somebody came here by boat, murdered the whole family, and then disposed of the bodies. Their own boat was still moored to the dock."

Nathalie murmured to herself as she ran her finger over the page. Something about a blond little boy, but Erica couldn't really hear what she was saying. She turned to look at the house.

"Aren't you worried that Sam might wake up and wonder where you are?"

"He fell asleep just before you got here. He usually sleeps for a long time," said Nathalie, sounding distracted.

Neither of them spoke for a while, until Erica suddenly remembered the other reason for her visit. She took a deep breath and said:

"There's something I have to tell you, Nathalie."

Nathalie looked up. "Is it about Matte? Do they know who . . . ?"

"No, not yet, although they have a few leads. But this does have to do with Matte."

"What is it? Tell me," said Nathalie. Her hand still rested on top of the article.

Erica took another deep breath and told her what had happened to Gunnar.

"No. That can't be true. Why?" Nathalie looked as if she could hardly breathe.

With a heavy heart Erica told her about the little boys who found the cocaine, about Matte's fingerprints on the bag, and about what happened after the press conference.

Nathalie started shaking her head. "No, no, no. That can't be, that just can't be." She turned away.

"Everyone says the same thing. And I know that Patrik was skeptical too. But everything points in that direction, and that might also explain why Matte was murdered."

"No," said Nathalie. "Matte hated drugs. He hated everything that had to do with drugs." She clenched her teeth and then said, "Poor, poor Signe."

"Yes, it must be terrible to lose both your son and your husband in a matter of weeks," Erica murmured.

"How is she?" Nathalie's eyes were filled with empathy and sorrow.

"I'm not really sure. All I can tell you is that she's in the hospital, and apparently not doing well."

"Poor Signe," said Nathalie again. "So much misfortune. So many tragedies." She looked down at the article lying on the table.

"Yes." Erica didn't know what else to say. "Do you think I could go up in the lighthouse?" she asked at last, wanting to change the subject.

Nathalie shuddered, as if she'd been lost in thought.

"Oh . . . sure. I just need to get the key." She hurried off toward the house.

Erica stood up and walked over to the lighthouse. When she stood at its base, she tilted her head back to look up. The white paint gleamed in the sunlight. A few seagulls circled overhead, shrieking.

"Here it is." Nathalie was panting a bit as she approached. She was holding a big, rusty key.

The key did not turn easily in the lock, but finally she pulled open the heavy door. It creaked and groaned on its hinges. Erica stepped inside and began climbing the narrow, winding stairs, with Nathalie right behind her. Halfway up, Erica was breathing hard, but when she reached the top, she saw that it was worth the effort. The view was spectacular.

"Wow," she said.

Nathalie nodded proudly. "Yes. It's amazing, isn't it?"

"But imagine spending hours in this cramped space," said Erica, looking around.

Nathalie came over to stand next to her, so close that their shoulders almost touched.

"A lonely job. Like being on the very edge of the world." She seemed far away in her thoughts.

Erica sniffed at the air. She smelled something strange, and yet it seemed familiar. She knew that she'd smelled it before, but she couldn't really place it. Nathalie had taken a step forward to look out of the window at the open sea. Erica moved closer too.

Her brain was working feverishly to identify that smell. Then she realized where she'd encountered it before. Thoughts continued whirling through her mind, and slowly the pieces began falling into place.

"Would you mind waiting here while I run down to the boat to get my camera? I'd like to take a few pictures."

"Okay," said Nathalie reluctantly. She went over to the small bed and sat down.

"Great." Erica ran down the stairs and then raced down the hill on which the lighthouse stood. But instead of heading for the dock, she dashed for the house. She tried to tell herself that this was all just one of her crazy ideas. At the same time, she needed to find out for sure.

After casting a glance over her shoulder at the lighthouse, she pressed down the handle and opened the front door to the cottage.

Madeleine had heard them yesterday from upstairs. She hadn't known they were police officers until Stefan appeared and told her. In between hitting her.

She dragged her bruised body over to the window. With great effort she pulled herself up and looked out. The small room had a slanted ceiling, and the only light came from the narrow window. Outside, she saw farmland and woods.

They hadn't bothered to blindfold her, so she knew that she was at the farm. This room had been the children's when they lived here. Now the only reminder of their presence was a discarded toy car lying in one corner.

She pressed her hands against the wall and felt the pattern of the wallpaper under her palms. This was where Vilda's crib had stood. Kevin's bed had stood against the wall at the end of the room. That all seemed so long ago. She could hardly recall living here. It had been a life filled with fear, but at least she'd had the children.

She wondered where they were now—where Stefan had taken them. Probably they were staying with one of the families that didn't live here on the farm. One of the other women must be taking care of them. Missing the children was almost worse than the physical pain. She pictured them in her mind: Vilda coming down the slide in the courtyard back in Copenhagen, as Kevin proudly watched his brave little sister, and that lock of hair kept falling into his eyes. Madeleine wondered whether she'd ever see them again.

Sobbing, she sank down onto the floor and curled up in a fetal position. Her whole body felt like one enormous bruise. Stefan had vented all his anger on her. She had been mistaken, terribly mistaken, when she thought that it would be safer to come back to Sweden, that she would be able to ask forgiveness from him. The second she saw him standing in her parents' kitchen, she understood. There would be no forgiveness, and she'd been a fool to think otherwise.

Her poor mother and father. She knew how worried they must be, and how they were probably discussing whether to contact the police or not. Pappa would be in favor of doing that. He would say that was the only option. But Mamma would object, terrified that it would mean the end, that all hope would then be lost. Her father was right, but he would allow her mother to win, as usual. Nobody was going to come here to save her.

She curled up even more, trying to shape her body into a little ball. But the slightest movement hurt, so she forced her muscles to relax. She heard a key turn in the lock. She lay perfectly still, trying to will him to leave. A rough hand grabbed her arm and yanked her to her feet.

"Get up, you fucking whore."

It felt like her arm was being pulled out of its socket, as if something broke inside her shoulder.

"Where are the children?" she pleaded. "Can I see them?"

Stefan gave her a contemptuous look.

"You'd like that, wouldn't you? So you could take my kids and run away again. Nobody, and I mean nobody, is going to take my kids away from me." He dragged her out of the door and down the stairs.

"I'm sorry. I'm so sorry," she sobbed. Her face was streaked with blood and dirt and tears.

Stefan's men had all gathered downstairs. The inner circle. She knew them all: Roger, Paul, Lillen, Steven, and Joar. Now they stood in silence, looking at her as Stefan dragged her through the room. She had a hard time focusing. One eye was so swollen that it was practically closed, and blood from a cut in her forehead was clouding the vision of her other eye. And yet she knew exactly what was going to happen. She could see it in the faces of the men—some of them stared at her coldly, while others looked at her with pity. Joar, who had always been the nicest to her, suddenly looked down at the floor. That was when she understood. She considered fighting back, trying to resist, trying to get away. But where would she go? It was hopeless. All it would do was to prolong the agony.

Instead she stumbled after Stefan, who still had a tight grip on her arm. They hurried across the field behind the house, over toward the woods. In her mind she conjured up pictures of Kevin and Vilda. Newborn, lying at her breast. And much later, filled with laughter as they played in the Danish courtyard. She chose not to remember the time in between, when their eyes became more dazed and resigned for each day that passed. That was the life they were now going to return to, and she couldn't bear to think about it. She had failed. She should have protected them, but she had grown soft and weak. Now she was about to receive her punishment, and she accepted that—as long as her children would be spared.

They had entered the woods. Birds were chirping, and sunlight seeped through the crowns of the trees. She stumbled over a tree root and almost fell, but Stefan yanked at her arm and she kept on going. Up ahead she caught sight of a clearing, and for a moment she saw Matte's face. His handsome, kind face. He had loved her so much, and he too had been punished.

When they reached the clearing, she saw the hole in the ground. A rectangular hole, four or five feet deep. The shovel was still there, sticking out of the heap of dirt.

"Move over to the edge," said Stefan, letting go of her arm.

Madeleine obeyed. She no longer had any will of her own. She stood on the edge of the hole, shaking all over. When she looked down, she saw several fat worms trying to burrow deeper into the dark, moist earth. With one last effort she slowly turned around so she was standing face to face with Stefan. He would at least be forced to look her in the eye.

"I think I'll put the bullet right between your eyes." Stefan raised the gun, holding his arm out straight, and she knew that he was speaking the truth. He was an excellent marksman.

A flock of birds took off from the trees in fright when the shot was fired. But they soon settled back onto the branches, and their chirping blended with the soughing of the wind.

༄

It was so tedious, plowing through all the documents: post-mortem reports, interviews with neighbors, notes that they'd made during the investigation. After three hours Patrik realized dejectedly that he was only halfway through. When Annika stuck her head in the door, he welcomed the interruption.

"The detectives from Stockholm are here. Should I bring them to your office, or do you want to sit in the kitchen?"

"The kitchen," said Patrik, standing up. His back creaked, and he reminded himself that he ought to get up and stretch once in a while. He couldn't afford any back problems now, especially since he'd only recently returned to work after being on sick leave.

He met them in the corridor and paused to shake hands. The woman, who was tall and blond, gripped his hand so hard that he thought his bones would break. The short man with the glasses had a more relaxed handshake.

"Petra and Konrad, right? I thought we could sit in the kitchen. How was the drive?"

They chatted some more as they took their seats, and Patrik was struck by what an odd pair these two were. Yet they seemed perfectly at ease with each other, and Patrik suspected that they must have worked together for years.

"We need to talk with Nathalie Wester," Petra finally said, having tired of the small talk.

"As I said, she's here. Out on her island. I met her about a week ago."

"And she didn't mention her husband?" Petra fixed her eyes on Patrik, who felt as if he were being interrogated.

"No, she never said a word. We went out there to talk to her about an old boyfriend. He was found murdered in Fjällbacka."

"We read about the case," said Konrad. He turned to look at Ernst, who had come into the kitchen. "Is he the station's mascot?"

"Yes, you might say that."

"This is quite a coincidence," Petra went on. "We have a husband shot to death, and you have an old boyfriend shot to death."

"I was thinking the same thing. But we have a possible suspect in our case."

He briefly told his colleagues what they'd found out about Stefan Ljungberg and the Illegal Eagles. Both Petra and Konrad looked startled when he mentioned the bag of cocaine found in the litter bin.

"Yet another connection," said Petra.

"The only thing we know is that Sverin had touched the bag."

Petra waved away Patrik's protests. "No matter what, we need to look into this. Fredrik Wester mostly dealt in cocaine, and his transactions weren't restricted to Stockholm. With Nathalie as the common link, maybe they got in contact with each other and started doing business together."

Patrik frowned. "I don't know . . . Mats Sverin wasn't exactly the type who . . ."

"I'm afraid there isn't a specific type," said Konrad. "We've seen it all: upper-class youths, mothers of small children, even a pastor."

"Oh, right, that guy," laughed Petra. She suddenly looked less intimidating.

"Yes, I realize that," said Patrik, feeling like a real country bumpkin. He knew that he was a novice when it came to this type of crime, and his instincts might be wide of the mark. He needed to trust the experience of his Stockholm colleagues instead of paying attention to what his gut was telling him.

"Let's hear what you've got, then we'll fill you in on our case," said Petra.

Patrik nodded. "Okay. Who wants to start?"

"Go ahead." Konrad got out a pen and paper, and Ernst lay down on the floor, disappointed.

Patrik paused to gather his thoughts and then from memory told his colleagues what they'd found out so far. While Konrad took notes, Petra sat and listened intently, her arms crossed.

"Well, that's basically all," Patrik concluded. "Your turn."

Konrad put down his pen and gave him a summary of their investigation. They hadn't been working the case very long, but they'd already amassed a lot of information about Fredrik Wester and the narcotics organization he'd been part of. Konrad added that they'd gone over a lot of the details on the previous day, when Martin Molin had phoned. Patrik knew this, but he had wanted to hear their report himself.

"As you can tell, we're working closely with our colleagues in the narcotics division on this investigation." Konrad shoved his glasses back into place.

"Yes, that sounds good," murmured Patrik. An idea was starting to take shape in his mind. "Have you run the bullets through the police database yet?"

Konrad and Petra both shook their head.

"I talked to the lab yesterday," said Konrad, "and they were just getting started."

"We haven't received a report yet either, but . . ."

Petra and Konrad stared at him. Petra suddenly realized what Patrik was getting at.

"If we asked the lab to compare the bullets from these two cases . . ."

"Then we'd probably get the results back quicker," said Patrik.

"I like the way you think." Petra glanced at Konrad. "Could you give them a call? You're on good terms with the lab, whereas they're not too happy with me lately because of—"

Konrad seemed to know exactly what she meant, because he interrupted her and took out his cell. "I'll call them now."

"Do that. In the meantime, I'll go and get the information you'll need." Patrik jumped up and ran to his office. He came back with a document that he set on the table in front of Konrad.

Konrad chatted on the phone for a bit, and then made the request. He listened, nodded, and a smile appeared on his face.

"That's fantastic. I owe you one. I owe you big time. Thanks!" Konrad ended the conversation with a satisfied look on his face. "I talked to one of the boys I know over there. He's going to do a comparison right away. He'll call back the minute it's done."

"Incredible," said Patrik, clearly impressed.

Petra seemed unfazed. She was used to Konrad's ability to accomplish minor miracles.

⌖

Anna had slowly made her way home from the cemetery. Erica had offered to drive her, but she wanted to walk. Falkeliden was only a stone's throw away, and she needed to collect her thoughts. Dan would be waiting at home. He was hurt when she told him that she wanted to visit the grave with Erica and not with him. But right now she just didn't have the energy to take his feelings into consideration. She was hardly capable of examining her own emotions.

The inscription on the headstone would be etched into her heart forever. Little One. Maybe they should have tried to come up with a proper name. Afterward. But that hadn't felt right. They had called him Little One the whole time he was inside of her and loved by them all. So that was what he would always be called. He would never grow up, never be anything except that little mite that she'd never even held in her arms.

She'd been unconscious for so long, and then it was too late. Dan had held him, wrapped up in a tiny blanket. He'd been able to touch the baby and say goodbye. Even though she knew that wasn't Dan's fault, it hurt that he'd had that experience and she hadn't. Deep in her heart she was also angry at him for not protecting them, her and Little One. She knew that she was being ridiculous and irrational. It had been her decision to get in the car, and he'd not been present when the accident occurred. There was nothing he could have done. And yet she was angry that even Dan had not been able to protect her from bad things happening.

Maybe she had allowed herself to be lulled into a false sense of security. After everything she'd been through, after all those awful years with Lucas, she had convinced herself that it was finally over. That her life with Dan would be a long, straight road, without any unexpected bumps or curves. She hadn't had any high-flying plans or big dreams. All she wanted was an ordinary life in a row house in Falkeliden, with dinner parties, mortgage payments, football practice for the kids, and the ever-present piles of shoes in the front hall. Was that asking too much?

In some sense she had viewed Dan as the guarantor for that sort of life. He was so steady and stable, always calm and with the ability to see beyond any problems that arose. She had leaned on him, without standing on her own two feet. But he had fallen, and she didn't know how she was going to forgive him for that.

She opened the front door and went in. Her whole body ached after the walk, and her arms felt heavy as she lifted them to take off her scarf. Dan glanced at her from the kitchen and then stood motionless in the doorway. He didn't say a word, just looked at her with a pleading expression. She averted her eyes.

"I'm going upstairs to lie down," she mumbled.

∽

Anders was slowly packing up everything. He had enjoyed living in this small apartment, which had come to feel like a real home. That was not something that he and Vivianne had experienced very often. They'd lived in so many different places, and just when they were settling in and making friends, it would be time to move on. They would have to pack their belongings when people started asking questions, when neighbors and teachers started worrying about them, and when the ladies from social services finally began to see through Olof's charms.

As adults, he and Vivianne had done the same thing. It was as if the two of them carried a sense of insecurity with them, as if it were in their bones. They were constantly on the move, going from one place to another, just as they'd done with Olof.

He'd been dead for a long time now, yet they still lived in his shadow. The pattern was repeated. Things were different but somehow just the same.

Anders closed the lid of his suitcase. He had decided to suffer the consequences. In his heart, he was already missing her, but it was impossible to make an omelet without cracking some eggs, as Vivianne liked to say. Though he knew she was right, it was going to take years to make this particular omelet, and he wasn't sure that he could predict the results. But he was going to tell her. There was no use starting something new without admitting to what he'd done. He had spent too many sleepless nights coming to this conclusion, and now he'd made up his mind.

Anders looked around the apartment. He felt both relieved and filled with dread. It took courage to choose to stay instead of running away again. At the same time, it was the easiest route to take. He lifted his suitcase off the bed, then set it on the floor. There was no more time for brooding. He needed to tend to the festivities. And he was going to help Vivianne to make sure the party was a huge success. That was the least he could do for her.

⌘

The time hadn't gone as slowly as Patrik had feared. They had discussed both cases while they waited for the phone call from the lab, and Patrik had felt the adrenaline kick in. Although Paula and Martin were highly skilled police officers, he noticed that his Stockholm colleagues had a whole different mindset. Above all, he envied the working partnership that Petra and Konrad shared. Patrik could see that they were made for each other. Petra was excitable, and she was constantly coming up with new ideas and firing out suggestions. Konrad was more tactful and introspective, and he was able to offer insightful comments to Petra's outpourings.

When the phone rang, all three of them jumped. Konrad answered.

"Yes? Okay. Hmm . . . Really?"

Petra and Patrik stared at him. Was he saying so little just to torment them? Finally he ended the conversation and leaned back in his chair. They kept on staring at him until he finally spoke.

"They match. The bullets match."

For a moment there was total silence in the room.

"Are they positive about that?" Patrik then asked.

"A hundred percent positive. There's no doubt whatsoever. The same gun was used in both murders."

"Bloody hell." Petra had a big smile on her face.

"Now it's even more vital that we talk with Wester's widow. There must be some link between the victims, and I'm guessing it has to do with cocaine. Considering the type of individuals that might be involved, I wouldn't feel very safe if I were in Nathalie's shoes."

"Shall we go out there?" asked Petra, getting up.

Patrik was so engrossed in his own thoughts that he barely heard what she said. Vague suspicions were starting to gel into a pattern.

"I need to check on a few things first. Could you wait a couple of hours before we go out there?"

"Okay, we can do that," said Petra, but it was obvious that she was impatient.

"Great. You can make yourselves at home here, or you could take a walk around town. If you're hungry, I can recommend the food at Tanums Gestgiveri."

His Stockholm colleagues nodded.

"We'll go and have lunch. Just point us in the right direction," said Konrad.

After Patrik had told them how to find the restaurant, he took a deep breath and went back to his office. It was important not to be too hasty. He needed to make several phone calls, so he started with Torbjörn. He wasn't sure he'd get hold of him, since it was Saturday, but Torbjörn answered his phone. Patrik briefly told him what they'd found out about the bullets, and then he asked Torbjörn if he could compare the unidentified fingerprints from the cocaine bag with the prints they'd found on both the inside and outside of Sverin's front door. Patrik also warned him that he'd be sending over a new fingerprint to compare with the others. Torbjörn started asking questions, but Patrik cut him off. He would explain later.

The next task on his list was to locate a specific report. He knew it was somewhere in the stack on his desk, so he began leafing through the documents. Finally he found it. Carefully he read the odd, brief report. Then he went into Martin's office.

"I need your help." He put the report on Martin's desk. "Can you remember any more details about this?"

Martin looked at Patrik in surprise but then shook his head.

"No, I'm afraid not. Although I'm not going to forget that particular witness for a very long time."

"Could you go back there and ask a few more questions?"

"Sure." He looked as if he would burst with curiosity.

"I mean now," said Patrik when Martin made no move to get up.

"Okay, okay." He jumped to his feet. "I'll call as soon as I find out anything more," he said over his shoulder. Then he stopped. "But can't you at least tell me why . . ."

"Go now. We'll talk about it later."

Two things taken care of. One more to go. Patrik went to the sea chart hanging on the wall in the corridor. After trying to pry off a thumbtack, he finally lost patience and yanked the map off the wall, tearing several corners. Then he took it into Gösta's office.

"Have you talked to that guy who knows the archipelago near Fjällbacka?"

Gösta nodded. "Yup. I gave him all the information, and he was going to mull it over. It's not an exact science, but it might give us a lead."

"Call him up and give him this information too." Patrik set the sea chart on Gösta's desk and showed him what he was talking about.

Gösta raised an eyebrow.

"Is this urgent?"

"Yes. Call him now and ask him for a quick opinion. All he needs to tell us is whether it's possible. Or reasonable. Then come and let me know what he says."

"You got it." Gösta reached for the phone.

Patrik returned to his office and sat down at the desk. He was out of breath, as if he'd been running, and his heart was pounding. Thoughts continued to whirl through his mind. More details, more questions, more speculations. At the same time, he felt that he was on the right track. But all he could do at the moment was wait. He stared out of the window and drummed his fingers on the desktop. The shrill ring of his cell startled him.

He answered the phone and then listened intently.

"Thanks for calling, Ulf. Keep me posted, okay?" Then he ended the conversation.

His heart was pounding again. This time from anger. That bastard had found Madeleine and her children. Her father had mustered the courage to call the police and report that his daughter's ex-husband had forced his way into their apartment and left with both Madeleine and the kids. Since then, they hadn't heard a word from them. Patrik realized that they must have already gone missing when he and Ulf were out at the farm. Were they somewhere on the property, locked up and in need of help? Patrik clenched his fists, feeling helpless. Ulf had assured him that they would do everything they could to find Madeleine, but he didn't sound hopeful.

An hour later Konrad and Petra appeared in the doorway.

"Are we ready to go now?" asked Petra.

"Not quite yet. There's one more thing we need to work out." Patrik wasn't sure how to explain. So much was still murky and hazy.

"And what's that?" Petra frowned. She clearly didn't want to waste any more time.

"Let's meet in the kitchen." Patrik got up and went to summon the others. After hesitating for a moment, he also knocked on Mellberg's door.

When everyone had gathered, Patrik introduced Petra and Konrad. Then he cleared his throat and slowly began explaining his theory, careful to include those areas that still had major holes. When he was finished, everyone sat in silence for a moment.

"What would be the motive?" asked Konrad. He sounded both hopeful and skeptical.

"I don't know. That's what we still have to work out. But the theory holds up, even though there are some gaps that have to be filled in."

"How should we proceed?" asked Paula.

"I've talked to Torbjörn and told him that we'd be sending over a new fingerprint ASAP, so he can compare it with the prints on the door and the paper bag. If it matches, everything else will be easier. Then we'll have a link to the murder."

"The murders," said Petra. She looked dubious but at the same time slightly impressed.

"Who's going with us?" asked Konrad, looking at the others. He was starting to get up, as if to head out the door at once.

"I'll go with the two of you. That should be plenty," said Patrik. "Everyone else will keep working on the new leads."

The minute they stepped out into the sunshine, Patrik's cell rang. When he saw that it was his mother calling him, he didn't want to answer, but finally he decided to take the call. Impatiently he listened to his mother pouring out her worries.

She couldn't get hold of Erica even though she'd tried ringing her cell several times. When she told Patrik where Erica had gone, he stopped abruptly. Without saying goodbye, he ended the phone call and turned to Petra and Konrad.

"We have to go. Now."

⌒∞⌒

Erica opened the door and nearly toppled over backward. She almost threw up, and she realized that she was right. It was the smell of a corpse. A suffocating and deeply disturbing stench that was impossible to mistake for anything else once you'd smelled it. She stepped inside, holding her arm over her nose and mouth as she tried to shut out the smell. But it was impossible. It was so penetrating, seeming to seep into every pore, just as it had clung to Nathalie's clothes.

She looked around, her eyes filling with tears from the stench. Cautiously she took a few more steps inside the small house. Everything was quiet and peaceful. Only the distant sound of the sea could be heard. Nausea threatened to overwhelm her, but she fought off the urge to escape into the fresh air.

From where she stood, she could survey the entire ground floor. There were only ordinary things to see. A sweater hanging over the back of a chair, a coffee cup on the table next to an open book. Nothing that could explain the cloying, disgusting smell that hovered like a blanket over everything.

One door was closed. Erica dreaded opening that door, but now that she'd come this far, she knew that she had to do it. Her hands shook and her legs suddenly felt like jelly. She wanted to turn around and run out the front door to the boat and go home. Home to the fragrant scent of her babies' hair. But she moved closer. She saw her trembling right hand reach out and take hold of the door handle. Still she hesitated to press it down, didn't dare see what was inside that room.

A sudden gust of wind on her legs made her turn around. But it was too late. Suddenly everything went black.

⌀

The guests of honor who had come from further away were chattering happily as they disembarked from the buses arriving from Göteborg. Sparkling wine had been served during the drive to Fjällbacka, with the result that everyone was now in a glorious mood.

"It's going to be great." Anders put his arm around his sister's shoulders as they waited to welcome the guests.

Vivianne smiled joylessly. This was the beginning, but it was also the end. And she was unable to enjoy the present moment when it was only the future that mattered. A future that no longer felt as certain as it once had.

She studied her brother's profile as he stood in the open doorway of Badis. There was something different about him. She'd always been able to read him like an open book, but now he'd retreated to a place where she was unable to reach him.

"What a splendid day, my darling." Erling kissed her on the lips. He looked rested. Yesterday she had given him the sleeping tablet at seven o'clock, so he'd slept for thirteen hours straight. Now he was practically bounding around in his white suit. After giving her another kiss, he hurried off.

The guests began entering the building.

"Welcome. I hope you have a pleasant stay at Badis." Vivianne shook hands, smiling and repeating her words of welcome again and again. She looked as if she'd stepped out of a fairytale, wearing a white, ankle-length gown, and with her thick hair hanging in a plait down her back, as usual.

When everyone had gone inside, and she and Anders were alone for a moment, her smile faded and her expression grew serious. She turned to face her brother.

"We always tell each other everything, don't we?" she said in a low voice. She ached with longing to hear him say what she wanted to hear. She truly wanted to believe him. But Anders looked away, and didn't say a word.

Vivianne was about to ask him again, but a late-arriving guest was approaching the entrance, so she plastered on her warmest smile. Inside, she felt ice-cold.

⁓⧼⧽⁓

"Why did your wife go out there?" asked Petra.

Patrik was driving to Fjällbacka as fast as he dared. He explained about the books that Erica wrote and told them that lately she had started researching Gråskär, just for her own amusement.

"She probably wanted to show Nathalie what she'd found."

"There's no reason to think that she's in any danger," said Konrad, sitting in the backseat and trying to reassure Patrik.

"No, I realize that," said Patrik. At the same time he had a feeling that he needed to get out to Gråskär as fast as possible. He had phoned Peter, who promised to have the Coast Guard vessel ready when they arrived.

"I'm still wondering what the motive could be," said Konrad.

"Hopefully we'll find out soon—if Patrik is right, that is." Petra didn't sound completely convinced.

"So you're saying that, according to a witness, Mats Sverin had a woman in the car with him when he came home on the night he was shot? How reliable is the witness?" Konrad leaned forward to stick his head between the front seats. Outside the car windows, the countryside was passing by at breakneck speed, but neither Petra nor Konrad seemed particularly concerned.

Patrik considered how much he should tell them. The truth was that Old Man Grip was not the most reliable of witnesses. For a start, he claimed that it was his cat who had seen the woman. That was the first thing that had occurred to Patrik when he heard that the bullets matched. In Martin's report, it said that the cat was sitting in the window, hissing at the car, and a few lines above it said: "Marilyn doesn't like women. She hisses at them." Martin hadn't noticed the connection, and Patrik hadn't either when he first read the report. But combined with the other details that had emerged, it was enough for Patrik to send Martin back to have another talk with Grip. This time he managed to get the man to admit that a woman was seen getting out of the car that had stopped in front of the block of apartments in the early hours of Saturday. After hesitating a bit, he had also confirmed that it was Sverin's car. Unfortunately, Grip continued to insist that it was his cat who had seen all of this. Patrik decided to omit this last detail for the time being.

"The witness is certain," he said, hoping that would satisfy his colleagues. The important thing now was to reach Erica as quickly as possible and have a talk with Nathalie. Everything else could wait. Besides, they had the boat. According to the expert that Gösta had talked to, it was not only possible but very likely that Sverin's boat had drifted from Gråskär when it ended up stranded in that inlet.

In Patrik's mind, a plausible chain of events had begun to unfold. Mats had gone out to visit Nathalie, and for some reason she had then accompanied him in his boat to Fjällbacka. They had driven to Mats's apartment, where she had shot him. He had trusted Nathalie, so he didn't hesitate to turn his back on her. Then she had gone back to the harbor, taken Sverin's boat to Gråskär, and let it go from there, causing it to drift off until it got stuck and was later found. That much was crystal clear. Except that Patrik still didn't have any idea why Nathalie would want to kill Mats and possibly also her husband. And why did they leave Gråskär and go back to Fjällbacka in the middle of the night? Did it have something to do with the cocaine? Had Mats been involved in business transactions with Nathalie's husband? Did the unidentified fingerprint on the bag belong to her?

Patrik stepped even harder on the accelerator. Now they were racing through Fjällbacka, and he slowed down a bit when he almost ran into an elderly man who was crossing the street near Ingrid Bergman Square.

He parked the car at the harbor near the Coast Guard vessel and jumped out. He was relieved to see that Peter had already started up the motor. Konrad and Petra trotted after him and jumped on board.

"Don't worry," Konrad said. "At this point, it's all speculation, and there's no reason to believe that your wife is in danger, even if your theory turns out to be correct."

Patrik glanced at him as he held onto the railing of the boat, which was speeding out of the harbor faster than was normally allowed.

"You don't know Erica. She has a talent for sticking her nose into everyone's business. Even people who have nothing to hide think that she asks too many questions. You might say that she's really persistent."

"She sounds like a woman after my own heart," said Petra, staring with fascination at the archipelago they were traversing.

"And besides, she's not answering her cell," said Patrik.

No one said a word for the rest of the crossing. They saw the lighthouse in the distance, and Patrik felt his stomach lurch with fear as they neared the island. He couldn't stop thinking about the other name for Gråskär, the name that the locals called it: Ghost Isle. And why it had gotten the name.

Peter slowed down and steered the boat over to the dock, next to the wooden motorboat that belonged to Erica and Patrik. There was no one in sight, either living or dead.

⁂

Everything was going to be fine. They were together. She and Sam. And the dead were keeping watch over them.

Nathalie hummed as she stood in the water holding Sam in her arms. It was a song that she had always sung to him when he was younger and couldn't sleep. He lay in her arms and felt so light because the water was helping to carry him. A few drops splashed upon his face, and she carefully wiped them away. He didn't like getting water in his face. As soon as he was feeling better, she was going to teach him to swim. He was old enough now to learn to swim and ride a bike, and soon he'd be losing his baby teeth. Then he'd have a big gap in his teeth, showing that he would soon leave the first years of childhood behind.

Fredrik had always been impatient with Sam and demanded too much of him. He thought that she coddled him, claiming that she wanted him to remain a child. Fredrik was wrong. She wanted nothing more than for Sam to grow up, but he had to do it at his own pace.

Then he had tried to take Sam away from her. In that arrogant voice of his, Fredrik had said that the boy would be better off with a different mother. The memory started encroaching, and she hummed louder to make it go away. But those terrible words had already crept into her soul, drowning out the song. The other woman would be better, he had told her. She was the one who would be Sam's new mother and accompany him and Sam to Italy. Nathalie wasn't going to be his mother anymore. She was going to disappear.

Fredrik's face had been filled with such smug satisfaction that she hadn't doubted for a moment that he meant what he'd said. How she hated him. Anger began growing somewhere deep inside of her and then took over her whole body before she could stop it. Fredrik had gotten what he deserved. He couldn't hurt them anymore. She had seen his rigid expression. She had seen the blood.

Now she and Sam could live in peace here on the island. She looked down at his face. He was sleeping. No one was going to take him away from her. No one.

⁓∞⁓

Patrik asked Peter to wait in the boat. Then he went ashore with Konrad and Petra. On the table in the open-sided boathouse they saw that someone had served coffee there. When they walked past, several seagulls flew up from a plate full of buns.

"They're probably in the house," said Petra, taking a good look around.

"Come on." Patrik was impatient, but Konrad gently took him by the arm.

"I think we need to be a bit cautious now."

Patrik realized that he was right. He headed for the house, walking calmly even though he wanted to run. At the house, they knocked on the door. When no one answered, Petra leaned forward and knocked harder.

"Hello?" she called.

Still not a sound from inside. Patrik pushed down the handle, and the door swung open. He took a step forward then nearly backed into Konrad and Petra as the smell overwhelmed him.

"Shit," he said, putting his hand over his nose and mouth. He had to swallow several times in order not to throw up.

"Shit," echoed Konrad from behind him. He too looked as if he were fighting back nausea. Only Petra seemed unperturbed, and Patrik cast an astonished glance in her direction.

"I've got a weak sense of smell," she told him.

Then Patrik entered the house and immediately caught sight of the person lying on the floor.

"Erica?" He ran over and dropped to his knees. With his heart in his throat, he put out his hand to touch her. She stirred and let out a groan.

He said her name over and over, and she slowly turned her head to look at him. Only then did he see the wound at her temple. With an effort she lifted her hand to touch it, and her eyes opened wide when she saw the blood on her fingers.

"Patrik? Nathalie . . . she . . ." Erica began sobbing and Patrik stroked her cheek.

"Is she okay?" asked Petra.

Patrik motioned with his hand to indicate that she was going to be all right. Then Petra and Konrad went upstairs to see what they could find up there.

"The place seems to be empty," said Petra when they came back. "Have you checked in there?" She pointed at the closed door behind Erica.

Patrik shook his head, so Petra cautiously stepped around them and opened the door.

"Bloody hell. Come and look." She motioned to them, but Patrik stayed where he was and let Konrad follow his colleague.

"What do you see?" asked Patrik, glancing at the partially open door, which blocked his view of what was inside.

"Whatever the smell is, it's coming from inside this room." Konrad came out, holding his hand over his mouth and nose.

"A dead body?" For a moment Patrik thought it must be Nathalie lying inside there, but then a thought occurred to him that drained all the color from his face. "Is it the boy?" he whispered.

Petra came out of the room too. "I don't know. There's nothing in there now. But the bed is a horrible mess and it stinks to high heaven. Even I can smell it."

Konrad nodded.

"It must be the boy. We saw Nathalie a week ago, and I'm guessing that the body must have been here longer than that."

Erica was struggling to sit up, and Patrik put his arm around her for support.

"We have to find them." He looked at his wife. "What happened here?"

"We were up in the lighthouse. I noticed the smell on Nathalie's clothes and started to wonder. So I slipped over here to check things out. She must have hit me on the head . . ." Erica's voice faded.

Patrik looked up at Konrad and Petra.

"What did I tell you? She's always sticking her nose in things." He smiled, but he looked worried.

"You didn't see the boy?" asked Petra, squatting down.

Erica shook her head, then grimaced with pain.

"No, I never got a chance to open the door. But you have to find them," she said, repeating what Patrik had said. "I'm fine. Go look for Nathalie and Sam."

"Let's carry her down to the boat," said Patrik.

He ignored Erica's protests and the three of them carried her to the dock and then carefully lifted her down to Peter.

"Are you sure you're all right?" Patrik didn't want to leave Erica when he looked at the bloody wound on her head and saw how pale her face was.

She waved him away. "Go on. I'm fine. I told you that."

Reluctantly Patrik turned away.

"Where do you think they've gone?"

"They must be on the other side of the island," said Petra.

"Yes, because their boat is still here," said Konrad.

They started walking over the rocks. The island seemed just as deserted as when they arrived, and except for the lapping of the waves and the screeching of the seagulls, there wasn't a sound.

"They might be up in the lighthouse." Patrik leaned back so he could peer up at the tower.

"Maybe, but I think we should search the island first," said Petra. She shaded her eyes with her hand in an attempt to look through the glass panes at the top of the lighthouse. But she didn't see anyone moving around up there either.

"Are you coming?" called Konrad.

The highest point on the island was only a short distance away, and they cast glances left and right as they walked. Once they reached the top of the hill, they'd have a view of almost all of Gråskär. But they were moving cautiously. They didn't know what sort of state of mind Nathalie was in, and she had a gun. The question was whether she was prepared to use it. The cloying smell of the corpse still clung to their nostrils. They were all thinking the same thing, but none of them dared say it out loud.

They climbed up to the crest of the hill.

⌘

They had arrived by boat, just as she thought. She heard voices from the dock, voices from the house. Their escape route from the island was blocked. She couldn't get to the boat to flee. She and Sam were caught.

Nathalie had thought that Erica was on their side, but then she tried to push her way into their world. So she had been forced to act, and she had done the right thing. She had protected Sam, just as she had promised him she would, the instant he was placed in her arms at the hospital. She had promised not to let anything bad happen to him. For a long time she had been a coward and failed to keep her promise. But ever since that night, she had been strong. She had rescued Sam.

Slowly she moved further into the water. Her jeans felt heavy against her legs, dragging her forward. Sam was so sweet, lying quietly in her arms.

Someone came over to her, wading alongside her and following her into the water. Out of the corner of her eye she saw the woman holding up her heavy skirts. After a moment she let her skirts drop so that they floated in the water all around her. She had her eyes fixed on Nathalie. Her lips were moving, but Nathalie refused to listen. If she did, she wouldn't be able to protect Sam any longer. She shut her eyes to make the woman go away, but when she opened them, she couldn't help glancing in that direction again, as if something were forcing her to look.

Now the woman was carrying a child in her arms. He hadn't been there a moment ago. Nathalie was sure of that. But now he too was looking at her with big, pleading eyes. He was talking to Sam. Nathalie wanted to put her hands over her ears and scream to shut out the voices of the boy and the woman. But her hands were holding Sam, and the scream stuck in her throat. Her shirt was starting to get wet, and she gasped for breath as the cold water reached her stomach. The woman was walking very close. She and the boy were both talking at once—the woman to Nathalie, and the boy to Sam. Against her will, Nathalie started to listen to what they were saying. The voices forced their way in just like the salt water was soaking through her clothes and reaching her skin.

They had come to the end of the road, she and Sam. Any minute now, those people would find them and finish what they'd begun. The memory of the blood spattering the wall and coloring Fredrik's face flashed through her mind for a moment. Nathalie shook her head to make those images go away. Were they dreams or fantasies? Or were they real? She no longer knew. She remembered only the icy feeling of hatred and panic. And a fear so great that it seized hold of her, leaving only the most primitive and furious of reactions.

When the water came up to her armpits, she could feel how light Sam was in her arms. The woman and the boy were very close. Their voices were close to her ear, and she clearly heard what they said. Nathalie closed her eyes and finally relented. They were right. A sense of certainty filled her body and made all fear disappear. She knew that they wished her and Sam well, and she stood there, letting a feeling of calm wash over her.

Far behind her, she thought she heard other voices. Others who were calling her, who wanted something, and who were trying to get her to listen. She ignored them. They were less real than the voices so close to her ear that were still talking.

"Let him go," said the woman gently.

"I want to play with him," said the boy.

Nathalie nodded. She needed to let go. That was what they had wanted the whole time, what they had tried to explain. He belonged to them now. He belonged to the others.

Slowly she released her hold on Sam. She let the sea take him, let him disappear beneath the surface to be carried away on the currents. Then she took a step forward, and another. All the voices were still talking. She heard them both near and in the distance, but again she chose not to listen. She wanted to follow Sam and be one of them. What else should she do?

The woman's voice was pleading, but the water rose up over her ears, drowning out all sounds and replacing them with a roar, as if from the blood that was rushing through her body. Onward she went, feeling the water closing over her head and the air being pressed out of her lungs.

Then something dragged her upward. The woman was surprisingly strong. She pulled her to the surface, and Nathalie felt anger rise up inside of her. Why wasn't she allowed to follow her son? She fought back, but the woman refused to let go and kept dragging her back toward life.

Another pair of hands grabbed hold of her body and pulled her up. Her head broke through the surface and her lungs filled with air. Nathalie uttered a scream that rose up toward the sky. She wanted to go back under the water, but instead she felt herself being dragged toward land.

Then the woman and the boy were gone. Just like Sam.

Nathalie felt herself being lifted up and carried away. She gave up. They had found her at last.

⚬∞⚬

The party went on all evening and well into the early morning hours. Everyone enjoyed the excellent food, the wine flowed, the guests of honor and the locals mingled, and new friends were made on the dance floor. In other words, it was a very successful event.

Vivianne went over to Anders as he stood leaning against the railing, watching the couples dance.

"We've got to leave now."

He nodded, but something in his expression made her feel more uneasy than ever.

"Come on." She tugged at his sleeve. Without looking her in the eye, he turned and followed her.

She had hidden her suitcase in one of the rooms that wasn't reserved for guests. She picked it up and headed for the door, ready to leave.

"Where's your suitcase? We have to leave in ten minutes, otherwise we might miss our plane."

Anders didn't reply. Instead he sank down onto the bed and stared at the floor.

"Anders?" She had a tight grip on the handle of her suitcase.

"I love you," whispered Anders. Those words suddenly sounded ominous.

"We have to go," she said, but she knew in her heart that he wasn't going with her. In the distance they could hear the thudding music. She set her suitcase on the floor and sat down next to him.

"I can't." He looked at her. His eyes filled with tears.

"What have you done?" She didn't want to hear what he said, didn't want to know that her worst fears had come true. But she couldn't stop herself from asking the question.

"Done? Good Lord, did you think I was the one who . . . ?"

Anders shook his head and began laughing as he wiped away his tears with the back of his hand. "Good Lord, Vivianne. No!"

She felt enormously relieved, but in that case, she really didn't understand what was going on.

"Why then?" Vivianne put her arm around her brother's shoulders, and he leaned his head against her. That conjured up so many memories of all the times they had sat like this, with their heads close together.

"You know that I love you."

"Yes, I know that." And suddenly she understood. She straightened up so she could get a proper look at him. Gently she took his face in her hands. "My dear brother, have you fallen in love with someone?"

"I can't go with you," he said, his eyes again filling with tears. "I know that we promised each other that we'd always stay together. But you'll have to make this trip without me."

"If you're happy, then I'm happy too. It's as simple as that. I'll miss you terribly, but there's nothing I want more than for you to have your own life." She smiled. "But you do have to tell me who it is. Otherwise I can't leave."

He mentioned a name, and Vivianne pictured a woman they'd worked with in connection with Project Badis. Again she smiled.

"You have good taste," she said, and then fell silent for a moment. "You're going to have to do a lot of explaining, and you'll be held responsible. Should I really leave you alone with all this? I'll stay if you want me to."

Anders shook his head.

"I want you to go. Bask in the sun and enjoy it for me too. I doubt I'm going to see much daylight for a while, but she knows about everything and has promised to wait for me."

"What about the money?"

"It's all yours," he said without hesitation. "I don't need any of it."

"Are you sure?" Again she took his face in her hands, as if touching him would help her to remember his familiar features.

He nodded and took her hands away.

"I'm sure. And now you have to go. The plane won't wait for you."

He stood up and grabbed her suitcase. Without another word he carried it out to the car and put it in the trunk. No one saw them. The hum of voices blended with the music, and everyone was focused on other things.

Vivianne got into the driver's seat.

"We did a good job, didn't we?" She glanced up at Badis, which glittered in the dim light.

"A damned good job."

For a moment neither of them spoke. Then Vivianne took off her engagement ring and handed it to Anders.

"Here. Give this back to Erling. He's not a bad person. I hope he finds somebody else to give it to someday."

Anders put it in his trousers pocket.

"I'll make sure he gets it."

They stared at each other in silence. Then Vivianne closed the door and started up the car. Anders stood there for a long time, watching as she sped away. Then he slowly went up the stairs to Badis. He had decided to be the last person to leave the party.

# 22

E rling was starting to panic. Vivianne had disappeared. No one had seen her since the party on Saturday, and her car was also missing. Something must have happened.

Again he picked up the phone and called the police station.

"Have you heard anything?" he asked as soon as Mellberg answered. When he received another negative reply, he could no longer control himself. "What exactly are you doing to find my fiancée? I'm convinced that something terrible must have happened to her. Have you dragged the water around the dock? Yes, I realize that her car is missing too, but who's to say that somebody didn't drive it into the harbor, and maybe with Vivianne inside?" Erling's voice rose to a falsetto as he pictured Vivianne trapped in the car, unable to escape as the water slowly rose. "I demand that you make use of all possible resources to find her."

He slammed down the phone. A timid knock on the door made him glance up. Gunilla poked her head in, giving him a frightened look.

"Yes?" He wished everybody would just leave him alone. He'd been out searching for Vivianne all of Sunday, and this morning he'd come to the office only because he hoped she might try to reach him there.

"The bank called." Gunilla sounded even more anxious than usual.

"I don't have time for things like that right now," he said, staring at the phone. She might call at any moment.

"It's about the Badis account, something that's not as it should be. They want you to call them back."

"I told you, I don't have time for that," he snapped. To his surprise, Gunilla was still standing there.

"They want you to call back, and they said it's urgent," she told him, and then went back to her desk.

With a sigh Erling picked up the phone and called their contact at the bank. "It's Erling. Is there some sort of problem?"

He tried to sound authoritative. He wanted to make the call as brief as possible so that the line wouldn't be busy if Vivianne phoned. He was hardly paying attention as he listened to the bank official, but suddenly he sat up straight.

"What do you mean there's no money in the account? You'd better check again. We deposited several million kronor, and additional funds will be arriving from Vivianne and Anders Berkelin this week. I know that we have a lot of suppliers that need to be paid, but there's plenty of money in that account." Then he fell silent and listened some more. "Are you sure you're not mistaken?"

Erling tugged at the collar of his shirt. He was suddenly having a hard time breathing. When he put down the phone, thoughts began whirling through his head. The money was gone. Vivianne was gone. He wasn't stupid—he could put two and two together. But he didn't want to believe it.

Erling had just tapped in the first three digits of the phone number for the police station when Anders appeared in the doorway. Erling stared at him. Vivianne's brother looked haggard and exhausted. At first he merely stood there without saying a word. Then he came over to Erling's desk and held out his hand, palm up. Light from the window shone on what he was holding and made tiny sparkles dance over the wall behind Erling. Vivianne's engagement ring.

At that moment all doubt disappeared from Erling's mind. In a daze, he tapped in the rest of the numbers for the Tanumshede police. Anders sat down in a chair across from him and waited. On the desk lay the engagement ring, glittering in the light.

# 23

On Wednesday morning Erica was allowed to leave the hospital and go home. It had turned out that the blow to her head wasn't serious, but considering the previous injuries that she'd sustained in the car accident, the doctors had decided to keep her under observation for a few days just to be on the safe side.

"Stop it. I can walk on my own." She glared at Patrik, who was holding her arm as they went up the front steps to the house. "You heard what they said. Everything looks okay. I don't have a concussion, only a few stitches."

Patrik opened the door.

"Yes, I know, but . . ." He fell silent when he saw the look Erica gave him.

"When will the kids be home?" She kicked off her shoes.

"Mamma is bringing the twins over around two, and then I thought that we could all go and pick up Maja. She's been missing you terribly."

"What a sweetie she is," said Erica, going into the kitchen. It felt strange to be home with no children around. She could hardly remember what that felt like.

"Sit down and I'll make some coffee," said Patrik, moving past her.

Erica was about to protest when she realized that she ought to make the most of the situation. She sat down at the kitchen table and with a contented sigh propped her feet up on the chair next to her.

"Do you know what will happen with Badis?" She felt as if she'd been living in a bubble at the hospital, so now she wanted to hear about everything that had been going on. She still couldn't believe the rumors she'd heard concerning Vivianne.

"The money and Vivianne are gone." Patrik was standing at the counter, making the coffee. "We found her car at Arlanda airport, and we're in the process of checking the passenger lists from the weekend. Presumably she wasn't traveling under her own name, so that makes things harder."

"What about the money? Can't you track it down?"

Patrik turned around and shook his head. "It doesn't look good. We've asked the fraud division in Göteborg for help, but there are ways of transferring funds out of the country that make it extremely difficult to track the money. And I'm guessing that Vivianne planned the whole thing very carefully."

"What does Anders have to say?" Erica got up, wanting to get something out of the freezer.

"Sit down. I'll get the buns." Patrik took a bag of cinnamon buns out of the freezer and put several of them in the microwave. "Anders has admitted to taking part in the embezzlement scheme, but he refuses to tell us where his sister and the money are now."

"Why didn't he leave with Vivianne?" Erica had sat back down at the table.

"Who knows? Maybe he got cold feet at the last second and didn't want to spend the rest of his life away from Sweden, in exile."

"Hmm, I suppose that's possible." Erica paused for a moment and then asked, "So how is Erling taking it? And what's going to happen to Badis?"

"Erling seems mostly . . . resigned." Patrik poured two cups of coffee and then took the warm buns out of the microwave and set everything on the kitchen table. "As far as Badis is concerned, nobody really knows what its future will be. Almost none of the suppliers or builders have been paid. The question is, which option would be more costly: to close the doors, or to continue operating the place. After the party on Saturday, reservations have been pouring in, so the town might try to run the spa and hope to make it profitable. At least that would be a way to recoup some of the money. I think it's possible that they'll decide to keep the place open."

"It would be a shame to close Badis after doing such a great job on the remodeling."

"I agree," said Patrik, taking a big bite of a cinnamon bun.

"How did Matte know that something wasn't right? You said that Annika's husband Lennart didn't find any irregularities. It does seem strange that no one from the town was the least bit suspicious."

"According to Anders, Mats wasn't positive, but he'd started wondering if something was wrong. On the Friday before he went to see Nathalie, he dropped by Badis and had a talk with Anders. He asked a lot of questions. For instance, he wanted to know why so many of the suppliers' invoices hadn't been paid. He also wanted to know when the funds that Anders and Vivianne had promised to invest would be arriving. And where that money was coming from. He wanted the names of contacts so he could verify the funds. Anders was really worried.

If Mats hadn't been killed, he probably would have uncovered the true state of the Project Badis finances and exposed Anders and Vivianne for the swindlers they are."

Erica nodded. She suddenly looked sad. "How is Nathalie?"

"She's going to be evaluated by a forensic psychiatrist, and I think there's very little chance that she'll end up in prison. She'll probably be institutionalized. Or at least she ought to be."

"Why were we all so stupid? Why didn't we realize what was going on?" Erica put down the cinnamon bun. She had suddenly lost her appetite.

"How were we supposed to know? Nobody knew that Sam was dead."

"But how did he die?" She swallowed. Her stomach turned over at the thought of Nathalie living in that house for more than two weeks while her son's body slowly decomposed. She was filled with both horror and compassion.

"We don't really know. And we may never find out. But I talked to Konrad last night, and apparently they discovered that another woman was booked on the flight to Italy with Nathalie's husband and Sam. They talked to the woman and found out that the plan was for her to accompany Wester, while Nathalie would disappear out of the picture."

"Did she know how Nathalie's husband was planning to accomplish that?"

"He was going to use her cocaine habit to blackmail her. He threatened to make sure she would lose all custody rights if she didn't voluntarily step aside."

"What a bastard."

"That's putting it mildly. He probably confronted Nathalie with the plan the night before they were supposed to leave for Italy. The police found two blood types when they did an analysis of the blood in the double bed. It's likely that Sam crept into the room and got into bed with his father. So when

Nathalie sprayed the bed and her husband with bullets from his gun, well . . . she didn't know that her son was there too."

"Imagine finding out that you'd shot your own son."

"I can't think of anything worse. It was probably so traumatic for her that she completely lost her grip on reality and refused to accept that Sam was dead."

Neither of them spoke for a moment.

Erica suddenly looked puzzled. "But why didn't the mistress call the police when Wester didn't show up?"

"Fredrik Wester wasn't exactly known for being reliable. So when he didn't turn up, the woman assumed that she'd been dumped. According to Konrad, there are some furious messages from her on Fredrik's voicemail."

Erica had already moved on to another topic. "Matte must have found Sam."

"Yes. And the cocaine. Nathalie's fingerprints are on the bag, and on the door to Mats's apartment. Since we haven't been able to interview Nathalie, we don't know for sure, but it seems likely that Mats discovered that Sam was dead and also found the cocaine in the early hours on Saturday. Then he forced Nathalie to come to Fjällbacka to contact the police."

"And she had to shoot him in order to protect her deluded belief that Sam was alive."

"Yes. And it cost Mats his life." Patrik looked out of the window. He too felt enormous compassion for Nathalie, despite the fact she had killed three people, including her own son.

"Does she know now?"

"She told the doctors that Sam is with the dead on Gråskär. She said she should have listened to them earlier and allowed him to go with them. So, yes, I think she does know now."

"Has the boy been found?" asked Erica hesitantly. She didn't want to think about what an awful state the child's body must have been in. It was bad enough that she'd smelled the horrible stench inside the house.

"No. He disappeared into the sea."

"I wonder how she could stand the smell." Erica could almost feel it in her nostrils, and she'd been inside for only a brief time. Nathalie had lived there for more than two weeks.

"The human psyche is strange. This isn't the first time that someone has lived with a corpse for weeks, months, or even years. Denial is a very powerful force." Patrik took a sip of coffee.

"That poor little boy." Erica sighed. After a pause, she said, "Do you think there's anything to the rumors?"

"What do you mean?"

"You know. What people always say about Gråskär, or Ghost Isle—that the dead never leave the island."

Patrik smiled. "No. And now you've got me worried that the blow to your head has addled your brain. It's an old wives' tale. Nothing but a ghost story. That's all."

"I suppose you're right," said Erica, but she didn't look entirely convinced. She was thinking about the newspaper articles that she'd shown Nathalie, about the lighthouse keeper and his family who had disappeared from the island without a trace. Maybe they were still out there.

❧

Nathalie felt so strangely empty inside. She knew what she had done, but she felt nothing. No grief, no pain. Just emptiness.

Sam was dead. The doctors had cautiously tried to tell her that, but she had already known. The moment the water had closed over Sam's head, she understood. The voices had finally reached her and made her release her hold, persuading her that it would be best if he was allowed to join them. They would take good care of him. And she was glad that she had listened.

As the boat carried her away from Gråskär, she had turned around to take one last look at the island and the lighthouse. The dead were standing on the rocks, gazing at her. Sam was with them, standing next to the woman. On the other side of her stood her son. Two little boys, one with dark hair, the other blond. Sam looked happy, and his expression assured Nathalie that he was fine. She had raised her hand to wave, but then lowered it. She couldn't bear to say goodbye to him. It hurt too much that he was no longer with her. He belonged to them now. To Gråskär.

The room she was in was small but bright. There was a bed and a desk. She spent most of her time sitting on the bed. Occasionally she was required to talk to someone, a man or a woman. Both of them spoke in kindly voices as they asked her questions that she wasn't always able to answer. But day by day she began to see things more clearly. It was as if she'd been asleep and had now awakened. Slowly she was being forced to distinguish between what had been a dream and what was reality.

Fredrik's scornful voice was real. He had enjoyed watching her pack for Italy before telling her that he was going without her. And that the other woman would be accompanying him instead. If she offered any objections, Fredrik said he would tell the authorities about her cocaine habit, and then she'd lose custody of Sam. In his eyes, she was nothing more than a weak woman. Superfluous.

But Fredrik had underestimated her. She'd gone into the kitchen and sat down to wait in the dark until he'd gone to bed. Once again he'd taken pleasure in crushing her and exerting his will over her. This time, however, he had made a serious mistake. She might have been weak before Sam was born, and she still was to a certain extent. But her love for Sam had made her stronger than Fredrik would ever be able to understand. She sat on one of the bar stools in the kitchen, with her hands resting on the cold marble of the countertop, waiting for Fredrik to fall asleep. Then she got out his gun, went upstairs, and with a steady hand fired it again and again into the bedding, into the bed. And it felt good. It felt right.

It wasn't until she went to Sam's room and saw his empty bed that panic took hold and a fog slowly settled over her. She knew at once where he must be. Yet when she lifted the blanket and saw his little bloodstained body, it came as such a shock that she collapsed in a heap onto the thick carpet. The fog intensified, and even though she knew that she was living in a dream, Sam still seemed so alive.

And then there was Matte. Now she remembered everything. The night they spent together, and the feel of his body against her, so familiar and beloved. She remembered how safe she felt, and how a possible future became linked to the past they had shared, erasing everything in between.

Then came the sounds from downstairs. She woke up to find Matte gone. The warmth of his body was still there, and she realized he must have just gotten out of bed. She wrapped a blanket around her and went downstairs, only to see his look of disappointment as he held up the bag of cocaine. She had put it in a drawer, which she apparently hadn't shut properly. She wanted to explain, but the words wouldn't come out. She really had no excuse, and Matte would never understand.

As she stood there, wrapped in a blanket, her bare feet cold on the wooden floor, she had watched Matte open the door to Sam's room. Then he turned around and gave her a look of alarm. He made her put on some clothes, telling her that they needed to go back to the mainland and summon help. Everything had happened so fast, and she had passively done as she was told. In the dream, in the world that wasn't real, she had protested with all her heart over leaving Sam behind on the island. But neither of them had said a word as they crossed the bay in Matte's boat.

Then they were driving in his car. Her mind felt strangely empty of all thought, except for her concern for Sam. And the fact that once again something was happening that would take him away from her. Without thinking, she had grabbed her purse from the house when they left the house and brought it along. Sitting in the car, she could feel the weight of the gun inside the purse.

As they walked toward the block of apartments, an insistent buzzing had started up inside her head. Through a haze she saw Mats toss the paper bag in a litter bin. Standing in the front hall of his apartment, she had reached into her purse and felt her fingers touch the cold steel. He hadn't turned around. If he had, and she had looked into his eyes, she might have been able to stop herself. But he was moving away, with his back turned, and she had raised her hand, gripping the butt of the gun, with a finger on the trigger. A loud bang, a thud. Then not a sound.

She had to get back to Sam. That was the only thought in her head. She went back to the dock, took Matte's boat over to the island, and then let it drift away. After that there was nothing to keep her from being with him again. Fog took over her mind. The rest of the world disappeared. The only thing left was Sam, and Gråskär, and the thought that they had to survive. That was her only refuge; otherwise nothing but emptiness remained.

Nathalie sat on the bed, staring straight ahead. In her mind she pictured Sam, holding the woman's hand. They would take care of him now. They had promised her that.

# Fjällbacka 1875

**M**amma!"
Emelie instantly stopped what she was doing. Then she dropped the saucepan on the floor and dashed outside as fear fluttered like a little bird inside her heart.

"Gustav, where are you?" She looked all around.

"Mamma, come here!"

Now she could hear that he was calling from the shore. She lifted her heavy woollen skirts and raced over the rocks that formed a ridge in the middle of the island. From on top she saw him. He was sitting at the water's edge, holding his foot and crying. She ran to her son and knelt at his side.

"It hurts," he sobbed, pointing at his foot. A big piece of glass was sticking out of his sole.

"Hush . . ." She tried to calm her son as she thought about what to do. The shard was buried so deep. Should she pull it out right now or wait until she had something to use as a bandage?

*Quickly she made up her mind.*

*"We'll go see your father." She glanced up at the lighthouse. Karl had gone over there a few hours ago to help Julian. She didn't usually ask her husband for advice, but she wasn't sure what would be the right thing to do in this situation.*

*She picked up Gustav, who was still sobbing pitifully. Carrying him like a baby, cradled in her arms, taking care where she set her feet. It wasn't easy for her to carry him, now that he'd grown so big.*

*As they approached the lighthouse, she called out Karl's name, but he didn't answer. The door stood open, presumably to let in some fresh air. It could get unbearably hot inside when the sun was shining.*

*"Karl!" she called again. "Could you come down here, please?"*

*It wasn't uncommon for him to ignore her, and she realized that she would have to make the effort of going up in the lighthouse to find him. She couldn't carry Gustav up the steep flight of stairs, so she carefully set him down on the ground, then gently patted his cheek.*

*"I'll be right back. I'm going to get your father."*

*He gave her a hopeful look and then stuck his thumb in his mouth.*

*Emelie was already out of breath after carrying Gustav from the shore; she tried to calm her breathing as she went up the stairs. On the top step she paused and raised her eyes. At first she couldn't understand what she was seeing. Why were they lying on the bed? And why didn't they have any clothes on? She stood there, frozen to the spot, and stared. Neither of the men had heard her. All their attention was focused on each other, on the forbidden place of their bodies, and Emelie saw with growing astonishment, that they were caressing each other.*

*She gasped, and now they noticed her. Karl looked up, and for a second their eyes met.*

*"You sinners!" Words from the Bible burned inside of her. The Holy Scriptures strictly forbade such things. Karl and Julian would bring misfortune and damnation upon themselves, and upon her and Gustav too. God would curse everyone here on Gråskär if they didn't atone for their sins.*

*Karl still didn't say anything, but it was as if he could see straight through her and knew what she was thinking. His eyes turned cold, and she heard the dead start to whisper. They told her to flee, but her feet refused to obey her. She was incapable of moving or tearing her eyes away from the naked, sweaty bodies of Julian and her husband.*

*The voices got louder, and something seemed to jostle her, so that she could finally move again. She raced down the stairs and picked up the sobbing Gustav. With a strength that she didn't know she had, Emelie ran, unaware of where she was headed. She heard Karl and Julian coming after her, and she knew she wouldn't be able to outrun them. The house wouldn't provide any sort of safe refuge. Even if she managed to get inside and lock the door, they could easily break it open or get in through a window.*

*"Emelie! Stop!" yelled Karl behind her.*

*Part of her wanted to do just that. Stop and give up. And she would have done that if she had only herself to think about. But she kept going because of Gustav, who was now crying in fear as she carried him in her arms. She had no illusions that they would spare him. Gustav had never meant anything to Karl. The boy existed only to placate Karl's father, to convince him that everything was as it should be.*

*It had been a long time since Emelie had thought about Edith, her confidante during those years on the farm. She should have listened to her friend's warnings, but she had been young and naive and hadn't wanted to see what was now crystal clear to her. Julian was the reason that Karl had returned home so abruptly from the lightship and been forced to marry the first available girl. Even a farm maid was good enough to save the family's reputation. And everything had been arranged according to his parents' wishes. The scandal concerning their youngest son never got out.*

*But Karl had duped his father. Behind his back, he had hired Julian to be his assistant on the island. He had decided it was worth the risk that he might again suffer the brunt of his father's anger. For a moment Emelie actually found herself feeling sorry for Karl, but then she heard his footsteps getting closer and she remembered all the harsh words and blows, and the night when Gustav was conceived. He hadn't needed to treat her so badly. But for Julian she felt no sympathy. He had a cruel heart, and he had directed all his hatred toward her from the very beginning.*

*No one could save her now, but Emelie's feet kept on carrying her forward. If it were only Karl chasing her, she might have had a hope of reasoning with him. He was once a different person; he changed when he was forced to live a lie. But Julian would never let her get away. Suddenly it was very clear to her that she was going to die on this island. She and Gustav. They would never leave.*

*She felt a hand reaching out toward her from behind, almost touching her shoulder. But she pulled away at exactly the right moment, as if she had eyes in the back of her head. The dead were helping her. They urged her to run toward the shore, toward the water that had been her enemy for so long. She now realized that it would be her salvation.*

*Emelie ran right into the sea, carrying her son in her arms. The water splashed around her legs, and after a few meters it got too hard for her to run and she had to slow her pace to a walk. Gustav had his arms wrapped around her neck, but he was no longer crying. He didn't make a sound, as if he understood.*

*Behind her she heard Karl and Julian enter the water. She had a few meters' head start, and she kept on going. The water now reached up to her chest, and she could feel panic taking hold of her. She didn't know how to swim. But then it felt as if the water were embracing her, welcoming her and promising safety.*

*Something made her turn around. Karl and Julian were standing in the water a short distance away, staring at her. When they saw her stop, they began moving toward her again. Emelie started backing up. The water now reached to her shoulders, and Gustav felt lighter, his weight buoyed up by the sea. The voices were speaking to her, calming her, saying that everything was going to be fine. No harm would come to them. They were welcome and would be given peace.*

*Emelie was filled with a sense of calm. She trusted them. They enveloped her and her son in love. Then they urged her to turn and head toward the endless horizon. Blindly, Emelie obeyed the ones who had been her only friends on the island. With Gustav in her arms, she struggled in the direction where she knew the currents would be strongest and where the bottom sloped steeply downward. Karl and Julian followed, heading toward the horizon and squinting into the sun, without taking their eyes off her.*

*The last thing she saw before the water closed over her and Gustav was how Karl and Julian were pulled under by the currents. And perhaps by something else. But she was certain that she would never encounter them again. She and Gustav would be staying on Gråskär, but those two would not. The only place for Karl and Julian was in hell.*